THIRTY ACRES

RINGUET **THIRTY ACRES**

Introduction: Albert LeGrand   General Editor: Malcolm Ross

New Canadian Library No. 12

McClelland and Stewart

Copyright, Canada, 1940
The Macmillan Company of Canada, Limited

Translated by Felix and Dorothea Walter

This edition published 1960 by arrangement with
The Macmillan Company of Canada, Limited

0-7710-9112-5

Introduction © 1970   McClelland and Stewart Limited

The Canadian Publishers
McClelland and Stewart Limited
25 Hollinger Road, Toronto

Manufactured in Canada by Webcom Limited

CONTENTS

INTRODUCTION

Thirty Acres, first published in 1938, is one of the most important books ever to come out of French Canada. Its interest is a lasting one. The years, if anything, have only added to its prestige, and the secret of this enduring power surely lies in the deep understanding, knowledge, and high artistry which the author brings to his study of man in relation to the soil. Here is a book which breaks the restricted boundaries of regionalism and reaches into universal significance. Ringuet belongs to that family of great authors who, from Hesiod to Vergil, from Ramuz to Barrès, have celebrated the nuptials of man and the land. This time the man was a French Canadian, the land was Quebec.

Do these nuptials, does this "ruralist humanism," constitute a new direction in French-Canadian writing? On the contrary. For decades, French-Canadian novelists had been idealizing habitant farmers against a romantic background of religious and national mysticism. Ringuet's revolution (and it *was* one) consisted in a new experiment which brought together for the first time two well-known elements: French-Canadian rural society and an artistic creed which holds that the purpose of art is to depict life with complete and objective honesty—in short, *realism*. It is amazing that French Canada should have waited so long for its Flaubert (but then, had English Canada fared any better?). This was 1938. Flaubert had introduced *Madame Bovary* to the world in 1857. Such a delay, however, merely gave Ringuet's book additional impact. It was eulogized as an impressive work of art by the best critics. As a social document it gained shocked attention from other circles. As a kind of therapeutic treatment it worked wonders with the failing health of the French-Canadian novel. Whatever one's feelings towards this book may be, it indisputably stands out as a major achievement and must be regarded as the watershed of the French-Canadian novel.

No book can attract this kind of attention without bringing its author into the limelight. Who was Ringuet? Even before the book's appearance, Canadian literary circles were buzzing with rumours. Max Fisher, Flammarion's literary director, had casually announced in Montreal in the summer of 1938 the forthcoming publication of an unusually important novel by a "Montrealer." When the book appeared, the secret came out. Ringuet was the nom de plume of

Dr. Philippe Panneton—and Panneton needed no introduction. Since 1917 his name had figured prominently in the leading periodicals, newspapers, literary journals, and medical reviews of French Canada. Linked to that of Louis Francoeur, a journalist friend, his name had also appeared on a book published in 1925: *Littératures . . . à la manière de.* Typically, this work was an iconoclastic take-off on some of French Canada's most respected names like Bourassa, Groulx, Camille Roy. (Long before 1925 Panneton's nonconformist nature had caused him to be eased out of one "collège classique" after another—without a degree. He felt, as he wryly put it, "none the worse for this." Sly jabs at the "collèges classiques" dot his books. He clearly looks upon the discipline of these classical institutions as somewhat narrow and culturally restrictive.)

In Quebec, where climbing family trees is a sport, Panneton can afford to feel at home. He traces his ancestors back to 1640 and 1688 when they settled in the Three Rivers district. His father was born close by, at Sainte-Marguerite des Trois-Rivières, on the ancestral farm. He himself was born in 1895, in Three Rivers, then a town of about fifteen thousand and entirely French-Canadian. At eighteen he left for Montreal, put in one year as a cub reporter, then switched to medicine, first at Laval, then at the Université de Montréal. In 1920 he was off to Paris and a few years of post-graduate work after which, back in Canada, he set up practice as an eye specialist. Over the next twenty years, all his leisure went to reading, writing, and travelling. He travelled extensively, but his wandering served only to bring his own land and its people into sharper focus.

Thirty Acres was begun more or less accidentally, as the result of a steady accumulation of random notes. Panneton at the time was a practising doctor in Three Rivers. Each week he would commute by train to Joliette where he kept another office. On these trips he would search out the farmers to chat and smoke with them. We can also guess that in the smoking car there was excellent material for a novelist whose literary creed was based on shrewd observation. The notes grew. The idea ripened. The book appeared in the late fall of 1938. It was, as we have mentioned, an immediate success and has since won many laurels for its author. To mention only a few: prix du Gouverneur général du Canada (1938); prix de l'Académie française (1939); prix des Vikings (1941); prix Duvernay (1955) for his work as a whole; and the Lorne Pierce Medal of the Royal Society of Canada (1959). *Thirty Acres* has been translated into German, Dutch, Spanish, and English.

The English title is a free translation of *Trente Arpents*. In Quebec, farms belonging to the old parishes are still measured in arpents. There are about twenty-eight arpents to a mile. In depth, Euchariste Moisan's farm stretched a little over a mile (thirty arpents). It was some five hundred feet wide (three arpents). It resembled those old farms that even today stretch their long and narrow strips along a river, a highway, or a back concession road. The pattern goes back to the French régime when the first seigneurs sought land grants along the province's great waterways. Moisan's farm lay on the north shore of the Saint Lawrence in a triangle between Montreal, Joliette, and Three Rivers.

The casual reader will no doubt find here "an excellent novel of habitant life in a small Quebec community" (as one critic put it). It is all of that. But it is also more. If we are to appreciate fully the significance of Ringuet's novel, I am afraid it will be necessary to run the risk of sounding a bit abstract. Let us examine some of the themes that had, before *Thirty Acres*, most consistently inspired French-Canadian life and literature. Briefly summarized, the legend runs something like this: "French-Canadians must remain faithful to the language, religion, and traditions of their forefathers." This was their mission. How could it best be accomplished? Through fidelity to the land, because on the land the national virtues responsible for French Canada's survival seemed to flourish most naturally and most vigorously. The soil became a sacred thing. Rural life assumed the proportions of a national myth complete with its heroes. Who were they? The sedentary habitant and the pioneering colonist breaking new land to handle the overflow of population from the old parishes. Thus a relationship of direct dependency developed between rural life in particular and French-Canadian life as a whole. What had so far been a historical fact (the predominance in Quebec of an agricultural economy) became a creed: this way of life was to be encouraged and its primacy upheld. The regional novel, grafted on to this ideological system, was put to preaching. Rural idylls always sermonized to the same end: staunch moral values, frugality, and industry were possible only in an agrarian society.

From the very beginning, in French Canada, the rural novel became the prey of this devouring ideology. In 1862 Antoine Gérin-Lajoie wrote *Jean Rivard, le défricheur*, a novel that reads most of the time like a sociological treatise on colonization. The romance and scientific data are mere window-dressing for the book's undisguised propaganda. Young French Canadians are urged to emulate the shining example of the hero, Jean Rivard. He goes out into the bush, clears the land and, by determined effort, finally achieves brilliant economic and personal success. The novel was a dull mixture of pioneering ruggedness and proselytizing patriotism. (About ten years earlier, Susanna Moodie had written *Roughing it in the Bush*. It would be difficult to imagine two books on the same theme further apart in tone and intention. Indeed, we might in this contrast find the measure of the disparity in thought and mood between the two Canadian cultures.)

Maria Chapdelaine is, in a sense, the feminine counterpart of *Jean Rivard*. Written in 1916 by an itinerant Frenchman, Louis Hémon, *Maria Chapdelaine* is an enduring work of art. But, like its predecessor, *Jean Rivard*, it is nevertheless a novel with a message —alas, the same message. And it was to become the archetype of countless rural idylls celebrating wholesome love and patriotic devotion.

It is against this tradition of the sentimental—and ideological—idyll that we must read *Thirty Acres*. Ringuet's book spans a period of peasant life from the late nineteenth century until the late 'thirties. The setting is thus an era of rapid change and world-shattering events. World War I reopens old racial wounds. Creeping industrialization lures people away from the farms and into the cities and a different way of life. New mass media of communication break down barriers that had made isolationism a natural phenomenon in a huge and sparsely populated country. Economic depression spreads disillusionment and bitterness everywhere. Then the first rumours of another war are heard in the land. These new forces and currents affected Canada as a whole but their impact on Quebec was that of a tidal wave. The time was ripe for Ringuet, for a new direction in the novel and in all the arts.

Thirty Acres is the story of Euchariste Moisan, whose life was filled by one great passion: a love for his "thirty acres" of Laurentian farmland. This passion was his whole moral universe. On the land he walked, talked, and lived like the master that he was. Away from it he was just an awkward farmer. Moisan has always been pictured as a simple man. Let us not oversimplify him. He is twenty-three when the story begins and he walks straight into an arena of dilemma, indecision, and change. His personality is made to mirror the ironic complexity of his small world—and the conflicts between the old and the new, between tradition and progress. Euchariste belongs both with the past and the future. Within him, tradition and progress are at war. Therein lies the drama of his life. Where will his choices take him? Where will they take the habitant? For Euchariste symbolizes more perplexities than his own. From the very beginning Euchariste clearly bears the marks of the modern man: he is shrewd, taciturn, pragmatical, ambitious, avid for success and prestige. A cold realist, he also worships progress. He is, therefore, one of the "new men." All his ventures are characterized by the same practical, "no-nonsense" approach to life. Love, marriage, the family, the land, religion, morality—it makes no difference—in all of these affairs one must be practical.

What sort of a lover is he? 'Phonsine is his girl. He realizes that she is just what he wants. Does he idealize her? Does he deck her out in any "dream-fabric"? "His conception of her was not in the least romantic." Pretty face, good figure, strong and sturdy. Good! He "knew" what to expect and had "allowed" himself to want her. He then drives the hard practical bargain with her father.

For marriage, especially for Euchariste, is clearly a practical arrangement. An orphan, he lives with his uncle Ephrem, a childless widower, owner of thirty acres of good alluvial soil that has been producing for some two hundred years. The farm becomes his sooner than anticipated when Ephrem dies suddenly. In short order, he has a farm, a wife, and an heir. Euchariste is indeed a fortunate man: "He, who just a few months before had been merely a nephew sheltered on someone else's farm, knew now that he had become, by the miracle of this begetting, the master of the land when yesterday he was a stranger." Now that the thirty acres are his by right of the flesh, Euchariste is a moneyed man. The earth—money. They are one. Out in the fields, he would lift some of the good earth gently in his hands, mingling it with his flesh. He would slowly "crumble it between thumb and fingers, with the gesture of a man counting out the minted coins of his fortune." The thirty acres are generous providers. Each year, Euchariste adds to his savings on which the village notary allows him five per cent. And over the years, his flesh, his land, and his money are together subservient to one burning purpose—the prestige of the Moisan name.

His avarice even extends to his religion. Should Oguinase, his eldest son, study for the priesthood? Euchariste has no objections, provided that the parish priest pays half of the expenses. Euchariste is not a pious man, yet the idea of the priesthood appeals to him. Why? A priest in the family would assure him of the highest and most lasting prestige. He was fond of saying: "There are two things in the world know a lot more than we do: the priest and the land." And who can say? Euchariste might get special attention from God in the way of good crops. . . .

Euchariste is quite indifferent to moral issues. Before his marriage he was not ashamed to lust after 'Phonsine and "he had once taken the Fancine girl on the spur of a chance encounter." As a father, his attitude remains noncommittal. His third son, Ephrem, a sturdy young man, is the local bully. He fights, drinks, and swears. Euchariste is secretly proud of this. Nor does he reproach his daughter Lucinda, although he knows a few unsavoury things about her and suspects more. In his small way, Euchariste has all the greed, the pride, and the lust of the new "economic man."

And, of course, he wants progress. "You have to keep up with the times," Euchariste advises an old-timer. "I'm all for progress," he tells Ephrem, "and everybody knows that."

Euchariste, as we shall see, is also a stoic and a fatalist. *Thirty Acres* is divided into four parts that answer the call of the four seasons. At once real and symbolic, the season-divisions stress the bonds that link the peasant to the soil and dictate the terms of his life. "The years go by with their succession of days and nights, their rotation of the seasons in a cycle just like the one men themselves apply to the crops." The days, weeks, months, seasons, and years roll by, yet for the habitant the pattern remains rigorously the same: "Out of bed in the morning, work, breakfast, work, dinner . . . And the day after that, out of bed in the morning, work, breakfast . . ." Euchariste accepts this rhythm as part of his inescapable destiny. But, happily, fate has been good to him. He has achieved his ambitions. "Lucky as 'Charis Moisan," had become a saying in the district. The first two seasons of the book, spring and summer, correspond with his youth and adult age. Progress and success embrace, as spring advances to summer, under the sign of Euchariste Moisan, the modern man.

Then the tale takes a tragic turn. In the symbolic autumn of the novel, the proud world of "lucky 'Charis" slowly crumbles.

Because of bad luck? No. Euchariste is slowly reversing himself. A suppressed second self rises to the surface. The man who had once stood up to Uncle Ephrem in the name of progress now takes sides with tradition against progress, against his own flesh, against his own son Ephrem. Cars noisily invade the farmer's quiet country roads, many of them with American licences. To the younger generation, to boys like Ephrem, they symbolize ease and luxury. The older ones, like Euchariste, look on resentfully, fearing for the traditional rural virtues of thrift, hard work, and respect for authority. The old gods are clearly losing their force. Young Ephrem wants to buy a tractor. The answer is no. A car? Still no. The inevitable happens. Ephrem directs his revolt against his father, against the land, against the Bishop who had suggested that "if you desert the land you're practically headed for hell." Euchariste Moisan had lost his authority. He stupidly hauls his neighbour, Phydime Raymond, into court, appeals the judgement which had gone against him, and again comes out on the losing end. Gone is the last mark of prestige. When the *Banque Nationale* opens a branch office in the village, Euchariste, with habitant prudence, continues to entrust his savings to a young notary who one day absconds with them. Youth, pride, power, fortune—all are lost.

As the novel moves into its last season, winter, the forces of progress have pushed Euchariste aside. He is cleverly manoeuvred into going to the States on a visit to his third son Ephrem, now established in Massachusetts. Etienne thoughtfully provides him with a one-way ticket. Literally transplanted overnight into a strange world, amongst strange people whose language he neither speaks nor understands, Euchariste Moisan, the master of thirty acres and father of twelve children, is suddenly nothing but a broken and forlorn old man. Bewildered and lost, rejected and hated by his daughter-in-law, the old man, now a night watchman in a garage (the temple of modern man), sits silent and alone, dreaming of the lost acres, waiting for death.

Thirty Acres will always remain a fascinating appraisal of French-Canadian rural life dictated by a refreshingly realistic approach. Some critics saw in this novel an inappropriate—and merely negative—pessimism. Others were gratified that art had at last begun to deliver shock therapy to Canadian sensibilities. Certainly, the trend to a fuller realism has acquired momentum with such recent writers as Gabrielle Roy, Roger Lemelin, André Giroux, Yves Thériault, and several others. Today, French Canada emerges as an increasingly complex cultural entity. The somewhat simple reasoning of the agrarian school of thought stands discredited. There are, if anything, too many "agonizing reappraisals" going on in French Canada today. But a birth-agony holds the promise of new life. And pain is complacency's enemy. If one book, more than any other, can be the cause of the present soul-searching in French-Canadian art and letters, that book is *Thirty Acres*.

ALBERT LE GRAND.

University of Montreal.

SPRING

1

"We're getting after the fall ploughing pretty soon, Mr. Branchaud. Just when I was coming away, Uncle said: 'Tomorrow we'll have to plough the field at the bottom of the hill.' If only the rain lets up for a while."

The two men sat in silence. Their chairs were tilted against the wall, balanced on two legs, and at regular intervals they took their pipes out of their mouths and, leaning over the edge of the veranda, sent a stream of saliva into the weeds. Then they took up their tranquil pose again and stared off into the distance.

Before them stretched the plain, splashed with colour by the first October frosts. Clumps of trees stood out in sharp relief, the black willows, already stripped of their leaves, blending into a pattern with the green beeches. In the distance ran the long belt of woods, the first outpost of the great Laurentian forest: a brilliant symphony in which the low notes were supplied by the dominant greens of the conifers, the high by the scarlet of the Norway maples.

Immediately in front lay the King's Highway, winding and deserted. The water stagnant in the ruts mirrored the sky in two long parallel blue ribbons. The road ambled off to north and south. Coming from the country, it was in no particular hurry; it curved aside to pass under a friendly old willow tree and made a bend to brush past someone's front doorstep. It would get there in the end; the later the better.

A buggy drove by, and when the horse passed in front of the house he broke into a smart trot. On the seat sat a courting couple, stiff and rather awkward in their Sunday best. The young man waved his whip in greeting. Branchaud and Moisan took their pipes out of their mouths in acknowledgement.

On the other side of the road the checkerboard pattern of the fields began again and stretched away until it came up against the russet fringe of alders, and here, through the gaps, there were glimpses of the steely sheen of the river.

As if riveted to the wide circle of the horizon, and suspended above all this colour, was the pale blue dome of the northern sky.

But neither of the two men was conscious of the face of the earth, the overpainted face of an old woman with the first signs of winter already visible. For it was their arms and not their eyes which linked them to Mother Nature—their thickset arms, that on Sundays seemed to become paralysed and to hang inert beside their chair legs. Only their hands emerged from the sleeves of coarse homespun—rough calloused hands, alike in both men, though they were of different ages. For hands age fast from contact with the handles of the plough or from wielding the pitchfork and the axe. Branchaud had the face of a man of fifty, the body of a man of thirty-five. Euchariste Moisan might have been anywhere between twenty and thirty.

"I guess it's better land round here than up by Sainte-Adèle."

"It sure is, Mr. Branchaud. There wasn't nothing but stones up there. We'd put in the potatoes and when we came to dig them up there'd be nothing but stones—big ones, little ones—and hardly no potatoes at all. It was kind of queer of the old man to go and settle up there. But Father Labelle came round here to where Pa was working on Uncle Ephrem's farm. I don't remember so well, because I was only five when we got burnt out. But I know sure enough that it was more of a stone-mine than a gold-mine. Just stones and stones."

All that he could now remember clearly was the mountain to which their house clung and whose folds bore abundant crops of blueberries, raspberries, and blackberries, which he ate in handfuls when he went to fetch the cows. What else? To be sure, the creek where the fishing was so difficult with all the bushes in which the line caught, and the flash of a too agile trout slithering down through the branches to fall back into the current. What else? A vague memory of a huge valley with mountains and still more mountains at the other end of it and one in particular with a hump standing out above the others. For a long time he had thought that it was here Christ had been crucified.

But those were the recollections of a child and he was a man now.

"So when the fire took in the barn after five weeks without a drop of rain, there wasn't much to burn. I got out, but nobody else did, and I don't know how it was. You see it was night-time, Mr. Branchaud. It all burned up—the barn, the stable, and the house. My poor Pa and my poor Ma too, and Agénor and Marie-Louise. Everything, everybody. But I don't remember well; I was pretty small."

"And then your Uncle Ephrem adopted you?"

"Yeah, sure," said Moisan, who seemed to be thinking of something else.

They spoke slowly and said little, as was their custom, for they were farmers and therefore sparing of words. But today there seemed to be an added hesitation—a groping for the right expression, as is fitting when you are discussing a matter of importance. They avoided looking at one another, each seeming to fear that the other might have too definite an idea of what was in the wind. It was the same idea with both of them—one that had been ripening somewhere outside the mind, as the seed ripens in darkness before it pushes proudly into the light of day as an ear of grain. Years of servitude to the land had made their every necessary gesture precise. But they did not possess precision of the mind, a luxury that is sometimes so hard to live up to.

"So your Uncle Ephrem kind of adopted you," said the old man again.

Branchaud seemed to hesitate and then took his tobacco pouch out of his pocket with a deliberate gesture.

"You must be getting on for twenty-two now, Euchariste."

He said the last few words quite simply, as he packed the bowl of his pipe conscientiously with careful thrusts of his thumb; it was done now and he had spoken. At any rate, it was just as if he had; and Moisan caught his meaning, for he saw him raise his hands to his knees. He had to bring the matter up, since that young slowcoach couldn't seem to make up his mind.

"Twenty-three next spring, Mr. Branchaud. . . . As long as my aunt, Uncle Ephrem's wife, was alive, I didn't hardly notice it. She always treated me like a kid. But now . . ."

He hesitated a moment and stared fixedly at a black knot-hole in the floor of the gallery.

"But now it's different. It's a big house for just Uncle Ephrem and me. And Uncle's getting old. He's broke up a lot the last two years. So . . . that way it makes quite a bit of work for one man all alone, as you might say."

"Yeah. You've got quite a big farm, sure enough. Pretty soon you'll have to start thinking about . . ."

He stopped speaking to light his pipe and was lost for a moment in a cloud of bluish smoke. But in Moisan's ears the words rang: "You'll have to start thinking about getting married, getting married!" It was like the rhythmic jingle of sleigh-bells on a horse trotting along a winter road.

"About getting a hired man," the old fellow went on without moving a muscle of his face.

But the very same words were drifting gently through his mind too. Both of them were as aware of the real issue as if the younger man had said: "It's time for me to get married and it's your Alphonsine I want," and as if the other had answered: "Why, sure! You've been hanging around Alphonsine long enough. Why don't you two get married before the spring seeding?"

Moisan would be heir to his Uncle Ephrem, who was a childless widower. In so many months, or so many years—what difference did it make?—the thirty-acre strip of land would still be there. The old Moisan property, rich and fat, generous to those who worked it, had been built up over thousands and thousands of years until the time when the river shrank and left its former shore—that ridge over there—but only after having patiently deposited layer upon layer of heavy alluvial soil.

Moisan was a good catch and they both knew it. But time doesn't count on the land, which teaches those who depend upon it that hurry doesn't get them anywhere. Of course, he was fond of Alphonsine. At first he had come to see the Branchauds merely in a friendly way, as any good neighbour, cut off all week by the exacting demands of farm life, which allows no respite, might come to get the news of the people round about, and above all to see how the neighbouring farm was getting on and what it was likely to yield. But then gradually, as the young people of his own age began to get married, he came to realize that this particular girl was just what he wanted. To be sure, he didn't idealize her or deck her out in any dream-fabric; his conception of her was not in the least romantic. On the contrary, he had a very good idea of what he might expect from her. She was strong and sturdy and not afraid of work; she would be able to run the house and help in the fields at harvest-time. She had a pretty face and a good figure and would breed him healthy sons after pleasures of which he sometimes thought without either embarrassment or urgent longing. That is why he had allowed himself to care for her, or, more accurately, to want her, even before he had made a habit of going to see her every Sunday. The whole concession knew she was his girl and would be his wife some day. Still, he had better not wait too long or someone else would come along and whisk Alphonsine away from under his nose.

And so old Branchaud had looked favourably on the young man's attentions to his eldest daughter. From the very first visits he had spoken of it to his wife at night, and tacitly they had hatched the everlasting plot of parents with a marriageable daughter. When the young people were on the veranda together, the members of the family, one after another, would think of something they had to do, so that they could leave them alone. For they were dimly aware that love grows more quickly that way. For months now Euchariste had been coming to the Branchaud's every Sunday at about two o'clock. They spent the long afternoons, until the time came for each of them to go and milk the cows, sitting side by side and had very little to say to one another after they had exchanged news about the farm and the neighbours. They did not deal in ideas, that paper currency of the mind that is all right for city folk, but in facts, which are metal coins, real gold and silver, and which there is no arguing about.

Sometimes one of Alphonsine's younger brothers or sisters would come and chat with them for a moment. Talk started up again whenever that happened. If it was one of the boys, Alphonsine was forgotten while they talked of work and mutual friends. If it was a girl, her elder sister fussed over re-tying her hair-ribbon or pushing back an unruly lock of hair under her hat-brim, while Euchariste tickled the little girl's neck with a long wisp of hay held between his teeth. But the mother's voice soon issued from the depths of the kitchen. The child was called away on some pretext or other and the lovers were left alone again, feeling awkward and trying not to look at one another.

Moisan hadn't answered when Branchaud suggested that he couldn't remain alone much longer. His gaze wandered over the countryside, patterned with autumn colours, and seemed to be looking for some object to dwell on. From between the islands, covered with a tangle of brushwood, came a wedge-shaped flight of ducks, instinctively fleeing the winter they had never known.

"Quite a shot that," he said, pointing with his pipe toward the bright steely surface of the river.

"Gosh, yes!"

And then after a moment's silence: "I guess you haven't had your gun out yet, 'Charis."

"Why, no, Mr. Branchaud! There's no time for it—too much work to do. We work a sight too hard for what it gets us. You just earn enough to get by. No way of saving a single cent these days."

He was a shrewd one. He had gone off on a wide circle to reach his goal, like a good hunter who only shows himself when he is sure of his shot. In spite of what he said, he must certainly have something saved up. Not in cash perhaps. But his Uncle Ephrem owed him quite a lot for the ten years he had been working on his farm. What did it matter? Although he was careful of his money, old Branchaud meant to do things properly. In the first place he would pay for the wedding—and it would be a real wedding: there would be enough to make the whole township drunk and kill off all the relatives with indigestion. But it was time to come to a definite understanding.

"You're a good lad, 'Charis; you don't often take too much liquor and you're a hard worker. I guess I know you pretty well. I ain't what you'd call rich, but I've still got a few dollars saved up. When it comes time for . . . a showdown, you'll see I won't haggle."

The young man did not move. But he was balancing himself now on the two back legs of his chair and his face had lighted up. Everything else was easy now that the old man had promised to give his daughter a dowry and pay for the wedding. And if it had to happen . . . it might as well be now as later. For some weeks his desires had been aroused every time Alphonsine went back with him after their courting, along the dusty road, as far as the weeping willow which marked the limits of the Branchaud property. He felt a great urge bubbling up inside himself and longed to take her, right there, without saying a word, under the canopy of branches, just as he had once taken the Fancine girl on the spur of a chance encounter.

It couldn't go on much longer. Perhaps if she had been willing to yield he might never have married her. It would have meant a few more years of liberty for him. Once he was married he certainly wouldn't be free any longer to come and go as he wished or, on an occasional Saturday night, to drink *whiskey blanc* with friends until there was nothing left in the crock or a heavy drunken stupor flung him into a ditch where he stayed, bound by sleep and alcohol, until the icy dawn. But Alphonsine was not like the Fancine girl. She was a good girl who laughed when he took her round the waist with his big clumsy hands; but she kept the rest for her husband, and it was he, Euchariste

Moisan, she wanted to marry. Besides, she was a farmer's daughter and knew that no one will buy something later on if they've had it for nothing the first time.

"If it's that way, Mr. Branchaud, I guess if Alphonsine's willing we could fix it for the spring, before the seeding."

"It's all right with me."

The old man still drawled out his words without a trace of emotion. But he had begun to tug at his reddish moustache with a nervous gesture.

The kitchen floor creaked under the cautious footsteps of someone moving away from the open window. Old Mrs. Branchaud smiled to herself as she left the cupboard where for some time she had been rummaging about to hear what the men had to say. Branchaud seemed to be gazing at the earth, all decked out in gold and purple for its own wedding in the spring, when the sun would fertilize it once again, after it had waited patiently all through the long winter under a white bridal veil of snow.

"I guess it's about time to go and fetch the cows," said Euchariste Moisan.

2

There was a fire burning in the Moisans' kitchen stove. For at nightfall it began to rain, one of those October downpours of cold steady rain that the east wind gathers up to hurl against the windowpanes with a noise like wet sheets flapping on the line. A useless autumn rain like a wicked old fairy arriving late and uninvited, furious because the abundant fruitful rains of June have been there before her; jealous, too, of the late August rains which in a single night can rot the grain left lying in the fields. An autumn rain can do neither good nor ill. It can only drum on the roof, stir up the mud puddles in the road, and tap undecipherable messages on the panes.

Mechanically the clock cut up the hours into minutes, the

minutes into seconds. The kettle sang on the stove, and the cat purred underneath it. Beside the stove, and just as sensitive to the cold, old Mélie dozed in her old-fashioned wing chair. The lighted lamp, which hung on the wall near the window to shine on the front steps, just showed up the round ball of her tight cap. Ephrem Moisan swayed gently to and fro in his rocking-chair to the rhythm of the clock. The only patch of light in the room, except for the lamp, was the reflection on his bald head between the two tufts of cottonwool above his ears. He was old and bent with the weight of sixty ploughings and sixty harvests.

There was a whirring sound that lasted for a few moments, and then the clock pretended to strike ten times in succession; but the hammer encountered no resistance, like an interrupted heart-beat. Mélie's shoulders twitched and the wrinkles stood out on the face she turned suddenly towards the light. Ephrem Moisan's rocking-chair creaked as he leaned against one arm.

"Sleep well?" he asked, knocking the bowl of his pipe sharply against his heel above the sawdust-filled spittoon.

"Well, I like that! Bless me! I wasn't asleep. I was listening to the rain. It's just pouring! It's getting on towards nine, Ephrem, and 'Charis will be back soon."

"Maybe you wasn't asleep, Auntie, but it's all of ten."

She was always "Auntie" to Ephrem, though they were merely very distant cousins—"thirty-first or thirty-second," he said when people tried to pin him down. But Amélie had been a member of the family for a long time, since ever so far back. For it was she who nursed Ephrem; and Honoré, Euchariste's father; and Eva, who died a Grey Nun in Montreal; and the others—the five children of Grandfather Moisan, whose portrait done in crayon hung on the wall. In it he looked, with his fringe of beard, like a jovial old fellow whom the itinerant artist was unable to depict with an air of gravity, for there were far too many little smiling wrinkles at the corners of his eyes. It was he who took Amélie into the household, where at first she lived almost as a servant. Then, as the old people died off one by one and the children grew up, she gradually became a member of the family. For a long time now there had been no one to whom she could sing:

> The old grey hen
> Has laid an egg again,
> She laid it in the barn . . .

But she had been the undisputed mistress of the house since the death of Ephrem's wife, Ludivine. For "her poor kids" she had kept a deferential, grumbling affection, allowing herself every now and then to mutter "It ain't possible!" or "Would you believe it!" but pleased, nevertheless, when one or the other, uncle or nephew, bullied her a little to tease her.

Someone was coming up the steps. Heavy feet clumped against the threshold and the door opened.

"That you, 'Charis?" said the old man instinctively.

Who else could it be in this house where only the three of them lived?

"It's me, Uncle."

Taking off his wet coat, he stood for a moment absent-mindedly with his arms still in the air. Aunt Mélie trotted over to him.

"Can you beat that! There you are all soaking wet, like a dish-rag. Where have you been? Were you at the fort?"

"Why no, Auntie."

She still talked about the "fort" when she meant the village, like the old colonists of days gone by, whose only refuge was a wretched palisade about their houses, against which Iroquois arrows thudded without warning. She asked the question as if unaware that he had been at Branchauds'.

She was always "Auntie" for him, as well as for his uncle. She had done the same for him as she had for his father and his father's brothers. At her knee he listened to the same immortal stories which are used the world over to send little children to sleep : "Tom Thumb" and the innumerable variations on the adventures of "Ti-Jean."

As Euchariste said to old Branchaud, they had rebuilt a family together. Uncle Ephrem : the widower of a woman rendered sterile by a chronic weakness and finally carried off by consumption which had attacked her late in life, at a time when he was still too young to give up the farm and, above all, bound to it too closely by centuries of servitude to consent to sell it. Amélie : a stranger, or almost one—Amélie Carignan, the great-granddaughter of some soldier-of-fortune come from Picardy or Maine with the regiment whose name had become her surname. Finally Euchariste : of Moisan blood, but come as a stranger, too, one day from the newly settled lands of the North to this parish of his ancestors that wasn't home to him, wasn't the little parochial fatherland which is the only one country folk recognize. These three had united, however, to form a new family; these different fragments had been knit together upon the web of the ancestral farm. The unfeeling and imperious land was the lordly suzerain whose serfs they were, paying their dues to the inclement weather in the form of ruined harvests, subjected to the forced labour of digging ditches and clearing away the forests, compelled the whole year round to pay their tithe in sweat. They had come together on, and almost in opposition to, the harsh soil, from which nothing may be wrung except by sheer strength of arm. They had, because of its dumb will, restored the human trinity: man, woman, child; father, mother, son.

And now that another cycle was ended with the coming of autumn, the earth, already lulled by the first frosts, was getting ready to transmit its slumber to the farm, which would cease to know anything but a restricted winter existence. The fields would pull a heavy blanket of snow over themselves. For five long months they would rest, forgotten by a puny fitful sun incapable of piercing with its diminished warmth the thick shell of cold which clung to the earth.

Such was the hibernation that was about to begin for all things, for men too, and to them it would bring a partial respite from the obligations of their servitude and a chance to think of themselves a little and to prepare future harvests of wheat and humanity. The winter was the season of the year when the wood was cut, buildings repaired, fences and harness mended; it was also the season for getting married.

Uncle Moisan was aware of all that. He knew the laws of the soil, though he might not be able to put them into words. That is why from one Sunday to another he expected Euchariste to announce his approaching marriage.

"What's the good news at the Branchauds' tonight?" he asked.

"Nothing special. They're busy digging the ditches of the corner field at the end of the farm. They're going to start ploughing tomorrow, like we are, if that damn rain only lets up.

But the rain continued to beat the retreat of summer, furnishing an accompaniment to the savage chant of the wind tearing dead leaves from the trees and, when balked, breaking the branches in two.

The old clock went on ticking off the minutes and no one spoke. Euchariste got up, went over to the pump, took a drink of water, sat down again, lit his pipe, got up once more, went over to the window, and then as he turned around let out the great news: "I was talking with old Branchaud the other day."

The uncle suddenly stopped rocking to and fro in his chair and, leaning towards his nephew with his elbow on his knee and his pipe hanging expectantly in the air, every nerve and muscle in his old body tense with curiosity, he asked in a non-committal fashion:

"Well, is he willing?"

"I guess we'll go through with it right after the spring ploughing. If it's all right with you, I can fix up Pa's old house this winter. When she's calked and a few missing shingles put in and a good pile of dirt set round the foundations, Alphonsine and me won't be so bad off till the children start coming."

Ever since his father had gone to seek his fortune in the newly settled lands, the old Moisan house had stood empty and lifeless, with the chimney gaping like a dead mouth and the windowpanes filmed over like glazed eyes. From this time on the real Moisan house was the new one built by Uncle Ephrem's father. The main building had a roof set cantwise and was flanked by a small wing of similar construction, which was set back a little and used as the kitchen. The whole thing was of wood roughly painted in a kind of yellow. On one side, behind the veranda which ran right along the front, was the parlour with its hermetically sealed shutters that were opened only on two occasions: on the annual visit of the parish priest, and on one of those rare days, New Year's for instance, when a Moisan from the city came to spend a few hours with the country Moisans. Beside it, and lighted by the second window in the front of the main building, was a spare room which served no particular purpose but which, when Aunt Ludivine was still alive, had sometimes been used for evening gatherings of friends. Behind the parlour was the bedroom with a wooden bed in the middle of it covered with a brightly coloured patchwork quilt; on the floor beside the bed lay a rag carpet. On the walls hung cheap lithographs: Christ and, on the opposite wall, the Virgin, both looking down into the room; the Son auburn-haired, the Mother fair. Both pointed with identical gestures to their hearts; one gaped open from a wound dripping blood and crowned with fire, the other was surrounded fanwise by the seven swords of sorrow. Over the bed hung the angular, tortured face of a Holy Visage, with a branch of fir that had been blessed fastened to the frame.

A good deal of space in the next room was taken up by a staircase which led to the bedrooms in the attic above. On the opposite side of this room was a door giving onto the kitchen, where they ate in summer and lived in winter, which they left in the morning only to start the day's work or in the evening, after a gathering of friends had filled the room with smoke, to stretch their tired bodies on their hard beds.

"It's only natural you'll want to be alone with your Alphonsine," said Uncle Ephrem, suddenly breaking the silence. "But I kind of think you'd be better off right here in this house; it's solid and comfortable. You could have the big bedroom. That room should certainly be glad to see babies again, since I never had that kind of luck with my Ludivine."

"Yeah, but what about you, Uncle?"

"I tell you what, boy—I'm beginning to feel my age. I'm all of sixty-four and getting on sixty-five. The rheumatism has got me bad the last three years, and I guess the farm's through with me. It don't treat me right no more. So I'd been thinking of going to live in the village with Mélie. You'll take over the farm as if you owned it; a little sooner or a little later, what's the difference? You can pay me a little money every year, say around ten per cent on the crop. I've got a few hundred dollars at the notary's; but I'd just as soon not touch it, because you never know what'll happen when you're getting old. How does it strike you?"

"Have it your own way, Uncle, but I hate to see you go."

"I won't be so far. Less than nine miles. You'll come and see us Sundays at the village with 'Phonsine. You'll be real welcome and I'll be glad to see the little Moisans. I was kind of scared the stock was going to peter out."

"With 'Phonsine and me there's no fear of that," said Euchariste.

He could see her in his mind's eye just as she was a little while before when he held her close to him on the Branchauds' veranda just before leaving, and more particularly as he saw her with the avidness of his desire: firm, full-breasted, with a rather heavy mouth, wide hips swaying with a motion like the rocking of a cradle. He felt all warm inside with contentment and waves of heat came throbbing rhythmically to his temples. He was going to reap far more than his imagination, constricted by the tight bonds of habit, had ever sown. His heart had already warmed once before, when he and Branchaud exchanged the words which assured him the possession of this fine young woman's body and her gentle loyal presence for many years to come. He had got the better of old Branchaud then and made him cough up his money.

And now he was going to own the old Moisan property into the bargain. From now on he would be the one to decide which field was to be seeded with wheat and which left as pasture for the stock; the hay would be cut and sold at his price. Everything would depend on him. And everything to do with the farm and with him would depend only on the earth itself and on the sun and rain. Too saving to hire help, too old to work hard every day, Uncle Ephrem, even with his assist- ance, had been unable, in his opinion, to get from the farm all the riches that lay hidden in its flanks. He, Euchariste, would now be able to give himself without stint to the tasks which the land requires. If he had to use paid help for a time, sons would soon be born from his wife's flesh and blood and his own . . . his wife's ! and his own !

"It's a good farm, 'Charis, a real good farm," said the old man almost in a whisper.

For his mind had accompanied his nephew's in a parallel flight. He had been thinking about each of his fields in turn, reckoning their yield and going over their history. For fields have their years of success and failure. The field next to the Mercure property, where the year after his father's death he harvested twenty bushels of barley to the acre. And that narrow strip of land along the river, that was flooded every year at high water and reappeared again, when the waters had receded, diminished in area, eaten away by the ice which carried off whole bushel-measures of good earth to the sea; that narrow strip of land which every year, though, yielded its hundred bushels of potatoes and became more generous as it shrank in size.

So he was going to leave all that to bask quietly in the sun, to smoke his pipe and play chequers through the long days and discuss the news of the land—other people's land. He had said what had to be said, sure enough, and, as he was quite decrepit and racked with pains at the least sign of rain, he couldn't think of staying on the farm. But he hated to leave it like that. Would his nephew know how to get the most out of it? Above all, would he be able to avoid exhausting and impoverishing it?

He had "given" himself to his nephew, as the saying went. He whose livelihood had hitherto been at the mercy of a sud- den shift in the wind, a cloud laden with hail, hated to be dependent on a fellow human-being whose whims were more unpredictable than those of the weather. For you can tell it is going to be a late winter from the fact that the squirrels have not yet begun to store their provisions in the hollows of the willow trees. The first cawings of the returning crows are a warning to get ready for the spring. But what sign foreshadows the weather that is going to prevail in the hearts of those on whom we depend?

Outside the rain had stopped falling, sucked up by round balloon-shaped clouds that the wind drove westward. Old Mélie, aroused by the silence, began to recite the evening prayers while still half asleep. The two men knelt with their pipes in their hands and made the responses, though their minds never ceased following the same train of thought. When they had carefully knocked out their pipes into the stove, and Mélie had drunk a mouthful of holy water, as she did each evening, the staircase creaked under the weight of the old woman and of Euchariste. In his bedroom on the ground floor old Moisan coughed, spat, and blew his nose at some length.

That was all, except that outside the wind flattened soggy leaves against the windowpanes; within there was nothing but the slow pulse of the clock and the winking of the last embers on the polished floor.

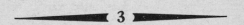 3

Old Moisan woke up at five o'clock from force of habit, fell asleep again, and then, when he slowly returned to consciousness, lingered a little in his snug bed. It was still dark, for November had come, eating away the days to lengthen the nights, each morning retarding the pale dawn whose dampness crept in even under the warm blankets. Little by little the frosty mist dimming the panes whitened and the window reflected a brighter, colder patch against the wall.

Gone was the spur of vibrant summer mornings when an early-risen sun beats the reveille. There was no longer any hurry. The fall ploughing was over, stopped by the early frosts which each in turn had hardened the soil to greater depths. There were only the animals to look after; "the chores to do," as they say—cutting the winter's supply of wood on the hill-side, finishing up odds and ends of work in the fields and on the farm.

Euchariste had already risen and was walking about up-stairs with a heavy tread; the noise of it filled the house still wrapped in slumber.

The old man threw off the blankets and sat up, shivering in spite of his night cap and his woollen underwear. But he fell back onto the edge of his warm bed. Suddenly the window and the furniture bathed in a chalky light started to go round and round at a terrific rate. He clutched the bedposts and closed his eyes as he felt the floor slipping away from under his feet like a trapdoor suddenly opened. Then he had to press hard against his chest with both hands as his heart beat violently, knocking against his ribs with a dull sound that reverberated in his poor old head.

A few minutes later he managed to get up. In the air heavy with cold his breath was expelled in little hurried jets of vapour. He went into the kitchen, started the pump-handle going, snorted violently at the shock of the icy water, sprinkled some of it over his neck, his shoulders, and his chest, and then felt better. His shirt, his trousers, his top-boots and his coat, and he was dressed. What were they going to do today? The weather would decide that.

He melted the film of condensed vapour which had formed on the windowpane by placing his hand on it at the level of his eyes, and it ran down his wrist and into his sleeve in long icy rivulets. The cross-bars framed a dull indistinct landscape: a frozen sky, showing through the leafless branches of the nearby beech trees that stood out in sharp black relief. Beyond, an opalescent mist clung to the edges of the farm-buildings, blurring the outlines, changing the shapes of objects, and bringing the horizon so close that it almost seemed as if you could touch it by stretching out a hand. The clumps of trees and the barn in the far background appeared only as dark smudges frozen fast in this whitish jelly that dulled the rays of a timid sun.

Once he had retired and gone to live in the village, he wouldn't have to worry any more about the weather. Rain or cold, he could stay quietly at home and take things easy.

During the next few days his dizzy spells recurred several times. They came upon him suddenly in all sorts of places; in a field, where he had to sit down until they passed off, or even in the stable at milking-time; on those occasions he would lean his head against the heedless animal's flank, taking good care that Eucariste didn't see him. For some time now he had noticed at night when he took his boots off that they left a deep pattern of white furrows on his legs, which had become heavy and swollen. A few days before, his feet were so numbed that he had to take his boots off at supper-time, but when he tried to put them on again he wasn't able to. The damp had shrunk the leather, he supposed.

As a matter of fact, what was there to worry about? He was still husky and would last for years, long enough to sow and reap a good many more times. He could still plough his ten sets of furrows before dinner without getting overtired, ploughing the furrows straight and parallel to one another and swinging the plough round at the end to start the next one. It sometimes made him feel slightly puffed, but nothing more than that. Moreover, he came of good stock. The Moisans were a tough lot and lived to a ripe age; they only took ill to die. His father had lasted to ninety-two. Of course, people nowadays were not so hardy. But he still felt quite young at sixty-four; six years ago he had almost got married again.

These morning attacks of giddiness worried him, though. He had earned a rest. After a few months of quiet in the village with Mélie he would recover his strength and forget his little discomforts.

One morning he came into the kitchen as usual. Old Mélie and Eucariste were there already, surrounded by the strong smell and the thick smoke of boiling lard. His breakfast was waiting for him and so was the rough wooden bench, which ran along beside the table that was covered with white oilcloth, where his place was set with pewter knife and fork and with bowl and cup of enamel ware.

"Pretty cold this morning."

"Pretty cold," replied Eucariste, who was warming his hands near the stove.

"It froze again last night, froze hard."

"Yeah, it froze all right."

"Looks like it's going to be a hard winter."

"Certainly does."

In silence the two men began eating their strips of bacon

and the buckwheat pancakes which Mélie made extra large to fit their appetites. Then she filled their cups with boiling-hot tea. When breakfast was over Uncle Ephrem took out his pipe, while Euchariste chopped up long twists of brown tobacco for the day's supply on a corner of the table. Suddenly the old man had a fresh seizure and fell heavily into his chair, his hands tightly clenched, his eyes closed, and his breath coming in gasps.

"What's the trouble, Uncle?" said Euchariste. "Are you sick?"

But the old man's senses had left him in this general dislocation of the world about him and he did not answer. It was useless for him to close his eyes, for it seemed that some evil power turned him upside down with his head dangling, while the four walls spun round and round and the floor heaved violently. A single thought floated on the surface of his consciousness : the annoyance at being surprised in this way, he who had always boasted of his strength. Mélie lost no time in reading him a lesson.

"There you go; now you've gone and got sick! It serves you right; that'll teach you. Where's the sense in a man your age working the whole day driving fenceposts like you done yesterday? Look at yourself in the mirror; you don't hardly look human."

"Uncle, why don't you go see the doctor in the village?"

Ephrem still did not answer, but Mélie reacted violently at the word "doctor."

"Doctor! Doctor! Just let me catch you going to the doctor's. A cousin of mine had pains all up and down his side; he went to the doctor's. The fellow told him there wasn't much wrong with him, and gave him some little bits of pills, and charged him a dollar and a half. But he had bronchitis the rest of his life, just the same, and died of the pleurisy."

She had that horror of doctors which is common to all country people. When you buy something, you take something away in exchange for the money. But you give the doctor your hard-earned dollars and get nothing tangible in return, except perhaps some miserable little ten-cent bottle.

"I'll go make you a good hot toddy. Then I'll go find some milfoil to make you some herb-tea."

"Hold your tongue, Mélie. Why don't you go get the priest and the notary while you're at it? I'm not sick. I never was sick. Do you take me for a namby-pamby like those young fellows you see round nowadays?"

Making a great effort, he pulled himself together and relit his pipe. Then, turning to Euchariste: "Let's get after the chores. Then you can harness the mare and go to the cross-roads for the new collar and the shafts Pitro was fixing. While you're doing that, I'll go look at the fences and see if there's any rails missing."

The week went slowly by with the days growing shorter and shorter. Morning and evening now they had to light the lantern to go and milk the cows. The deadly breath of the cold November wind shrivelled the weeds along the edges of the ditches; and almost every day there were downpours of rain that forced the cows to take shelter against the fences, where they stood motionless with the water streaming down their flanks and their rumps to the wind. Soon they would have to shut them up in the stable.

The first snow fell, stayed a while on the ground, and then melted.

One evening when he had gone up the hill to cut wood for the winter supply, the old man was late in getting back. It was already dark and time for the chores, and he still had not returned.

"Maybe you'd better go look for your uncle," said Mélie. "It's getting dark. Where's the sense in coming home so late? He'll be all wore out when he does get in. I've a kind of a hunch; suppose he's had something happen to him."

"I'll go, Auntie."

Euchariste lit his lantern and started out. Ten minutes went by, a quarter of an hour, half an hour. Standing anxiously in the kitchen doorway, Mélie peered into the night, looking for the tiny pale gleam of the lantern.

Then suddenly: "Mélie! Mélie!"

The voice came to her anguished and breathless through a thick wall of darkness; and because of the blackness of the night it seemed to come from every direction, from every corner of the horizon.

Suddenly the glow of the lantern appeared between the pig-sty and the shed, where the road came in from the fields. But the light bobbed up and down in a peculiar way, like a will-o' the wisp hopping about in one place.

"Holy Father in Heaven!" cried Mélie with the premonition of disaster.

Her old legs shook under her; she wanted to run, but she couldn't. Then all of a sudden she felt herself lifted up and found she was dashing towards the patch of light, which was still moving towards her, gliding noiselessly, close to the ground.

It was Euchariste coming back with the lantern in one hand, weighed down by the body he was carrying over his shoulder like a sack. He had found Uncle Ephrem on the other side of the creek, lying on the ground near the cool water towards which he had probably tried to drag himself. A few feet away were his axe and a little pile of wood already cut. He must have lain there since one in the afternoon. In all probability a stroke had seized him as he worked, his axe swung high in the air.

"I don't think he's dead yet; he was breathing a while back."

But Mélie wasn't listening to him. Dry-eyed, she was running about the house in a childish frenzy, pulling the bed about, picking up a lamp she set down at once unlit, smashing dishes in her haste to find some medicine or other on the shelves of the side-board, exclaiming, "Dear God! Dear God!" over and over again in an anguished voice.

But she suddenly stopped short and stood rigid. Euchariste, who had been leaning over the bed, slowly straightened up.

"I guess his troubles are over in this life. He's with God now."

A storm of tears burst from under Mélie's wrinkled eyelids, as from heavy rain clouds. She began to sob, with her head hidden in the folds of her blue apron. She was bent over by the gale of her grief like the old beech trees outside by the autumn winds. Euchariste did not cry, just as he had not done so when he lost his whole family at one blow. He was too young then for tears; now he was too old. His grief was the grief of a man used to struggling against the elements, getting the better of them sometimes, but who feels powerless in the face of death. He stared at the body of his uncle—of his father actually, for he was losing a father this time more truly than he had the first—this body, thrown on the disordered bed, which seemed to have been suddenly lengthened by death.

So the poor old man would never go to live quietly in the village.

He had died pressed close to this farm of his that could not consent to a divorce.

"It's too bad; poor old fellow !"

He would leave his house, the house his father had built, only to follow the road to the village for the last time, never to return.

A black wooden box; the slow winding procession of carriages following the hearse in the drizzling rain; the church full of people; then the heavy shovelfuls of earth on the coffin, falling with a hollow sound like a sledge-hammer, pressing poor Uncle Ephrem down into his grave.

How big and empty the house would be. And the farm, too, with him, Euchariste, all alone on a thirty-acre strip of land. He would have to work hard and get a hired man. There was the corn to put in the silo for fodder, and the turnips. The cellar had to be tidied up. By the way, he'd do that tomorrow. There was less of a hurry for the hen-house, and while he was fixing the cellar Uncle Ephrem could . . .

Why, no—Uncle Ephrem was dead. Poor old fellow ! He didn't get much rest when he was alive.

And then there was the winter supply of wood which hadn't been brought in yet.

The neighbours would get a surprise. Davi Touchette and Thomas Badouche, and old Branchaud. . . . Branchaud ! Why, of course ! Alphonsine.

Alphonsine !

Old Mélie's sobs were subsiding now, though her shoulders still shook from time to time as she spread a clean handkerchief on the bedside table, set a crucifix on it, lit a candle, and poured a little holy water into a saucer—into which she dipped a small branch of fir.

Alphonsine ! The old man won't have to make way for him. And he, Euchariste, won't go to see him on Sundays in the village, except at the cemetery on All Souls' Day, with Mélie . . . and with Alphonsine.

Mélie called him to hold the chair while she climbed up on it; with her trembling hand she stopped the pendulum of the clock, which was the proper thing to do. Just exactly what death had done just now to Uncle Ephrem's heart. And as soon as the ticking, which no one usually noticed, was stilled, silence filled the house with a velvety quietness, like something congealed coming from the dead man himself and spreading out over everything.

Mélie rearranged the bed, stretched out the legs in their proper posture, put her hands for a few moments over the eyes to close them, and tied a big red handkerchief round the head, one of the old man's own, so that the mouth wouldn't gape open any more. These duties were hers by right, as is the custom in every country where the dead are entrusted to the women. In birth and in death.

Euchariste turned back towards the bed, attracted, like all human beings, by an experience which doesn't frighten simple people but which sets them face to face with the ineluctable mystery of all things. With his arms dangling by his side, he let this new idea take shape in his mind: Uncle Ephrem is dead, *dead*. Uncle Ephrem will never cut wood again, never eat again, never speak again. The house seemed big now. . . .

Alphonsine ! . . .

His thoughts turned back to living things and were borne down the wind towards the waiting animals and towards the patient earth, that was indifferent to the death of the man it nourished and who was now to unite with it.

Furtively Euchariste's thoughts tried to escape from this room. But at once they came up against a black wall.

Uncle Ephrem is dead.

He became aware again of the dead man's face. The red handkerchief made him think of a toothache.

Only hope he won't change too much before the funeral. No, it's autumn.

Alphonsine ! . . .

If they got married before the spring, it wouldn't be so bad. In January perhaps.

He'd have to speak to the priest about it.

Poor old fellow; who'd have thought it !

4

When the service and the burial were over, Euchariste had to go to the rectory to pay the funeral expenses and then to the carpenter's for the marker, the simplest possible kind: a wooden board which would be set upright at the head of the grave with the dates of birth and death and the name Ephrem Moisan, "who lies here awaiting the Day of Resurrection," painted in black letters.

"How are you, 'Charis," said the people he met on the way. "Poor old Moisan; it's too bad!" The young ones added: "He went off pretty quick, did he?"

"Poor Ephrem," said the older ones. "He wasn't so old. Not sixty-five!"

The women who were still clustered together in little groups near the church, where they had attended the funeral service, greeted him from a distance. They were talking of sickness and death, which is the most fruitful subject of conversation among country people of every race and every land. Then they talked about Alphonsine, who was going to fill the empty place at Moisans'. Birth, marriage, sickness, death: the outstanding events of their calm even lives. Above all, death.

They never said: "Such and such a thing happened in 1862," but rather: "It happened the year after old Mrs. Chartrand's death," or, less frequently: "It was two months after the twins were born to Joseph the son of Clophas." The road leading from the past was measured by the deaths left scattered along the way. As for the future, it was best expressed in terms of the earth or of the heavens, which make or mar earthly harvests. "It'll rain tomorrow for sure and my wheat ain't in yet." "It'll be a good year for potatoes if the dry weather keeps up." And there were all the folk-prophecies about the weather, and the deductions based on signs observed by the old people and on laws that have been tested through generations: "It poured cats and dogs on Ascension Day; now we're in for forty days of it." "Somebody saw a bear day before yesterday; spring'll be along any time now." What is more important in country life than the life and death of kinsfolk, unless it be the life and death of the crops?

When his business was done Euchariste climbed back into the carriage beside Mélie, and the mare set off at a lumbering trot for the farm. A cold wind, harbinger of imminent winter, brought more tears to their eyes than they had shed for Uncle Ephrem. A few hours before they had followed the hearse, through whose glass panels the shining handles of the coffin could be seen; behind them wound a long line of carriages that grew longer as they passed each farm and drew nearer to the village. When the road made a bend Euchariste had only to lean out of his carriage to see how many of them there were, and their unusual number gave him great satisfaction. A Moisan was certainly somebody.

They were going back by the same road now alone. The carriage drove along in the two parallel ruts, hardened by the first frosts, between the weeds and bushes in the ditches, which were of a uniform rust colour. It was four o'clock, and the sun was already about to set behind a bank of low leaden-coloured clouds in a fiery stream of molten metal. High up in the faded blue of the sky a flock of little clouds as curly as new-born lambs, hung suspended, and towards the east the waning moon looked like another isolated tuft of cloud.

A little while before, when all the others were with them, the old man's absence had seemed less real; in any case, he had been with them there, up in front, in that sinister black vehicle, which was the head of a procession whose tail wound to and fro with every whim of the road. Now Euchariste was alone with Mélie; each was the other's entire family and living kin.

He hadn't dared consult the parish priest about his marriage. It would hardly have been proper at a moment when the freshly turned earth on the old man's grave still stood out in a long livid hump. How hard it is to broach a subject sometimes!

He thought of it continually on the days that followed, as he sat near the stove smoking his pipe. Quite as a matter of course he had taken possession of his uncle's chair as he had taken possession of his property. But all his recent experiences and, above all, the fact that he was now obliged to decide the fate of all sorts of lesser beings on the farm had suddenly aged him. Already certain of his gestures were those of Ephrem Moisan, so much so that Mélie had commented on it.

"Sometimes when I look at you I think it's Ephrem." And, indeed, at night, in the dim light, he seemed to assume the same posture and to use the same rhythm when he rocked himself in his chair, and he had the same way of stopping suddenly to spit and then of striking his heel on the floor to start rocking gently again.

He still slept upstairs, though, and the big bedroom remained vacant. He would move in there after the wedding, when Alphonsine had come to live in the house. He wouldn't have dared to use it in the meantime. Uncle Ephrem's death was so recent that it didn't seem real to him yet; it was as if the departed might suddenly come back to recover his authority and his property. Though Euchariste gradually took over the dead man's possessions, it was done warily, with a kind of anxiety which made his advance a series of furtive nibbles. Each partial encroachment was given time to consolidate itself, as if with too great haste he might run the risk of bringing the old man back to life again.

He wasn't yet used to ownership. He had the notary's word for it; he had even seen the papers. Yet, in conversation, he would say "the farm, the barn, the cows" instead of "*my* farm, *my* barn, *my* cows." It was just as if these possessions had come to him by some devious process which a gesture or an incautious word might interrupt. Sometimes, though, he would lean against a fence he was repairing and repeat aloud, as if for practice : "*My* farm . . . *my* farm . . . *my* farm." But he would look round immediately for fear Uncle Ephrem might have heard him.

A day or so later Mélie told him that somebody was ill at the Faribeaults', who lived at the other end of the concession. "I guess it must be Amanda; she's had lung-trouble a long time now, and maybe she's dying. They've sent for the priest to come tomorrow morning."

It occurred to Euchariste then that the priest would be passing by their house next day. He might stop him, perhaps, and try to speak to him. He'd been promising himself every Sunday to call at the rectory, but this seemed easier. For every Sunday his courage had failed him. He'd make sure of being there when he passed. Oh, of course, not on the way there, when the priest would come by in his surplice, with the bell ringing, his face radiating majesty, his hands crossed over his stole and bearing the Blessed Host. But on the way back . . . maybe . . .

Next day he was on the watch beside the highway, seemingly engaged in digging a ditch but in reality keeping a sharp eye on the clump of elms near the road, round which the carriage would first appear. When it came by he knelt down, scarcely daring to look at the priest's face, to which the Blessed Sacrament lent a halo of awe-inspiring dignity.

But when the carriage passed again, an hour later, he was standing in the middle of the road as if by accident.

"Hullo, Euchariste," said the priest.

"Good morning, Father. Things not going so well at the Faribeaults' ?"

"Not so well, son."

He reined in his horse, guessing that Euchariste had something to say to him.

He was no longer the imposing priest of a while ago, but just a man; a man with a rugged face and a decided corpulence, which his beaver coat, now buttoned up, seemed to accentuate; he had never ceased to be a peasant, and he had the peasant's knowing smile. He was, indeed, from the country and marked for life with the brand of the soil. And this in spite of his years at school, his four years at the seminary, his eleven years of priesthood. During the latter period he had been in charge of a parish and was at one and the same time pastor, judge, and adviser to the whole flock, arbiter of all disputes, intercessor to the Throne of Heaven, which sends good weather or bad; in fact, the real soul of that tightly knit, closed community—the French-Canadian parish. The same avid, suspicious, Norman blood ran strongly in his veins too. He had the same restrained gestures as the members of his flock, the same laconic speech, the same reticence, and, on that account, the same ability to understand things without their being put into words. Nevertheless, his office and his awareness of his importance had left the stamp of authority upon him.

Euchariste had only to hint at how hard the work had become since the old man's death for him to understand that young Moisan was neither able nor willing to remain a bachelor any longer. The wedding could take place in March; yes, that's right, in March, early enough so that the ploughing would not be delayed by the marriage festivities.

"You're marrying a fine girl; you're a good lad. You'll get on well together, and I hope you have lots of youngsters."

"Don't worry about that, Father. And if God's willing I'll try to have one raised for a priest, if I'm not being too bold. And I hope he'll be like you are, always kind and ready to help us poor people."

"That's fine, Euchariste, that's fine. I'll try and fix it up for you. Say hullo to Mélie for me."

He clicked his tongue and urged his horse into a trot.

"By the way," he shouted, "come and see me Sunday after Mass about the banns."

"I sure will, Father; I'll be there."

He stood there a while with one foot on his shovel, dwelling complacently on the idea that had come to him for the first time a few moments ago. Yes, he'd raise one of his sons to be a priest, and he'd sing Mass and preach on Sundays and drive along the road carrying the Blessed Sacrament while people knelt as he passed. And later, when he himself was old, he'd go to see him in his fine rectory in the heart of some comfortable, prosperous village. Why not this one? Everyone would take their hats off to his son; everyone would look up to him, as is proper; and a little of this glory would be reflected on him, the father of a priest.

In the meantime one thing was settled—Alphonsine and he were going to get married in the spring.

Fine!

December came with its feast-days. Midnight Mass with the runners of the sleighs grinding on the hard snow. Midnight Mass, when, under the northern lights, dancing in honour of the Christ Child, the night was filled with the clear sound of bells tinkling in every direction, while in the distance the church appeared magically set out on the white napery of the snow, its windows blazing with light; the church under the stars winking in the black sky, towards which all wended their way, like kings of the East journeying to seek the new-born Christ across a desert undefiled.

Then came New Year's, with visiting relatives and friends drinking rounds of Jamaica rum in a thick cloud of pipe-smoke, with the high-pitched laughter of the women.

The sun sank low on the horizon, hesitated there for a few days, and then began to climb back towards the zenith. February heaped the snow still higher on the roads. The farm-buildings wrapped themselves in snow-flakes, like a sick man in a woollen blanket, while day and night the breath of the house issued white from the chimney. Sometimes the whole country-side was seized in the grip of a snow-storm, driven by a fierce wind rushing down from the north; eddies of fine snow swirled about like smoke, sealing the doors and windows and shaking the black skeletons of the trees until they creaked.

March at last, when the promise of summer battles winter's rearguard to an accompaniment of showers.

Old Branchaud did things handsomely. People ate and drank for three days to the health of the newly married couple, who, on the very first night, went off to the Moisan house. It was a fine wedding and not likely to be forgotten for a long time.

5

Now that he had taken an outsider under his roof, it seemed to Euchariste that he was clothed with a more absolute authority and it gave him, along with a feeling of his own importance, the assurance that he was at last in complete possession of the Moisan heritage. The house that had been so dull a little while before now knew a brisker rhythm, set by Alphonsine's alert footsteps.

And Mélie could take a rest at last. She readily seized the opportunity to spend her days sitting up against the stove, in a state of complete bliss, her simple mind relieved of all the cares of material existence; her fingers alone moved as she mechanically told her beads.

The young couple had opened up the big bedroom and spent their evenings there; but during the day-time Alphonsine busied herself in the roomy kitchen, where they all lived. At first Mélie had to show her where everything went, but it didn't take her long to learn, for farm-houses are all pretty much alike. From now on she also called the old woman "Auntie," adopting all her husbands family as her own, just as she spoke of the bedroom as "my bedroom," the bread-oven as "my oven," and the stove as "my stove." That was all part of her domain, where her man ate at her pleasure and what she of her own free will decided to give him.

As for the farm-buildings, they were for her as for her husband "our buildings"; and the fields, "our fields." For at milking-time she, too, would go to the warm stable, where, in the strong smell of straw, the dim light of the lantern lit up the heavy muzzles of their cows, who looked at her wearily as they shook their chains and blew into the water which ran past their nostrils in the long wooden trough.

Euchariste lazily enjoyed his happiness. Now that March was nearly over, a sun that grew hotter every morning darted its rays into the crust of snow that had lost something of its whiteness and each day revealed more and more the shape of the earth. Warm rains slowly rotted the coating of ice on the river, and black patches began to show where the water gushed up with a dull sound under the pressure of all the invisible rivulets of melting snow. But there was a long time to wait yet before the earth was stripped naked and was quite ready for spring cultivation. And so Euchariste could spend whole afternoons sitting in the old man's chair, puffing at his pipe, and, without seeming to do so, watching Alphonsine going to and fro, calm of face, with her chestnut hair neatly done up and with something heavier, freer, more sensuous in her movements that did not belong to Alphonsine Branchaud but to the Alphonsine who was Mrs 'Charis Moisan.

It made him happy to think that all their winters would be spent as tranquilly. He was content to put up with that immobility which the northern winter forces on everything. Sometimes Alphonsine would stop and look at him with amusement.

"Don't get all tired out, 'Charis! If you work so hard, you might strain yourself!"

Her voice had a sort of husky veiled quality, like those early autumn skies that shed a warm light. The expression of her love was also something clouded and unconscious.

'Charis usually made no reply to this teasing, which was the only form of tenderness they knew. All the delightful caresses, which married people are allowed, were kept for the evening, when Mélie had gone to sleep upstairs and they had closed the door of their room. Then Euchariste would suddenly take Alphonsine round the waist with a bold clumsiness which she would resist with an eager laugh. But in the day-time they dared not kiss each other because of a kind of bashfulness which made them look away when the impulse came to them. Sometimes, though, desire would come upon them in the dimly lit work-shop, where Euchariste was repairing a piece of harness, or in the loft, amid the heavy odour of hay, and she would come out, fixing her hair, to be met by a smile and a sidelong glance from Mélie. Two months went by, and little by little her gait grew heavier. When she walked, her hips swayed like those of a woman carrying a burden. One fine day he came upon her as she was cutting out pieces of white cotton and making them up nimbly into a sort of long and very narrow dress.

As a matter of fact, he had had his suspicions. But he was afraid to believe it was true and still more to put his thoughts into words. He leaned over towards her.

"Are you making me a Sunday shirt so I can go and see the girls? Let's have a look."

And he tried to take away the piece of material she was sewing. But with an instinctive gesture she held it against her bosom, which was already noticeably fuller, and answered unsmilingly: "It ain't you who'll be going to see the girls, 'Charis, but somebody else when he grows up."

"When ... when will it be, 'Phonsine?"

"Maybe you'll have it for your New Year's present, if you're good!"

"Say ... that's fine! I'll do my best, Ma."

He used that name for the first time, calling her the mother of his unborn children, of the son she had already promised him—"Ma", which is what Canadian farmers call their prolific spouses; they bear no other title but this one, which recalls their supreme function.

Euchariste was filled with a strange feeling of well-being. He felt strengthened, fortified, and at the same time much more mature. He, who just a few months before had been merely a nephew sheltered on someone else's farm, knew now that he had become, by the miracle of this begetting, the master of the land where yesterday he was a stranger; in a sense the guardian of this thirty-acre strip of which, by a mysterious process, he was at one and the same time serf and suzerain. He had done the spring seeding with a heart lightened by the thought that he was sowing for two, for Alphonsine and for himself. He had ploughed a smaller acreage that year, since he didn't wish to hire help for the harvest. As for the moment, they could live without thinking of any future beyond the immediate one—tomorrow's work and the forthcoming crop.

Now it was another story. His future was no longer the restricted, short-dated one he had envisaged so far; that was now over and done with. He suddenly saw his task unfold before his eyes, as day-break discloses the fields and reveals a new world.

His grandparents, his father, his mother, Aunt Ludivine, Uncle Ephrem—all his protectors and guardians had disappeared one after another. All those who, when he was a child, had stood between him and the harshness of the seasons, the cold at night, the fatigue of work which ended each day only to begin again the next; those whose hands he had felt touch his to reassure him in the dimness of his childhood, just as old trees interlace their branches over the tops of the saplings. He was now the only tree left from the destruction of the family thicket, and he stood alone in the middle of the plain, surrounded in spring by furrows, in summer by golden waves of grain, letting the grazing cattle rub against his scaly trunk in autumn, and in winter struggling with every one of his black branches against the north wind and the blizzards. And like this tree he would be a shelter and a refuge to the harvesters and these harvesters would be his own sons, until the day came for the lightning to strike him down and dry up the sap of life as it had done for Uncle Ephrem.

Poor Uncle Ephrem. So he had been denied the long-anticipated joy of seeing those grandnephews to whom he would have been a grandfather. Mélie would be there to sing "The Old Grey Hen" to them, and to make them shriek with laughter as she recited the old jingle: "Five little pigs went to market." But the old man sleeping over in the village cemetery would not be there to tell the wide-eyed children of the astounding adventures he and the men of his generation had experienced; of the feats of "Tiribe" Moisan, who could bend a silver coin with his fingers; and of his fight one night with a were-wolf, from whom he had only escaped by drawing blood with a penknife, to discover next morning, by a gash he had on his cheek, that it was his own cousin. And the story of granduncle Gustin Lafrenière, who fought against the "red-coats" at Saint-Charles in '37 and was then arrested and imprisoned for ten months by that old fire-eater Colborne.

"A penny for your thoughts, 'Charis," said Alphonsine.

"I was thinking of the barn roof; it's leaking. I didn't fix it last winter because I didn't feel much like working right after Uncle died. And the year before, I guess you remember, I just about got my arm cut off at the mill. And there's the cabin in the sugar-bush needs fixing too. I'll have to get after that in the fall, when the grain's in."

"So you're aiming to do some sugaring next spring, are you?" asked Alphonsine.

"I guess so, if it's a good winter. But no snow, no sugar. And there ain't been such an awful lot of snow for a few years back. There seems to be less and less of it."

"It's nothing to what they had when I was a youngster," Mélie broke in. "When I was a little bit of a thing at Lavaltrie, up at Pa's place, we all woke up one morning with snow pretty near blocking the upstairs windows. We was just about buried alive. Pa had to go up the chimney to dig us out. And it's the truth I'm telling you. You folks sure don't know what a real winter is."

"She's not lying," put in Euchariste. "I saw what it was like when I was up in the mountains at Sainte-Adèle. Not where we lived, because we was on a slope. But down in the valleys. I've seen Sundays they couldn't go to Mass because the horses went in up to the back-strip in snow-drifts. After every storm they had to dig out the trees for marking the roads and stick them in again."

"Say, that's nothing," retorted Mélie. "In the old days it was like that all the time, not just once in a while. But the winters just seem to be getting milder and milder."

"That's right, Auntie; the winters ain't so hard now," Alphonsine agreed as she bent over her sewing.

Every now and then she straightened up, with shoulders thrown back and head erect, and instinctively put her hand to her waist.

<hr>

6

"'Charis! . . . 'Charis!" A voice vibrant with pain filled the silence and the night. "'Charis!" Euchariste was sleeping heavily and snoring from time to time. "'Charis! . . . Aaaah! . . . 'Charis!"

He started, turned over suddenly, and mumbled indistinctly out of his dream: "Leave go of that. I told you to let the mare alone."

But Alphonsine was persistent and dug her elbow into him. "'Charis! Get up!"

"All right!"

He sat up in the middle of the tumbled bedclothes, his head suddenly clear but his limbs still heavy with sleep.

"What's the trouble, 'Phonsine? Are you sick?"

"My stomach pains me something terrible. Aouh! It hurts!"

Only half awake, he hated to leave his warm bed for the

room that was icy-cold because it was winter and which the darkness made colder still. But a groan from his wife brought him to his feet with a start. Aunt Mélie, wakened out of the light sleep of the aged, came in carrying a lamp. She leaned over Alphonsine, who was moaning softly, with her teeth clenched, as each fresh spasm of pain tore at her entrails and made her limbs contract.

"Where's it hurting you?" asked the old woman.

"It gets me in the back and it . . . Aouh! . . . It twists my insides. I can't think what I ate for supper last night, but it seems like it was poison."

"Have you been that way long?" asked Mélie.

"My kidneys felt kind of sore yesterday, but it's only been hurting me like this tonight."

"Well, why didn't you say so?" the old woman answered. "Go and hitch up, 'Charis, and get the doctor right off. And don't you worry, 'Phonsine. It's a belly-ache all right, but a married woman's belly-ache. Get a move on, 'Charis."

"Auntie, Auntie, I feel like I'm going to die!"

The words came to her instinctively; they expressed not so much the fear of death as the desire for it, to escape the martyrdom which awaited her: this way of the cross whose every anguished station she had guessed in spite of the reticence and the encouragement of those who had gone before her. In the last weeks of her pregnancy she went from one woman to another under pretence of borrowing, here a loaf of bread, there a spool of thread. And she timidly asked each one the same question. They all answered: "It's pretty bad but it don't last long," and then changed the subject, leaving her standing there with beads of perspiration on her forehead, sick with anxiety.

And now her time had come, and the long waves of pain which, she felt, were merely a prelude of what was to follow.

"Don't stay in bed, 'Phonsine," advised the old woman, who had begun to bustle about. "Get up on your feet and grab the back of a chair. When the pains get you, hang on tight. While you're doing that I'll go light the stove, and then I'll rub your stomach with butter. There's nothing better!"

It was still going on when the buggy came with the doctor, who had to be brought all the way from the village. They shut the door in Euchariste's face and he stayed by himself in the kitchen, much more upset by his uselessness than by his anxiety, while from time to time a more than usually piercing shriek made him grip his chair.

It lasted until noon; and then the door opened and he saw Mélie leaning over the disordered bed, where his Alphonsine lay motionless, her eyes closed, and looking with her pallor and her two long braids as if she were dead. The old aunt held a little wailing creature wrapped in white swaddling-clothes.

"It's a boy, 'Phonsine, and a fine one!"

Alphonsine made a feeble effort to look at her son, and could not get over her surprise that this tiny being, almost lost in his infant clothes, should have caused her such terrible and protracted suffering. But at the same time she was filled with deep triumphant joy, the indescribable joy of creation.

She would never have believed that she could regain her strength so quickly after her confinement. Five days later she was back in the kitchen, still a little weak, of course, in spite of her courage, but drawing fresh vigour from nursing her child, from every occasion on which she bared her swelling breast to his greedy mouth.

What was he to be christened? There was a lot of argument about that. First of all Joseph, of course, for all boys are called Joseph and all girls Marie. But what else? Mélie wanted Ephrem in memory of his uncle. Euchariste had suggested Barthélémi, because it seemed to him a real he-man's name. It was probably because he had once known a husky fellow called that at Sainte-Adèle, and it seemed to him that by some process of magic this name would endow his son with exceptional strength. But Alphonsine had an idea of her own and that was to call her first child, this exceptional being who was the fruit of agony, by some unusual name which would be particularly his. He couldn't be called Jean-Baptiste or Etienne or Louis-Georges like just anybody. He must be given the dulcet mysterious name of Oguinase, which she vaguely remembered having heard a long time ago in church, in the course of a sermon preached during a retreat. Ever since, she had promised herself that if ever she became a mother her first-born should bear that name. And so the child was christened Joseph Ephrem Oguinase.

The birth of this child made a great change in the Moisan household. Particularly in Alphonsine, who, in spite of her spirit, had felt somehow deadened in this atmosphere dominated jointly by the memory of old Uncle Ephrem and the frail presence of the old aunt. In Euchariste's case, living with these people had already considerably dampened the liveliness which one might have expected to find in a young man of twenty-five. But all that fell away from Alphonsine as soon as the child was born. She became a child again herself and played with this living doll and spoke to it in that unintelligible language which mothers, and all those with strongly developed maternal instincts, use to the very young. It was the same with Mélie, for she was used to sharing the motherhood of others. Each wanted the child for herself and both their lives henceforth were centred on Oguinase. He became the cause of all sorts of arguments: how he was to be dressed, for instance, for the old woman, who was always afraid he would catch cold, kept wrapping him in thick swaddling-clothes, flannel dresses, and blankets, which his mother patiently removed in spite of Mélie's protests. But the old woman became the despot as soon as Alphonsine had turned her back, and took the child away from the window, where it had been put by its mother to keep it amused, saying: "If you put him in the light like that, he'll get cross-eyed."

But it was Euchariste's existence that changed most. His authority on the farm was untouched and so was his relationship to the land. But this addition to his family made him take a back seat in matters affecting the household. Now there were questions discussed about which he was ignorant, arguments in which he timidly ventured an opinion only to be told quite clearly that men knew nothing about such things.

The little fellow did nothing much but smile prettily when they tickled him under the chin, and sometimes he made inarticulate noises that were interpreted in various ways and gave rise to fresh disputes. His only effective way of protesting against his environment was by mysterious illnesses that overwhelmed Euchariste with a sense of his helplessness and terrified Alphonsine, but which enabled Mélie to triumph. For the old woman would take advantage of the situation to bring out another traditional remedy from the store-house of her experience; it was she who cured him of whooping-cough by hanging a hazelnut with a worm in it round his neck by a red thread. By the time the worm had shrivelled up, he was better.

Alphonsine and Euchariste had returned to the humdrum existence of ordinary people, from which they had escaped for a while during the first months of their marriage. They were a part of a family now and each one had a definite share in the common load of cares and daily tasks. All this conformed to an order established thousands of years ago, when man renounced the freedom of a life devoted to hunting and fishing to accept the yoke of the seasons and subject himself to the yearly rhythm of the earth, his team-mate. Euchariste had the farm; Alphonsine, the house and the child. Life passed from the earth to the man, from the man to his wife, and from her to the child, who was the temporary end of the chain.

Except when there was a great deal of work to do, at which seasons he even had to hire help, Euchariste, now that he could stay away from home without being missed so much, got into the habit of going to spend the evenings over near the cheese-factory, where a little settlement was gradually growing up. It was seven miles and more from the Moisan farm to Saint-Jacques, which was their parish, and over ten down to Labern-aide. So the two churches lay at least eighteen miles apart.

The cheese-factory had been built twenty years before by the father of the present owners, who was the second cousin of Euchariste's grandfather on his mother's side. In order to tap the largest possible area, he had built at the cross-roads. In one direction ran the main road, the King's Highway, which followed a course more or less parallel to the river; in the other, the secondary road, which joined the first concession and the farms lying farther back. This next concession was generally called the *Rang des Pommes*, perhaps because a certain number of the farmers there had planted apple trees, but more probably for the reason that one of the first settlers was called Bernard Peaume. The family still lived there, but, as often happened, a nickname had taken the place of the original surname. They now called themselves Lebeau.

The population of the rural parishes remains fairly constant in the Province of Quebec: the number of families on the land doesn't vary a great deal, for the country people don't like to divide up their farms. Generally the father prefers to have his younger sons settle in districts newly opened to colonization, leaving the eldest son in undisputed possession of the family property, rather than split it up between his children. Moreover, the original method of portioning out the land in long narrow strips makes subdivision practically impossible. But as forests are gradually cleared away to widen the narrow belt of arable land, squeezed in between the river and the rugged flanks of the Laurentian chain, new concessions are opened up. That is why a certain Labarre, known to everybody, because of a limp, by the nickname of *La Patte*, decided to set up a blacksmith's shop opposite the cheese-factory, and "Pitro" Marcotte a harness-maker's shop.

Then when Maxime Auger died his widow opened a store in her house. On a set of shelves in the window stood lamp-chimneys, shoe-laces, spools of thread, bags of salt, penknives, and, in a box, little chocolate-coated marshmallow pigs, which the children bought to play butcher. Her business gradually expanded. Little by little the farmers' wives stopped spinning and weaving, while their husbands no longer made their own heavy top-boots; they bought city-made goods instead, which they found almost as lasting, smarter, and certainly cheaper. From the moment the local member of parliament, to whom she was distantly related—some never spoke of this without a knowing wink—got her a post-office, her store became the meeting-place for all the idlers of the neighbourhood. With the excuse of going to call for the very occasional letter, all the carriages stopped there on Sundays on the way back from Mass. And the men used to meet there in the evenings to indulge in endless games of checkers. The Widow Auger supplemented her income by the bootleg sale of *whiskey blanc*. But as she was an intelligent woman, both cautious and reasonable, and as no one ever left the place too much the worse for drink, there were never any complaints.

It was she who brought a nephew of hers from her native parish on the lower St. Lawrence and set him up as a baker. With the widow's money he bought a little plot of land behind the cheese-factory, on the road leading to the *Rang des Pommes*; then he built himself an oven and a sort of shed and transformed an old second-hand buckboard into a delivery wagon. But since every farm baked its own bread once a week, where were his customers to come from? However, the farmers' wives began to patronize him one after another and without too many objections from their husbands, for the bread, which was delivered three times a week, was fresher and in many cases better. The result was that Antoine Cloutier paid off the debt on his little bit of land, built himself a house, married a local girl, and brought up seven children on a property enlarged by two new lots which he purchased out of his profits.

The cross-roads was the place chosen for all these establishments and they, together with the farm-houses, made up a group of low, one-storey buildings, built of planks nailed vertically to a framework and blackened by exposure to the weather; because of their proximity to the cheese-factory they were constantly pervaded by a sour smell of butter-milk. The Widow Auger's store was recognizable from the fact that it had a platform in front and a short flight of steps, and there she usually sat in summer, knitting all through the afternoon, while she observed what went on in the neighbourhood and kept an eye on the passers-by. Above the door was a yellow sign swinging in the wind, with the words: "General Store".

It wasn't far from the Moisan farm to the settlement. First came the Raymonds; then the Gélinas; then Maxime Moisan, who was a very distant cousin of Euchariste. To distinguish the two families the grandfather's given name was added to the father's and they were called *les Maxime à Clavis*, just as people often referred to *'Charis à Noré* (Honoré).

Then came the Zéphir Authiers, whose next neighbours on the way to the settlement were a family with the curious name of "Six." This wasn't a nickname, though, but a corrupt form of their family name as it had been handed down from father to son. They were descended from one of those German mercenaries who crossed the seas under General Riedesel, some of whom, because they had married local girls, settled in the Province of Quebec. Since it was too difficult to pronounce, Schiltz had become "Six." In the course of generations who would remember that a few drops of alien blood flowed in their veins? They were as Canadian as anyone, for they tilled the Laurentian soil as the others did and got their living from it. Country is a matter of soil and not of blood.

The cross-roads was three properties further on; the long line of farms, one very like another, continued on beyond, each with its house with a butterfly roof and a group of buildings standing further back. And this went on for nine or ten miles, as far as Labernadie, whose metal-covered steeple glistened above a ridge like the mast of a ship buried in the sand.

Euchariste got into the habit of going to the settlement fairly often. He went off after supper always with the same excuse: "I guess I'll go see if there's any mail." It was a stock phrase and was easier to say than: "I guess I'll go and play a game of checkers at the store." There never were any letters Country people don't write many and, when they do, it is only in cases of absolute necessity such as sickness or death. Business matters? They are best not put down on paper; they should be settled orally and preferably over a drink. That's why a letter is a cause for alarm when it does come. The last one the Moisans had received almost frightened them out of their wits. Euchariste brought it home without daring to open it. But there was nothing inside but a request from a cousin in the States for a copy of the record of his baptism, which he needed to get married.

So the long winter evenings were spent pleasantly at the store. When Euchariste came into the low-ceilinged, smoke-filled room, the noise he made stamping his snow-covered feet on the threshold generally caused one or more of the checker-enthusiasts to look up. These consisted of five or six farmers, most of them middle-aged, grouped around the players, who held the checkerboard on their knees and from time to time thrust forward a rigid finger to make a threatening move, which brought exclamations of admiration from the onlookers. Some-one would remark: "Why, hullo, here's 'Charis!" while the player in jeopardy, with his mind all on the game, would merely exclaim: "You old son-of-a-gun, you won't catch me that way!" Then they all leaned over the checkerboard again, Euchariste among them.

When a game had been hotly contested and resulted in a brilliant victory, the winner would turn to Moisan, who was one of the best players in the concession. "Come and take a licking, 'Charis. I'll take you on for a shot of whiskey." The loser, and it was rarely Euchariste, would pay for the drinks and get the offer of a return match. It's true they had cast-iron throats and stomachs, but after seven or eight games the Widow Auger usually had to intervene to keep the peace. She would put them out and they would all go home under a sky studded with hard, bright stars, in the immeasurable silence of a winter's night, which made them lower their voices and sobered them up.

There were never any young men there. For when the harvest was over they almost all went up to the lumber-camps. They left at the end of September, right after the threshing, and gathered in little groups in the villages. From there they made for the forests of the upper Saint-Maurice or the Gatineau for the lumbering. At sixteen, or even fifteen, they left the farm, with their belongings in a bundle, and set off in squads, singing along the road and drinking in turn from a big demijohn of whiskey.

Some might be mere children when they left, but they were all men when they came back. This was not so much due to the hard work in the winter camps, or the forty-below-zero weather, but rather to the toughness of their companions. This quality prevailed from the moment they set out, when each group pitted its best fighter against the champions of other groups as they arrived, until the return, six months later, when, as lumberjacks from the North with their pockets full of money, they rang their quarters on the bar. The innocent-eyed boys, who were among them when they left, came back able to drink, fight, and swear like men.

Euchariste had never been conscripted into this reserve army of young men who went from home every year. Perhaps because the Moisan household would have seemed too empty without him, Uncle Ephrem never once let him go off with the others. He would have liked to go, though. Those six months of hardship, of living in huts buried in the snow and handling the woodsman's axe and the cross-cut saw, had no terrors for him. On the contrary, the tales of the men who had been there gave him a thirst for this strange existence in the north woods, with its epic combats man to man, its monotony relieved by a rare glimpse of the "Flying Canoe," that Pit' Gélinas had once seen, or by the cries of the "Banshee of the Saint-Maurice"— that invisible being that strikes terror into the hearts of those who haven't told their beads on Sunday at the hour their folks at home are at High Mass. He, too, would have liked to see those marvellous and diabolic nights when the northern sky was alight with shifting curtains of fire, which a fiddler can compel to dance to a tune of his own playing, though only at the risk of his immortal soul.

The men, when they sat out, sometimes made jokes at his expense, and his feelings were hurt. It made him ashamed, as if he were a cripple and people were making fun of his infirmity. He was rather embarrassed now at not being able to rattle off a string of fantastic oaths like theirs and at being the only one who would begin to feel light-headed after a few drinks, while the others told stories of their wonderful adventures that he was unable to cap. It had even got to be a habit with the others to turn to him when they wanted to tell a story about the lumber-camps. "Listen, 'Charis, you was never in a lumber-camp; here's a swell story, and it's the God's truth." Even now he would have gone off if it hadn't been for Alphonsine and the baby.

That is why at the Widow Auger's he sometimes tried to outdo the others, just to show them he was as much of a man as they were, even though he had never spent a winter in the woods.

Alphonsine made no complaints when he came home a little tipsy. He was never violent if he had too much to drink and, in any case, she was used to that sort of thing and it seemed quite natural in a man; a good fellow like Euchariste would grow out of it. It didn't mean that he wasn't a good husband; he wasn't any the worse for it and knew when to stop. Besides, when he had been at the store, he always brought her news of the people in the parish or, if he had won at checkers and there was some extra money in his pocket, some bit of finery to wear on Sunday.

7

Every Sunday afternoon Euchariste hitched up his mare, Mousseline, and went off with Alphonsine to see her parents. Mélie stayed at home to look after Oguinase and his little sister Héléna. Alphonsine was expecting another child soon; it would be the third in four years.

At her side he travelled the same road he so often took when she was his girl and he was on his way to court her.

In the summer-time the carriage usually drove along in deep ruts under a broiling sun, whose rays accentuated the green of the trees and the golden yellow of the ripe oats. The horse's hoofs and the carriage-wheels sank with a soft muffled sound into the thick dust; Euchariste, clicking his tongue, urged the horse into a trot and a fine powdery film rose and settled on the weeds beside the ditch, dulling their vivid green.

Euchariste looked at each farm as they drove by and was able to tell at a glance how things were going. The earth answered his unspoken questions as fully as those who tilled it might have done: the Picards were beginning to take in their corn; the Arthème Barrettes were draining their pasture.

"Say," he would remark to Alphonsine, "the Touchettes are through weeding their potatoes."

"They're further ahead than we are," she would reply.

But today winter had made them drowsy with cold and rather like the animals who hibernate in hollow trees. Life had become a long wait for spring, with looking after the stock and cutting firewood its only diversions.

The sleigh glided along over the snow, which the wind had shaped into dunes of dazzling brightness, topped with a plume of fine white crystals at the slightest puff. This limitless white beach was streaked with a pattern of curved lines like a sandy shore lapped by the waves. The steel runners made a continuous shrill sound like the squeaking of a badly resined bow and the sleigh was shaken violently every time it fell into a trough between two drifts. As the horse plodded along at a heavy trot, both Euchariste and Alphonsine kept silent. For they seemed bound and gagged by the intense cold, which made their foreheads ache and caused them to huddle up half-numbed under the pile of blankets, coats, and bear rugs.

Over the whole expanse of the plain the only living things in this sparkling cold air were the horse, the sharp clear music of the sleigh-bells, the little spirals of white vapour; and those which hung above the horse's head, or were breathed out by the two in the sleigh, were the more evanescent. But here and there was a vertical plume rising from a chimney, like a feather stuck in the roof of the house.

Winter had buried everything under a layer of fine white powder. The trees stood sentry, with their wild skeleton limbs in sharp outline and the tops of the fence-posts just showing in a serried row; a black patch turned out to be a sturdy little fir tree, like a piece of flotsam on this lifeless, boundless, white expanse, beside which the shifting, changing green of the sea seems the very essence of life.

The mare shied suddenly. A red fox darted under her nose and loped slowly away, trailing a long shadow cast by the sun shining low on the horizon. A hundred yards further on he stopped with his tail in the air, turned to look back at the sleigh, sniffed the wind, and then went off with his lithe silent gait towards the woods.

"We'll have to look out for the chickens, 'Phonsine; there's a prowler looks mighty suspicious to me."

Aroused out of her torpor, Alphonsine untied the woollen scarf, patterned with hoar-frost, in which her head was wrapped.

"Say! 'Charis, I think the end of your nose is froze!"

"Shouldn't be surprised."

He reigned in the mare and climbed out of the sleigh, only to sink in snow up to his knees. When he had turned down the collar of his coat and taken off his tuque, he rubbed his nose vigorously with snow. Then he threw the last handful in his wife's face.

"Cut it out, you poor simp, what's the sense of doing that!" she shrieked.

But he started pelting her with snow-balls, which she tried to ward off with her arm as best she could. She was all tangled up in the rugs and shrieked with laughter every time a particularly well-aimed shot hit her full in the face and sent a shower of cold snow down her neck.

They behaved like children let out of school for the holidays; they were making the most of their respite from farming, for winter had freed them from worrying about rain that rots the crops, gales that tear the roofs off the barns, or the stock whose pranks might force them out of bed in the middle of the night.

Euchariste got back into the sleigh.

"Go on! Giddap!"

When they got to the Branchaud house, Mousseline slowed down to a walk and got ready for a special effort. With a good pull she dragged the sleigh out of the ruts and started for the stable.

In the open shed stood three sleighs with their empty shafts in the trampled snow. A little man, all bundled up and with a bright-coloured woollen sash round his waist, was unharnessing his chunky little horse.

The mare had come to a standstill of her own accord.

"Say! What do you know about that! Looks to me like Phydime Raymond. How are things, Phydime?"

The little man turned round and displayed a pair of shifty eyes framed by bushy, greying whiskers.

"Not so bad, 'Charis," he replied.

"Well, and what's the latest?"

"Oh! Nothing much; same as usual."

"Your folks all well?"

"Oh, sure. Yours all right, 'Charis?"

"Yeah, they're fine too."

Both were really thinking of something quite different as they exchanged these customary greetings. Phydime Raymond was the Moisan's next-door neighbour. Their long narrow strips of land ran side by side all the way from the road to the hill, where each ended in a small wood. Now Euchariste knew that his neighbour wanted his bit of sugar-bush to round out his own further up. Phydime's father had hankered after it in his day, so it was an old story. Not that he had ever mentioned it to Uncle Ephrem. But things of that kind can be guessed, or sensed, if only from the detached manner in which someone says: "Those maples over there don't look so good." When the same neighbour remarks a few months later that it's hardly worth his while making sugar because he has so few trees, it is quite clear what is meant. Euchariste knew pretty well that the subject would be broached one of these days.

Raymond's wife had been even more explicit at haying-time the year before. She had actually said to 'Phonsine: "Did you ever notice, 'Phonsine, how your farm cuts into ours up in the woods? It means we have to go round to get to the sugar-cabin."

As matters stood, Phydime and Euchariste kept an eye on each other, each waiting for the other to speak first. And it came to head all of a sudden while Euchariste was undoing the traces.

"Say," said his neighbour, "I'll have to see you one of these days about the fence up in the woods."

"Fine! You'd better come round to our place some night and bring your pipe. We can talk it over."

Alphonsine had already gone off towards the house. Euchariste opened the stable-door and the mare went in of her own accord, more than glad to find herself enveloped in the heavy acrid heat of the other animals, with the soft straw underfoot and, overhead, the low ceiling, which echoed muffled noises and from time to time the sound of a shoe knocking against the stall.

At the Branchauds, as in all the other farm-houses, the whole family was gathered in the kitchen round the stove, which was heated red-hot and roaring away at full blast.

"Hullo, you two," said Branchaud.

"Hullo, Pa. Hullo, everybody."

"Take your things off. Cold, eh?"

"Cold enough!" replied Euchariste, as he took off his fur coat and shook the snow from his boots.

Each new arrival had done the same thing and there was a little puddle round the stove.

"Say, 'Charis, didn't you see we had company?"

From the moment he came in the door Moisan suspected as much, for he noticed the demijohn of whiskey standing on the table. Suddenly through the thick cloud of pipesmoke he saw someone who wasn't one of the neighbours and whom he recognized as he came forward.

"Well, if that don't beat the devil!" exclaimed Euchariste. "If it ain't Willie Daviau! What are you doing down this way? Look who's here, 'Phonsine!"

Alphonsine, who had gone over to talk to her mother in the corner where the women were gossiping, turned round and let her arms drop to her sides with a gesture of mock despair when her eyes lighted on Daviau.

"If that don't beat all!" she said, shaking her head. "As if there wasn't enough nuisances hanging on round here now!"

"Oh, yeah?" Daviau retorted. "Some girl she is! I was her fellow for six months; I guess that's how she knows I can hang on."

Alphonsine's embarrassed protests were drowned in a burst of laughter.

"Ain't that just like him!"

"Darned if it ain't the same old Willie!"

"Ain't he the bastard!"

Old Branchaud's voice made itself heard above the hubbub and reduced the others to silence.

"Well, never mind about that, 'Charis; come and have a drink. Bring a tumbler, Ma," and as Phydime Raymond appeared just then : "And a bucket for Phydime."

They all burst out laughing again, this time at Raymond's expense. But he merely shrugged his shoulders. He didn't know how to take a joke and had never been known to laugh.

Old Mrs. Branchaud brought two glasses. The men were silent while drinks were poured out all round.

"Here's to everybody !" said Branchaud, who knew his manners.

"Here's to the girls," said Willie, no less polite, with a wink in Alphonsine's direction.

They all drank, emptying their glasses at one gulp. And the younger ones, whose tender throats were burnt by the raw spirits, tried not to make a wry face. They wiped their mouths on their sleeves and, in the ensuing silence, the smoke from their pipes rose again to the blackened rafters, where it hung in clouds.

The low voices of the women, rocking gently to and fro over in their corner, were accompanied by a rhythmic creaking. They were talking about Pétrusse Authier, who was dying of lung-trouble, about the death of the two little twin girls up at Armand Grothé's place. Then one of them proclaimed the efficacy of a potato carried in one's pocket as a cure for rheumatism. Finally the conversation came round to the illness of "Jésus" Lafleur's wife, whose time according to some was due in five months, while others maintained it was four. They merely referred to it as an illness, but not because they were prudish; for the children who were seated quietly in a corner of the room, so as not to dirty their Sunday clothes, took too active a part in the life of the farm, in the life of the land, where everything is simple and aboveboard, to be unaware of the fundamental laws of nature to which both man and beast are subject. They did so rather from an instinctive reticence towards things of the body, or perhaps because one should use precise terms only for matters connected with the land : birth, illness, death.

Euchariste cleared his throat noisily.

"Say, Willie, aside from coming to see if the girl who threw you over is being treated right, what brings you down our way ? Are you aiming to stay ?"

"Me ? Not on your life ! I've still got my job in town with

good pay. I'd sooner live with people than with the cows and pigs, if it's all the same to you."

They all laughed at his wise-cracks, except, of course, Phydime Raymond and Moisan himself, who thought Daviau eyed his wife rather too often. It wasn't that he was capable of jealousy. The women he knew were not much inclined to be interested in anything outside their housework and their children. If there were any others, Alphonsine certainly wasn't one of them. Not that the women of his acquaintance were conscious of any special loyalty, but they could not be lured away from their own menfolk by glamour or by sentiment.

Euchariste had never thought all these things out, for they were the answer to questions he had never considered. His type of jealousy was rather envy of Daviau himself.

The latter had prospered since he had left the farm to find a job in town, and had freed himself of the land's tyranny, its whims and its stern law. Starting as an ordinary day-labourer, he had become a foreman on city pay-roll. He was also known as a ward heeler, one of those electoral agents whose undercover work is far more useful to a candidate than all the speeches made in parliament. That was enough to make him a man of importance, but the fact that he was no longer bound to the soil was a still more cogent reason.

When the harvest was at its height and everybody else was hard at work from early morning until late at night, he had actually spent three whole days loafing about the district, strolling from farm to farm, sitting on fence-rails with his legs dangling and a pipe in his mouth while he watched the farmers and their families spreading hay and sweating profusely in the sun. During the brief pauses, when one or another would stretch himself out in the shade of a wild-cherry tree beside the ditch to swallow a drink of cold water from the earthenware jug, Daviau would chat about farming conditions and then switch the subject, apparently by accident, to François Auger, the member in the Quebec legislature, "who works so hard for the people in the country." Every now and then he would give a hand to the farmer and his numerous sons and daughters, particularly if one of the girls had a pretty face and a promising smile. But he knew how to be just awkward enough in helping for people to realize quite fully that he was now a gentleman from the city.

It suddenly dawned on Euchariste that this wasn't just an ordinary gathering of neighbours, met together by accident;

today the whole atmosphere suggested a political meeting. All those present were well-known party men. They and their families before them had always been Liberals, for in the country districts of Quebec political opinions are handed on from generation to generation just like farm-lands. They are almost as much a part of an inheritance as property or religion. People considered it quite natural to say: "No need to ask if he's a hundred per cent Grit; he's a real Moisan," or: "The Touchettes? Why, they've been Tories since Adam." These party loyalties formed the only factor in politics that was really understood, and every collective action flowed from this source. Whether it was a question of choosing a school-mistress or building a water-main, these two rival clans, Liberal and Conservative, were to be found facing one another, so full of political feeling that they were ready to battle one another to the death on election day.

Aside from Branchaud and his two elder sons, Anthime and Jean-Paul, and Euchariste himself, Pit' Gélinas was there and so were Jérémie Godin and Phydime Raymond and Baptiste, the son of Maxime Moisan, and Toine Cloutier and even old Badouche, who had witnessed electoral struggles in which people walloped one another over the head for or against Confederation.

But Willie had started talking again.

"I was just telling them why I was down this way when you came in, 'Charis."

"Do you know what! Maybe there's going to be a provincial election in the spring," said Anthime Branchaud, eager to show off his knowledge.

"I'd like to know what good that'll do," put in Godin whom they all called "Bébé" Godin. "With all these elections they keep having a man can't get his work done. When it ain't a provincial election, it's a federal election; and when it ain't a federal election, it's for the mayor. Last time I went and voted I'd all my hay to turn. While I was away it rained and it just about all spoiled on me."

"Maybe so," admitted Daviau diplomatically. "But if you've got a parliament you've got to have members. And if you want members you've got to have elections. No elections, no members."

"Good riddance," interrupted Godin.

"And don't forget one thing, Bébé; and that is if we don't

have real men with guts down in Quebec it won't be long before the English up in Ottawa tan the hides off us."

That was a masterly argument. Willie knew quite well that they could all be united against the English, those hereditary enemies of the French-Canadians, who, after a century and a half, have not forgotten that they were beaten and conquered.

But although he was shaken by this appeal, Godin stuck to his original idea.

"I guess you're right. But I think they ought to fix it up between them some way or other; a real good fight some Sunday afternoon, something in the line of a cock fight. The winner to be boss for keeps. You'd see, with two or three husky French-Canadians, the English would get an awful licking."

"Or you could have them chosen by the Bishop, just like the priest does all the time for the church-wardens," suggested Edouard Moisan. "It wouldn't take him long."

"You must be crazy, Edouard. No Grit would stand a dog's chance with Bishop Laflèche."

"Say, Willie," asked old Branchaud, "is it true they're going to spend a whole lot of good money to build a railroad for the fishermen down in Gaspé?"

"They're surely not going to do that," said old Badouche.

"I'll swear it's the God's truth, Badouche."

Up to that moment Phydime Raymond hadn't opened his mouth. Now he knocked out his pipe on his boot-heel in such a way that Daviau's attention was caught and he turned towards him.

"Say, Willie, you know a whole lot more than we do down here ..."

This got under Daviau's skin, but he was careful not to show it.

"How about telling us why it is no farmers ever get elected. They have lawyers, doctors, notaries, travelling salesmen, but never any farmers. It don't look so hard; I don't know if it's true, but I've heard they get eight hundred dollars just for getting up and talking once in a while and then sitting in a rocking-chair and smoking in the parlour all fixed up with gold things in the parliament buildings. Of course, that's too good for poor bastards of farmers. When we've worked all year yanking out tree-trunks and ploughing and sowing and cultivating, we've maybe a hundred and fifty dollars profit if it's a good year. And that's if the hail don't get in ahead of you, and the sheep don't get the strangles. But it seems to me if they had more farmers and fewer lawyers down in Quebec they might hear something once in a while about the land and the poor devils who work their guts out farming it. They might fix it so the price of potatoes would go up instead of getting people to fish for cod by rail. But what the hell does Mr. Auger care if potatoes sell for fifty cents a bag; he lives in Montreal!"

He stopped abruptly and took a deep breath, rather embarrassed at having said so much and particularly troubled by the silence that greeted him when he spoke of the land and on its behalf.

"By God, you're right, Phydime!" shouted Pit' Gélinas, whose liquor had given him courage.

"The farmer never gets a chance," insisted Edouard Moisan.

"And it's always been that way," summed up old Badouche, as he leaned over to spit emphatically in the direction of the stove.

A murmur of general agreement went round the room and even included the women, who had stopped talking in their corner and turned round to listen to Raymond's speech.

Daviau was the only one who said nothing. He let them calm down, waited a moment longer, and then said with a good-natured smile: "Well, I'll be darned, Phydime; you know how to talk! I'd never have guessed it. It would be fine if there was a few farmers like you in parliament."

"Not for me! That ain't why I talked the way I did. But it strikes me there's a limit . . ."

Still he was pleased by the impression he had made and by the compliment too.

"Good. Now let me tell you something." Daviau continued. "Suppose the county sends you down to Quebec to tell them all about it. Who's going to look after your farm?"

They all sat silent, as if they were gagged. They hadn't thought of that. They had forgotten their serfdom for a moment and the fact that though a doctor can leave his practice, a notary his office, a merchant his store, and even an artisan his workshop, the farmer alone cannot absent himself from the land, so close is the bond between them. The soil does not bear fruit without man's assistance, and it is this necessity that links him to it and can hold him prisoner to a thirty-acre strip.

It had begun to get dark and Rosa-Alma, Alphonsine's

younger sister, got up to light the lamps; a smell of coal-oil filled the room.

Alphonsine came over to her husband.

"Don't you think it's about time to get going, 'Charis?"

"Sit a while and smoke another pipe," said old Branchaud politely but without much insistence. "It ain't so late."

"It's getting kind of dark. Time to go and milk the cows," said Euchariste.

They all got up and put on their hats and coats.

"Have to talk about all this again some other time," said Daviau.

He would have liked to have gone on to make sure of his triumph. But he knew it was no good trying to keep them from leaving. Out of doors a cruel wind, blowing from the north over frozen forests, nipped their cheeks and made their eyes water.

The evening star was already visible, twinkling in the sky, and in the silence could be heard the long muffled mooings of the cows, complaining at the heavy burden of their udders.

9

Their third child was born a few weeks later. Oguinase was already running about all over the place on his little short legs, to the great apprehension of Mélie, who up to now had always kept him close to her, like a mother-hen her chicks. She was getting more and more fearful and had become a bit childish recently; no wonder, she must be over eighty!

The little boy was beginning to give her the slip and to make his own contacts with the animals and inanimate objects on the farm. He would follow her when she went to give oats to the chickens and liked to scatter little handfuls clumsily and step on the golden grains so that he could feel the hens pecking between his bare toes. All day long he played about in the big kitchen, which was his domain as well as that of the women-folk, until nightfall brought Euchariste in from his chores, fill-ing the room with a warm smell of stable-litter. Then Oguinase would climb up into Mélie's lap to listen to the wonderful stories she told him. Gradually he would fall asleep to the rock-ing of the chair and the lilt of the quavering old voice. When she thought he was fast asleep Mélie would stop, and the only sound was the creaking of the rockers. But he would wake up at once. "What next, Granny, what did 'Ti-Jean' do in the wood?" And this happened every night until he really fell sound asleep.

After Oguinase there was a little girl, christened Héléna. Then came another boy, Etienne.

The first child had been a revelation for Euchariste; Oguinase had satisfied his parental instincts and natural pride in seeing himself reincarnated in someone who would grow up to manhood. He felt he had added something to the Moisan farm, something that was its due and for which it had been waiting a long time. From a bygone age there survived in him the dim impulse to personify the earth, who was still the daughter of Heaven, the spouse of Time, the beneficent and fruitful goddess to whom one offers the first-born of the flock and the first fruits of the harvest.

But, above all, Oguinase confirmed Euchariste in his sway over the heritage of Uncle Ephrem. The child's birth definitely consecrated the continuity of the family, and for Euchariste he was also the crowning incident in a whole period of his own life. His betrothal, his uncle's death, his taking over the property, his marriage and the birth of the child—all these things took place in the space of a few months. Almost from one harvest to another he ceased to be Euchariste Moisan, an adopted son on a farm to which he had no claims, and became Euchariste Moisan, husband, father and undisputed owner of the land which was now his.

So many changes in so short a time.

Anything that could happen now would only be a repeti-tion. This period in his life would always seem to him a kind of heroic era, filled with decisive happenings which he could never forget, while the future would unfold without bringing him anything but one day's work very like another and the eternal round of the seasons. He could look back and say: "The year I was married." But in future he would record time not so much by what he himself had done as by the exceptional doings of wind and weather: "The year of the big hail-storm." "The autumn it rained so much." Each year would follow much the same pattern as the one before it. Ploughing, seeding, harvesting, and in winter a rest with no work to do. Then the same thing all over again, with, probably, a birth, that would no longer be the birth of the child but merely of a child.

He accepted these births without enthusiasm, but also without regret. The farm could support as many Moisans as were likely to arrive. If there were to be ten of them, well, there'd be ten; if fifteen, then fifteen. Just like everybody else. What would be must be. Alphonsine would have to bear her appointed number.

He soon got used to it and accepted things with that passivity that men and animals acquire when their lives are conditioned—conditioned, in the case of man, by wind and snow and rain and by all these things, plus the whim of their masters, in the case of the animals. For a while it had amused him to watch Oguinase learning to walk or trying to imitate the sounds of human speech. It was a new experience for him, as he had never had anything to do with children. It made him laugh at first when Mélie said: "Look at the nice cow," and the child lisped: "Ithe cow." Then the pleasure palled and the farm claimed his full attention again.

Héléna, however, hadn't learned to walk yet, though she was over fourteen months old. She remained sickly and, though at six months she seemed for a time to be growing stronger, for some weeks now she had been losing weight. Lying in the bottom of the cradle, from which she would soon be driven by the new baby, she looked, with her wrinkled face, like a little old woman and day by day her eyes sank deeper into their sockets.

She died a few days after the birth of Etienne. One morning her mother found her lying quite cold in the bed where she had been put after the arrival of her little brother.

Euchariste and his wife were much distressed. Alphonsine particularly, for she mourned in her first daughter a child of her own sex, whom she had thought of as helping her with the housework in the years to come and then marrying some honest lad, who, in her vague day-dreams, had the broad shoulders and the mischievous eyes of her own man.

For a few days Euchariste went about looking more preoccupied than usual and Oguinase, who didn't know what it was all about, was neglected by all except Mélie, for whom death was a familiar visitor. Then they turned their attention to the new baby; even Alphonsine consoled herself with the thought that she would certainly have other daughters, as she knew she was not barren.

Continued child-bearing had already broadened her hips and made her heavy-breasted. But her step was as alert as ever as she went to and fro in the low-ceilinged kitchen or in the stable, filled at milking-time with the purposeful sound of the milk spurting into the metal pails. She would stop sometimes and, staring into space, would, with an automatic gesture, push back a wisp of hair that was tickling her cheek. And whenever Euchariste looked at her with an expression of shy satisfaction, as sometimes happened still, she would smile a brave gentle smile, though otherwise she smiled rarely now.

The work was hard, to be sure. Even though Mélie could look after the children a bit, Alphonsine had all the house-work; the meals to get, as she leaned over the red-hot oven, often with the child she was nursing held in her left arm; the floors to be scrubbed; the sewing and the mending; the family wash to be done; and, once a year, the brown oily soap to be made in a cauldron hung over a big fire in the yard.

She had the kitchen-garden too, where sometimes Euchariste came and gave her a hand, a service she repaid by going to milk the cows with him and carrying back on a yoke from the stable to the house the buckets brimming over with creamy milk.

She did all this work without pleasure, but without distaste. Weren't all these a woman's usual tasks? And when the harvest-time came round with the need for hurry, she would leave everything to go and work in the fields with Euchariste and the man they always hired at this season, straining away with them to get the grain in before a storm broke.

But it was early April now. Not three days before the first crows had appeared, flying from the south to herald the tardy spring.

After hesitating some time on the horizon, the sun began to rise higher each day and, as it grew stronger, to thaw the frozen ground still covered with melting snow. Its warmth brought out black patches on the icy crust of the river, which the water was furtively eating away underneath. Here and there the earth was beginning to tear aside its shroud, to undo its bonds, before appearing newly risen in the bright sun of Eastertide. Along the road the runners of the sleighs already scraped the hard ground in places where the winter winds had blown away most of the snow; and the ruts were full of water, which still froze at night, but broadened out further and further each noon to mirror the fresh blue of the sky.

The nights were milder, and in their bedroom Euchariste and his wife sometimes talked for a little; that is, until sleep came to stifle the words before they were spoken.

"Say, 'Phonsine, I was talking to Phydime Raymond today."

"Is that so? What's he got to say?"

"One of these days I think he's going to ask me to sell him my bit of sugar-bush, up on the hill."

"Why, sure, 'Charis, but wasn't you going to make sugar this year? You ain't made any yet. And they say the sap's running well this spring."

"It's this way, 'Phonsine. Every year I aim to make some, and every year it works out different. Anyway, it ain't worth while tapping the trees. I had a look round when I went to see about the fence. From the north end of the hill down to the end of our place I don't think there is sixty fair-sized maples. That way, if Phydime puts it up to me, I guess I'll sell. And, anyway, that red earth don't make good land."

"What do you think he'll want to give for it?"

"Oh . . . for all the use I get out of it, it would pay me to take twenty-five dollars. It's as wide as the farm, three acres, but taken the other way it's not much more than half an acre. Anyway, I'll let him speak first."

Alphonsine didn't answer.

She was asleep.

Phydime Raymond's desire to get possession of this little wood was genuine. The two farms stretched out side by side, separated only by the fence of cedar rails and by the narrow creek, which wound along at will from one farm to the other and back again. Up at the top the ground climbed suddenly to a steep sandy hill, to which a few trees clung, and there the bed of the creek ran in a deep gully. The hill rose slantwise, so it was less than an acre in depth on the Moisan side and more than that on Phydime's. Above all, the Raymond wood had more maples, whose new sap in spring oozed from the tap-holes to give a tart fragrant sugar. Actually the land was impoverished and there was no use cultivating it; first of all because the soil was red ochre, in which wheat and clover don't grow well.

Matters were settled a few days later. Raymond came over

to Euchariste's place one evening "to see if the sick cow was getting better."

As they smoked pipefuls of strong tobacco they discussed illnesses and the weather, the ice-bridge that was becoming unsafe, the coming elections and François Auger's chances of being re-elected member.

Then as Phydime got up he said: "I guess I'll have to be getting back to the wife."

But Euchariste, who saw him hesitate, said nothing.

"Say, 'Charis, while I think of it, what are we going to do about the fence up on the hill? Is it your turn to fix it this year, or mine?"

The discussion begun in this way wasn't long in taking shape. Raymond, who wanted Moisan's lot, began by offering to sell him his own. Euchariste, who wasn't at all interested, replied that "maybe it wasn't a bad idea." The former declared that his own bit of land wasn't worth ten dollars; the other countered by saying that as far as he, Euchariste, was concerned Phydime might just as well tap the three or four Moisan maples while he was about it, for all the good they did him. It was his intention, though, to try and clear it one of these days and seed it in hay.

There matters stood for the next few days. Then Phydime came back and finally offered twenty-five dollars. Moisan asked seventy-five. They talked about the weather again and at last settled on fifty.

"It's an awful lot of money," sighed Phydime. "I can't pay you all of it right off. I'm going to maybe sell a horse, but I still won't have enough. Crops haven't been so good. Times ain't like they used to be."

The great difficulty was to draw up an agreement. Phydime suggested, without much enthusiasm, that they should go before a notary. But why make a trip to Saint-Jacques and pay fees when it was so much easier to arrange matters on a friendly basis? They agreed it really wasn't worth while and, on the spot, Euchariste, who could write fairly well, got out a sheet of writing-paper and set a lamp on the corner of the big kitchen table. It was set forth that "Euchariste-à-Noré Moisan sold to Phydime-à-Charles Raymond the sugar-bush at the top of the hill at the end of his farm for fifty dollars, payable in twelve months."

Before signing, they both reread the document carefully and had Alphonsine read it too, for they had the farmer's mistrust of anything set down in writing. For something signed is a bond that cannot be broken. Then Phydime folded the paper twice and slipped it into his vest pocket.

"To start with I'll bring you ten dollars, anyway. Sunday after Mass," said Phydime.

"That's all right with me, Phydime."

And they changed the subject.

The fifty dollars would be banked with the notary. They would go to swell the thousand-odd that Uncle Ephrem had left at his death and which constituted a little secret fund that was never referred to but was kept for an emergency and which increased twice a year with interest, at five per cent

In the autumn Raymond kept his promise and came to pay off the remainder of his debt. He counted out the coins on a corner of the table; eighty fifty-cent pieces, shining and smooth and warm. 'Phonsine put them into the knitted purse, which she hid under the sheets in the big linen-cupboard in the bed-room.

And that year there was an abundant harvest into the bargain.

In foreign countries, whose exotic names were given in the newspapers, on the far-away banks of the Volga, drought had killed the wheat and men were dying of hunger in their fields parched by the sun.

For that reason wheat and oats sold at prices never reached before. And Euchariste, well satisfied, was able to add more than a hundred and fifty dollars to Phydime's fifty next time he went to Saint-Jacques to see the notary.

SUMMER

1

The thread of days is wound onto the distaff of the years with an even continuous motion, each today enveloping a yesterday. When the skein is finished the spinning-wheel of time at once begins another.

Sunrise follows sunrise and brightening skies melt the snow and free the earth, which in turn thrusts up towards the heavens shoots born of hot June days, when the sun's rays shine almost directly down onto the furrows and burst open the seed embedded in the soil. The crops grow taller and taller, until men come to rob the ear of the grain which Nature meant for its perpetuation, but which they arrogate to themselves and devour as a reward for their trivial intervention in the order of the universe.

The seasons follow one another and men notice the altered face of things; they stop and lift their earth-bent heads from time to time to scrutinize the heavens, clouded or clear, for threat or promise.

The years go by with their succession of days and nights, their rotation of the seasons in a cycle just like the one men themselves apply to the crops. And through these two cycles, man's and Nature's, the earth, that otherwise would become impoverished, recovers its fertility.

The Moisans, like their neighbours, had bad harvests and good ones, but mostly the latter. There were gales like the one which tore the roof off the old barn, frosts that killed the buds on the fruit trees, and a tremendous flood which turned the whole lower plain into a huge lake, as the creek rose again to its original banks and took on the appearance of a river. When the waters fell they left behind a gift more precious than gold: a coating of rich black humus.

The family had grown. Every woman must bear her allotted number and Alphonsine did not fail to do so. After Oguinase, and Héléna, who died, and Etienne, came Ephrem; then a little girl who only lived long enough to be baptized; then Malvina; then another child who died before it was many months old; then Eva; and finally Lucinda, still in her cradle. A tenth child was expected. These births occurred regularly, so regularly that they could almost be used to reckon the years. And yet they rarely said: "The flood came the year Malvina was born," but rather: "Malvina was born the year of the big flood"—as they said "the year the wind blew down the old barn," or "the year there was no sugar." In the same way it was always: "He will be such and such an age when they cut the hay," or, "when they pick the apples."

As for Mélie, she slipped away quietly, a little light-headed towards the end and continually muttering to herself, huddled up in her rocking-chair near the stove and making a sort of indistinct purring sound like a cat. One fine morning Oguinase, who had been sent to wake her, came back and said that Aunt Mélie was fast, fast asleep and wouldn't get up. And, indeed, she never woke again. For a few days the big rocking-chair seemed empty without her shrivelled little body topped by a white cotton cap.

One after another the children followed the road to the country school-house. First of all Oguinase alone; but before long he was leading his little brother Etienne by the hand, both of them shuffling along in step, trying to raise as much dust with their bare feet as a horse would. Etienne gave his left hand to Oguinase so that his right was free to clutch at the weeds and the wild iris in the ditch. Then Ephrem came along to take the other hand and another link was added to the chain. Soon there were four of them and they could raise as much dust as a cart. The youngest was Malvina, a fresh, pink-cheeked little girl with two short brown braids tied end to end like the handles of a basket that bobbed up and down amusingly, like a skipping-rope, when she trotted along behind her three brothers.

With the passing of time Oguinase had grown up to be a sturdy little fellow of eleven, broad-shouldered and rather stocky like his distant Norman ancestors, but able now to give a hand in the fields, while the women—Alphonsine and the little girl—looked after the kitchen-garden: Alphonsine, with her face hidden by an enormous broad-brimmed sun-bonnet, and the little girl, more interested in the insects than in the weeds. From time to time Alphonsine straightened up with a movement of her hips which threw her shoulders back and outlined her prominent girth. She looked out absent-mindedly at the landscape bathed in a warm light. From far off, deadened by the heat, came the low drone of the mowing-machine, borne along with the heady honeyed fragrance of the clover. The little girl jumped up suddenly among the tall tomato plants, where a moment before all one could see of her was her red-flowered calico dress, looking like a huge fruit standing out against the blue and gold background : the blue of the sky and the gold of the fields of oats. For a moment she stood erect with smiling eyes, for her figure was not yet bent by much stooping towards the earth and, in her eyes, the round of the years, the seasons and the days offered something else besides an eternal repetition.

"Ma ! . . . Ma, when's Oguinase going ?"

"What do you want to know for ?" asked her mother, while her hands continued their work mechanically.

"Because we'll have to get his things ready."

This time Alphonsine as she straightened up put her hands to her aching back, for she was more wearied by each fresh pregnancy and particularly by this last one.

"Well, I guess he'll be off next week; because the priest told your Pa college would be starting next Wednesday. So they ought to be leaving Tuesday, I suppose."

Euchariste's plan was about to be fulfilled; his eldest son was being sent to the seminary. Alphonsine herself found it hard to become reconciled to the idea, though the thought of seeing him a priest one day seemed wonderful, if a bit frightening. But it was all so far away and he'd be at college such a long time. Such a long time and the priesthood so far off that it didn't seem to her as if the day would ever come when her son, the child she had borne, would don the cassock and become almost a stranger to his mother, a person like the parish priest, a sort of distant relative of God himself. When that time came, would she be able to love him as she did now and wouldn't even maternal love for a priest be something of a sin ? Her love was placid, silent, hidden, like the waters that idle in the bend of a river; a love without external signs of tenderness, but vital enough to make her reluctant to let him go out of her life for an indeterminate number of years.

If it had rested with her, his departure would probably have been postponed indefinitely. Although the priest and Euchariste had settled the matter already, she still thought Oguinase was too young. But how could she, who was only his mother, oppose the concerted wishes of the priest and the boy's father ?

A series of good harvests had made the Moisans fairly prosperous—though they didn't advertise the fact—and they had never had to touch the money banked with the notary. Yet sending Oguinase to town was an expensive undertaking, and they hesitated a good deal. For months at a time Euchariste was even more silent than usual, particularly during the evenings, when he sat in the kitchen in Uncle Ephrem's rocking-chair, forgetting even to smoke, as he wavered between his ambition to have his boy enter the priesthood and his unwillingness to let him go just when he was of an age to contribute his much-needed help on the farm. If he sent him off, would he not be depriving the land of its due?

When a second son came and then a third, he was more willing to consent; in a sense these births freed him of his obligation to the farm. However, he had not yet quite made up his mind. It was the parish priest himself who finally turned the scales. One fine day after High Mass he asked Euchariste to come to his study in the big cool well-scrubbed rectory.

At first they talked about everything except Oguinase. But very soon the priest asked: "And how are the youngsters? Your eldest boy?"

It was then that Euchariste realized what was afoot.

"He's just fine, Father."

"The teacher says he works well."

"She did, did she?"

"I guess you're pleased."

"Why, yes, Father, I guess I am."

A silence fell between them, broken only by the distant clatter of pots and pans and the sound of something frying.

"What are you going to do with the boy, 'Charis?"

His parishioner lowered his eyes, put his head on one side, and started to examine the stitching of his cap, held between his knees. He was ill at ease; his ready-made suit made him feel awkward and so did his unaccustomed surroundings, which seemed to conspire against him: a coloured plaster crucifix that looked down on a desk piled high with registers and papers, the flowered linoleum on the floor, the two shelves crammed with books and, above all, the almost religious hush of the room in which his voice sounded strange. He did not dare lift his eyes from his own dusty boots and the priest's thick-soled shoes, which tapped the floor with a dull sound in time with the rocking of the chair.

He really hadn't made up his mind about what he was going to do with Oguinase. He still remembered his conversation with the priest and the half promise he had made when he met him on the King's Highway one day shortly before his marriage. He had often thought about it, but as one thinks of those things one never expects to get—things which have nothing to do with the farm, or the crops, or ordinary everyday life. What was the use of planning years ahead? For fate decides whether a child will live or die, just as a crop may rot on the ground or shrivel up from drought, depending on the weather.

And then there were the years at the college—six, seven, he didn't know how many—and the expense they entailed. The very idea of it terrified him. He would like to have pleaded that times were hard, as farmers always do, but didn't dare, because of the money banked with the notary. It's true he had never breathed a word of this matter to anyone. But he felt dimly that the priest couldn't help but know, since he knew so many things; in fact, everything.

Seeing that instead of answering Euchariste had started to stroke a white patch on his cheek where the razor had scraped away the tan, the priest went on: "I don't know whether you've thought about it yourself; but I've been thinking about it for you, as it's my duty more or less to think for everybody in the parish. You once said you wanted a priest in your family, 'Charis. Haven't changed your mind, have you?"

"Why . . . no . . . Father. I guess not."

"Because, you know, it won't be you who'll be making a present to God, but He who'll be doing you an honour—the greatest possible honour. Euchariste Moisan, let me tell you something that'll surprise you, maybe. I've sometimes thought I'd like to have been a father of a family like you are, just so as I could dedicate one of the children God might have blessed me with to His service. And, listen, I once knew a man who wouldn't let his son go through for a priest, though he had been called by God. Do you know what happened to him? God punished that man. Less than a year later the boy fell into a threshing machine and was cut to pieces right there in front of his father."

Euchariste still didn't answer. He sat listening to the priest, admiring in him what he himself would so much have liked to possess: the gift of words, the ability to express the things you feel inside you and which are struggling to get out. He started drawing circles on the floor with the toe of his boot and then stopped when he realized he was being rude. But he still hadn't a word to say.

"What hurts me most, 'Charis, is that there isn't a single

son of the parish in the seminary right now, and there hasn't been for quite a while. Not since Father Emilien Picard, who's assistant to the priest at Saint-Bernard-du-Saut. This is a good Christian parish right here, only they seem to forget to give God His due. It's all very well to pay tithe on the crops, but if you want the family to be blessed you have to pay tithe in children too. Euchariste Moisan, don't you think you owe it to God? How does it strike you?"

"Well, as far as I'm concerned, Father, it would suit me fine. But . . ."

This time he had to give an answer.

"But what?"

"Well . . . I'm wondering if I can afford it. Sending Oguinase off to the college—that'll be seven or eight years, and all that time there's that great big farm of mine to work. Just when he was beginning to be a help too."

But the priest had an answer to everything. Up to now Euchariste had been able to work the farm alone and it had been generous to him.

In any case, there were two other boys—"and I hope there'll be more to come"—and the eldest of them was pretty nearly as strong and hard-working as Oguinase. As for the expense, well, he himself, the priest of the parish, though he had no private means, would pay half the college expenses out of his own pocket. For he was ashamed never to see his parish included in the list of those which sent up pupils.

And that is how the question had been settled a year before.

They set off very early on the morning of the appointed day, as soon as they had rushed through the chores and just as the pearly grey of the sky was beginning to glow towards the east. The prospect of seeing the town at last delighted the child, who knew nothing of the world beyond the village of Saint-Jacques, where they went to Mass on Sundays. He imagined the town as a sort of larger Saint-Jacques, with, or so he had heard, two churches and several stores. When he learned what had been planned for him, he plagued his father with questions for days; for he was the only one who knew anything about the town, having been there once in Uncle Ephrem's life-time. From his father he gleaned a few vague and almost incredible notions. "What's it like in town? Well, there's houses on both sides of the street and there are streets and streets like that.

And everybody goes round in their Sunday clothes all the time." With this slender stock of information he built up a picture which he proceeded to embellish with all the beauty he had ever imagined.

In school he had, of course, been taught the names of other towns, which were said to be even bigger. There was Quebec, for instance, which really meant something to him, for they had once been visited by a distant relative of Alphonsine's who lived there. And there was Montreal, where Willie Daviau was. But as far as all the others were concerned—New York, Lowell, Paris (which he had been taught in school was the capital of France), London, Vancouver—they had not the same reality for him as the house where he lived or the river that ran by their farm. Even Rome, which had a special prestige because that was where the Pope reigned, was actually nothing more than a dot on a wall map, whose variously coloured areas, he was told, stood for Europe, the United States, Germany . . . It never entered his head that a given blue patch on the map might represent the things he saw every day: the earth with its trees and ploughed fields.

And now what he was going to see was this little black dot right beside a winding black line that was supposed to be the river. The thirst for knowledge latent in every human being began to awaken in him. And it seemed to him that when he had once seen the town he would know all there was to know; for he was already familiar with the land and the rhythm of its existence, which he had learned from his father and more particularly from the constant teaching of Nature herself.

He took his place on the buckboard, that vehicle, peculiar to the country districts of Quebec, which consists of three long boards of some hard but resilient wood fastened to the two axles, with a seat, roughly upholstered and stuffed with horse-hair, on top of them. His father set about securing several parcels and a box containing the boy's outfit onto the back.

Alphonsine came out of the house carrying a basket into which she had put cold pancakes sprinkled with maple-sugar, a loaf of bread and some salt pork; as they weren't going to reach town until the middle of the afternoon, they would eat on the way.

She seemed rather sad, with that listless and deep-seated sadness which is like those long summer hours heavy with storms that never break. Not that she was about to burst into a storm of tears; in any case, tears were futile by comparison with the magnitude of the forces surrounding her: the immeasurable indifference of the elements that express their passions by cataclysms such as gales, floods and conflagrations.

"Is everything ready, Ma?" asked Moisan.

"Yeah. Look out for your money."

"Don't worry, Ma, I will."

He climbed in and the horse started off when he clicked his tongue and shook the reins.

Just as he turned left into the highway, Alphonsine shouted after him: " 'Charis, don't forget to say hullo to Uncle 'Phirin if you get a chance."

Moisan waved his hand and so, for a few moments, did Oguinase. Then the horse settled down to the jog-trot he could keep up for many miles.

Just then Etienne ran up.

"Ma, Ma! Pa's forgot his tobacco-pouch."

She didn't hear him and stood motionless until they passed the clump of beech trees and went out of sight round the bend in the road, leaving behind a cloud of dust that trailed out in a long shining veil.

"Come along, Etienne," she said in a gentler, more subdued voice than usual.

She gave him her hand, unconsciously wiped away a speck of dust from the corner of one eye, started off towards the house, and then suddenly took Etienne in her arms and hugged him so hard the child began to howl.

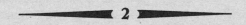

2

Oguinase had fallen asleep when, towards the end of the afternoon, the tall main steeple of the little town first came into view. It stood up above the nearest rows of houses, towards the summit of the ridge, on which the whole town was spread out so that you could see it from a long way off. The silver and black mosaic of tin and shingled roofs, inlaid here and there with the green of tree clumps, shone under the slanting rays of the sun against the scenic backdrop of a slate-grey wrack of cloud driving towards the north. The steeple stood out above all this and looked like a vertical shaft of light in the setting sun. At this sight the child immediately forgot the long journey under a pitiless sky and the dust that caked his face.

Over on the right the dark-green muddied waters of the river flowed towards the distant sea. A little schooner moved slowly along, begging a breeze with its limp sail and shaping a pair of white wings with its reflection in the water. A bit further down, a long raft of timber just showed above the unruffled surface.

The road seemed to be playing a game with the river; at times it sauntered along beside it, twisting around the shores of the bays, running out to meet it when the land jutted out in a spit overgrown with reeds and lapped by the current, and then it turned away all of a sudden and, making a sharp bend to the left, ran on until the river was only a distant reflection between the trees. But it always came back and sometimes passed so close that if you leaned out of the carriage you could see the waves like quick little tongues licking at the yellow sand and the rotting trunks of trees.

A ridge rose about a mile to the left and came slanting down to meet the town and the river. Between the river and the ridge was a triangle of land with the town crowning its apex, and the richness of this wedge was so apparent that Moisan looked at it with pleasure. Beside the road were houses just like the ones in Saint-Jacques, most of them of wood, some of small stones set in mortar in a style reminiscent of the architecture of the French province of Berri, while still others were of new brick. A few of these even had a second storey.

Right over at the foot of the ridge ran another concession with its long string of farm-houses and their whitewashed outbuildings. And all of them—road, river, ridge and concession —converged very gradually until they met, drawn together by the attraction of the little town and its shining steeple.

There was one last farm just like all the others; then the carriage bumped over a level crossing, with the wheels grating on the rusty rails, and then the steeple disappeared behind the sudden cluster of houses forming the town.

Country had become town with startling suddenness. Circled by the belt of the railway, whose emerald-green buckle was the harbour, the houses clustered close together, alike in their meanness: one storey with a door and a window on either side of it. The door was just one step above the ground. The houses, built of rough unpainted boards, nailed vertically to the framework, were protected against the cold of the approaching winter by a bank of earth freshly built up around the foundations.

The sidewalks on either side of the street consisted of a few thick planks laid end to end and between them stretched the roadway, which a recent shower had turned into a bog. Middle-aged housewives in blouses or loose flannelette jackets stood gossiping on their doorsteps or shrieked at their offspring playing somewhere in the street. And Oguinase noticed with astonishment that people scarcely turned to look at them, that nobody said hullo to them, as they should.

And now the street seemed more lively. The houses were still unfinished-looking and not much larger than the ones on the outskirts, but they had a second storey and three dormer windows in their low, slanting roofs. They seemed older, though; and their age was accentuated by the fact that their front walls had been torn out in part and replaced by plate-glass windows, which revealed all sorts of things Oguinase had never seen, or even imagined, and which he had no time to look at properly as they drove by. Above the crowded sidewalk hung shop-signs that were easy to comprehend: an enormous golden spool for the dry-goods store, a wooden bottle for the wine merchant's, a top for the place where they sold toys and all sorts of odds and ends. Others pictured the name of the shop: "The Golden Fleece," with a lamp swinging squeakily from a bracket, "The Ball," "The Shears," and so on.

Now they had reached the heart of the town, at the intersection of the two main streets; one of them ran steeply down to the river and a boat at the dock looked as if it were stranded right in among the houses. Over one door hung a big wooden mortar and a pestle.

"Look!" said Euchariste. "I guess this is where the priest's brother lives, Dr. Demers."

There was a press of vehicles of every kind: the ornate carriages of purse-proud farmers, the buckboards of the humbler ones, drays with loads of clattering barrels, buggies, two-wheeled carts, wagons, hay-carts with their high racks swaying unsteadily. They stopped when somebody started ringing a hand-bell. All eyes and ears were turned to a big man standing up in a gig, who was shouting out an announcement about a lost article and another about the death of a Mr. Joseph Grandbois.

Streets and still more streets, houses and still more houses. Then to the right and then to the left and then to the right again, until Moisan finally admitted: "It's a funny thing, but I don't know where we are." An obliging passer-by had to tell them how to find the street where Cousin Edouard lived.

Their cousins were in the Rue Plaisante, a quiet street with a pretty name which was probably given to it by some early landed proprietor with a poetic soul. From the far end it looked like one long private garden, enclosed by a fence which was topped by the spreading branches of the trees; the lower branches hung over and dropped down to form a leafy archway above the red-brick sidewalk, a shady passage like a cloister. In the distance the two rows of low houses tapered away towards the sandy ridge, bathed in bright sunlight.

They felt more at home in this quiet pleasant street; it seemed more like their own deserted road, and the sandy hill in the distance had a familiar look. Moisan read the numbers out loud. . . . There!

But Oguinase was disappointed by the house. When Cousin Edouard came to visit, he seemed to him a person of importance, with his fine clothes and the gold watch-chain strung across his vest; Cousin Zoé had a hat with flowers, a silk dress and gloves. And that is why, ever since entering the town, he thought each more pretentious house, bigger than its neighbours, must be theirs, their "Louvre", as Aunt Mélie used to say when speaking of a fine house. And it was this mean-looking place!

Euchariste slowed his horse to a walk and, recognizing his whereabouts, turned into a narrow driveway which ended in a small yard. Cousin Zoé was there bending over the wash-tub and up to her elbows in soapsuds. There were two urchins pulling each other about in front of the shed and on the bare ground sat a younger child eating mouthfuls of dust.

When she heard the sound of wheels the children's mother raised her head. At first Oguinase did not recognize this woman in slippers and a dirty dressing-gown; his father had to prompt him by saying: "Come on, Oguinase, don't you remember your cousin?"

"What!" she said as she kissed him. "This your eldest?

Gosh, how he's grown! Bernard! Go get your father and tell him Euchariste's here!"

Soon after Edouard Moisan turned up, wearing the white apron of a grocer's clerk. They told him why they had come, but it was only after Euchariste had explained to him that he had to start back next morning that he became really cordial. At first he had been afraid his cousins had come to stay for several days, as often happens when people from the country come to visit their relatives in town. It wasn't that he was in-hospitable; but, after all, the house was pretty small and two country appetites added to their own numerous family!

"You're in no hurry, 'Charis. Why don't you stay a few days? We haven't seen you in quite a while."

"Well, I can't make it right now. There's nobody to look after the farm. I'm just up here to take the boy to the college and . . . to get some business done, then I'm going back home."

"What kind of business?"

"Oh, business . . ."

Euchariste started to laugh as a man does who is just about to reveal a well-kept secret. For he had had an idea. Hay and grain were all very well; but he couldn't grow much of either, all alone the way he was, waiting for his children to grow up. That made him think of the money banked with the notary. Oh, he wouldn't need much of it, just enough to buy a cockerel and a few pullets and start selling eggs and perhaps even poultry.

"The other fellows are going to get a surprise. I didn't tell them a thing about it for fear they'd pinch my idea. As it is, they'll likely think the joke's on me. Reminds me of the time I got Uncle Ephrem to buy a mowing-machine; it was quite a job. He was all for the sickle, like in the old days. To his way of thinking, mowing-machines cut the grain too close and didn't leave enough stubble to plough under.

"There's nothing you can do about it," he added philo-sophically. "They're all the same."

They meant all the others, the ones who didn't have *ideas* like Euchariste Moisan, the *dumb-bells* who remained stuck in the rut of tradition and enviously watched the smart fellows make money.

Then he started to explain what was wrong with farming: how it didn't pay; how Edouard Moisan should consider him-self lucky to be living in town "with real folks" and getting his pay every Saturday night, regularly, "rain or shine," in real money and not in grain that has to be cut or potatoes to be dug up. Edouard didn't protest, for he had vanity; and the half-specious, half-genuine compliments of Euchariste strengthened the feeling of superiority which he, the town Moisan, felt towards the Moisans from the country. As a matter of fact, he had never regretted that at twenty he had left the farm on which he was born to marry a town girl against his father's wishes; the attraction of town life had counted for a good deal in his decision and so had a rather happy-go-lucky, lazy streak in his disposition that made him think clerking in a store more congenial than the hard drudgery of farming. It never occurred to him to think of the satisfaction of working one's own land, the stimulus of broad horizons, the thrill of a good harvest—all compensations which exist in theory but of which the farmer is hardly if ever aware. He thought still less of the triumphant beauty of the early morning, when the dew lies on the pastures; of all the poetic aspects of rural life, which are enjoyed only by those for whom they are not a part of the daily round. The things he remembered best were the feeling of tired arms driven by menacing storm or frost, the anxiety over a harvest threatened by hail. Of course, he did appreciate the grandeur of nature; but this grandeur overwhelmed him by its immensity. He preferred to be dependent on human beings. And the only part of his early life he really missed sometimes were the long winter days with nothing to do. His shop gave him a special feeling his cousin could never appreciate, that of dominating the little world about him. No, he had never for a moment been sorry he left the country.

And, as he spoke of his life with a touch of self-satisfied superiority, in accents that were still quite countrified, though sprinkled with anglicisms whose meaning escaped Euchariste, the latter began to feel rather envious of him. The farmer felt sorry for himself and longed for the town, where human beings constantly rub shoulders and are not separated from one another, where life is full of contacts, where work, instead of scattering the human herd, draws it closer together in harmony with man's gregarious instincts. He felt attracted by this regular, ordered existence, in which Sundays are always free and evenings uninterrupted. Hitherto he had had the same ambitions as Uncle Ephrem and all the other farmers : to retire to a little house in the village when the time came to rest his old bones. And now, like a wild animal attracted by a saltlick, he had begun to dream of the town. Who knows? . . . If raising chickens brought in as much money as he hoped . . .

This took him back to the purpose of his journey.

"I wanted to buy these hens. So I drove up and didn't come by train, though that would have been a lot quicker."

Oguinase entered the college next day. The evening before, Edouard got together various people—distant relatives and acquaintances who hadn't seen Euchariste for a long time. It was a merry gathering and Cousin Edouard insisted on Oguinase being present; everyone must realize that a member of the family was going to the college. If only to show how well off the Moisans were.

In the morning Cousin Zoé took them to the seminary. Parents and pupils were walking about in the courtyard and among them were a few seminarists, freshly tonsured and wearing their long black cassocks. Oguinase would look like them one day. Zoé showed Euchariste the prominent citizens who had come to bring their sons. One of them greeted her with a "Good morning, Mrs. Moisan" that made her redden with pleasure; it was her husband's employer.

At the end of the courtyard a block and tackle attached to a bracket was being used to hoist the baggage up to the dormitories. The loads spun round as they went up : solid metal trunks painted black, old-fashioned convex ones of tawny leather and, from time to time, the rough padlocked box of a farmer's son.

They waited to see the prefect of studies, who had received a letter from the parish priest announcing their coming. Moisan was touched by this and started to tell him the whole story of his son's vocation. The priest listened politely for a few moments and then excused himself on the grounds that he had a lot of people to see; father and son found themselves out in the courtyard again, feeling lost and rather bewildered. The melancholy horse went on hoisting the baggage; Euchariste walked over towards it, pleased at finding a familiar object.

"I guess I'll have to go now," he said at last.

"You going to go and buy your hens, Pa?"

"Yeah, and I'm going to try and get away by noon if I can make it."

"All right."

Moisan put his hand on his son's shoulder in a sort of restricted embrace; it was the only way he was capable of expressing his feelings at leaving him.

"We'll be up to see you often," put in Cousin Zoé. "So you won't be so lonely."

"Don't forget to write us once in a while. It'll please your Ma, you know," said Euchariste.

"Sure I will, Pa."

Oguinase felt like crying; he felt so lost already at being separated for the first time from his family, from his familiar surroundings, from the animals and fields, which had hitherto constituted his sole occupation and the whole of his experience. All this was being torn away from him and was receding into the past. It was going to be pushed into the background and divested of any importance by new experiences and new people. Already the life he had been accustomed to had become an unreal memory and the new unknown gripped his innermost being. It wouldn't have taken much to make him say: "I don't want to stay. Take me away. I don't want to be a priest; it takes too long. Take me back to the farm. Take me home."

At this moment his father, too, felt that if his son were only to give the word he would have put him in the buggy and they would both have galloped off as hard as they could, far from the town; far from this cramped horizon, where everything—trees, grass, houses, people and even the sky— were hostile and foreign to them.

"Well, good-bye, son!"

His hand tightened once more on Oguinase's sturdy shoulder.

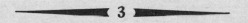

3

And so each year Oguinase travelled the road that led to the college in the town. Both Euchariste and Alphonsine felt that these absences broke up the household to some extent. At the beginning, particularly, Euchariste missed his eldest boy, whose help in recent years had become increasingly valuable. Indeed, he had to take on a hired man, a curious sort of fellow from some place over in Europe, who spoke their language but not in the way they did. He just turned up one day, going from house to house along the sun-drenched road. People took him for a tramp at first and offered him a piece of bread and some salt pork, but he turned it down and asked them to give him work.

They didn't want to hire him on any of the farms. Not that on some of them there wasn't plenty of work for this husky male, who was willing to take on any sort of job however hard it might be. But a foreigner is always suspect and no one dared to take him in. Their neighbour, Phydime Raymond, put him off the premises and went so far as to threaten him with his rifle.

It so happened that fate led him to the Moisans' the year after their eldest son's departure and on a day when Euchariste had had to do all the work almost single handed and had not been able to cope with it. He came in from the fields at noon of an autumn day to find this fellow with his sloping shoulders and the fringe of beard, which gave him such an unusual appearance, seated at a corner of the table, eating the meal which Alphonsine had served him out of the kindness of her heart.

It didn't take them long to come to an agreement.

Using expressions that Euchariste couldn't always understand, the man complained that in spite of his willingness no one would give him any work to do. And yet he'd seen plenty of fine farms, as prosperous and smiling as any man could wish, though it was autumn and though often enough they had rickety fences, buildings that needed white-washing, and unpruned orchards in which the trees had reverted to their wild state. It was true he didn't know anything about local methods of farming; but he was quite experienced in market gardening, a profitable branch of agriculture which seemed to have been overlooked in this part of the country.

He spoke slowly, but fluently and without hesitation, and his hands, instead of being used only to accomplish manual tasks, had a strange eloquent life of their own and gave shape to words which anyone could understand even before they had been spoken. He insisted on showing the muscles that quivered on his arms and seemed eager for work. Half an hour later he went out to the fields with Euchariste.

But every time Euchariste looked at him he felt a vague bitterness against his son, whose departure had forced him to take on a hired man. Just as if Oguinase had taken the money right out of his pocket to give it to this homeless creature.

During the summer everyone worked, including Oguinase. He used to turn up at the end of June, looking pale and tired after the ten months of study that were never crowned with any particular success. He got through each year and never had to repeat, because he worked hard and his teachers knew he was destined for the priesthood. When he came home to the farm and took off his tunic and his green woollen sash, he became a farmer again to all outward appearance and by the following morning he was at work with the others. But it took his father a few days to get used to his presence again. In his mother's eyes he was always the first-born, the son set apart in a sense from the others, whose departure had upset the mechanism of normal daily life and created a void which could not be filled by the other seven: Etienne, Ephrem, Malvina, Eva, Lucinda, Orpha and Napoléon.

Ephrem was now the one his father relied on most; he used to take him out to the fields with him in preference to Etienne, who was now the oldest of the boys on the farm. And, strangely enough, the foreigner seemed to prefer to talk to Ephrem too. Sometimes, during the long winter evenings which set in so early, he would get the child to sit down beside him and tell him stories of extraordinary adventures in strange countries. They all began the same way: "Well, son, if you want a story, I'll tell you about something that happened a long way from here to a man I knew." Then he would start talking about Africa and Asia and islands lost in tropic seas and fantastic countries against the background of which appeared yellow men and black ones, too, and, in the midst of it all, a single ever-recurring character, only vaguely outlined: the picture of a man distraught who left every place he visited carrying the same burden of weariness and boredom. Euchariste was the only one to guess who the man was. He and Alphonsine listened willingly enough to these long tales of distant lands, though they didn't always understand them. But all these unfamiliar things made them feel rather ill at ease; at these times the fellow seemed almost of a different species and not quite human. Besides, he didn't go to Mass and didn't join in the evening prayers, though he was polite enough to kneel. If he hadn't been willing to work hard for so little, they would certainly never have agreed to the arrangement which allowed the foreigner to stay at home on Sundays and look after the children while they went to High Mass in the village.

Each year brought its round of major activities on the farm: ploughing and harvest, effort and reward; the ploughing arduous and almost agonizing, the harvest every bit as trying —both bought with the same sweat and the same sacrifice.

Oguinase, who was growing up fast, still did his share of the work quite as a matter of course, and each summer he took up the axe and the pitchfork again as naturally as if he had laid them down the night before. But his mind strayed a little further each year from matters connected with the farm, even though all his life his body would bear its imprint in his plodding gait and a certain stoop of the shoulders, common to those whose boots are heavy with rich soil and who, at any moment, may have to bow beneath a pitiless rain of hail.

He was on his way up to the priesthood by the rungs of the ladder called grammar, mathematics, Latin, Greek and, finally, philosophy, that mysterious science that lifts man above the physical world. At first his father had tried to keep up with him and had him explain the various stages. But as his son progressed farther and farther along the road, a cleft opened between them and in it ran a river which grew ever deeper and deeper, more unfathomable from year to year, against the time when it would develop into the abyss which separates the priest from all other human beings. Even now, when at the beginning of the holidays, they went along together to pay a visit to the parish priest, Euchariste felt that, though Oguinase might not yet be a member of the priestly caste, he was no longer an ordinary person like himself. And he felt himself more and more supplanted by the parish priest.

One day, between seed-time and harvest, as they were both repairing a fence under the shrill-voiced cross-fire of the mosquitoes, Moisan questioned his son.

"Say, Oguinase, don't you get lonesome sometimes with the folks round here; they're not like your friends in the college?"

That isn't what he really meant to ask him, but rather whether his boy didn't sometimes long to come back home to the farm and his parents; to turn his back on this unnatural life of books and study, which to him seemed absurd, and return to the normal existence of manual labour; to contact with the austere land, where every gesture has a meaning and where, because of the very nature of things, only the most necessary ones matter. But he knew that this was now impossible, for his son's life had become in a sense predestined, beyond human control, something as unalterable as the flow of the river towards the gulf and the sea.

"Why, no, Pa! Of course not."

But that was all he said.

And it so happened that the same question was put at the same time to another person when Ephrem asked the foreigner: "Say, Albert, why do you stay on with us?"

"Well, son, that's the way it is."

And his answer ended in a gentle laugh—a laugh edged with secretiveness like the shifting foam on the crest of a wave. Then he looked up with his clear gaze, which had seen so many things, and he stopped laughing suddenly as he realized where he was. So many horizons had succeeded one another in his past life that he paused for a moment to weigh them one after another, to feel the rough and the smooth of them, before answering so difficult a question.

But Ephrem tried again.

"Don't you feel lonesome sometimes at our place?"

"No, son. I've knocked about all over. It's years since I set off down the road and left my native village behind me. I've never been back. Every day I live and every new village I see dims my memory of home a little more.

"I can hardly remember what it's like now. I don't belong anywhere any more.

"And I get a feeling now I haven't had for years. I know I'll still be here tomorrow. I know that in five weeks I'll be cutting the hay in that field, that one and not some other field. And I know that next year I'll be cutting it again. Though I can't be so sure about that."

"And you never think of leaving, Albert?"

"No, Ephrem, I don't think I ever do. But how do I know?"

He had gone off again too many times, after thinking that he had at last settled down in one place, for the future to have any certainty. And that is what made him seem abnormal and elusive to these people chained to their thirty-acre strips of land. That is what sometimes made him aware of his surroundings so that he looked at them as a man does when he sees them for almost the last time.

"But you must find it lonesome round here. Nothing ever happens."

"Nothing ever happens anywhere, son. You see, at first

everything seems wonderful. You come across houses that aren't of stone or wood; trees that haven't any branches; people of a different colour, wearing clothes you've never seen before and talking strange languages. And it never strikes you that those are just houses, trees and people with little unimportant differences. What attracts you at first is the way things move and change and flow. Then one day, somewhere or other, you notice that it's the same for all these things as it is for the sky and water. Look at the clouds. Well, the clouds go by; but it's always the same sky and the same sun. Water flows on and you never see the same water twice, but the river doesn't change. We're the only ones that change, son, and not much at that. As for the rest . . ."

But the little boy couldn't understand. He had never left the place where he was born; but he refused to believe that this horizon, hemmed in by the belt of the forest and the fluid barrier of the river, was neither more nor less attractive than any other, though it might be pleasant enough at this particular moment. To his way of thinking, there was this horizon and then the innumerable other ones, the thousands and thousands of pictures from the album of the world, and their skies couldn't be the same blue, nor their trees the same green, nor their men of the same flesh and blood. It seemed to him that no one who had known all these wonders could possibly consent to remain captive between these two walls of sky and earth, a prisoner of this farm-land whose appearance never changed.

The man had stopped working and stood with his mallet in his hand. And now he began to share the little boy's uncertainty and was no longer sure that he would stay forever imprisoned between the same earth and the same sky, fenced in by the palings of the forest, with the moat of the river in front of him.

The air was full of the heady perfume of honey from the ripe clover. In the distance, framed by the green of the beeches, the black roofs of the farm-house and its outbuildings were flattened in the glare of the sun.

After Oguinase had left and Albert appeared on the scene, life at the Moisans had resumed its slow-moving course and remained as uneventful as the changeless round of the seasons. Except in summer, the children went off to school every day, or at least the young ones did, for from necessity—or the pretext of necessity—the two eldest boys, Etienne first and then Ephrem, one fifteen now and the other fourteen, had cut short their brief schooling. Their places in the chain had been taken and there were still five children—Malvina, Eva, Lucinda, Napoléon and Orpha—who walked hand in hand along the road now covered with dust and now with snow. But nature was their real teacher and it was from things rather than from people that they learned what they needed to know about the world in which they lived. And that process began as soon as they left their mother's special domain, for it was from her they learned first of all to talk and then to walk and then to say their prayers. That was their mother's province, together with everything else connected with the house. From the moment they left the narrow limits of the kitchen and the farm-yard, which is an annex to it, their father showed them the way to the stable and then to the fields and it was from him that they found out what laws of nature must be obeyed and how to profit by them.

As they grew older, the differences in their characters became more sharply accentuated and each one reacted in his own way to the experiences of everyday life. The next oldest boy after Oguinase was Etienne, who had inherited his gentle expression and rather far-away voice from Alphonsine and the Branchauds. He was submissive and, like a true farmer's son, became more and more attached to the land, which meant more to him than his family or his own person. As a matter of fact, he was too close to the farm, too much a part of it, to be aware of his devotion. But his moods reflected the earth's changing fortunes; he was uneasy when a storm threatened the crops, quietly happy when, just at the right moment, the sun shone and the young green shoots of the oats forced their way through the clods of earth.

Ephrem, on the other hand, pleased his father by his manual skill and appealed to the hired man because of his curiosity, which sometimes made him rather a nuisance. He was obstinate and threw himself into his work impetuously, but he often went about things the wrong way and would lose his temper when Euchariste tried to show him his mistakes. And if the leaves of a tree he had planted too late withered in August, or a cow got loose in a wheatfield through a neglected fence, he just lost interest and would do the most necessary things only if his father kept after him all the time. But he was skilful, resourceful and very amusing and entertaining when there was company.

Now that his sons were growing up, Moisan could get the

most out of his farm and it sometimes occurred to him that he would be able to do without Albert one of these days. One good harvest followed another and the farmer, whose thick hair was now streaked with one white lock, wore the thoroughly satisfied expression of a man whose farm is behaving as it should. His buildings were always in good repair and were freshly white-washed every year. Once a year the glossy coats of his prolific stock were distended and they dropped their young, while in the henhouse the famous "Moisan chickens" increased in number under the care of Alphonsine and the little girls. People were beginning to say : " 'Charis Moisan ! Oh ! He doesn't have to worry !" To be sure, he hadn't in the least lost the habit of grumbling over the farmer's hard lot. And when one year prolonged rains had washed out the grain, he hadn't failed to complain : "Ain't it hell to be born unlucky like this? It's all fixed so a farmer can never save a cent without he has to spend it next day !"

But when some neighbour, with a mortgage on his farm, would say to him in a voice hoarse with envy : "You're darn lucky, 'Charis. You've no money troubles and you don't owe nobody a cent," he would agree : "Yeah, that's right; I don't owe a damn cent." For this is the kind of tribute one accepts willingly from others.

It was the same story when one of the neighbours' sons came to say good-bye before going off to the United States. Not a year went by without the news that at least one man, and sometimes a whole family, had gone off to join their cousins in New England towns, where the mills and factories clamoured for new hands.

How could it have been otherwise? Children kept being born into each household, ten or twelve to a family, and each farm could only belong to one of the sons, generally the eldest. The others had to go elsewhere, either to the village or to the city. Some of them, the brave ones who could only conceive of life as a struggle between man and the land, went off to the virgin territories of the North. The others went where anybody was sure of finding work and an easy life.

As a matter of fact, in preference to exile some of them willingly chose the new lands of the North, up around Sainte-Agathe, or even further on, towards Roberval or Amos. But it was hard for anyone who had known the amenities of life in the old settled parishes to go off to the rock-strewn country round Saint-Faustin or to endure the harsh climate of Lake St.

John and the Harricanaw, where the earth is only really bare and accessible from May to October.

"Those other fellows ain't really men at all," the old-timers used to say, Badouche among them. "In my day nobody thought of going to the States. They went up to the new lands, right into the woods, with a horse and an axe. In two years they had enough to keep a family. Nowadays all the young fellows think of is running off to the Yanks, though right here there's lots of good land laying round idle."

But Anthime Branchaud, Alphonsine's brother, who was just on the point of leaving, had this retort to make: "That's all very well, Grandpa. But I'll be earning three dollars a day, right from the start, summer and winter. And it's all very well for you to talk, but it's no kind of life to go off all alone into the woods and make land and half starve to death for three or four years. Look at Jos Paquette; he went up to that North Country of yours. When he came by here about two years later, he was pretty well all in. I saw him and he looked like a lead Christ on a crucifix he was so pale and skinny. Then he went off to the States and he's still there."

"That's just what I was getting at. The young fellows nowadays ain't real men at all; they're just dish-rags, softies. It's a darn shame."

"No wonder neither," added Athanase Giroux, grumbling into his beard as usual. "That's what comes of changing everything. If people farmed like they used to in the old days, the young fellows wouldn't fool around with these here machines that just cause accidents."

He had never forgotten the day when one of his grandsons was brought home after losing three fingers in a new binder.

"See here, Grandpa," put in Euchariste; "you have to keep up with the times. If you want the young fellows to stay on the land, you have to go ahead. You can't harvest with a sickle any more. And the day's gone by when you just sowed hay and grain. That's why I've started keeping chickens. If one of my family wants to take it over, there's a lot of money to be made. At any rate, if I can manage at all, I'm going to keep all my boys on the farm."

Perhaps one of these days he would be able to buy the Bertrand farm, whose untilled fields made one sick at heart and which was inhabited only by an elderly brother and sister.

From across the empty expanse of the river came a far-away sound of bells, the midday Angelus muffled by the distance. The air was heavy and humid.

"I guess it's going to rain," said someone. "You can hear the bells of Saint-Janiver over on the other shore."

"Looks like it, all right."

"It rains all the time now," mumbled old Giroux.

They were repairing a culvert in the road and they all stopped work. Euchariste swung his coat and his shovel over his shoulder.

"Got to go and bring in my barrow out in the field. So long, everybody!"

"So long, 'Charis!"

They stood there for a moment without speaking, listening to the mellow pealing of the bells, as Moisan went off.

"He looks out for things, all right, Moisan does," said Anthime.

"Sure he does. He's making quite a pile of money with his chickens, the old bastard!"

"You don't say."

"There's more to it than that," Baptiste Fusey insisted with an air of mystery. "I had to go and see the notary last fall. I ran into 'Charis just coming out. When he'd gone the notary says to me, he says: 'There's somebody now! If Euchariste Moisan goes on the way he's going . . .' "

"The notary said that, did he?"

"He sure did. As true as I'm here."

"Well!"

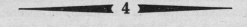

4

The men came into the big kitchen with the strong smell of the animals still clinging to their clothes; they had taken off their reefer coats in the porch used as a summer-kitchen. Euchariste had absent-mindedly forgotten to scrape his boots, and the fringe of sticky soil that adhered to the soles left smears on the floor.

"Watch out, 'Charis! Look what you're doing!"

"Hey! Don't get mad at me, Ma. That's just good clean dirt!"

She went back to her pots and pans. The children were squalling in the living-room; Napoléon was pulling little Orpha's hair and she was yelling, and this, added to the clatter of the tumblers and dishes which Malvina and Lucinda were setting out on the table, made a deafening din, typical of the end of a happy day.

Two long backless wooden benches, polished by constant use, stood on either side of the table. Euchariste took the chair at the head. The younger children sat against the wall. Alphonsine and the eldest daughter were kept busy serving the meal and would eat later.

"Let the girls do it, Ma. You're getting all tired out!"

"No, I'm not!"

She did feel tired, though, more tired than she had ever been. None of her other pregnancies had seemed such a burden to her, but perhaps that was because she had had time to forget what it was like a little in the last four years. This respite, coming after the twenty years during which she had been continually carrying or nursing one or other of their twelve children, of whom eight survived, had led her to believe that she had borne her allotted number.

And now, at forty, she must carry her burden again just as if she were a young woman. Once she had got over the first birth and the anxiety that preceded it, the other ones had almost always left her more or less indifferent. After all, it was as natural as eating or sleeping or working. In fact, it was when she was carrying a child that she felt most energetic and contented. But this time things weren't the same. Every now and then she felt worried and upset, as if her whole being had been thrown out of balance; at such moments she would slow down in the middle of her work and, if she were alone, would sit for a while, staring into space, anxiously conscious of this womb of hers which had so often been fruitful. Was she going to have twins, perhaps?

Now, though she had reached an age when one is more often a grandmother than a mother, she would have to nurse a child again and rock a cradle as she sang. How gladly she would have done it if this unborn child had been her son's, Oguinase's, child! But that would never happen. Why had it to be her eldest son who became a priest, and not one of the others: Ephrem, Etienne or Napoléon? What difference could it have possibly have made to God which one it was, while for her . . . Oh, well, things were fated to be that way!

And yet it wasn't so long ago—last year, or so it seemed to her—that she was teaching him to talk, and then to walk; that she was showing him how to kneel down and fold his little hands before this God who was taking him away from her—had already taken him, in fact. That tall distant youth, who came home once a year to spend a few weeks with them, was not the little boy that only yesterday she was dressing as though he were a doll.

Euchariste tapped his plate with his knife.

"Hey, Ma, what's got into you?"

She started up and went over to the stove. Just as she was about to take a dish out of the warming oven, she saw, reflected in the little nickel-framed mirror on the front of it, the image of a woman with lifeless hair and a dried-up face: the Alphonsine of today, who had nothing, or hardly anything, in common with the mother of Oguinase as a baby.

At the table Euchariste was explaining something to Albert.

"These pies are still called *tourtières*, though they're made with ordinary meat; nowadays it's just a kind of meat-pie. But it didn't use to be that way. There was a bird they called *tourtes*, a kind of pigeon, and were they good to eat! They used to come along in the fall, whole bunches of them, like flocks of starlings, and the whole sky was just black with them. My old man used to say that when he was little and these *tourtes* showed up, they used to go out into the fields with sticks and just keep on killing them till their arms got tired. And that's what they used for . . ."

There was a yell from the children and a loud swishing of wings that filled the room with a roar like that of a waterfall: a swallow had flown in through the open window and was dashing itself in blind terror against the walls. The children got in one another's way and upset the chairs as they ran after it, but suddenly the bird escaped again through the window.

There was silence once more and the contrast was so great that the whole house seemed uneasy and brooding.

"What's the matter, Mrs. Moisan?" Albert exclaimed.

Alphonsine, pale and rigid, was leaning up against the door-post.

"Was you scared, Ma? Brace up," said Euchariste.

"Let's kneel down and say our beads," she answered. "You know what a bird in the house means. It's a sign of bad luck . . . it's a sign of death."

"All right. But you do scare easy."

As a matter of fact, he didn't feel any too happy himself. They all knelt down; even Albert, to be polite, though he shrugged his shoulders imperceptibly as he did so.

Alphonsine didn't mention the fact that she saw the bird of ill-omen fly close above her husband's head.

In spite of the effort they all made to be cheerful, they finished their meal in silence. Then Euchariste and Etienne filled their pipes, while Albert, who was always different from the others, rolled himself a cigarette of strong tobacco. As for Ephrem, he took his cap, which was hanging behind the door, and started to go out.

"Where are you off to?" his father asked. "You're not going out again tonight?"

"I'm just going to the store for a while to see the fellows."

"Can't you stop home once in a while! You're always going off. Why don't you stay with your folks for once?"

For some time now Ephrem had been going out more and more often in the evening; almost every night, in fact. His father was beginning to be worried by this flight from the family circle, this habit his son was getting into of spending as much time as possible with the boys, some of whom, as he knew, were evil companions. One of Ephrem's great friends was Ti-Jos Authier, whose reputation was notorious for thirty miles around and who nearly got arrested once for being mixed up in some sheep-stealing. Then there was a son of Eusèbe Six and "Red" Mercure, a young scamp who was always egging the others on to fresh mischief.

Ephrem was only sixteen; but he was full-grown, deep-chested, rather squat and square-shouldered, with hands like paddles hanging from his muscular arms. This physical maturity made him conceited and, at the same time, gave him a precocious feeling of independence, a veiled obstinacy, behind which one could discern the underhand promptings of others.

He went off more and more frequently in the evenings to the settlement, where the Widow Auger's store was still running. At first he used to come home early, after a couple of games of checkers and a half-hour or so of loafing about. But one Saturday he came in drunk at two in the morning. His father didn't say much about it; that sort of thing can happen to anybody and he had not forgotten his own youth, which was not so very remote. But then the boy came home drunk three times in one week and once, after a fight, with an inch long gash in his cheek. Moisan had just found out what everybody knew except himself; his son was becoming the bully of the neighbourhood and picked a quarrel with anybody and everybody when he had too much to drink. Worse than that, he had actually become friendly with some people who lived in the *Rang des Pommes*, a family with a lot of shameless hussies who were no better than they should be. He tried to be firm with him that evening. But he found himself face to face with a violent and obstinate Ephrem, with hard eyes and clenched fists, changed out of all recognition. He almost felt afraid of his son and left what he had meant to say unsaid. Still, he felt a kind of pride in this strength which others respected in Ephrem, in this fear inspired by his cheeky swagger. Men admired the boy for it and girls turned round with timid looks and inviting eyes when he went by. But his feeling of authority was wounded, all the more because, now that Oguinase occupied a special place outside the family and was in too lofty a position to be compared to any one of them, Ephrem had become his favourite son.

And tonight once more, and once more without any hope of success, he made a feeble attempt to prevent him from going out to join the gang of youths who looked on him as their leader.

"What are you always going to the store for? At your age I stayed at home."

"Say, Pa, I'm not a kid any more. . . . You coming along, Albert?"

"No, not tonight; I'm pretty tired."

"All right, don't if you don't want to!"

He went out and they heard him whistling as he walked away.

Over in a corner near the lamp Napoléon whittled away at a piece of soft wood. Whenever he was left to his own resources he would immediately get out the penknife he had been given for New Year's and carve crude replicas of running animals or cunningly fitted pieces which he assembled into tiny carts. At such times he would sit bent over a bit of willow or birch, with his tongue sticking out of one corner of his mouth and his brown hair of the same shade as that of his mother, whom he so strikingly resembled, thrown back in a mop above his temples. As soon as he had finished what he was doing he would hand it over to one of his brothers or sisters, for he worked for the sheer pleasure of it.

"Say, 'Phonsine, look at that boy of yours whittling again!"

"What are you making, Pitou?" (That was Napoléon's nickname.)

"A doll for Lucinda," the child replied, without raising his eyes from his work. "But she ain't very pretty; my knife's on the blink."

"It don't matter," said the little girl. "I'll make her a nice velvet dress."

"It's easy to see all she ever thinks about is clothes and dressing up."

She was a pretty little thing, all pink and white, with the colouring of the Christ Child in his manger. She was big for her age, too, and though only nine almost a woman now.

"Mr. Moisan," said Albert, who, in spite of the child's efforts to retain it, had picked up the doll before it was finished. "Do you realize your boy has real gifts as a woodworker?"

"Huh! When it comes to whittling he's no slowpoke."

"Do you realize he could earn his living by it later on?"

Moisan pondered for some time without saying anything, and then remarked: "I guess that's right. He'd make a good farmer, but maybe he'd make a good carpenter too. We'll wait and see."

Ephrem had arrived at the Widow Auger's, where, as usual, everybody hailed him.

"Hey!" said Red. "Thought you weren't coming over tonight."

"Christ! Why not? It's dull enough round here without stopping home all the time."

The gathering was larger than the ones in those already distant days when Euchariste used to attend—larger, noisier and, above all, more loud-mouthed. Little by little more and more houses had been built at the cross-roads and there was now a real village stretching along the road on either side of the cheese factory, which had become a butter-factory. There was even talk of splitting up the parish of Saint-Jacques and building a church somewhere in the vicinity. There would just be a rectory, first of all, and a temporary church. Some of the old people in the surrounding countryside would probably build houses there when they retired, and the village would grow until it resembled all the others—all the villages stretched out along both sides of the river like the beads on a rosary.

Only one thing had really hardly changed at all : that was the Widow Auger's store. It had been patched and repainted a few times but was more than ever the centre of community life, the place where people met to exchange gossip about everyday events, a substitute for the public square in a country whose climate compels people to live indoors. Sons followed their fathers to the Widow Auger's and she still reigned over her domain, though now old and decrepit. But she was beginning to give ground to her daughter-in-law, a Grothé who had married her eldest son Deus. He was the one who had gradually transformed the business. The post-office was still the biggest asset, but ever since someone else had started up a dry-goods and shoe store, the grocery end of things had taken on added importance. It was an American-style grocery, where they sold chiefly cigarettes, soft drinks, patent medicines and postcards; in a little room at the back there was beer and *whiskey blanc*, which Deus urged the customers to buy, sometimes by word of mouth and, when necessary, by the example he set them.

Someone was telling a story over in a corner.

"He didn't even try to stop, the bastard! Before I knew it, all there was left was a cloud of dust and my poor old Black howling, with his hind-quarters dragging in the road. It was terrible; I shot him through the head. It sure was awful."

"Last month they killed two of my hens. At first they used to stop and pay the damage like folks ought to. But nowadays the more there is of them, you might say, the less they care. One of those damned automobiles comes by every day now pretty near. And they tear along like mad too. You ain't got time to get out of the road before they're on top of you."

"Yeah, I broke a wheel on my new buggy! My horse was so scared he went into the ditch."

"And I see in the papers where it says in a hundred years there won't be nothing else on the road."

"You're crazy, Red! There's no sense at all buying them contraptions instead of horses. What'll they do in winter? Can you see one bucking a snow-drift!"

"Sure! After that four days' rain we had last week, I had to yank out three of them in a row with my horses; they'd got stuck in the boggy patch over in front of our place."

"That reminds me. We got a letter from Uncle Anthime;

he lives in Central Falls, down in the States. Well, do you know what he's doing now? I bet you can't guess. He works in a place they call a garage; it's where they fix automobiles. Seems they pay good wages."

"Must pay better than here, anyhow," said Ephrem.

"There you go! Why don't you go and get a job in one of them garages?"

"Maybe I will too. Think I'm going to stick here and rot all my life?"

"You've got no kick. It's not so bad here after all. Specially if you're lucky enough to have an old man who's well fixed."

"It makes me sick to hear you talk that way! What good does it do me? Anyway, I can tell you he never gives me a damn cent. I've had about enough."

"See here, Ephrem, you're no worse off than the others in your family," prompted Red, who saw that his friend was beginning to get excited.

"That's what you think. Well, take Oguinase; it's all right for him, he's going to be a priest. Good clothes, good eats. Lord and master of the parish. He takes the cassock next year. And Etienne, he's going to get the farm. Where do I come in?"

They all listened, though nobody dared to agree with him openly, as they could not understand how anybody could wish to struggle against the eternal, predestined order of things or how one of their number could strike out on a path other than the one imposed by nature and custom. But still they felt a kind of startled admiration for the rebel, that hot-headed Ephrem Moisan!

As for Euchariste, he understood his son less and less. He felt there was something hidden, something disquieting stirring deep down inside him. And sometimes in the evenings, on those rare evenings when his son stayed at home, he would, without seeming to and without saying a word, watch him as he sat sullenly smoking his pipe in a corner. Obviously something was worrying Ephrem, like a noxious animal crouching in its hole and waiting to spring out into the light of day.

How could Moisan know that this something was his son's determination to speak his mind one of these days? Ephrem was tired of having to make a fuss every time he wanted to get a few cents out of his father, who couldn't understand that there was any need to spend money when one had everything one could want: a roof, plenty to eat and, as an added luxury on top of that, a well-filled tobacco-pouch. Of course, when he had to hand out a few dollars for the household, the farm or the animals, Euchariste, though he hesitated a little, would do what was needful and willingly enough too.

But he felt that his children lacked nothing. Quite recently he had bought Ephrem a good Sunday suit, though he hadn't yet outgrown his old one. And as for Etienne, he never asked for anything; like a true farmer he knew that money is hard to earn; and it wasn't because he was counting on eventually getting the lion's share, as Ephrem once said when they had a quarrel. No! Ephrem was the one who was always asking for money, using as an excuse all sorts of vague needs which his father utterly failed to understand.

"What, you want fifty cents again? What did you do with the quarter I gave you last week?"

"Hell! What do you expect me to do with a quarter? When you're out with folks you have to be polite and pay your shot. Anyway, I do enough work round here."

And so Ephrem had decided to settle matters once and for all. Every evening he made up his mind to speak, and every evening he avoided doing so on the pretext of waiting for a better opportunity. He lacked the courage, even after fortifying himself with alcohol, for he guessed how indignantly his father would refuse the monstrous request for a regular sum of money, a fixed salary.

Euchariste soon had other things to worry about. Alphonsine, whose "illnesses" had always been so uncomplicated, was really far from well. They had to fetch the doctor a month before her time. He reassured them all but advised her to stay in bed; as if that were easy, with the housework and all the chickens to look after!

It all occurred so suddenly that Oguinase hadn't even time to get home from college. And before Euchariste had fully realized what was happening, he found himself in the big bedroom, standing at the foot of the bed, where a vaguely outlined form and a waxen bloodless mask were all that was left of his Alphonsine. The children huddled in the doorway, the elder ones sobbing and their small brothers and sisters wondering why they were being kept there at a moment when the warm sunshine called them all out of doors. In a corner of the kitchen the eldest daughter, Malvina, sat rocking a baby girl who had robbed her mother of the last spark of life.

For three days and two nights the house was invaded by relatives and neighbours. Fortunately her death had occurred during the relatively slack period between seed-time and harvest; still, they had to feed the animals as usual and do a number of necessary chores during the day. At night they kept watch beside the body and neighbours came in turn to say a prayer at the bier and spend the rest of the evening sitting round the table, where they were waited on by Malvina, who suddenly found herself mistress of the household. As long as Euchariste and the children had not gone to bed, the mourners kept their voices low and tried to speak in compassionate tones, though from time to time they forgot to do so. Then, little by little, their constraint disappeared as they gradually forgot why they were there. They began to swap stories. Voices rose, though the first laughs were stifled until a round of jokes and broad stories, which everyone tried to cap, released that hysterical laughter which springs from the unhealthy, uneasy tension of a house where death is present.

This would go on until someone said : "Just the same, it ain't right; with poor 'Phonsine lying there in her coffin. Let's say our beads."

And they all knelt in the silence which fell heavily on them like a lid; there were no sounds other than the low drone of the responses, to which Euchariste's snoring supplied a bass accompaniment from upstairs.

When Oguinase came home for the summer holidays, which were to be the last before he entered the seminary, he was surprised to see how little things had changed. It was now Malvina who reigned in the kitchen and she was helped by Lucinda, now almost eleven, whose blonde prettiness was becoming more noticeable every day. He found that his father was seriously considering the purchase of the Bertrand farm, an abandoned tract of land that had been left to a cousin living in Ontario, who said he would like nothing better than to sell it at almost any price. And yet Moisan hesitated, though the harvest looked pretty good and a dealer from the city had agreed to take all his eggs.

On Sundays, Euchariste wore a black tie.

5

Each year, now that his sons had grown to manhood, Moisan planned on getting rid of Albert; but he kept putting it off from one season to the next. He was doubtless waiting for some event to make up his mind for him, for he was used to things happening that way.

Eight years had gone by since the day the foreigner stopped for the first time in front of the unknown house, which he expected to be the hundredth to turn him away, though actually it was there that work and shelter were waiting for him. He had knocked at the front door, like a visitor or a stranger who has no access to the familiar regions at the back. Then they made him sit alone at the end of the table like a beggar. And it was only when he crossed the threshold of the back door that he began to share the farm-yard and the buildings and the fields and finally the whole farm with the others; for a farm is an entity, which, though possessed by men, in reality possesses them still more completely and ties them down by their hands and feet for life to a given tract of land.

But unlike the others, and though his work seemed to give him a sort of title to this farm, he never made the total surrender of himself to which the land is accustomed; he never gave up his liberty to the Mother of Harvests. And probably that is what kept him looking different from the others through all these years and prevented the sort of intimacy springing up between the Moisans and himself that arises from a common subservience. Between him and the little world he lived in there was merely an alliance, a tacit and reciprocal contract, not domination on the one hand and on the other servile attachment to a mistress.

It was precisely because he lacked certain traits which might have made him one of them that he was worth his salt. Moisan couldn't bring himself to do without this skilful pair of hands, this fertile mind which drew on a varied experience for quick and unexpected solutions to the little everyday problems of the farm. For this man knew nothing of the traditions that compel the people of a given locality to bow beneath an unchanging yoke and lead them blindly along a beaten track. It is true they and he were of the same blood, for Laurentian blood flows from French blood as from a parent stream. But though he came from around Lyons, he must have had a few drops of some strange, unstable, nomad blood. Perhaps in days gone by, some ancestress of his yielded to a handsome gypsy and it was from him that he inherited the love of wandering which one day tore him from the gentle valley of the Loire, from those Monts de la Madeleine whose delicate feminine lines still stood out sometimes against the far horizons of his memory, and sent him off across the world to feel at home nowhere and everywhere; unless, as Phydime Raymond maliciously insinuated, he had run away after committing some crime or other!

Euchariste used to attribute such slanders to envy, though he himself had never been able to get rid of a feeling of suspicion towards this extraordinary man who had no ties to any given place or tract of land. On the other hand, the fact that the Moisans needed a hired man gave them a certain prestige, which they did not fail to appreciate; it was further evidence of their prosperity. The crops sold well; the hens were a paying venture, Euchariste took care to be seen going to the notary on his annual visit. What more was needed to arouse jealousy? Yet no one dared to complain when he was elected school trustee.

Now that the boys were old enough, it was decided that Ephrem was to accompany Etienne to the lumber-camp the following autumn. They were to go off together to the headwaters of the Saint-Maurice or to the Gatineau, to the distant Rivière-au-Rat or the Tomassine. During that time the farm would hibernate like a torpid bear in a hollow tree, while Euchariste and Albert pottered about in a leisurely way, spinning out the hours, with nothing to worry about after supper, nothing to do but smoke their pipes in the company of one of the neighbours. But the two boys would live the hard masculine lives of lumberjacks in the North Country, handling axes and cross-cut saws at a temperature of forty below zero, all through the short days when only seven or eight hours separate the late dawn from an early twilight. They would be far from everything, from men and domestic animals, from the village and the snug farm, from their girls too.

It was Arcadius Barrette, hiring men for Mr. O'Leary, who suggested that a husky fellow like Ephrem shouldn't stay home all winter with nothing to do. Moreover, there was going to be a lot of lumbering that year and the pay would be good: twenty-two dollars a month. The season before, Etienne had come home with more than a hundred dollars, which he had handed over to his father; it represented all his earnings, less ten dollars or so spent celebrating on the way back from the lumber-camp. After all, it was better to keep Albert on.

On New Year's Eve Oguinase came home as usual to spend the holidays with his family. Euchariste went to the station and waited on the platform for the train to arrive, bundled up in his heavy 'coon coat and protected by the telegraph office from the keen northeast wind which blew the snow along in a spindrift of sharp cutting particles. A few passengers got out, among them the whole Azarie Picotte family—father, mother, and six children—all wrapped up in red and blue scarves. He looked about in vain for his son, who was already standing beside him; he hadn't recognized this tall, pale, sharp-featured young man with a black cassock showing beneath the hem of his overcoat.

"Hullo, Pa!"

Even his voice had changed and had become slower, deeper and more incisive too.

"Why, hullo!"

But Euchariste stood there rooted, in front of this man who looked so much like Oguinase Moisan but in whom he somehow failed to recognize his son. It was the first time he had seen him in the black robes of a seminarist and it was the first time that he fully realized his boy was a priest, that he himself had fathered a child who was now far above him and belonged to another world. The fact that he wore the sacred habit was enough; after all, there seemed to be little difference between a priest and a seminarist.

He would have liked to talk to him as he used to, as father to son or, at least, as one man to another, and inquire quite casually about his health and the college. But he couldn't think of anything to say; he couldn't recall any of the usual meaningless phrases that establish a contact between human beings. What he really couldn't manage to do was to find the right way of addressing this taciturn, godlike person and yet keep from falling into those familiar modes of speech which now seemed so unsuitable.

"Well, so . . . so everything's all right up at the college? Not too sorry to come home and see your old father?"

"Why, no, Pa. Of course not. It's nice to come and see you."

And he seized his father's arm with cordial familiarity.

Albert and the children were waiting for him at home. The former offered to shake hands, a habit he had never lost and which always surprised the farmers, for whom a handshake is something reserved for New Year's Day or for a first meeting with a stranger; in the latter case it is used to establish acquaintanceship once and for all. The seminarist, though taken aback, gave his hand in return; but he did so without cordiality and with a certain mistrust, which Albert didn't fail to notice. The children fell silent when their brother arrived, and during the whole evening there was a feeling of awkwardness that never entirely disappeared. He was no longer one of them and he himself was aware that his cloth set him above those who up until now had been his brothers and sisters.

Indeed, how could he be one of them, how could his feelings be in tune with theirs, since he had assumed not only the priest's robes but something of his measured dignity and unction? Besides, they had merely to see the village priest treat him almost as an equal and carry on long and mysterious conversations with him to realize that the only bond between him and the family was the memory of another Oguinase, who dressed and talked like one of themselves, who had the same thoughts and, like them, was mainly interested in the farmbuildings and the fields. He was no longer a farmer and so he was a man apart; he was almost a priest and therefore a superior being.

And he was aware of this himself. He proceeded to wield an authority over his brothers and sisters that surprised them and treated his father with a touch of condescension, which was fostered by Euchariste's growing respect for him.

That year they got a letter with the unexpected news that a cousin in the United States was coming to visit them in the summer-time. He was a Larivière, the son of a first cousin of Uncle Ephrem. The latter used to talk about her sometimes: Cousin Annie. Euchariste had never set eyes on any of them, and all he knew about Cousin Annie was that the older people all agreed that in her day she had been the most attractive girl in the township. She had married Aegédius Larivière against her parents' wishes and with a haste that subsequent events made readily understandable. On his father's death Aegédius came into a little money, but he soon lost it through the failure of a small business he started up in the city.

After that the two of them went off to the United States with the children they had had in the meantime. Cousin Annie had been dead for a long time and they only once heard from her descendants: that was fifteen or twenty years previously, when a short letter arrived from Alphée Larivière asking for his baptismal record, which he needed down there for getting married.

But the unexpected news of his visit unloosed a regular flood of surmises. Euchariste quite looked forward to meeting his relatives, for he had far fewer than his neighbours. There were only Cousin Edouard, who lived in town, and the Moisans in the same concession; and he didn't get on with them. To explain Alphée's visit, Etienne had at once suggested that perhaps he was coming back to farm.

"You never know, Pa; perhaps they're fed up with the States and want to come back and live here. Specially if they've money to buy a good farm."

"Come back and live here!" exclaimed Ephrem with a jeer. "The hell they will! They'd have to be awful damn fools to leave Lowell, where they get good wages—regular too—all year round, to come and work their guts out on a farm."

But this was going too far. Euchariste snatched his pipe out of his mouth to reply: "In the first place, you're just guessing. Wait a while till I get through reading the letter, then maybe we'll find out. . . . And you ought to be ashamed of yourself, Ephrem, talking that way. The Moisans are farmers. Farming's always been good enough for the Moisans and they've always been pretty good at farming. Farming never lets you down."

"Except when there's no rain and the wheat gets burnt up or else . . ."

"You shut your mouth! I can't hardly believe it's you talking that way. And you was there last spring, wasn't you, when the Bishop came to visit the parish? Don't you remember what he said? Didn't he say it was us, the people in the country, who are the real Canadians, the real folks? He said when a man loves the land it's just like loving God, Who made it and Who takes care of it when we deserve it."

He stood very erect, as a son whose mother had just been publicly insulted might have done. He forgot all about the feelings he had once had, the wave of suppressed envy of the people who lived in towns, the time he drove Oguinase to the college.

"And he said if you desert the land you're practically headed straight for hell."

"Yeah, sure! It's all very well for him to talk. No chance he'd ever . . ."

"You going to start talking against the Bishop now? If your poor Ma, if my poor dead 'Phonsine hears you, she'll turn in her grave. You watch out, son. For there's one thing sure: the land can get even with the ones who talk too much. You go and ask Pitro . . ."

"The cripple?" Malvina asked.

"Sure! He can tell you a thing or two. One day when it hailed his father cursed the land. He hadn't hardly finished when there came a clap of thunder. His mother let Pitro drop and he broke his leg and put it out of joint. And the funny thing about it is, though they had all the best bone-setters, even the Ground Hog who's a seventh son and has some Indian blood too, nobody's ever been able to fix his leg right."

"You oughtn't to talk that way," Etienne added.

But Ephrem shrugged his shoulders and made no reply. However, he felt a little uneasy.

It was Albert who brought them back to the subject in hand.

"Well, anyway, Mr. Moisan, what do your cousins say in the letter?"

Euchariste mopped his forehead, picked up the letter with hands that still trembled, tried to read, and then said: "Here, you take it," as he passed it to Etienne.

Dear Cousin,

I take my pen in hand to let you no everythings fine heer and we bought a car. So I thought Grace Billy and me could visit with the Canadian cousins to rest up a bit from the factry. We wont stay long because its a long ride three or four days. It will be at the end of July if thats alrite with you. I hope the children and Mrs. Moisan is well and we wil be real glad to see the Canadian cousins and my wife wants to meet you to.

Your cousin
(Alphée) Walter S. Larivière

There was silence in the room for a few moments. There were obviously some things that Euchariste couldn't understand.

"What's he mean when he says he bought a car?"

"It must be an automobile he means. Guess they're not so bad off, though they've quit farming," said Ephrem, returning to the attack.

"An automobile!" Euchariste shrugged his shoulders. "They can't be so rich as all that! Anyway, they'll see we can get along too, though we may be just farmers. Maybe they'll get a bigger surprise than we do."

But he was just trying to keep his courage up.

In the meantime nothing special happened except the departure of the eldest girl, Malvina, who entered the Franciscan sisterhood. She was quiet and gentle and merely did what they had always expected her to do. During the holidays before she left, she often spent whole afternoons alone with Oguinase while the others were out in the fields and they had long conversations which they broke off abruptly whenever anyone else appeared. It was the seminarist who told Euchariste of the decision his daughter had taken.

June went by, nibbling away at the summer in little even bites; then July came with its overpowering heat, which yellows the young grain and threatens to burst the ears; then August, when the sower wins his wager against the soil and the weather. In the early part of the summer, before the heavy work of reaping and getting in the crops, when everybody has to help, the children had started to fix up the house in anticipation of the arrival of the Larivière cousins, whom they expected from day to day.

"Maybe they changed their minds," said Moisan every now and then.

At first he used to add: "If they're going to come in harvest-time, I'd sooner they stopped home and waited till next year. It wouldn't be so much bother."

But as the days went by, the delay began to seem unbearable. There was feeling of suppressed irritation against these people who hadn't kept their promise. For Euchariste, to a certain extent, and, above all, Ephrem had gone about all over the place telling people they were expecting a visit from their cousins the Larivières, who were pretty well off and were coming in a big automobile.

And now the neighbours and those who were jealous of the Moisans were beginning to say with knowing smiles: "So those rich Larivières ain't showed up yet. Perhaps they was going so fast in that automobile of theirs they went right on by!" Or: "Is it true the Larivières automobile got stuck and they had to hitch a horse to it to drag it here?"

Ephrem went about in a rage.

One day in August, when they were out in the fields, they heard someone calling from the house and a beaming Pitou came running towards them, breathless and red in the face.

"Pa, Pa! There's an auto just stopped in front of our place."

But when Euchariste and his helpers, who left the horses and the mowing-machine standing in the field, reached the house, all ready to welcome their cousins, the car, which had only stopped to get water for the radiator, had gone off again.

The following Saturday night Ephrem, who had got roaring drunk in a blind-pig, half murdered a fellow from Labernadie who had the misfortune to mention a Larivière family he hadn't seen for a long time.

The crops had been harvested, the grain threshed, and the season for the fall ploughing was approaching when, one night, there was a violent knocking at the door. Etienne, who slept on a folding-bed at the foot of the stairs, got up to see what it was all about. A few moments later the whole household was awakened by a clamour of voices. The Larivières had arrived.

There was "Walter" S. Larivière, the cousin, whose ready laugh displayed a row of gold teeth. There was his wife, a lanky American, whose white face-powder failed to conceal her freckles and whom Euchariste disliked from the very beginning. Not so much because of her appearance; but she spoke in a halting brand of bad French that only her husband could understand, and she spoke only English to him. They hadn't been there five minutes when she jabbered off a long sentence which made her husband smile in a knowing way. Euchariste felt sure they had been making critical remarks about the Moisans and their home. It made him feel humiliated and that is something one never forgives. Finally out of the auto they produced a little boy of about five or six, who woke up from time to time to stare at all the people and at his surroundings with frightened, uncomprehending eyes.

When all the degrees of relationship had been straightened out by references to family history, Euchariste, who now felt a little more at ease, put a question: "Say, what's your real Christian name anyway?"

"I was christened Alphée; but they can't pronounce those

kind of names down in the States, so I had to let them call me something else. And now they call me Walter."

He made this declaration in an amused tone of voice, as if to show his cousins from the back country of Quebec that he belonged now to the American nation, to that terrifically vital race which is composed of the overflow from all the other nations, like those colourful patchwork quilts made up from scraps sewn together anyhow.

But he hesitated a moment before going on.

"It's the same way with our family name, Larivière 'Course we didn't give it up. But folks could never get it. So we just sort of translated it into English. It's Rivers in English and that means the same thing. Larivière, Rivers, there ain't no difference."

"Then you ain't hardly a Canadian any more!"

"Well, what of it! If you live down there, well, you have to act like they do in the States. Everybody does. There's the Bourdons, they're called Borden; and one of the neighbours, a Lacroix, he calls himself Cross."

But this time his words lacked conviction and betrayed a certain embarrassment. For it was evident that your given name belonged to you; and if you changed it, it was your own business. But if you changed your family name, the one you inherited from a long line of ancestors, it was a bit like repudiating your descent and stripping the name of its honourable reputation for hard work and persistence in the face of every obstacle, which generations of the family had built up. And if going off to the United States was a kind of desertion in any case, he felt that this final surrender was in some ways a denial as bad as St. Peter's, an act of treason like the treason of Judas.

This Canadian of Norman origin had done more than shed the name of Larivière when he crossed the border. Alphée Larivière, who had become Walter S. Rivers, no longer spoke the old-fashioned colourful French of the shores of the St. Lawrence. Besides his American accent, which made him pronounce words as if his mouth were full of glue, he generally used strange English terms, which he made a half-hearted attempt to frenchify and which no one could understand—not even Albert, who was educated and knew all the French words there are. When Larivière said: *"Mon grand fille Lily alle est comme ouiveuse dans une factrie sur la Main. Alle a pas venue parce qu'all doit marier un boss de gang du Rutland,"* Moisan hadn't the heart to say he couldn't understand a thing.

To change the subject he asked another question: "Why didn't you bring along the other little Larivières?" After all, he couldn't very well call them the Rivers!

"There ain't no others. Just Lily and Billy."

"Why?" asked Moisan naïvely. "Is your wife sick?"

Rivers burst out laughing and translated the question for Grace, who opened her eyes in astonishment and hid an almost irresistible impulse to laugh behind a wry and rather superior smile.

"Well, cousin, two's plenty for us, a boy and a girl."

"I guess I'd sooner not have had thirteen myself. But there's nothing you can do about it."

"Damn it, my wife and I figured we'd put on the brakes," he said with an air of finality.

Moisan was taken aback and felt embarrassed, so he said nothing. How could people talk about such things openly? He hadn't understood all the words they used; but he was pretty sure they had been referring to one of those wicked practices, which the parish priest had mentioned once at a retreat for men and which seek to interfere with the designs of Providence. He looked away.

Alphée's wife was sitting at the table, where Lucinda had set out an impromptu supper, and Ephrem slipped into a place beside her. He kept looking at her out of the corner of his eye, and his surreptitious glances showed that he had lost all his boldness in the presence of this woman of another species. Every time he looked at her furtively he took in a detail of her face with its rather clouded grey eyes, her thin-lipped, somewhat vicious mouth and her flaunting bosom, whose charms, when she bent over to drink from her tea-cup, her low-cut blouse failed to conceal. Every now and then Grace looked up at him with an amused and knowing expression which made him lower his eyes at once. These two had sized each other up from the very beginning. She was attracted by the obvious physical strength of this well-set-up country bumpkin and guessed at the boldness concealed behind his subdued exterior, while he saw in her all that was most alluring to him in a woman: clothes not made for work, an ability to talk about other things than farming, interests which lay beyond crops and stock. Above all, he felt that she was the sort of woman who was used to living in proximity to all kinds of men, aware of their desire pressing close against her breast and flanks and constantly struggling to fight it off. He was sure she was the sort of woman who would yield without hesitation, doing so of her own free will and not through terror or ignorance like girls he had had so far. At least, that is what he imagined women from the world outside were like.

The two had become participants in that eternal duel which draws the sexes together only to separate them almost immediately, that conflict which, in the cities, takes the place of the more forthright struggle which, in the country, man wages against the earth, who is a female too. For neither earth nor woman are ever entirely mastered.

Moisan made them all sit down round the table, except the smaller children who had been put back to bed. At the end Euchariste, Etienne and "Walter" got talking, or rather the visitor started telling Moisan about the life he led down there in the huge brightly lighted cities of the American Republic; and both used the familiar form of address, for they felt drawn to one another by the mysterious bond of blood. From time to time they filled their empty glasses from a bottle that Lucinda, who knew the rules of hospitality, had set down on the table. Without saying a word the youngster looked after everything. She brought in the dishes and added hot water to the tea-pot. But she, too, couldn't take her eyes off the American woman. The blue blouse Grace was wearing would have suited her own fairness so well. Ephrem went on talking in a low voice and sat beside his cousin's wife while she listened as much with her eyes as with her ears, for she did not understand the countrified locutions and the harsh accent. But she was pleased with the striking impression she was making. And that made her begin to feel a little less contemptuous of them all.

Albert looked in only for a few moments, just long enough to greet the visitors. They disposed of the children, including Alphée's boy, as best they could by putting them three to a bed so as to make room for the grown-ups. And soon, in the whole house, the only room still awake was the warm kitchen where the smoke from the pipes rose into a thick cloud under the heavy beams of the ceiling.

6

Larivière said they had come to Canada for a fortnight's visit, but when scarcely a week had gone by he announced that they were leaving. His wife couldn't bear to stay on any longer with these lowly ignorant peasants, the descendants of a race which she despised with all the arrogance of an American of English stock. Even her husband began to feel that she looked down on him, too, for claiming relationship with these people.

It had been a relaxation, though, for an American like himself, who lived in the narrow streets of a city, to stay in a country that was so foreign and which seemed so not merely because of the distance from his home, which was not very great, nor because of the language, which he had not entirely forgotten. Up till now he had hardly ever left Lowell and its busy streets, where, in the daytime, a grimy sun melts the asphalt and where the night is stripped of its shadows and its mystery by multicoloured electric signs. When he did leave, it was only to go to other towns which resembled it in every respect, where the dust had the same oily taste and the people the same strained, hurried look. He had never come in contact with the country, had never got to know it. It made him feel funny now and he would sometimes stop short in the middle of a field, surprised to realize that he stood out above the meadows and that there was nothing above him, no tall build-ings, no factory chimneys, no network of parallel wires; noth-ing but the occasional spiky tuft of an ash tree or the queer twisted branches of a willow. Beyond, sheer empty space stretched to the clouds, which passed by up there at an in-credible height in stately procession. He felt bewildered and at the same time relieved by this disappearance of everything which usually interfered with his vision or his movements. When he stretched out his hand, there were no walls there. The ground yielded gently beneath his footsteps, like an ex-pensive carpet. He was happy, though not quite at his ease.

Euchariste, too, was rather looking forward to their leav-ing. Yet they got on very well together. Every night, bursting with laughter and conversation, they visited a different house, going as far as Labernadie and even further. And everywhere the cousins' auto made an excellent impression.

But Moisan, who at first had been delighted when Ephrem stayed at home evenings in honour of the Larivières, was much less pleased when he began to realize that his son seized every opportunity of leaving his work to go back to the house to be with Alphée's wife. So much so that one night he couldn't refrain from saying jokingly: "See here, Ephrem, Alphée will be getting jealous if you don't watch out."

His son blushed to the tips of his ears and his eyes suddenly clouded with anger.

But his cousin burst out laughing and merely said: "Well, 'Charis, that's a good joke."

But Grace didn't even smile.

So when they spoke of leaving, Ephrem was the only one whose protests were not merely polite. And on the eve of their departure he disappeared for a whole hour in the middle of the afternoon, just at a moment when the threat of a storm was spurring them all on to fresh efforts. Then Euchariste saw him coming slowly back through the fields, but he was with Cousin Alphée and they were both absorbed in a conversation that brought them to a halt every twenty paces. They stopped talking when they came within earshot. What could it be about? Surely nothing to do with that woman! But they didn't seem to have been quarrelling.

The only person to protest against leaving was the little boy, Billy. He had never even dreamed of such a holiday, for so far the horizon of his fancy had been bounded by cramping walls. At first his mother tried ineffectually to get him to live up to his station, but soon they had had to lend him old clothes so that he could go along with his cousins to the fields, the stable and even to the pig-sty, where he used to spend long hours talking to a young pig which he was very anxious to take home with him. Twice a day he dragged Pitou off to swim in the river and, though they couldn't understand one another, they kept up an incessant chatter and always managed to guess the other's meaning with that intuition and gift for friendship that all children have.

Just as they were leaving, Alphée kissed all the children and said: "It's up to you to come and see us at Lowell. When are you coming, 'Charis?"

"Oh, I don't get around much, Alphée, and a farm ain't

like a factory. It's not that I wouldn't like to, but it don't look as if I'd be leaving here for a while yet."

"Well, if you're too slow, send one of the boys for a few weeks. Maybe we could find him a job that would pay for the trip. Then it wouldn't cost nothing."

"Oh, I guess I can find the money all right," Moisan replied, feeling that his self-respect had been wounded. And in a voice full of meaning added : "I've got a few dollars put by with the notary. I'll think it over."

"Thank you very much, cousin, and *au revoir*," said Grace.

"Good-bye."

"*Bonjour. Bonjour.*"

"*Au revoir.* Good-bye," said Ephrem last of all.

Euchariste imagined that he saw his son exchange a last knowing smile with Grace.

Life on the farm reverted to its ordinary humdrum pace and the only change was that Ephrem left the house less frequently than before to go roistering here, there and everywhere. But what his father couldn't understand was that he asked for money just as often, if not oftener, than before. Until one day he thought he had guessed the reason : Ephrem was saving up.

This unexpected change in his son's behaviour made his happiness complete. To look at, Euchariste Moisan was just like any of the neighbouring farmers. Like them, he worked long hours and was always grumbling about hard times. His brow was like a field of heavy soil, furrowed by cares, anxieties and sweat; his skin had a texture like clods broken by the harrow; and his thick arms ended in gnarled fingers. His clothes were old and worn; it cost so much to cover the buildings every year with a fresh coat of white-wash and the fields with their garment of red clover or golden grain that he could not think of wasting money on things for the owner of these fields and buildings to wear. As a matter of fact, in comparison with people from the town he looked almost like a beggar.

But he was no such thing and his eyes gave the lie to his appearance. His glance flowed with an even assurance like a stream which has turned the mill-wheel and runs on, well satisfied, between the bushes on its banks. That's exactly how it was with him. There was a stream flowing gently through the Moisan mill. The winters went by, leaving the Moisan farm rested, restored, eager for the seed and ready to labour again. Springs came and went, and as they hovered on the threshold of June a delicate velvety green covered the Moisan fields. When the summers were over, all this burden of wealth was swallowed up by the Moisan barns and hay-loft, and the cattle were turned loose in the bare fields. And each year, at the beginning of winter, Euchariste Moisan paid a visit to the notary's at Saint-Jacques.

"Morning, Mr. Boulet!"

He pronounced the name Boulé as did all the people in that part of the country.

"Oh, it's you, 'Charis. What can I do for you?"

The procedure was always the same. The farmer would take the bank-notes and silver out of his old leather purse, and these would go to join their predecessors in the notary's strong-box. And when the money had been counted and recounted in his presence and before it had disappeared out of reach into the safe, he would say: "How much does that come to now, Mr. Boulet?"

Mr. Boulet got out a big ledger. And his client sat there hardly daring to breathe and with his eyes screwed up, as if the money might fly out through the door if he allowed his attention to wander for a moment during the checking over of his annual deposits.

He relaxed a little towards the end when he heard the notary say: "Plus this year's interest at five per cent . . ."

But he never got up to go until the strong-box had been shut tight.

Apart from Christmas and New Year's, that day was the only one in the year on which Euchariste Moisan came home a little drunk and it was more due to happiness than to *whiskey blanc*.

It would probably have been impossible for him to explain what instinct impelled him to hoard his savings like this. He didn't have to worry about his old age, because his capital was there at hand: a fine thirty-acre strip of farm-land, with no mortgages on it, paying a generous annual income and asking only what it is natural for a man to give and which costs nothing; namely, work. Now that his Oguinase had finished his studies he had no further need for money, since his sons could go on living off the farm. And yet, without being a skinflint, he was careful of his cash and, rather than spend it freely, preferred to hide it away in the notary's strong-box. The impulse was too strong for him and was like one of those instinctive urges that affect both men and animals: ants, for instance, who store food in their ant-hills for generations they will never see and of whose future existence they are not even aware. It was a compelling, vital instinct, inherited from his ancestors, those Norman or Picard peasants, whose race he perpetuated and that would be carried on after him by his sons and grandsons and those still distant generations which are the future made flesh.

Etienne took after him in this, for he was thrifty and hard-working and incapable of reckoning hours of work, the sweat of his brow, the weariness of his arms and legs in terms of money, since work, sweat and weariness cost nothing, while money is worth a great deal. Not that either of them, nor any of the other farmers for that matter, were really miserly. By no means! But they were governed by the vague feeling that the money that comes out of the land belongs to it and must not be diverted. Every bale of hay, every bushel of wheat they sold bound them more closely to this kindly mother, who was both generous and exacting.

Etienne was thinking of getting married; but he would never have dreamed of choosing any other time but the autumn, in case even the founding of a new home should interfere with the work.

In his spare time he patched up the tumble-down house where Euchariste had thought of settling down with Alphonsine long ago. He was doubtful about the place for a time, for the floors were rotten and the walls eaten with damp; but the framework was still solid after a century and a half.

He spoke to his father about it, half hoping that he and his wife could live in the big house. She was a Lamy he had met at a party and whom he visited twice a month at her father's place at Notre-Dame-des-Sept-Douleurs, seventeen miles up the river. But his father's house was only just large enough for the immediate family. Aside from Euchariste and Etienne there were Albert, Ephrem, Eva, Lucinda, Pitou, Orpha and Marie-Louise, without counting Oguinase, who had to have the best bedroom when he came home at New Year's or for the summer holidays. So for the moment it was decided that the newly-weds should live in the old house that had been fixed up. His father gave him to understand that later, perhaps, when Ephrem's turn came to get married, Etienne, as the eldest, would get the new house. As for Ephrem, he could move into the old one.

But Euchariste did not mention that he had an idea at the

back of his mind. He didn't like to think that Ephrem, who in spite of everything was still his favourite son, might one day be less well housed than his brother. When the time came, he could advance him enough to buy a farm. The Bertrand property had slipped through his fingers and had been sold to a stranger while he shilly-shallied in the hope of getting it without having to pay cash and tried to get over his dislike of coming to a decision. Oh, well, when he needed it he would get one that suited him, and next time he wouldn't let it escape him.

The wedding took place in October and, as was fitting, there was no undue expense. The only hitch occurred when Euchariste went out of doors to get a breath of fresh air and almost bumped into Lucinda, who was being hugged by one of the young wedding guests. And it wasn't the first time either. But he had never been willing to believe his own eyes, or, for that matter, his ears when neighbours made half-teasing, half-malicious remarks. She had sprung up a lot in the last three years and was now almost as tall as her father. She had also developed a bosom which she was at no pains to conceal and had the inviting eyes of a pretty, tame animal. To him she was still a child, but others probably already realized that she was a woman.

One day, during the following year, Ephrem was reading the weekly paper when he looked up and remarked: "Say, here's a piece of news; looks like they're going to have a war in Europe."

Europe was everything outside Canada or the United States, everything far away and mentioned in the school histories.

Euchariste and Albert were sitting at the table playing checkers.

"Whereabouts?" asked Albert, advancing a man.

"Wait a second. . . . The Russians against the Aus . . . Austrians."

"What's their trouble?"

"It doesn't say."

Euchariste took advantage of Albert's inattention. "One, two, three, four and King," he said, cutting a swathe through his opponent's men. Then, well pleased with himself, he turned to Ephrem.

"Well, let them fight it out. It won't bother us any!"

But the Saturday evening following, Ephrem had hardly

sat down before he announced the big news he had read in the paper he brought back from the post-office :

"Do you know what? They've gone crazy over in Europe. They're all fighting each other. There's Russia and . . . some other country and another one and England, too, and Germany."

Albert turned right around to face him. But his voice remained perfectly calm.

"And what about France?"

"Why, sure. I just told you; France too."

In the silence there was a distant sound like a tocsin: it was an empty tin on a fencepost, banging to and fro in the wind. Under the low rafters the cloud of pipe-smoke seemed to become motionless and then to billow down over the men sitting in the room. Euchariste suddenly remembered that Albert came from Europe, though he had never said exactly where. He turned towards him instinctively, but avoided looking right at him. Albert picked up the paper and scanned it quickly without any change in his expression.

"Who's fighting who, Albert?" Lucinda asked.

"Well. On one side there's Austria-Hungary with Germany and Turkey and probably Italy. On the other there's France, Russia, England, Serbia, Belgium and . . . and pretty well everybody."

"Whatever for, that's what I'd like to know. But . . . how about? . . ."

Albert guessed what the question was going to be as well as if he had asked it himself.

"In the first place, it just isn't possible; it's too crazy. And if it is true, it won't last more than a couple of months. And anyway . . . anyway, I'm a Canadian. I've been a Canadian for twelve years now; it's none of my business. And what's more, let me tell you, I don't give a damn !"

Moisan said nothing and himself felt torn by two contrary feelings of which he was just becoming dimly aware. France! It had been upsetting to hear that one name among those of all the other countries mentioned. It was only a name to him, but it had a special savour. He had only to remember how gently the old people pronounced the word France, even the roughest and surliest of them, giving it the inflection one uses for the name of a woman once loved. On the other hand, he just couldn't bring himself to visualize what was happening so far away among these unknown people, who were a prey to passions and hatreds which he, Euchariste Moisan, had never experienced. How could they think of going off to fight before the harvest was all in?

The sensuous, humid, enervating heat of a midsummer night came in through the wide-open door; the air throbbed with the rhythmic chirping of the crickets hidden between the boards of the veranda.

Then he recalled the words the parish priest had used on one occasion: "France will be punished for expelling the priests." Now he understood.

Albert sat down in the big rocking-chair and said with unusual emphasis: "Oh, well! If they want to fight, they'll have to get along without me."

Through the open door and the windows the pipe-smoke drifted off into the night in long tenuous ribbons.

But Ephrem was looking at the newspaper again.

"Pa, Pa! You won't believe me maybe, but do you know hay's selling at fifteen dollars in Montreal?"

"Say, Ephrem, there must be a mistake somewhere," said Euchariste, now really interested.

"No, it's on the level; here's oats up to a dollar and a half a bushel."

What a soft and fragrant night it was! Euchariste thought of his thirty acres by three lying close at hand and of the tall serried ranks of oats and hay rustling gently under the sombre canopy of night; tomorrow they would quiver with ecstasy under the noonday sun. Soon, in a fortnight's time, the mowing-machine would come through and mercilessly cut down the stalks and lay them in long even swaths before the ears were ripe enough to open and spill their seed on the ground.

Good!

It would be a fine harvest and it would sell well.

7

When the haying was over and the appointed day and hour came, each stalk of grain was severed by the reaper-binder, drawn by three horses, and all day long its clatter could be heard in the distance. Perched on his metal seat, Euchariste could hear the faint rustling of the ears of grain as they fell onto the canvas of the conveyer-belt. He sat enthroned above the plain, with the reins round his neck and his hands on the controls, and the arms of the beater revolved in the air above him. There was an abundant yield of both oats and wheat, and every five seconds a yellow sheaf bound with yellow twine fell to the ground. All the men of the household—Albert, Etienne, Ephrem and Napoléon—followed behind and they stuck their pitchforks into the sheaves and piled them up in stooks until the whole field looked like a village of straw huts. At last there was nothing left but the close-cropped carpet of golden stubble.

But when the time came for threshing, Albert was no longer there. Though formerly he never used to read the newspapers, he had begun to follow the course of events over on the other side. At first, when the news arrived of the early Allied victories in the valleys of Alsace, he was merely interested. Then whenever, in spite of optimistic reports, a dispatch made it clear that the Germans were advancing, he would shrug his shoulders like a man trying to throw off a sack too heavy to carry.

But one evening he turned very pale, got up suddenly, hesitated, and then threw down the paper he had been reading and went out into the night without saying a word. Euchariste picked up the paper and looked to see what it was that had upset his farm-hand. He read the headlines, which mentioned names of unknown places as usual; there didn't seem to be anything there that could disturb a man as calm as Albert generally was. Euchariste turned to the inside pages, looked for the listings in the prices of hay, saw that it had touched eighteen dollars and twenty-two cents, and smiled as he thought of his hay-loft, which was filled to the rafters.

But when Albert, who didn't come home all night, took him aside next morning and said quite simply: "I'll have to go, Mr. Moisan," he realized that what was happening over there, so far away from them, had reached out to a quiet Quebec parish and there touched a peaceable man who, seemingly, had never wanted to harm anybody, who had never coveted either his neighbour's land or his house. He understood then that war meant going away. His own sons wouldn't have to go, since it had nothing to do with them. But things might be different in the case of this fellow here, who had never been altogether one of them—and that in spite of the twelve years he had lived with them on this thirty-acre strip of farm-land.

"Just as you like, Albert; you know what you're doing."

"I can't stay any longer, Mr. Moisan. I just can't when I think of those damned Boches in France."

"Yeah!"

"I'm off now. It won't be for long. Don't worry; at the latest I'll be back next year in time for the haying."

"Do as you please, Albert; you're your own boss. You know what you're doing. But"—he hesitated to ask so direct a question—"I thought you didn't want to go back there."

"Oh! That's what I thought, Mr. Moisan. I don't mind admitting it now—I left there so I wouldn't have to be a soldier. I deserted; it was easy enough. But now . . ."

He couldn't find words to express himself, though usually he was so fluent. He gazed round and wondered how it was that a few words of print on a piece of paper could suddenly make this sky and this horizon seem so foreign to him, all these things which had become so familiar that he had ceased to notice them. And now he turned to look at this man who, though his hair was just beginning to turn grey, was in the full flower of his strength and with whom he had spent twelve years of his life. What troubled him was not why he, Albert Chabrol, a French deserter, was going off, but why this other man had not a word to say and was remaining behind. Wasn't he the real deserter, this man who had French blood in his veins, too, but who seemed quite untouched by the misfortunes of the mother country?

They parted next day. And both realized that whatever happened they would never meet again.

As a matter of fact, Euchariste Moisan did not greatly

regret this departure. Of course, indirectly he owed a good deal of his reputation for modest wealth to Albert. He himself was fond of saying: "The more people there are on a farm, the better it pays."

But he found it pretty hard to have to pay out wages to his hired man at the end of the year. Not to mention that with some people, the envious ones, respect was not unmixed with criticism. Albert had never been really popular in the tightly knit group which surrounded him and he had always remained aloof from this society, which restricted itself to the immediate neighbourhood and looked upon a man even from the next parish as almost a foreigner. People from outside were never fully accepted by such a group, nor were their sons. Complete fusion took place only after two generations.

What they were most suspicious of were his religious opinions. Not that he ever discussed them. But that was the first thing they suspected in any outsider, and particularly in a Frenchman from France. Ultimately he conformed to local custom and went to Mass on Sundays every now and then, but less from any religious conviction than because he had nothing better to do.

Of course, all this wouldn't have really mattered so much to Euchariste if the parish priest hadn't let him see that he secretly disapproved. And Oguinase, too, once asked why he kept this foreigner on and hinted that he might have a bad influence on Ephrem. He even mentioned Lucinda, but Euchariste couldn't make out what he was driving at. Lucinda was just a child! He had found it hard, though, to be passed over for the honourable office of church-warden, to which it seemed that his position and his age—he would soon be fifty—gave him an undeniable right. His envious neighbours let him know that the reason why he wasn't elected was because he had an un-believer living under his roof.

This was shown to have been the real cause at the very first elections after Albert's departure, when the priest had him appointed to the church-wardens' pew.

When Athanase Picard nominated him after coming to a previous understanding with the parish priest, there was a slight stir in the corner where Phydime Raymond sat. But before anyone had time to rise the priest said:

"Euchariste Moisan has been nominated as church-warden for the year. Any objections?"

And nobody said a word. The envious ones just had to keep their mouths shut.

The following Sunday, when the priest was reading the announcements for the week, he gave notice of "a solemn High Mass offered by Euchariste Moisan for the repose of the soul of the late Ephrem Moisan." Euchariste hadn't thought about the poor old fellow for a long time and he owed him at least this much. He sat right up in front, next to Athanase Picard, in the church-wardens' pew, which was the only upholstered one in the whole church.

From now on, when he came out of church, one of the last to leave, he would stand for a bit on the steps, where the men gathered in little knots to light up their pipes and exchange news of their farms.

"Hullo, Mr. Moisan." "How are you, Mr. Moisan?" "Morning, Mr. Moisan"—the young men would say politely.

"Why, hullo, 'Charis!" "Darn old 'Charis; he's got a new hat again." "Listen here, 'Charis, what do you think we ought to do about the school?"—said the men of his own age. And what he found most flattering was that nothing was done now in the concession, or even in the parish, before he had been consulted—he, Euchariste Moisan, a fatherless and motherless orphan who had been taken in out of charity by Uncle Ephrem but who since then . . . It was only natural to seek the advice of a man who had been so successful in his own affairs. Everybody knew he wasn't a "no account," not by a long sight; just imagine—here was a man who had thousands of dollars at the notary's, or so people said who ought to know.

But he was happiest on those rare occasions when Oguinase came home on a visit. The latter had been ordained nearly three years now and was assistant to the priest of a distant parish, which was new and rather poor. It certainly didn't live up to Euchariste's dreams of what his son should have, and he had been greatly disappointed when he went to see the little church, with its roof of unweathered shingles, standing in a forlorn cluster of shacks. Fortunately the presbytery was more imposing, with its windows set in new brick. But he wasn't really satisfied until he managed to have his son come on a Sunday. Father Moisan sang High Mass, which is the one all the parishioners go to, except the women in the village, who have to be content with Low Mass when they don't attend both.

Euchariste wept with emotion; it was like a partial realization of his dream, in which he saw Oguinase as parish priest of

Saint-Jacques, one of the fattest livings in the diocese. Perhaps this crowning reward of his life would come to him before very long and then he could die in peace, respected and, above all, envied, after a successful existence which had been the reward of his labour.

What made him all the more anxious for this to happen was that Oguinase was wearing himself out in his backwoods parish doing all the work of the old semi-invalid priest, an uncouth person who was hard to get on with. It did no good to urge him to take things easy, for each time he saw him he seemed thinner, his face more drawn, his eyes more sunken, hollow-chested and with a cough that shook him every now and then when he was speaking.

"Well, Oguinase, I guess they don't look after you right in your parish. You've got thinner again."

"Why, no, Pa. You're wrong. I get well fed. There's always more than I can eat."

"Yeah! Maybe. You ought to get a new house-keeper; the one you have now spends all her time making fancy dishes. But that isn't what you need to set you on your feet; good pea-soup, thick enough to stand a spoon up in like this here—see! —and good pancakes with salt pork. And no getting up in the middle of the night."

"Yes. But listen, Pa; you have to go out and visit the sick, and a priest can't let a Christian die without the sacraments."

"That's so!"

What a wonderful person a priest was after all.

His other sons had given him satisfaction too, except for a few arguments now and then with Ephrem, who had taken it into his head to try and get him to buy a machine called a tractor to take the place of the horses.

"Listen, son," Euchariste replied, "I'm all for progress, and everybody knows that. I was the first man in the parish to get a cream-separator, and I almost had a fight with Uncle Ephrem to get him to buy a binder. But some things ain't necessary. I once met a fellow who had one of them gasoline tractors. Just ruined his farm with it."

"Now listen, Pa. Who told you that? I bet you can't tell me who it was."

"That's got nothing to do with it. We've got our horses and one of those things couldn't do the work they do. While you're at it, why don't you suggest we buy an automobile?"

"Why not? The Barrettes have one, haven't they?"

"Yeah! More fools they! You'll have everybody laughing at you."

Except for such crazy ideas and the occasional reference to the United States, Ephrem worked as well as Etienne did. The latter was already the father of three children and the old Moisan house, which had been patched up, had come to life again.

Etienne was a real peasant, both because of his gravity and his industry and because he seemed to have no particular age, like many people who live close to the ageless earth and are constantly bent towards it with mingled feelings of affection, respect, and perseverence but without fear. The workman crouching over his machine is not like that. For the machine can be crafty and mean. But the earth does everything on a grand and generous scale, whether it accepts man or rejects him, allows the plough to penetrate its fertile womb, or, indifferent to human despair, arches its back to the hail pelting down on its fleece of yellow wheat. When drought threatened and then when the long-awaited rain beat down for days and weeks on end from overcast skies, Etienne was just like all the others, like his father and the neighbours, and could only hang about the house or the stable and look towards the rain-soaked horizon in the west for signs of a change in the weather. And it was quite clear that he counted on becoming the owner of the farm, which was bound to come to him in due course. Every now and then Euchariste thought he could detect symptoms of this attitude in his son; he occasionally had the feeling that someone—namely, Etienne—was treacherously trying to shoulder him out of the way and deprive him of the farm, which after all still belonged to him.

And it was partly for this reason that he had not lost the habit of regarding Ephrem as his favourite son. And one day when his younger boy answered a reprimand with: "What's the use of breaking my back on a farm that'll go to someone else anyway?" he gave him clearly to understand that he intended before very long to give him a farm of his own, for he was delighted to see that he was still interested in farming and had apparently given up the idea of going off.

The youngest of the boys had begun to follow his chosen profession.

Now, instead of carving useless and childish objects out of soft wood, Pitou was learning to handle the plane and saw under Barnabé Boisclair, who had built a house in the settlement and went about the concession with his apprentice doing odd jobs of work.

Lucinda had lived up to her early promise and was now the belle of the township. She had plenty of suitors, but seemed in no hurry to set the church-bells ringing; she would have her pick of them all when the time came. That left Eva, Orpha and Marie-Louise, though the first-named wouldn't be at home for long; it was easy to see that she would soon be off to join Malvina in the convent. Two nuns and a priest; God would be well pleased and would surely be generous in return.

Apart from a few unimportant favours from time to time, such as a little rain or making a sick animal well, all that Euchariste asked of Him was that life should go on just as it was, with good harvest and high prices. "Lucky as 'Charis Moisan" had become a saying in the district.

Twice a week he went to the station with crates of eggs which a dealer in the city paid a good price for. Euchariste was a shrewd business man, careful and never in too much of a hurry; he seemed to know when to sell and when to hold his produce. He capped his reputation for business ability when a government purchasing-agent from the remount department came to buy up all the available horses for the army, for Ephrem and he passed off a mangy five-year-old on him, which they had faked so cunningly that the buyer was completely fooled. Some people said that not all the profits of that deal went in Moisan's pocket, but there was only one thing that mattered: he had made a good trade. As usual, the lucky devil!

In any case, everything was selling well: hay, grain, eggs, cream, and vegetables. It seemed as if the more the land produced the more people there were to buy. One wondered where it all went. But what did it matter? All the farmers cared about was to increase their savings tucked away in an old stocking or on deposit at the notary's. The Banque Nationale even opened up a branch in the village, but Euchariste was rather dubious about it. He was quite satisfied with the notary, for at least he could talk to him personally and he knew that once a year he added on the interest in the ledger. No, the land had never been so fruitful. And when the parish priest, acting on instructions from the Bishop, conducted public prayers for peace, the farmers in the congregation couldn't help wondering why people were so keen on bringing back the days when farm-produce had almost to be given away for nothing. They prayed, though, from obedience and force of habit; but they kept their voices low, in the childish hope that Heaven might not hear them, or would at least realize that they were not very anxious to have their prayers answered.

Sometimes, when he was out in the fields, Euchariste would stop working to exchange a few words with a neighbour or with one of his sons, and would stoop down instinctively and take up a handful of this blessed and inexhaustible earth, this Moisan earth, which no one could have harmed without at the same time wounding the men who were rooted in it through all their past and all they owed to its generosity. He hefted it gently in his hands and some of it clung, so that his flesh and the earth were mingled. Then he would begin to crumble it between thumb and fingers, with the gesture of a man counting out the minted coins of his fortune.

AUTUMN

1

While for some the future, right to the end of their days, remains subject to the sudden storms of human caprice and ordinary chance, Euchariste Moisan could look with complete satisfaction on his road through life. It stretched straight behind and straight before him, across the rolling fields of the years; in one direction it lay bright with the memory of bountiful harvests, and in the other heavy with the promise of even larger herds. It was a quiet road, marked with the deep ruts of habit; there were occasional dips or clouded puddles, many shady patches and a few lengthy sun-baked stretches. It was a long peaceful road, a trifle monotonous, perhaps, but it ran as true as a well-turned furrow; it rose gently towards the horizon and there one day, sometime in the future, it would break off sharply at the top of the hill under a cloudless sky.

He knew this because he had learned it from the land. As his roots did not go deep and he was at the mercy of the winds and the seasons, his part in life was passive; he had to submit to events as they arose and profit by them when he could. For he was dimly aware that all these ups and downs were merely the fleeting expressions of a single face. Storms? A frown. Winter? A nap. And underneath all this there was always the earth, ever a virgin and yet each year bearing fruit. This made him feel certain of enduring in that succession of generations which marks the years for men of the soil. People who live in towns are always restless and moving about in the midst of shifting and transitory surroundings, which they themselves build up and pull down and build up again, and so the lives they live are precarious and fleeting.

Like his uncle, his father and his grandfather, like all his relatives, he was satisfied with the quiet happiness of people who never question their existence; who understand the futility of any gesture which has no practical purpose, of any thought that does not lead to action.

He was fond of saying: "Let the land guide you, son; it won't take you far, but anyway you'll know where you're headed." Or else: "There are two things in the world know a lot more than we do: the priest and the land."

And so Euchariste Moisan, firmly rooted to his thirty-acre strip of Laurentian farm-land, plodded on towards old age and the tranquil end of a peasant, sure in the knowledge that when he was gone there would always be a Moisan working the land —always. At least one.

Oguinase had taken the only path that can raise a man above earthly existence. Until he was ordained, his brief vacations brought him back to the farm for a few days every summer. On these occasions the whole house took on a sort of sacerdotal air, very like that of a presbytery, where women, following the rules of the Church, had to keep in the background. Oguinase was going to undergo more than a second baptism in the awe-inspiring sacrament which would exalt him, ennoble him, and set him above and beyond ordinary humanity; and he had the austerity of all neophytes.

But his last stay was spoiled and cut short very suddenly through Lucinda's fault.

Her youth had lived up to the promise of her childhood. She got even prettier as she grew older; but she never had the shy gentle eyes of a timid animal that so many country girls have, who bravely face work and child-bearing, but are timid and fearful in the presence of a stranger.

Oguinase in his zeal hoped for a long time to be able to persuade her to follow the example of Malvina, her elder sister, who for nearly six years now had worn the conventional habit of a Franciscan nun; Eva had followed her down the saintly, tranquil path. Weren't there whole families who died to the world only to live again in God? The Racicots of Labernadie had two priests, one of whom was a missionary in China, and four nuns. But his efforts were in vain. Indeed, he felt, just as in the case of Albert, that he had no influence over her either. And he began to resent the fact that she treated him merely as a brother.

The last straw was when she announced one day that she was going off to town to take service in the house of old Dr. Demers, the brother of the former parish priest. Then, a few months later, she drifted to the textile factories, like so many other girls.

And after that she sometimes came home on Sundays, though more and more rarely. At first, at the doctor's, she was dazzled by her wages of twelve dollars a month and by the fact that she had more real cash in her possession on pay-days than she had ever seen in her life before. So each month she lent her father a few dollars, for which, as was proper, he gave her a written receipt. And when her younger sister Orpha needed some piece of finery or other, they generally asked Lucinda to bring it from town. More often than not she wouldn't take the money for it, as she was proud of being able to show off her wealth.

But she changed quickly, and now it was she who asked her father for loans on the most extraordinary pretexts. After she got her job in the textile factory she dressed just like a lady in artificial silk and wore brightly coloured clothes. But her cheeks had grown paler under the make-up.

The storm broke some weeks later. Oguinase came to spend a few days at home and that morning the whole parish attended the High Mass sung by the son of Euchariste Moisan. Euchariste himself, in his capacity as officiating church-warden for the year, sat and beamed in his pew. That afternoon Lucinda dropped in with a boy friend from town, who wore yellow gloves and a gaudy tie. She had on a new sleeveless dress of green taffeta which showed off her inviting bare arms. When he saw her rigged out like that, Father Moisan stood up with a forbidding expression and reproved her in front of everybody.

"You ought to be ashamed, you, the sister of a priest, showing yourself off half-naked like a wanton and in front of me, too!"

But town life had given her an extraordinary amount of cheek.

"Well, if it bothers you, you don't have to look at me!"

Everybody was aghast and Oguinase went white. Euchariste was completely paralysed and felt doubly wounded, in his pride as the father of a priest and in his reverence as a Catholic.

But before he had time to intervene Oguinase burst out: "Very well! I am leaving this house, where neither decency nor my thrice sacred habit are respected."

And without stopping for an instant, he picked up his hat and his bag and went off along the road to the village.

Since then neither he nor Lucinda had come home again.

It was Euchariste, accompanied by one or other of the younger children, who had to go the twenty-seven miles to Saint-Isidore in the back concessions, where his son was curate; the farm-work and the weather prevented him from making the journey often. Of course, it was very far from coming up to his expectations. He sometimes thought of the disappointment his wife Alphonsine would have felt at not seeing her priest officiating in some rich parish close at hand. And, in addition, the poor boy seemed to be just killing himself. His parish priest was an old man, worn out by thirty years of work in a series of bleak, poverty-stricken parishes and this had made him a bit of a crank. He suffered from liver-trouble and chronic catarrh and believed that turnips and carrots cooked without salt, with a strict monastic fast on Fridays as the only variation, made an ideal diet for mankind. As, in addition, Oguinase had to shoulder all the work of a widely scattered parish, he had grown thin and pale, with a sickly yellow complexion. He had also begun to develop a cough. Of course, he never complained. But he no longer allowed anyone to complain in his presence either, for nobody had a right to feel sorry for themselves when he bore his martyrdom with such striking resignation.

At least he lived in a fine red-brick rectory that looked prosperous by contrast to the wooden chapel which had, because of the meagre revenues of the parish, not yet been transformed into a handsome stone temple worthy of the Lord. That was the curate's whole aim in life; to get enough money out of his parishioners to build a church that would be the envy of all the neighbouring parishes and even of the city people. He dreamed about it and often, when he was walking on the veranda of the rectory reading his breviary, he would peer through the branches of the lilacs, searching for the twin steeples roofed with sheet iron and shining like polished silver. But all he saw was the squat belfry of the chapel with its poor solitary bell.

He didn't let a Sunday go by without reproaching his flock from the pulpit. Even the plans had been drawn and were left posted on the wall of the parish office; they showed the church in vertical and horizontal sections, and the architect's drawing had the twin towers rising from a terrace with flower-beds and tourists gazing in admiration. But it all took time and the money could only be drawn very slowly from households which had a dozen mouths to feed and could barely wrest a living from the poor soil of the back concessions. In the meantime the two priests saved every cent they could get, even though it meant that their health had to suffer.

Euchariste would like to have seen his son surrounded by the splendour befitting a man of God. He longed to see him wearing a beaver coat like Father Bourdon's. Once, on a previous occasion, he had gone so far as to criticize the curate of a rich parish who visited Saint-Jacques in an automobile, but now he said quite openly that the Bishop should see to it that his clergy lived in greater comfort.

His happiness would have been complete but for that and for the absence of any sign of life from Lucinda. But he was getting used to it, just as he had accustomed himself to the escapades of Ephrem, who still did foolish things from time to time. The lumber-camps had toughened his son but had not made him any more sensible.

He was more taciturn than ever and in his father's presence rarely alluded to his plan of leaving for the United States; he only spoke of it when he was drunk and lost his temper. But as soon as these bouts were over he seemed to forget all about it. He said nothing when a letter arrived from his cousin, Larivière, in which he spoke of the business boom and the marvellous wages the war had introduced in the neighbouring republic. As a matter of fact, these beneficial effects were also felt in the remotest corner of Quebec. Hay was up to twenty-two dollars and even at that the farmers had to be coaxed to sell, for they hoped for still better prices in the near future.

There was a moment, though, when the breath of war seemed to threaten the peaceful Laurentian countryside. As the war went on, now favouring one side and now the other, it began to be rumoured that there would be conscription soon. All the men of military age, at least those who were single, were to be called to the colours. The local member had to make a special visit to reassure them. It simply couldn't happen and anyway, as he said, if the worst came to the worst, agriculture was so important that farmer's sons would have to be exempted.

There were a few volunteers: Ti-Noir Corriveau, one of the Labernadie Corriveaus, who had tasted adventure before when he fought with the Americans against the Spaniards in Cuba and with the French Foreign Legion in another war somewhere in Africa—away off beyond the States somewhere. One of the Mercure boys, who enlisted in town, came home once or twice to strut up and down the concession in his uniform and show off in front of the girls of the township; but he had been over on the other side in England for the last six months, and from there he wrote a couple of letters that were enough to discourage anyone from following his example. In any case, his folly took no one by surprise; he had always been considered a pretty irresponsible person.

It was even rumoured that the Authiers of Saint-Stanislas-de-Kostka had had a son killed over there. But nobody had heard of anyone else.

At any rate, Moisan wasn't at all worried; it all seemed so ridiculous. Ephrem would certainly stay at home. And as for Etienne, he already had three children. Besides, they were needed on the farm; they were part of it and this conviction fully satisfied him. Napoléon was still only sixteen.

But people had plenty to say about it all when they met in Deus's store, where the memory of the Widow Auger still hovered. They liked to loaf about there, because cars stopped to fill up with gas and brought a supply of rumours which generally gave them enough to chew on for several hours. They never had much to say as long as any strangers were about. For it's hard to tell who you are dealing with. But Deus, as he worked the pump, would put a few pointed questions. And then, as soon as the car had driven off, he would come in and spill his news which was received with a shower of comments.

"Well, anyway," said Eutherius Badouche, "if they come to get me they're going to have one hell of a time. In two shakes I'll be up in the woods and they'll never find me there."

"I'll shoot the first Englishman in uniform that tries to grab a hold of me; just like my Granddad in '37."

"See here," said Etienne Moisan, whose usual calm was all the greater as he knew that he was perfectly safe, "they're not crazy enough up in Ottawa to do a thing like that."

"You never know with those damn English."

"And don't forget they're Protestants. They're liable to do it on purpose just because the Pope told them to quit fighting."

A horn sounded outside. They all stopped talking. Eutherius moved cautiously over to the window and peeped out from behind the screen furnished by a monster advertisement for cigarettes.

Deus came back again and without waiting to be questioned burst out excitedly: "Do you know what? Bourassa made a speech in Montreal. . . ."

"Bourassa! . . . Bourassa? . . ."

"Yeah! And he told them they had no business mixing up in those scraps over in Europe. And he said the French-Canadians wouldn't go, neither."

"And Bourassa's no light-weight!" said Eutherius.

But Deus waited for complete silence before hurling his real bomb-shell.

"That's not all," he continued in a slow voice that cut through the heavy silence. "It seems they're going to arrest the two of them, him and Lavergne!"

There was a moment of complete consternation!

"The bastards!" Ephrem growled between his clenched teeth.

"They came to get Pit Lafleur, all right," said Joe Grothé.

"What? Pit Lafleur?" Etienne asked. "I thought he was in town."

"Say! Haven't you heard?"

"Heard what?"

"Well, he got drunk one night and let them kid him into signing up. Next morning when he woke up he was in khaki: a soldier."

"You must be crazy. What did he do?"

"Well, he watched for a chance and one night, when they let him out, he ran away. He had to walk for two nights to get home. And was his father glad to see him! He sent him off to the woods right away and they hid him in the sugar-cabin up above the Bois-Franc. He won't stick his nose out till the damn war's over."

"I'd be pretty scared if I was him, just the same."

"Scared!" shouted Ephrem, turning suddenly on his brother. "I'd just like to see them if it was me!"

"Yes, yes, that's what you say, but suppose they did come."

"Let them come, by Jesus! Let them come! I'll roast in hell if I don't shoot down the first one that even tries to get near me. And just let me get my hands on one of those bloody English sons-of-bitches!"

But at bottom all this blustering wasn't very dangerous. The only anxious moment was when the government distributed cards which every man of military age had to fill in, giving his age and his profession and stating whether he was married or single. To be on the safe side and as no penalties were provided in the law, nobody in the country districts, or hardly anybody, filled them out.

There was a general election, however, and though conscription was not specifically an issue, everyone knew it was in the offing. The result was to split the country in two and to shatter the fragile bond that held English and French Canada together. The people of Quebec believed that all the soldiers, who had been given the franchise, and all the "English," whose sons were already at the front, had banded together to force every recalcitrant into the war. Every French-Canadian in the Province voted against the government.

It didn't help. As soon as parliament met, it passed the law. But the exemption granted farmers' sons and, particularly, the absence of leaders prevented the feeling of revolt from taking shape and spreading. The events of '37 came within an ace of being repeated a little less than a century later. Stormy meetings were held in Montreal; in Quebec there was open rioting. But it all died down pretty soon.

It was sufficient excuse, though, for all the war profiteers, brass hats, politicians on the make, armament manufacturers and army contractors to set up a howl about cowardice. But when Bourassa agreed to stop campaigning and the Catholic hierarchy, true to its age-old policy, counselled obedience to constituted authority, there was no one left to interpret and explain the feelings of this racial minority that had been dragooned into participation against its will. No one to show how simple the whole question really was.

Rooted in the Laurentian soil, which is the only one they had ever known, without contact for a century and a half now with the distant world of Europe, the peace-loving people of Quebec were not in the least interested in the Great European Madness. The people of Flanders could see their blazing homes, their shattered woods and orchards; Englishmen could feel the presence of hostile battleships just over the horizon; other countries could seize the colonies of an enemy helpless to defend them, but they . . .

Britain? All the name meant to them was a double conquest : the first one cruel and complete, cutting deep into the living body of the French nation to separate mother and child; the other conquest, which was still going on, was slow and underhand but even more cruel, as it crushed the life out of a little race of farmers and workmen under the weight of economic pressure and kept on snatching away and assimilating their most successful sons.

France? The only France they knew or cared about was the France of another age, the France of the days before she forsook them and became an apostate, the France of Christ and the King. They had nothing in common with the France of today, whose very writings were poisonous. That is what they had been told so it must be true.

They knew nothing at all about the other countries.

What had they in common with those far-away peoples, some of them dominant nations thirsting for murder and loot, and others, quite humble like themselves, probably, but drunk for generations with the wine of patriotism and fed on military glory?

Of course, if they were forced to re-enact their own history and fight again the backwoods campaigns of an Iberville, a Montcalm or a Chénier, it would be easier, and even then . . .

All they asked was to be left in peace to till their rich fields and cultivate their fruitful, familiar acres; they had no other ambition than to harvest their crops and pasture their stock.

And, in spite of the advice and the pastoral instructions they had received, they felt that the country priests—who were the ones they really knew, as they were of their own flesh and blood and lived side by side with them—were animated by the same likes and dislikes. Their thinly veiled utterances showed that they were ready to protect them, that they watched over them with affection, and that they shared their indifference and their tacit resistance.

The young men from the towns were less fortunate than the farmers' sons, as their only way of escaping conscription was by deserting. Some of the luckier ones, who were just finishing their studies and who came from well-to-do families, donned the black cassock which put them above the law.

In the woods of the North Country, deserted lumber-camps were full of young men who preferred dangers that were familiar to them—intense cold, hunger and sickness—to that unimaginable and terrifying unknown : war. And this attitude was strengthened when it was rumoured that crafty old England was sending colonial troops to the slaughter and husbanding her own soldiers.

They fled like deer, bear or moose, the bravest denizens of the forest, when a tide of crackling flame sweeps through the woods.

Nobody referred to it again when the storm had passed. No one, or hardly anyone, was missing from the ranks of the farming population. But in country districts, particularly, the gulf yawned wider than ever between the "English" and the "Habitants" : between the Canadians of the greater British

Empire and the Canadians of the little nation on the banks of the St. Lawrence, the French-Canadians of Quebec.

The thunder rumbled on in the distance and there were a few flashes of lightning from time to time on the horizon. People went on with their work, forgetting everything except the sky above them and the price of oats and hay.

2

As the weather was doubtful they decided to do the threshing in the barn. The tread-mill and the threshing-machine were set up side by side on the threshing-floor. And all day long the two horses, gripping the treads with their shoes, blocked up the barn-door, while the golden dust clung in large sweaty patches to their rumps. Their efforts raised an acrid cloud which caught you by the throat and there was a continuous rumbling sound like thunder. When the men and the horses stopped to rest, you could hear the pigs grunting in the sty beside the barn.

The whole family was there, their faces plastered with grain-dust mixed with moisture and sweat. Euchariste fed the ears onto the beater-drum. Etienne looked after the controls. And the others—Pitou, who had left his carpentering for that day, Orpha and Marie-Louise—dumped the sheaves onto the conveyor-belt. Ephrem stood at the other end and filled the sacks. They had even hired help in the person of "Bizi", who had been lent them by the Barrettes; he was a poor creature, crippled in mind and body, and no one knew why they kept him on.

"Hold on, Etienne!" shouted Euchariste all of a sudden. "And, Ephrem, you look out for the horses!"

Ephrem jumped up and rushed over towards the tread-mill, which was cracking under their weight. It looked as if Brillant, who had the bad habit of hanging back, had caught a shoe in one of the treads. He had pulled the shoe loose with a sudden jerk and had slipped back onto his team-mate. Then Rougette started pushing with all her might and shoved Brillant against the railing of the gangway, which started to give.

"Whoa, there!" Ephrem yelled, but it was already too late.

The framework, though solid enough, began to yield. With a final heave Rougette upset Brillant, who, with an ear-splitting crash, toppled off the tread-mill in a cloud of dust.

"You can't do a thing with that mare!" said Etienne, when it was seen that there were no bones broken and the panting animal had scrambled to its feet again and stood up on trembling legs, its flanks heaving like a bellows. "Rougette just won't work on the tread-mill."

And it was a fact that the mare, who was so quiet and tractable in all the other farm-work, was more and more obstinate each year when it came to threshing. She would get up onto the tread-mill without balking. But once it was put in motion she would use any excuse to bump into her team-mate, and under cover of the noise, when the men were busy with the machinery, she would wickedly take a few sly nips at him.

"We'll have to put the partition in between them," said Etienne, wiping the streaming sweat from his forehead.

"Yeah . . . but she's liable to go through that too!"

Just the year before they had rigged up a solid bar reinforced with iron to separate the two horses. It had been no use.

"Pa! Pa!" said Orpha gently.

Moisan swung round. Under the overhanging roof which ran along the front of the barn stood two well-dressed men, obviously from the city. What on earth did they want? Moisan was in a bad temper because of the accident with the horses and didn't bother to put himself out. He merely looked at them questioningly and said: "Well?"

"I'd like to talk to Mr. Raymond," said one of the men in French, but with a strong English accent.

"Raymond? What Raymond?" Moisan asked grumpily.

He was annoyed enough already, and the idea that he had apparently been taken for Phydime Raymond was not calculated to soothe his feelings. His neighbour kept getting more envious and more quarrelsome and he had been at odds with him for years.

The two men carried on a consultation in English for a few moments. One of them took a note-book out of his pocket and turned over the pages.

"Phydime Raymond," he said, pronouncing the name with difficulty.

"He don't live here," Euchariste answered testily. And added, gesturing over his shoulder: "Next-door neighbour."

But Ephrem came over and gave them by gestures more specific directions for reaching Raymond's house.

They all stopped working to watch the strangers walk away and get into the big car which was waiting for them and that did, indeed, drive off in the direction of Raymond's place.

"What's it all about?" said Euchariste. "The old bastard must have done something he didn't ought to."

But as the men were out of sight now, they went back to work and started fixing the tread-mill. Ephrem didn't go in with the others.

"Ain't you ever coming, Ephrem?" his father shouted.

Now what was the matter with him? His son had been glum and secretive again for some time. Euchariste thought for a while that the letter from the Larivières had something to do with it and that once more Ephrem was hankering to go off to the United States. But the weeks went by and there was no mention of the matter.

"The men are going out into the fields with Phydime," Ephrem remarked.

"What the hell is it to us? Come and get on with the work."

He would have liked to ask him what he was brooding about. Perhaps he was fed up with having no real place of his own and was thinking of setting up house. But he knew what his son was like; he'd get nothing out of him. And, anyway, he was more than half afraid that if he got an answer it would be an unwelcome one.

And then one evening Ephrem brought the matter up of his own accord.

It was during the quiet spell that intervenes between the last of the threshing and the first of the fall ploughing. After the feverish activity of harvest-time it was nice to be able to loaf around and do odd jobs about the place, in the stable or the work-shop, or to split firewood. The day's work finished early and then there was plenty of time to sit and smoke on the veranda. There was a nip in the air as daylight waned and down by the river the last of the wild geese were flying past over the bronze fringe of the beech trees. Euchariste started talking about old times that people of the younger generation knew nothing about.

"Farming was mighty hard back in those days when you had to do everything with an axe, a flail, a sickle and a hand-rake. Nowadays all you have to do is sit on the driving-seat of a reaper-binder and 'Giddap, there!' And another thing is that harvests are earlier now with this new seed that ripens quicker than the old kinds used to."

There had been a lot of changes in fifty years; the old-timers would hardly know their way around.

"Why, sure," said Etienne, getting up to go into the kitchen. "Two men will do where you used to need five before, and even they don't have to use much elbow-grease!"

Ephrem waited till Etienne closed the door. He sat looking at a red blossom, which had escaped the frost and that grew on a Scarlet Runner that climbed up a post of the veranda, as he said: "It's that way on this farm too; you don't need so many people."

Euchariste pricked up his ears, but he avoided looking at his son for fear he'd stop. To encourage him he merely remarked: "We've got a good farm all right, but it's not so big."

Now there was going to be a show-down. Ephrem was coming to the point. It made his father feel pleased and just a trifle uneasy. They were going to have to speak out and some things would be hard to say. There was a moment's silence.

"I've been thinking, Pa . . ."

Another pause.

"That I'll have to make up my mind one of these days."

"Well, why not? You're old enough. You'll have to decide sooner or later."

Ephrem wiped his nose on the back of his hand. He looked as if a great weight were off his mind.

"Well, if you're willing, I guess I know what I'd like to do. I've been hanging around long enough now. If I've got to do it, I might as well do it now!"

They could really tackle the question now, as at last they understood one another. And Euchariste recalled a very similar encounter he had had with old Branchaud; at that time a few hints had made his meaning quite clear. It would seem as though he was going to have his own way again. He bowed his head and his stout heart beat with a quiet satisfaction; a feeling of relief rose in him and overflowed like the water that floods the deep ditches in springtime.

"I tell you what. I'm not a rich man, but I've got a few dollars saved up. I'll help you out, son."

"You will!" Ephrem exclaimed.

"Sure I will. The Picard farm's for sale pretty cheap. If you'd put a little work into it, it would make a mighty good farm."

But Ephrem looked up in bewilderment.

"A farm? Whatever for?"

"Well, say, that's a fine question! To live on, of course, with a nice little wife like Edouard's daughter, Louisette, for instance."

The silence was so intense that they could hear the wavering chant of the frogs from down in the hollow where the purple loosestrife grew. Now it was Euchariste's turn to look up and his eyes met those of his son and saw they had grown suddenly hard again.

"What's all this about Louisette and the Picard farm? You just said you knew I was going off to the States."

"To the States?"

"Sure, to the States! The Larivières found me a good job in Lowell; that's where they live now."

So that is what Ephrem had been thinking about all along. That's what he had been brooding over for such a long time: going away and leaving them all. A Moisan was going to desert the land and his native Quebec and leave everything that had always been theirs to go off into exile, off to work which had nothing to do with farming, to stay with people who gabbled a foreign language and lived in distant cities where no attention was paid to the message of the skies or to God's commands. It hurt him more than anything could and particularly because it was Ephrem who was leaving.

For now that Oguinase was no longer his, Ephrem had become his favourite son, though he would have found it difficult to say just why. He never acknowledged this predilection, for, like all simple people, he never in word or gesture betrayed his deeper feelings. He was aware of it only from the warm glow he felt when anyone praised his boy's strength or even his escapades, that were always manly ones.

He liked him better than his elder brother Etienne, who was a real farmer's son, though, and close to the soil. For that very reason perhaps. Etienne was only one farmer among many, one Moisan among all the Moisans who farmed for a living. Etienne was just Etienne-à-'Charis, but Ephrem Moisan was always called Ephrem Moisan. Perhaps his friendship for Albert Chabrol, who had gone off to the war, had endowed him with something that made him more a freeman than a serf: an impatient gesture with his hands, a flutter of the eyelids, whenever he spoke of distant, unfamiliar places or things. While your real farmer purses his lips stubbornly at such times, since for him anything that lies beyond his narrow horizon is suspect if not actually hostile.

But Etienne was intuitive enough to sense his father's preference for his younger brother. The sturdy tree of his nature became covered with a deceptive coating of moss; he assumed a kind of ferret-like vigilance where Ephrem was concerned and followed him around everywhere at his work, pleased when he could quietly correct some blunder or finish a job that Ephrem had left uncompleted. This malicious pleasure became the spice of his existence. To counterbalance the unspoken alliance between his father and his brother, he sought to contract an enduring union with the farm itself, the old Moisan farm, that became more truly his with everything he did, was branded as his by every furrow he traced and closed off more completely from others by every fence he repaired. Each year it became more absolutely his mate and his mistress, his suzerain and his slave.

So it made him jealous when his father took Ephrem's advice about sowing a piece of land with Indian corn, or cutting down a tree, or selling one of the animals. Even when Moisan bought the chickens with the excuse of giving the girls something to do, he realized that his purpose was to amuse Ephrem, to interest him in the farm which without these trimmings was not enough to keep his mind occupied.

Euchariste walled himself up in a stubborn silence. He seemed to have no interest in anything but the farm animals, though hitherto, in the evenings, he had liked to play with Etienne's children before they were put to bed and dance them up and down on the end of his foot, while in his husky voice he sang the old children's songs he had learned from Aunt Mélie. He spun the farm-work out to make it last longer. And then, in the evenings, he sat motionless in his rocking-chair, smoking continuously and trying not to look at Ephrem, who always stayed at home now. The young man felt rather uncomfortable, rather put out by this silence and this domestic excommunication before his departure; it made him think he ought to feel ashamed of himself. There was also something else at the back of his mind. The money he had been saving up for a long time now might just be enough to pay for his trip, but he wondered if his father was going to give him anything more. As a matter of fact, hadn't he a right to his share of the inheritance? He didn't dare ask for it, but he ought to get it just the same. Etienne was to have the farm, but what about him? Shouldn't he get some sort of a salary for all the years he had spent doing this farm-work that didn't really interest him?

Three days before Ephrem was due to leave, Moisan hitched up the horse and drove into the village. And later, taking advantage of a chance moment when they were alone in the stable together, he handed over a little roll of bank-notes without saying a word.

But that evening at supper-time Euchariste found an excuse to give way to his annoyance.

"Do you know what's happened? Well, I've just found out why those fellows from town came to see Phydime Raymond a few weeks back."

"What's he been up to?" asked Napoléon, who, though the youngest of the boys, was almost seventeen now.

"He's sold them some land at the end of the farm, some of his and some of ours. They've found out there's red ochre there. And do you know how much they paid for all that junk? Eight hundred dollars! God Almighty!"

"Eight hundred!" said Etienne. "Eight hundred dollars. That's a lot of money all right."

"Yeah! Eight hundred cash; just like that! The notary told me about it. I'd like to know what that bastard Phydime did to God to have that kind of luck. Not a damn chance anything like that would ever happen to me. But haven't I got a boy who's a priest and two girls nuns? I guess I was just born unlucky. Damn it to hell, there must be a curse on me!

"And when I think I sold that bit of land for fifty measly dollars! Holy Jesus! If it wasn't for Oguinase I'd turn heathen on them."

He pushed his plate back with a sudden gesture that scattered the beans all over the oil-cloth. He got up and grabbed his chair by the back, but it came apart in his hand. Then the storm broke with a vengeance.

"You damn lazy good-for-nothings, how many times do I have to tell you to fix that chair. You can't even keep things running at home, but you want to . . ."

His words didn't seem to be intended for anyone in particular. But as he didn't want to address Ephrem, or even look at him, for fear of an outburst, he turned towards Etienne and Napoléon, who had sat down to play checkers as soon as supper was over.

The back of the chair was hurled across the room and it crashed into the stove. Euchariste grabbed the lighted lantern and, without even turning up the wick, stalked off to the stable.

Napoléon raised his eyes in surprise at the outburst. But Etienne did not budge. He looked at Ephrem out of the corner of his eye, as the latter took short puffs at his pipe to get it started. Orpha went over and picked up the back and put away the broken chair.

"I jump this one and these two here and I get a King," said Napoléon.

But Etienne had lost interest in the game. He had been aware for the past three days that he had won a more important one and that for the time being, at any rate, he was boss of the farm after his father.

On the morning of his son's departure, Euchariste went off early to cut wood. And it fell to Etienne to drive his brother to the station. He hummed a little tune to the clear-cut rhythm of the horse's hoofs striking the frozen ground. The train was late and they waited for it in silence.

"Well, good luck in the States, Ephrem !"

"Thanks a lot, Etienne."

He didn't leave the platform until the rear coach with its two little green flags was only a black splotch disappearing round a bend in the line.

"Fine day today !" said the station-master as he went by.

"Yeah, mighty fine !" Etienne replied.

3

After his departure Ephrem became more real to Euchariste Moisan. He would often turn round to call his son and was always surprised to find he wasn't there. Ephrem was like some familiar object which, when it disappears, leaves its outline for some little time in the space it once occupied.

One by one those who sat around the big table had left. There had almost been a return to those silent days when Uncle Ephrem and Aunt Mélie sat alone at one end of it, while the other was lost in untenanted shadows. Alphonsine was gone, but she had decked it with a circle of newcomers. Then Oguinase left, then Albert the hired man, then Etienne, then Malvina, then Eva, then Lucinda, and now finally Ephrem. According to custom, Euchariste sat at the head, facing the road; but on the benches on either side there were only Orpha and Marie-Louise and sometimes in the evening Napoléon, "Pitou" for short, who went from farm to farm with his employer Barnabé Boisclair, the master carpenter.

But things couldn't go on like that. Euchariste wasn't alone for very long with his two daughters, who were now eighteen and eleven respectively. Until then Etienne had lived in the old house with his four children. But one day he and his whole family simply came and sat round the big table. His wife, Exilda, took over the cooking, while Orpha quite naturally helped to look after Etienne's children. When the cold weather came, the whole brood moved into the upper rooms to save the trouble of heating two houses and the two families huddled close, the better to withstand the onslaughts of winter.

The house was almost crowded again. It comforted Euchariste and cheered him up to have the newcomers filling up the empty spaces left by those who had gone. He didn't often mention the absent ones. Why should he? Nobody could have said anything about them that he didn't know already. Their names were merely used as landmarks to fix the succession of events: "When my poor Alphonsine was alive"; "when Oguinase was at college"; "before Malvina became a nun." But since her going away to live in Montreal, Lucinda's name was hardly ever mentioned, and Ephrem's never, precisely because his father thought of him most often and most distinctly. He thought of him particularly every time he looked at these children round him, who were not Ephrem's children. It annoyed him sometimes and made him feel angry with Etienne.

He had other worries besides; he was secretly tormented by this business of the deposits of red ochre that were going to bring in money to Phydime Raymond. But his eldest son's health caused him even greater anxiety. Oguinase had had to give up parish work. He came to spend a few weeks at home on the farm in an attempt to regain his strength. It might have made his father forget Ephrem's absence if only Oguinase's health had been better. But they hardly recognized him when he arrived. He had gone into a decline and in the mornings he had big circles round his eyes, while at night his cheeks seemed to burn from an inner fire. He spent his days huddled in the rocking-chair next to the stove, coughing like an old man, though he was only thirty.

As his health got worse and worse, he went off to town and wrote to say the doctor had advised him to go into hospital.

His father was relieved. Now that he no longer had to keep looking at his son's drawn face and sickly frame, it all seemed less real to him; the invalid's departure broke the anxious tension. And when people in a sympathetic tone of voice asked him for news, there was nothing to prevent him from imagining Oguinase was in good health, or at least convalescent.

But this Phydime Raymond business was much more troublesome. To think that he had had a small fortune right there at the end of his farm and that a stupid trick of Phydime's had made him let go of it! Moisan had not said hullo to Phydime since the latter had put through the deal and Raymond never met him without giving a little soundless chuckle. When they were working in adjacent fields, they would sometimes stop and stare at one another across the fence, until Euchariste, choking with anger, suddenly turned his back on him. He had been robbed, for he persuaded himself that Phydime had known all about it ever since the day they had signed that damned paper.

A gang of men were on the job now. The road that climbed gently to the hill on Phydime's farm was deeply rutted by the wheels of the wagons carting the red earth to the station.

One day Euchariste could stand it no longer. Pretending there was a fence that had to be mended, he went off very early in the morning to the triangular field at the end of the farm. He sauntered along, like a thief spying out the ground, and kept stopping every so often to see if anyone was watching him from Phydime's place. Suddenly he heard a wagon coming down to the road with its axles creaking under the weight of the load. He dashed through a clump of brushwood and landed in the middle of the creek.

When he got to the end of the farm, he was confronted by a gaping hole in the side of the hill, an open wound in the earth from which the red ochre streamed. He stood there motionless for a moment, feeling in his own heart the wound in the land that was his, the old Moisan land ravished by an out-sider—by Phydime Raymond.

And suddenly the whole thing came home to him; it was "his land" that his neighbour was carting off and selling shovel-ful by shovelful. Because what he had sold him, he remem-bered now, was "the piece of land *on the top* of the hill." But the excavating was being done on the slope; the pit was about halfway up. And now that he knew for sure that this outrage was an actual fact and that he had been really and truly swindled, it wasn't the bitterness of anger he tasted but the strong savour of imminent vengeance. He went up to the top of the ridge and from this piece of ground he felt he had reclaimed the silent challenge to Phydime and his loaded wagons.

He would like to have had him there for just one minute, the dirty skunk! He would have given him one of those looks, so that Phydime would realize he was being threatened and would be worried because he wouldn't know how or when the blow was going to fall. For he intended not only to stop his plundering his farm, but to make him cough up too. They had been carting off his rightful property for days now, whole wagonloads of it.

He had to make up his mind what to do. He suddenly felt relieved of a great burden and he flung his head up as a horse does when his collar has just been taken off. It was no good going to talk the matter over with Phydime; he would only get insulted for his pains. No, the best thing to do was to take it to court and then that damn robber would have to pay the costs.

Of course, it was a long trip and quite a nuisance to have

to go to town and get a lawyer. But suddenly his hesitation vanished; he could go to see Oguinase, who was ill in hospital.

Only once before, and that was a long time ago, when he took his son to the college for the first time, had he travelled the full length of the long road that led to town. And, as a matter of fact, that is as far as he had ever been, that was the limit and the most distant boundary of his world. He was a true farmer in that the farm was all he needed, while he on his part tried to do everything that was needful for the farm. There was a real communion of spirit, a real physical bond between the two of them. His farm was a little inhabited island in the surrounding archipelago. His universe did not extend beyond this patch of ground and this little cluster of humanity, that were linked together by strong mutual attractions.

You only left your own house to go to another for very urgent reasons. And, from now on, what could he possibly hope to find anywhere else? When he was a young man he had to go and get himself a wife. Later, he went to the Widow Auger's store to hear the news and find out if anything was happening. Now, at fifty-five, he had discovered that nothing ever did happen; at any rate, nothing that mattered as far as he was concerned. The war had come to an end before its shadow fell over his part of the world; the valley of the St. Lawrence was not touched by it. People everywhere else were all talking about peace; but it was never mentioned here, for here a quiet fruitful peace had always been taken for granted.

It needed the sharp spur of a Norman's greedy vindictiveness to make him take this trip to town and cross the border line which separated him and his from all the rest of the world. And that border line wasn't far off; it ran along the ravine, in the bed of the creek, that separated his farm from Phydime's— that son-of-a-bitch Phydime!

He travelled the long road again but failed to recognize it. It was no longer a narrow, dusty, unhurried way, meandering across the fields, narrowing at a culvert every few rods, turning aside to wind around a barn. The banks of the ditches on either hand used to be overgrown with wild raspberries and dog-roses, while in the swampy parts the brown distaffs of the bullrushes stood sturdily erect. In those days when an occasional buggy drove silently along you could see it from a long way off because of its wake, which rose in a cloud of dust as fine as wheaten flour.

Today his poor horse clumped along so heavily on the

asphalt that every now and then he had to drive off along the shoulders of the road, where there was no pavement, to rest it a bit. And every few moments he felt the swish of air from a car hurtling by at breakneck speed.

Euchariste, whose memory was excellent, had a good recollection of the town and expected to be able to find his way around it without any trouble. And yet, when he thought he was still a good six miles away, the houses suddenly began getting closer together. They were evidently summer cottages and, as it was early spring, they still looked rather dreary, with the paint peeled off by the cold weather, the windows boarded over with rough planks, and last year's flowers rotting in garden-beds among unkempt lawns. But fortunately from a long way off he caught sight of the steeple pointing up into the blue sky, which looked like a huge blue leaf ribbed by the bare branches of the trees.

He was completely lost by the time he got to where the town really began. Formerly you passed from the scattered fringe of farms to a row of little one-storey houses, rather poor-looking and unpretentious ones with their gables somewhat askew. But now the road at this point ran right into a regular mountain of lumber, a whole forest sawn into logs and lying prostrate along the way. It made the road turn sharply aside like the jams of criss-crossed tree-trunks in the North, which block the rivers and force them out of their beds. And the whole town was covered with a pall of heavy rank vapour, which stung your nostrils and made you feel sick. This stench of the acid used to dissolve the pulpwood was familiar to him, because sometimes, when the northeast wind blew straight in the direction of Saint-Jacques, he got a whiff of it at home. But he had never smelled it so strong and so nauseating. "It can't be this way all the time," he said to himself. "You couldn't stand it."

The town had changed so much that it almost seemed like a real city, Quebec or even Montreal. He remembered that it had been partly destroyed by a fire about twelve years before. The whole central part now consisted of streets so wide that they looked empty between the pretentious rows of three-storey multicoloured brick buildings with stores on the ground floor.

It took him a long time to find out where his cousin Edouard Moisan now lived. He inquired of several people he saw, but it was no use. The first one didn't speak French and the two others looked at him in surprise and said they had never heard of any Edouard Moisan. After searching for an hour and a half, he finally wound up in the marketplace, quite at a loss as to what to do next. A policeman came up to him.

"You can't park there !"

Euchariste didn't understand and started to explain what had happened. At the policeman's suggestion a clerk in a store looked the name up in the directory and found there were two Edouard Moisans listed.

The first place he went to was at the other end of town, in one of the new streets that had grown up round a factory, and, of course, the Moisan he found there wasn't the one he was looking for. Towards evening he did find the right one, or rather he found where he lived, but there was nobody at home. The neighbours told him that Mr. Moisan and his daughters usually got back at six. And as no one invited him in, he sat down on the doorstep, while his horse nibbled at the bark of a scraggy-looking tree.

His cousin arrived at last; he was a widower now and looked much older, but the pleasant smell of spice still clung to him. He seemed glad to see Euchariste, for impending old age, which feeds on memories of the past, drew them together. After supper, like all their neighbours, they sat in their shirt sleeves on the front steps. Edouard's daughters changed from their working clothes and went off, chewing gum, to a movie.

His cousin gave him the name of a lawyer : a Mr. Bouchard, who was one of the customers of the grocery store where he worked.

Euchariste went to see him next morning, a little nervous at having to deal with a lawyer and quite put off by the stenographer, who stared at him and burst out laughing when he inquired politely if she were Mrs. Bouchard.

But he came away from the office feeling reassured. His case was an excellent one and the lawyer had promised to take it in hand just as soon as he had finished with a couple of lawsuits he was fighting at the moment against two big companies.

So he went off to the hospital to see Oguinase, feeling very much more cheerful. The pleasure of suing Phydime and of starting a lawsuit that was bound to succeed prevented him from noticing that sickly smell of drugs and surgical dressings that hangs about in hospital corridors.

A nun knocked at a door just like all the others and told him to go in. At first he wasn't conscious of anything but a strong smell of creosote and a very high white bed that filled the room. Then, in the hollow of the pillows, he made out an old man's sharp-featured face with two sunken eyes, while on the bedspread lay a wan hand, which was raised when he came in.

He must have got into the wrong room.

"That you, Pa? I wasn't expecting you."

My God! it wasn't possible! That couldn't be his son, the priest.

"Come closer, Pa, and let some light in so I can take a look at you."

Oguinase took his hand in a grasp that was lifeless and leaden and he could feel every bone in his fingers.

"Say . . . what have they been doing to you, son?"

"Why, nothing, Pa. It's just the opposite: I've been feeling a bit better lately."

"Well, just the same, I never knew you was as sick as all that."

"Well, the doctor told me there was something wrong with my lungs and it was threatening to turn into tuberculosis. That's why he's keeping me here in the hospital. But it seems my lungs aren't so bad now; it's my insides are all upset. When that gets better I'll be all right."

Moisan listened to the poor hoarse voice without taking in a word. All that he was aware of was that his son was going to die between these four cold walls, far away from his own people and his own home. How was it they didn't realize that his son, Father Moisan, was dying? From the corridor came the sound of the quick footsteps of a nurse and the slower muffled ones of a nun, with the clicking of the beads of her rosary as she walked. All these people went by without stopping. They were hurrying off somewhere else, though his son, Father Moisan, was at the point of death. Then there was a heavy silence again, broken by a terrible fit of coughing, and it sounded as if he were tearing his lungs with the effort.

"Come, Pa, sit down and stay a while."

He dropped listlessly into a low rocking-chair beside the bed. He would have had to raise himself up from where he sat to see his son's face: that anguishing, unfamiliar face. It was a relief to look at the unfeeling walls of the hospital room; at the large cross on which Christ lay stretched, stiff and bloody in death; at the statuette of Saint Theresa in a corner, her arms filled with gaudy flowers below her pink-enamel face. Then there was the deep recess of the window, which framed the uniform pattern of the grey stone wall opposite. It was good stone-work, though, well pointed, and two or three years old at most. The three windows were a nice bit of carpentering too.

The coughing began again, thin and dry at first, but developing into a violent upheaval which shook the bed before the sick man could clear his throat with a rasping sound and fall back onto the pillows.

It brought Euchariste's gaze back to the face he couldn't avoid any longer. But, as his chair was low and the bed very high, he had only to keep looking down and then all he could see was the white bedspread with that mummified hand he tried in vain to imagine was not his son's.

But he couldn't just sit there without saying anything. And for ten minutes he talked quietly about the house and the farm, the fields and the stock, and the family and their neighbours. And he kept on until he had nothing more to say and could only go on sitting there hypnotized by that cadaverous hand.

It was a relief when the nun knocked at the door and told him the chaplain wanted to see him. It was from him that he learned that his son had only six more weeks to live. It was longer than he had thought possible. Then both of them, the priest and Euchariste, went to acquiesce in the sacrifice and ask God for resignation. In the chapel, where the horizontal rays of the sun streamed in and lit up the pink paper flowers, the chaplain in a steady voice, that was rather too theatrical and practised, recited the act of submission to the Divine Will. Euchariste Moisan felt completely crushed and no prayers came to his heart or to his lips, for he could not imagine that all this concerned his son the priest, Father Oguinase Moisan.

4

The doctors were right. Oguinase died five weeks later, just at the last of the ploughing. He seemed to be getting better right before the end. This sometimes happens with persons who are dying and leads those who are with them to hope there is just a chance they may recover. The sick man himself thought it was a miraculous cure brought about by the intercession of the Blessed Canadian Jesuit Martyrs. His father got a letter from him about it and was beginning to believe it was true when the news of his son's death arrived; it came just too late for him to get to town in time, though. Besides, it would have been difficult for him to go, for troubles never come singly and the mare had stumbled on a culvert and hurt herself badly.

So all he could do was to go to the station and fetch his son's body. The whole concession was there. The baggage men hauled out a wooden box enclosing the coffin and on it were pasted, just as if it were an ordinary shipment, the name of the consignee and a description of the contents.

The carriages fell into line behind the humble village hearse and started off along the side road which led from the station to the highway. There was a whole swarm of vehicles of all kinds; there were even two automobiles, which they put at the head of the procession to give it tone. Euchariste and his brother-in-law, Jean-Paul Branchaud, rode together in the same buggy.

A warm sun shone down on the freshly turned furrows, where flocks of starlings twittered as they feasted among the dead stalks of last year's stubble. On nearly every fencepost sat a solemn-looking crow, all in black like a beadle, watching the funeral as it approached and then flying off to settle further along. On either side of the road, where spring had just touched the banks of the ditches, the starry white flowers of the wild strawberry gleamed in the short grass and there were, here and there, occasional clusters of bachelor's button and pleasant patches of early-flowering catkins on the particoloured branches of the willows.

As they turned into the highway, Euchariste's brother-in-law leaned out of the buggy.

"I'm telling you, 'Charis, there's an awful lot of people."

"Yes, it's a nice funeral. There's a lot of people."

"Sure is, 'Charis, a fine lot of people."

Euchariste leaned out too, just far enough to be able to see the long procession winding away behind, but not too far to offend the proprieties. And then, feeling a little more cheerful, he looked out straight ahead again at the patch of landscape visible to him above the quivering rump of his yearling, whose short tail whisked the air.

"Looks like it's going to be a pretty good year," said Jean-Paul Branchaud. "The fields is in fine shape."

"Yeah, there was enough frost to break the earth up good."

"Please God there'll be a good crop, if our luck holds out."

"Yeah, the crop shouldn't be so bad."

But his heart wasn't in it.

This death had struck him a cruel blow. He had lost his first-born. In itself that wouldn't have been so hard to bear, easier perhaps than Ephrem's departure. For it was a long time now since Oguinase had left home and quit farming; his death had been a gradual process stretching over many years. They had got used to his absence, because they knew it was final ever since that first day when he had left for the college.

But what Euchariste Moisan had just lost was his son the priest and that was hard to bear. It was for him he had painfully sacrificed so much money; it was he who had been his pride, he who had made him feel more important than other people when somebody asked: "Well, and how's your son, Father Moisan?" This loss threw him back into the crowd of ordinary people whose families can boast only a nun or two or a son in a teaching brotherhood. He had hoped that some day later on he would be able to go and live with his son, who by that time would be the priest of a well-to-do parish, or perhaps even a canon, like the priest of Saint-Antoine-de-Padoue, who wore a beautiful violet sash round his middle.

In the weeks that followed, he thought he noticed that his son's death had lowered his own prestige. And for the first time, too, he began to feel his age weighing on his shoulders and stiffening his limbs. Everything made him aware of it: the dull pains he had in his joints after working out in the rain and a tired feeling he never mentioned, but which showed itself by the way he dropped into his arm-chair in the evenings to get a little rest before supper. Sometimes, if he dared, he would have liked to stretch out on his bed right in the middle of the day. And then there was the fact that Etienne was taking more and more upon himself in connection with the farm.

And yet Etienne was only twenty-nine; hardly more than a child. Of course, he, Euchariste, had been only twenty-three when he inherited the farm on his Uncle Ephrem's death; six years younger than Etienne. But he had belonged to a different generation. It was easy to see that young people nowadays were really just children.

Etienne had a special way of saying certain things to make them seem quite innocent.

"If you like, Pa, I'll go and dig the ditch along the field where the oats are. You don't have to come. It's pretty hard work and, anyway, I can manage by myself."

But the real reason was that Etienne almost always took advantage of his father's absence to change things about to suit himself. The time Euchariste went to town, he was flabbergasted on his return to find the pigsty had been scrubbed out and scoured as though it were a kitchen. And his son was always talking of making changes. "Say, Pa, how would it be if we put a new floor in the hay-loft?" "Say, Pa, what about building a real good hen-house in the fall?" "Did you notice, Pa, the Gélinas have bought a pedigreed bull? We could do with one of them bulls too."

Every day he had to fight harder against these crazy notions. The farm had no need to follow fashions. Progress? As a young man no one had been more in favour of it than he. Why, look at his discussions with the old folks who didn't want to use reaper-binders, manure-spreaders or seed-drills. He had been the first person to use a cream-separator and a fodder-press.

But that was a very different story from turning everything upside down. Besides, had anybody invented anything worth while in the last fifteen years? Things were pretty nearly perfect and all this new stuff was just nonsense. Anyway, what was the use of building stables finer than houses, with cement floors that only hurt the animals' feet? And now the government was talking of examining livestock with the excuse that they were looking for tubercular cattle! And tractors! Machines that cost a small fortune and did no better work than the horses they used in the good old days. Who ever heard of a farm without horses! People nowadays really didn't know what to do with their money any more. A lot of good it would do them when they'd ruined their farms!

As for him, he preferred to leave his money with the notary. At least that brought in some returns, particularly with the new notary, who was an "A-one" business man.

He had turned up when Boulet, the old notary, died and had taken over his practice. Of course, at first people hesitated, and some of them even went to see him with the firm intention of withdrawing their money. But the way he spoke to them soon restored their confidence and now he had just raised the rate of interest, thanks to some investments he had made through one of his brothers in Montreal, who was also a notary. In three months he had become a man of consequence, especially since he was seen going to communion every Sunday and had taken part in a retreat.

But Moisan had had to fork out a certain amount of money, though, for his lawsuit against Phydime Raymond: "advance payments on costs" was what his lawyer called it. Fortunately he would get it all back when he won his case.

Months went by and still nothing happened. And then one day he got a notice saying the case was coming up the following Thursday.

He drove into town and went to the court-house. There he suddenly caught sight of Phydime sitting on a bench and talking to a young whipper-snapper in a gown. His own lawyer was much more imposing-looking; that comforting thought restored his ebbing courage. Before that he felt awkward, out of place and rather lost among all these strangers. He would never have believed so many people could be mixed up in lawsuits.

Suddenly Phydime looked up at him. Moisan took advantage of this to make the most of his triumph. He stared at his neighbour with a gloating expression and felt quite cocky. Raymond didn't seem at all put out; on the contrary, he gave one of his little mocking smiles again, just as if he, too, were quite confident of the outcome.

At all events, this facing up to one another led to nothing that day. The case was postponed for a fortnight, though nobody knew exactly why. Moisan and Raymond both felt crestfallen at having to go back to Saint-Jacques. Their two buggies drove along one behind the other hour after hour and every time they turned out onto the side of the road, Euchariste had to swallow the dust kicked up by Phydime's mettlesome horse.

They had to go back to town again and this time the trial really took place. After a two-hour wait the case was called and Moisan went into the witness-box.

As long as he was being questioned by his own lawyer and in spite of the terrible stage fright which made his knees shake and his speech falter, things went fairly well. Though Phydime had the cheek to sit right opposite him and stare at him with his thieving eyes. But everything went wrong when his lawyer tried to get him to make definite statements and bring out all the points he had confided to him in the privacy of his office to show him how it all happened. He never dreamt that he would be asked to repeat them in open court, in front of this distrustful-looking judge, who kept writing all the time.

But that was nothing compared to the cross-examination. The young whipper-snapper started asking him one question after another, interrupted him each time he began to explain what he meant, and did his best to get him to make a speech when he didn't want to answer. Moisan felt like a pig being turned round and round in a vat of boiling water and having his hide peeled off. Finally he was asked about his relations with Phydime and then at last Euchariste had a chance to unburden himself. All they had to do was just to let him talk. The whole court learned what his real feelings were. It was useless for his lawyer to make frantic signs and even to interrupt him; he was off at full speed like a toboggan down a steep slope. When it was all over, he went and sat down, feeling relieved and rather pleased with himself.

Then it was Etienne's turn, but he hadn't much to say. Phydime came next. He gave his evidence in a self-righteous manner, lied like a Turk, and even went so far as to pretend that he had never had any but the most friendly feelings for Euchariste up to the time when the latter tried to pick a quarrel over a piece of land that belonged to him, Phydime. He almost gave the impression that it was he who had been robbed.

Then some of the neighbours gave their evidence. They were embarrassed and reticent, and avoided answering direct questions as long as possible, while the judge, who seemed to have made up his mind in favour of the plaintiff, stared absent-mindedly out of the grimy window, where a few flies clung in the damp heat. Those damn lawyers . . . They had such a way of twisting your words round that even when you were sure you hadn't answered they made it seem as if you had said something compromising. The defence wound up by proving without much difficulty that since the sale, twenty-eight years before, Raymond had apparently considered the hillside "bordering the sugar-bush at the top of the hill" as part of his property and that he had acted accordingly. Of course, that was precisely what it was all about! Otherwise the case of "Euchariste Moisan versus Phydime Raymond" would never have started.

A few moments later Moisan was out in the street with his lawyer, who assured him, but without much conviction, that they would win their case. Euchariste would have liked nothing better than to believe him, but he had seen Phydime and his lawyer go by and they had looked just as confident. Besides, his own attorney didn't seem to have taken things sufficiently to heart; he hadn't realized what a crook Phydime Raymond was. He had seen him talking to his colleague for the defence in quite a friendly fashion, and he had even gone so far as to greet Raymond!

In any case, the only thing they could do was to wait.

He waited at home on the farm, day after day, week after week. The seeding was over, the hot sun hatched out the seed-grain, lengthened the stalks, and headed the ears. But for the first time Euchariste was busy thinking of other things. When they were doing the harrowing and he came to the end of a field where he had to turn the horses, he was so absent-minded he would just let them come to a stop. And when the July sun yellowed the wheat, the barley and the oats, Euchariste looked out over his fields without really seeing them, for his gaze was fixed on Phydime's crops, which he would have gladly seen burnt by the sun or flattened by hail even if his own had to suffer the same damage. It wasn't right for a man like that to have crops as good as his.

Orpha's marriage made him forget his troubles for the time being. He wanted to make an impression and he showed the whole concession what a first-class wedding was really like. Expense? It seemed well worth it when he thought of the wry faces his neighbours must be making.

But they missed poor Oguinase, for they had been counting on him to perform the ceremony. And Ephrem, and the two nuns, Eva and Malvina, and Lucinda, who had given no sign of life for two whole years now. There was another empty place at the table, but it was soon filled by Etienne's eighth child. There were five of them now; three had died in infancy, but these had been forgotten as soon as they were replaced. Of

Euchariste's own family, apart from Etienne, there was only Marie-Louise and occasionally Pitou. Etienne's brood swelled silently like a flood and invaded the table, the whole house and even the fields. Moisan was becoming more and more the grandfather and what hurt him more than anything was to hear the young people say: "Etienne Moisan's place" when they were referring to the farm and the house that belonged to him. Etienne's wife, Exilda, now reigned over the whole household. There were times when the old man almost felt he was in the way.

The last straw was when Etienne disapproved of the lawsuit against Raymond. One day when his father was seeking an encouraging word, he said: "To my way of thinking, Pa, all this law business is no good. Of course, it's a damn shame to have Phydime rob you like that, but where's it going to get you if you let the lawyers rob you too? You know darn well, Pa, that lawyers just eat up money."

This piece of advice might have influenced his father, if he hadn't been tactless enough to add: "Those damn shysters will maybe swallow up our whole farm, lock, stock and barrel."

"In the first place the farm's mine. It's my farm. And it's me that'll be robbed. I aim to see if there's any justice round here!"

After the trial he was at pains to tell his son how he'd spoken straight out about their neighbour and also about the lawyer's high hopes, though he exaggerated these.

But as time went by without any news, his confidence began to wane. It was particularly puzzling not to hear from his lawyer. Perhaps the case had been settled and he'd kept all the money for himself. But surely people would have heard about it.

The harvest was nearly over when he got the news; his suit was dismissed with costs. And in case he failed to understand the meaning of that last word, the lawyer enclosed a statement; five hundred and seventy-five dollars which had to be paid within thirty days. Unless . . .

Unless, it was suggested, he wished to appeal the judge's verdict. It was explained in the letter that the judgment was not final and that there were sufficient grounds to lodge an appeal. In any case, it would be better for Mr. Moisan to come to town, where it would be easier for him to decide what was the best thing to do.

Euchariste stood there holding the letter and the statement

and looking from one to the other with a sick feeling in his stomach. Phydime had won! Besides being robbed, it was going to cost him plenty—a whole lot more than he had ever imagined.

He stood there panting like a horse that has just been pulling a heavy load and he was so suffused with rage that he thought his head was going to burst. He could just see Phydime, who at this moment was probably having a good laugh at his expense with all the neighbours and who would laugh at him on Sunday when they came out from Mass, this Sunday and all the other Sundays, forever and ever. And now he had to pay Phydime, "that god-damn bastard Phydime," the money to pay his own lawyer. That was the limit!

He looked up and saw his family, Etienne and the others, staring at him. They were all in their Sunday best, for they had just come back from Mass in the village. He flushed to the roots of his hair, slipped the papers into his pocket and went out without saying a word.

He reread the letter when he got outside. It wasn't all over yet. Should he carry the case on to the very end and hope for an honest judge? Was it worth while risking additional costs, hundreds and maybe thousands of dollars?

Looking across the roof of the hen-house, he could see Phydime's place beyond the creek which separated their farms. His horse was still harnessed to the buggy, which was standing behind the house; but Raymond had got out and was standing by the side of the road talking to some of the neighbours, who had pulled up in two carriages. It seemed to Euchariste that he was pointing over his shoulder at the Moisan house. He clenched his jaws and gnashed his teeth.

"I'm going to stick with it, by Jesus! I'm going to stick with it! You ain't through with the law yet, you old bastard. Even if I have to sell the farm I'm going to stick with it right to the end!"

5

Agriculture did not suffer from the war. In Europe the bodies of two generations of men had enriched the fields. In Quebec farmers sowed, harvested and marketed their produce to feed other farmers across the sea, who had been busy fighting. This course of events made the people who raised crops and livestock something more than mere cogs in the economic machine; as never before, the man who fed the nation was king.

Farm produce fetched fantastic prices, for everywhere people needed to satisfy a hunger that had lasted four years. Wheat was at two dollars a bushel. And hay touched thirty dollars a ton! Mankind had never demanded so much of the land, and the land had never been so generous or given so abundantly. And it still went on, long after the war was over, as if this cataclysm had given birth to a new order of things. It went on so long that at last farmers began to believe that their good fortune was permanent, not knowing that on the other side of the ocean, in shell-torn fields watered by the Marne and the Vistula, women, children, and soldiers had re-formed the family group and were stooping again to their accustomed tasks.

It was hardly worth while storing the crops in the barns; lots of people sold them before they were harvested, though they might regret it later on as prices continued to rise.

Euchariste was almost the only one who hadn't sold his crops yet. One after another his neighbours hesitated and then accepted the offers made by the buyers. Moisan's barn was full to the rafters and, confident in his business acumen, he waited and waited. People looked at him enviously nowadays, especially Phydime, who had accepted the first price bid, it seemed so good.

Three times a day, in the morning, at noon and at night, Euchariste went out to the barn to take a look at all this wealth of his. Often, instead of coming from the stable straight into the farm-yard, he would find an excuse to go through the store-

room to enjoy the sight of his riches and especially to con-
gratulate himself on his cunning. He was careful to see that the
children were not allowed to jump about in his precious hay;
animals won't eat hay that has been trampled. And the last thing
he did at night, when the stock had been looked after, was to
make another trip to the barn to gaze at the huge mass of
fodder, and its acrid perfume went to his head a little. The light
from his lantern only lit up the broad base of the column,
whose tangled summit was lost up there among the rafters,
where the birds had their nests.

Sometimes at night he would wake up out of the light sleep
of the ageing—for he was getting on in years—and think he saw
a glow or smelt something burning. The fear of fire, which is
such a nightmare for people in the country, would bring him
out of bed to the window, where he could see that the only
flames visible were the shimmering blue streamers of the
northern lights. At other times he would rush downstairs and
find that someone had put some damp wood in the stove and
that it was smoking.

His obstinacy in holding out for higher prices gave him a
sense of triumph, particularly where Etienne was concerned.
His son was timid and lacked assurance when it came to
matters of this kind and was always imagining that prices were
just about to drop. But each time they got a better offer
Etienne was proved to be wrong. Moisan felt he had got his
own back from this son of his with whom he had been having
more and more frequent disagreements. Secretly and in an
underhand way, he seemed to be out for nothing less than to
supplant his father as boss of the farm.

Spring had come, according to the calendar, and it was
quickly followed by the real spring. It burst upon them early,
heralded by all the usual signs there is no mistaking. It was still
too soon for the first crows, but someone saw a bear and everybody knows that bears come out on the twenty-fifth of March
and don't go in again if they see their shadow. It's a sign of a
warm short spring.

Euchariste dreamed one night that he was living in the
village and that a fire had broken out. All the neighbours were
there, including his old uncle Ephrem, the other Ephrem, his
son, and a number of old people he didn't recognize. They had
formed a chain and were trying to put out the fire by pouring
water out of buckets that were empty, though they seemed not
to be aware of the fact. They must be told about it and he was

running off to do so when Phydime got in his way and kept him from passing. They struggled with all their might and he cried out as Phydime crushed him under his weight in a suffocating cloud of smoke. Suddenly he found that he was sitting bolt upright in bed, choking and covered with sweat. His own frantic shouts woke him abruptly out of his dream.

There was no smoke in the room and a red dawn was just breaking. He was wide awake now and jumped out of bed.

A flood of crimson light streamed in through the window and was reflected redly on the polished edges of the furniture. Just then the door shook and was almost broken in under a hail of blows.

The whole barn was blazing away in the darkness. It made a purring roar like that of a contented animal and this was punctuated by sharp reports that sounded like exploding fire-crackers. From time to time sparks shot up into the black sky, where the stars were blotted out by the smoke, whirled about in the wind and fell sizzling into the damp snow and expired.

The blaze was already surrounded by a wide area where the snow had melted away. Here people were running about, sharply lit up by the fire, though at times they just stood, outlined against the flames, with their arms dangling and their heads bowed, as if hynotized by this tragic midnight sun.

At the stable near by a devoted group of neighbours was trying to save the animals, whose shrieks could be heard high above the roar of the blaze. But they reared and kicked and refused to be rescued. From the stable-door, which was already breathing out little puffs of smoke, two figures burst: a man struggling with a frantic horse.

There was nothing to do now but watch the progress of the fire. Fortunately they were able to get most of the animals out and save the equipment in the cart-shed. They could do nothing but just look on and try to save the other buildings, such as the house and the hen-run, where the rooster stood and crowed, thinking it was sunrise. Luckily the wind was blowing straight from the east, bringing with it a light sprinkle of rain that helped the men trying to stamp out flying embers on the shingle roofs.

The neighbours were all there, staring in wide-eyed horror at the blaze. They stood silent and motionless with their backs to the cold drizzle brought by the east wind; their faces were scorched by the heat from the leaping flames, which were now beginning to die down. Behind them the reaper-binder, which had been dragged out of the shed by the first comers, stood with its naked canvas arms outstretched imploringly to the sky.

When the roof fell in, another burst of fire-works shot up into the blackness, throwing into sharp relief the leafless trees, the remaining buildings, and even Phydime Raymond's house. Phydime was there, but standing on his own property, on the other side of the creek, leaning against the boundary fence as he watched the consummation of his triumph. There was his neighbour's crop going up in smoke, while his own, in the shape of good hard cash, was tucked away safely somewhere or other. He never left his money with the notary, preferring, in his foolish way, to do without interest rather than run what he believed to be a risk. When he did lend it, it was always at very high rates.

Moisan quickly spied his enemy. He guessed instinctively at his cruel delight and knew that this marked the climax of their rivalry and of his own defeat. And then he noticed that Phydime was the only one of the neighbours who was completely dressed, as though he alone had not been roused from sleep when the alarm was given.

It had not occurred to him that Raymond could see everything that was going on from his window while he took his time getting dressed. So far he had felt crushed by the disaster, but now it served to redouble his hatred. Phydime was quite capable of setting fire to the barn from jealousy! He had only to reflect how pleased he, Euchariste, would have been to see Raymond's place burn down—crops, stock, buildings and implements—to realize in a flash who the author of the crime must have been.

So Phydime wasn't satisfied with stealing his property and wronging him before the courts, while he, Moisan, had to pay the costs of the injury!

Euchariste directed his violent, impotent rage towards Phydime. He cursed the wind for not turning south-west and carrying the sparks in a rain of hatred over the Raymond house instead of dropping them on his own, where three times already they had had to put out the beginnings of a fire.

He turned on one of the Mercures who was standing beside him.

"Look at him over there, the bastard !"

"Who do you mean ?"

"That son of a bitch Phydime. He done it."

"Come, come, Mr. Moisan," said Alphonse Mercure. "There's no sense to that."

The shock must have made him slightly crazy.

"Mustn't say things like that, Mr. Moisan," he said, when Euchariste became violently insistent. "It's pretty serious. He might make a lot of trouble for you."

Just then Etienne rushed up to his father. He was dressed any old way and wore a pair of trousers and a tattered sweater. His shoes were undone, his hair, eyebrows and moustache singed, and his face and arms covered with smudges where sparks had fallen. Even his voice was unrecognizable; it was so choked by the anguish of his despair.

"We hardly saved a thing, Pa! We hardly saved a thing!"

He had been repeating the same words over and over again for an hour as he went from one silent knot of spectators to another. He was so overwhelmed by the disaster that he could neither think nor speak nor act.

"We hardly saved a thing, Alphonse. It's terrible; we hardly saved a thing!"

"How did it happen, Etienne?"

"Perhaps," one of the family suggested, "perhaps it was when Pa went to the barn last night to have a look round. He had his pipe with him."

"Yeah, I guess that's what it was. But we hardly saved a thing, hardly a thing."

And then Etienne turned and faced his father and, though he said nothing more, his eyes blazed angrily in the light of the dying fire. That hard glowing spark was for Euchariste Moisan, whose negligence had consumed the wealth they had worked and scrimped and saved for throughout a whole year.

Like a flock of sheep bewildered by peals of thunder and the violence of a storm, the children huddled close round Euchariste.

Etienne turned on his heel suddenly and went off towards the hen-house, where there still seemed to be work to do.

But Euchariste went on staring at Phydime.

The catastrophe seemed to have broken something in Euchariste Moisan. He spent the next day and many others prowling about the ruins as though he were looking for a buried treasure, though actually all that remained was a blackened mass with charred fragments of the walls and here

and there a wisp of smoke from the hay that went on smoulder-
ing underneath.

Etienne was the first to get over it. After a few days he
decided a new barn would have to be built, and a good one at
that. He said nothing to his father about it and, in fact, took
advantage of the old man's stupor to get in touch with one of
the Fusey boys, who was Provincial agronomist, and together
they drew up plans for a new barn and a new stable. The loss
of the old buildings was not very serious in itself, for Etienne
had been thinking for quite a while of replacing them by more
modern ones and would have done so if his father had not been
so stupidly obstinate about holding the crop and running the
terrible risk of fire. As long as the barns are full the very
thought of a fire keeps a farmer from sleeping.

Although Etienne had insisted several times that they ought
to accept the dealers' offers, his father stuck to his guns and
didn't seem to realize that he was getting old and, above all,
that he belonged to an earlier generation. It was Etienne who
was to inherit the farm by right. Then why shouldn't he be the
one to make the decisions?

It was time for him to take over. The barn would not be
covered with cedar shingles, in the old-fashioned way, but with
sheet iron and a gable roof. The stable was to have a cement
floor and foundations and a skip to carry the manure to the
outside platform. And while they were about it they might as
well build a real hen-house. They would set the buildings
further apart to lessen the risk of fire. Fine. Except that . . .

Except that they would have to have money and the old
man had all the cash.

It wasn't until ten days after the fire that Euchariste first
mentioned the subject of rebuilding. Etienne was greatly relieved, for he didn't know how to bring up the problem of
financing.

To Euchariste's mind all that had to be done was to recon-
struct the old buildings and, in a sense, wipe out all trace of the
fire by putting everything back into its normal state and place,
just as it had always been.

So he was flabbergasted when Etienne showed him the
plans he had got from the agricultural engineer and even more
aghast when he realized that his son had made up his mind
before he had had a chance to say a word and without taking
him and his opinions into account.

He realized then how much had been shattered by the

disaster and how many new, unbelievable factors it had introduced—factors which it was high time for him to fight against
and overcome. Fight! Fight when he felt so old and tired! But
not too old or too tired yet to resume the struggle on and for
the farm, for this conflict was his whole life from birth to
death. But how could he fight against other people, against his
own family?

He did try, however, strong in the conviction that everything still depended on him, since nothing could be done without his money. He tried to prop up his crumbling authority,
until Etienne got tired of his stubbornness and tired of arguing
with him and explaining things and told him quite plainly that
his carelessness had been responsible for the disaster. So they
were all turning against him now!

Etienne even called in the agronomist to help him and the
latter, who was a farmer himself and understood farmers,
managed to arouse Euchariste's pride by taking him to see the
buildings of the Experimental Farm at Parentville and the ones
on the Lacroix place. But it was Etienne's unyielding obstinacy
and his own loss of spirit which finally turned the scales.

On this occasion, for obvious reasons, he hated going to
the notary. For the first time in his life the object of his visit
had nothing to do with piling up money.

The notary received him with his usual warmth, though
his face fell a little when he learned that Euchariste wanted to
draw out the rather large sum he needed. He explained to him
how difficult it was to convert such profitable investments as
the ones he had selected for his clients' savings.

"I've got a better idea for you, Moisan," he said after a
moment's reflection. "Perhaps I ought to explain first of all
that since last year the money you left with me has been earning not five or six per cent but seven. If I were you, this is
what I'd do. I'd go and see the priest and, as you're a church-
warden, the parish would be glad to lend you the money at
five per cent. That way you'll make the difference. Five from
seven leaves two; you'll get two per cent a year. How does that
strike you?"

Euchariste was amazed at this suggestion. Notary Boulet
was no business man; to think that for years he had only paid
him five per cent!

Still . . .

"Why, sure. But . . ."

"But what?"

"Well, I don't much like the idea of borrowing. I never owed nobody a cent, nor put my name to a note. I guess maybe . . ."

"Suit yourself, Moisan. It's up to you and it's your money. I can give it you whenever you want it—the day after tomorrow if you like. I don't give a damn. I won't charge you anything for the advice and I'm not going to force you to make money if you don't want to. A fellow's either born smart or he ain't. That's your affair."

This time he had touched a tender spot. Euchariste was soon persuaded.

The new buildings began to rise. From their concrete foundations the framework of new yellow lumber mounted up and up until the day when the roof-tree was decked with a bouquet of lilac-blossoms and spruce branches blessed by the priest.

6

Though the burning of the barn had been a great blow, the construction of the new buildings filled Euchariste with even greater dismay, largely because it was the expression of a will other than his own. It changed the very appearance of the old Moisan farm.

He didn't feel at home any longer. For the last few years, when he sat smoking in his rocking-chair near the stove, he had been surrounded by a family that was not his but his son's. The stable, the barn, all the old familiar buildings, of which he was master, had been a kind of refuge then; but now nothing was in its accustomed place. He had to keep asking Etienne where things were, just like a stranger.

So now instead of pottering about among the horses and cows under the old friendly beams, where the same pair of swallows came each year to build their nest, he would go out, as much at a loss as they were, and wander across the fields, hoping to rediscover what really belonged to him, hoping to find himself again. But whichever way he turned he met with something hostile. If he looked away from the brand-new farm buildings it was only to light on the hill-side, from which Phydime, jeering and triumphant, had taken his stolen wealth. Over to the left, beyond the farms of the neighbours, oblivious of his troubles, the spire of the church where his son the priest slept rose above the trees. And beyond that were the distant cities that had robbed him of Lucinda and Ephrem.

Looking north, it was worse still. The very sight of Raymond's fields and cattle made him catch his breath and filled him with a bitter jealousy that made him do stupid, spiteful things. One day when the crows were pecking at his oats he caught himself shooing them over towards his neighbour's field.

The land was the only thing left to him, but the land was changeless and unfeeling, without tenderness or compassion. He would have liked to feel that it was an ally against hostile people and hostile things; but he found it as willing to multiply the grain of the unjust, like Phydime, as it was to increase his own, as ready to fill the new barn, Etienne's barn, with generous bounty as it had been to stock the old one.

Yet no one knew the old Moisan farm better or loved it more than he did. He was familiar with every clod of earth and every bush. On the very first day he had come, fifty-four years ago now, he had given himself to the farm, taken it in marriage, and had had no thought, or care, or toil for anything but the farm, which now, thinking only of its fruitfulness and indifference to the sower of the seed, was about to give itself to someone else. He was aged and worn at sixty, though he hoped that contact with the land would give him back his strength and authority and send coursing through his faltering limbs a little of that sap that it so generously gave to the buckwheat and the millet-grass, the couch-grass and the liverwort. He was the only one it would give nothing to; he whose sole disasters and triumphs had been the disasters and triumphs of the farm, whose whole idea of country was confined within his thirty-acre strip of Laurentian land.

"Something wrong, Pa? You seem pretty far away these days," said Etienne.

"Pa's getting old," he said to his wife when Euchariste had clumped off heavily. "He ought to take a rest. If I was him I'd go and live quietly somewhere, or else . . ."

"Or else?"

"Or else in the States, with Ephrem."

"The States? That's a long way off."

"It'd be a change for him."

Etienne took advantage of the situation to edge his way gradually and perfidiously into a position where he was more or less in control of the farm. Though outwardly they both remained calm, they had long bitter discussions. And when Etienne wanted to reduce his father to silence, he had only to allude to careless people who set fire to buildings. Euchariste would stop arguing then and stand rooted; for actually he was not quite sure that the charge was unfounded, though he never lost an opportunity of hinting at Phydime's guilt.

And every time Etienne got his own way, Euchariste would start hoping again that the farm would give its verdict and side with him against his son by proving that he was right. But earth and sky were deaf to their disagreements. The field that Etienne sowed in clover, against his father's advice, yielded a bumper crop. If the rain could hardly fall on Euchariste's farm without coming down just as abundantly on Raymond's, so the grasshoppers recognized no border line separating the property of the thief from that of his victim. It all seemed monstrously unjust. And he even got to the point of hoping the drought would scorch his crops along with Phydime's rather than see them both equally plentiful.

He was sitting near the house with Etienne, choking in the smoke from a smudge of green wood they had lighted to drive off the mosquitoes. Pitou, who had gone to the village to deliver some eggs, was just back and came up to them with a letter in his hand.

"Here you are, Pa. Here's some news from town. Looks like it might be about your lawsuit."

"Yeah? Let's have a look."

He took the letter without apparent eagerness and weighed it in his hand.

"Would you like for me to read it out to you, Pa?" said Etienne. "It's getting kind of dark."

But Euchariste didn't answer. He hesitated about opening the envelope. Formerly he would have been quite sure of himself; everything that happened to him in those days was favourable, but now that he was dogged by bad luck he was always expecting the worst.

He began to tear the end off the envelope very slowly.

shaking it well first so as to be sure not to tear the letter along with it.

Then he started to chuckle to himself; it was silent laughter and his shoulders shook to it.

"Well, I guess it's good news, Pa," said Pitou.

He stopped speaking abruptly when he noticed the expression on Euchariste's face. It certainly was a good joke to have hoped and believed even for a moment that there was such a thing as justice for a good honest French-Canadian farmer.

He had lost his appeal, just as he had lost his original action; the only difference was in the amount of the costs, which this time far exceeded anything he had ever imagined. That's what filled him with such savage mirth: it was the satisfaction of seeing his misfortune finally completed.

Etienne took courage from the growing darkness and spoke out in a voice touched with bitterness: "I told you so, Pa. . . . Well, now we're in a fine mess!"

Moisan still did not answer and sat with one side of his mouth twisted in an absurd grin. Etienne took advantage of his silence to goad him still further.

"First you won't sell the crop. Then you set . . ."

But he didn't dare finish the sentence he had begun.

"Then the barn burns down and the crop along with it. And now the money's gone. I'd like to know what it will be next time."

"Next time?" said Euchariste, who didn't understand.

"Yeah, next time! We're all going to wake up one fine morning and find ourselves out in the road, sold up by the sheriff, with no more farm and no more nothing. I ought to have gone off to the States like Ephrem done, with a nice pile of money like you gave him. Yeah! I know all about it. I saw you that morning he left."

"Listen here, Etienne!"

"There's no 'Listen here, Etienne' about it. I'm old enough to know what I'm doing. If you'd listened to me, none of this would have happened. But it's always the same, children are just there to work, but aside from that they've got no say at all."

Etienne talked on and on, working up his anger in the hope that a retort from his father would give him an opportunity of proposing his own solution, the one he wanted so badly that he believed it now to be real and imminent.

He succeeded a few days later. With the excuse that his

father ought to look after his health, that no one knew what Phydime would be up to next, that there was even talk of an action for slander because of what took place when the barn burned, that Pitou's future had to be provided for, that the family possessions must be safeguarded and for a lot of other vague reasons, Etienne calmly proposed to sacrifice himself. He would take over the farm by deed of gift and give his father "two hundred dollars a year, plus firewood, tobacco, meat, butter and peas." He would help Pitou build a house on the farm and pay him a salary.

All this had taken shape stealthily in Etienne's mind and had now developed into a definite plan, buttressed by all sorts of reasons, each one better than the last; but the root of it all was his secret desire to own the farm and run it, to be its only master and its only servant.

In any case, his father was getting old; he was losing his grip and his step was beginning to drag. Above all, though he didn't realize it himself, his mind had lost that capacity to make sound clear-cut decisions, which is so necessary to a farmer. He was ageing visibly too. Actually it never occurred to Etienne that he was really trying to dispossess his father; he had no thought for anything but the farm and, after all these years, was using the very same arguments that Euchariste had applied to Uncle Ephrem. It seemed to him his father wasn't giving the farm its due and wasn't getting the most out of it. Besides, Euchariste had got into a rut and took no account of modern methods. He refused, for instance, to have anything to do with chemical fertilizers and insisted peevishly that they only burned up the soil, though some of the neighbours had used them to advantage.

Etienne began to make more and more obvious allusions to his father's age.

"Do you know what, Pa? I was looking at some of the folks in the village on Sunday, some of the old ones. They're not so bad off; they can sit on the veranda and smoke and watch people go by the whole blessed day."

"Why, Etienne, you ought to be ashamed of yourself talking that way at your age. Who wants to be a loafer? Besides, it must be awful lonesome!"

"I wasn't thinking of myself, Pa. I've no right to take a rest yet. But I've been thinking that when I'm your age, if I can afford it . . ."

"My age! I'm not so old!"

"Yeah! That's what you say. But it's too late to have a good time when you're dead. It's bad enough for a poor man to have to work so long. Why, just look at old Barrette! It's true he's pretty well fixed."

"Old Barrette? Say, I'm as well fixed as him. He ain't got any money at the notary's. But, of course, his boy pays him something every year."

Etienne had to leave it at that. He felt it was all too early to broach the subject, as he merely said: "That's right: some people have all the luck."

And that ended the conversation.

For some time now Euchariste had seemed absent-minded. He would ask for the salt at table when it was right under his nose, or rummage about in the stable for a halter that was staring him in the face.

It was Napoléon, "Pitou," who took his older brother aside one night and drew his attention to it.

"Say, I think Pa's getting kind of old."

"What makes you think that, Pitou?"

"Haven't you noticed? He can't hardly see straight no more. He can't hammer a nail in without banging his fingers."

"You don't say!"

"Well, it's only natural; he's all of sixty."

Etienne's eyes followed a pair of bobolinks skimming the ground above their nest hidden in the long grass. He was thinking of what he must say and how to say it.

"Pitou, don't you think Pa ought to take a rest?"

"Yeah, maybe he ought. But how could he? He'd be lonesome with nothing to do. So long as he's on the farm he might as well do a bit of work."

"Work! Work! He thinks he's a help, but every time he does anything you have to do it all over. Besides, he's killing himself. He looks pretty sick these days."

"Do you know what I think would do him good? A trip. He keeps thinking about Ephrem all the time."

Pitou stood with one hand on his hip and scratched his head with the other.

"A trip to the States? You must be crazy. That costs a lot of money."

"In the first place, Pitou, Pa has the money. Anyway, it wouldn't cost him no more than it does to hang round here and have a whole string of lawsuits. Besides, we might fix something up . . . if he's willing."

He left his sentence suspended in mid-air, like a truss of hay on the end of a pitchfork. Etienne would have preferred to have his brother frame the suggestion, but Pitou said nothing. He started to pick up some planks that were rotting away beside the barn.

So Etienne had to make the plunge.

"If he wanted to do things the way I said, you and me could run the farm together. All he'd have to do would be to sign a paper or something, and I'd be willing to pay him an allowance, not much, because times are bad."

"Yeah! You want him to deed himself over to you, like they say."

But Etienne didn't let him finish. Put like that it sounded too crude and embarrassing, too shameful and dishonest.

"Hell! Not right away. Where would I get the money to pay the allowance? Prices are all shot nowadays."

"Times are bad, sure enough."

"Bad! If it keeps on this way we'll be using up all we've got put by. All Pa will leave us will be the farm, if that ain't mortgaged."

Pitou turned this over in his mind in the days the followed. Etienne had hit on the right idea.

The farm would go to Etienne, as he was the elder son. So what would he get? His father's money, if there were any left over. But if things went on this way much longer his father wouldn't be able to work and would have to live on the remains of his capital, while if Etienne started paying the allowance now they would be that much ahead. And as soon as Etienne got possession of the farm, he, Pitou, could ask for a salary; his father would never dream of giving him one. Or else he could ask for his share of the nest-egg banked with the notary and go and get a job in town.

Napoléon Moisan wasn't in the least attracted by the repose of country life, the satisfactions of farming, the magic of free and boundless horizons, for he knew nothing about such things. Neither, for that matter, did his brothers and sisters; nor Oguinase, whom his father and the parish priest had set on the blessed road to the priesthood; nor Ephrem, gone off to a better-paid job; nor Etienne, who was still there and intended to stay; nor even Euchariste, his father, whose time was getting short. It anyone had asked them if they loved the land, meaning by that the broad fields where men and animals are thinly scattered as if by the wide sweeping gesture of a sower—had asked them if they loved the untrammelled sky above their heads, the winds, the snows and the rains that brought them riches, and that distant flat horizon—there would have been merely a look of surprise. What Euchariste cared for was not *farming* but *his farm*; Etienne wanted it too, and felt it was going to be his—was his by a plain and unquestionable right. They were attracted to their own farm and not to country life in general.

The others, the younger sons and daughters, didn't care. The attachment they felt to all this was nothing more than their instinctive suspicion of the unknown world outside. They stayed on because that is where they got their daily bread and where the people and ways of life they were accustomed to were to be found. But they didn't mind leaving provided they could be sure of similar security, even in some far-away unknown place. Until now they had remained where life had no surprises, no sudden ups and downs, and was lived with a minimum of stress.

Napoléon Moisan, who was now a carpenter by trade, stayed on his father's farm through sheer force of habit, and he knew that one day when business picked up he was bound to leave it again and go off with his hammer and his plane. As he was not the eldest son, he had no claim to the farm and he expected to get his share of the inheritance in good hard cash, which can be felt and handled before it is exchanged for the worth-while things of this life.

He would soon have to think of marriage. He would be twenty-five next haying-time, an age at which most of the young men were already fathers of families. They took to it as naturally as birds do when they build their nests, bees when they cluster in a hive, the solitary stag when he mates, eels when they swim blindly down in countless hordes to the unknown sea, the pistils of the lilac-blossom when they strain to the pollen drifting through the air. It happened without their giving a thought to those who would follow after. It happened because it was natural and proper in their case that it should, natural and proper for a man to choose himself a wife.

Pitou himself had never been much of a hand with women. He had had a few girls like everybody else; but he always sheered off as soon as his visits gave rise to gossip and expectations of marriage, and that generally occurred sooner or later. Anyway, what had he to offer to the woman of his choice? At least, that was the excuse he gave himself.

He finally made up his mind, though, and overcame the

strange feeling of distaste that made him feel ill at ease in the company of women. As he had to get married, it might as well be Louisette Lacroix as anyone else.

He spoke to Etienne about it.

"That's a good idea, Pitou; you better speak to Pa about it."

"Yeah, I guess I'll tell Pa."

Etienne had been oiling the mowing-machine and he stopped with his oil-can in one hand. What would Napoléon do once he was married? What would he live on and where?

"Yeah, you better tell him."

There was a pause.

"Say, Etienne, I was thinking of going to work for the railway and getting a brakeman's job on the C.P.R.; but it looks like it's going to fall through. In the meantime I guess I'll have to stick around here for a while."

"At any rate . . . yeah ! . . . Say, listen, Pitou; it's a damn shame we can't do what we want here on our own farm."

"What do you want to do?"

"Well, Pitou, I was figuring on building another house where that old one is that's all falling down. A nice little home for you and Louisette."

"Well, Etienne, I certainly would like to have my own place."

"Oh! If the land was mine I'd have it up in two shakes. I'd help you build it and then, if you wanted to work with me on the farm, I'd just as soon pay you wages as some hired man."

"Say, that would be an idea!"

"Yeah, but first of all Pa would have to . . ."

7

"I can't help it, Pa, there's no work round here. My carpentering doesn't even bring me in enough to eat. And farming's worse still. I'm going to Quebec, where I can get three dollars a day right at the start."

Here was another one going off to answer the call of the city, dazzled by the winking lights of the electric signs, by easy money easily earned and easily spent. Napoléon had chosen the daily round of factory life with its humdrum safe security.

He meant to leave, as the farm could no longer support those who worked it, the very people who had faith in it. Not that it had lost its fertility; it was more prodigal and generous than ever, though this very abundance had become a source of poverty. Prices were slowly subsiding under the curse of a succession of rich fat harvests. What was the good of reaping a hundred-fold if the buyer had only to wait until the farmer, in his anxiety to empty his overflowing barns to make room for the new crop outside, was ready to sell at prices that sank lower and lower?

There were now nine members of Etienne's family on the Moisan farm; and, in addition, there were Euchariste, Marie-Louise, Napoléon and his wife, the latter already pregnant. The farm was more than able to feed these thirteen mouths. But they needed money and still more money to clothe these thirteen bodies and provide shoes, both big and little, for these thirteen pairs of feet.

But seeing the prices meat, vegetables, eggs, and butter fetched, they might just as well be eaten on the spot. The farm could no longer produce enough to satisfy all the new human needs. Besides clothing and boots and shoes, there was gasoline for the engine and spare parts for the farm implements. All too often a horse or a cow fell sick and you can't always do without the veterinary; sometimes people were ill too, and brews and herb remedies won't always cure them.

Marie-Louise was taking a long time to get married, particularly to Etienne's way of thinking, and he was always making sarcastic allusions to the matter.

"What's the trouble, Marie-Louise? Can't you find a man to suit you? If it goes on like this you'll start running to seed and end up an old maid."

"You leave her alone, Etienne," said Euchariste. "She's only nineteen; there's no hurry."

But during these years prospective husbands were in no hurry either. She wasn't bad-looking, though her face was covered in freckles and she had a slight squint—what the country people politely called "loving eyes." She had a gentle expression like her mother, whose placid manner and quick smile she inherited.

It annoyed Euchariste that his daughter was not more sought after. But at the same time he was glad to have her there at home with him. When she went off none of his family would be left. He would still be living in his own house, but in the home of another—the home of his son Etienne.

It was bad enough that he hardly knew where he was, there had been so many changes about the farm. He could hardly recognize anything any more. Not even Etienne, who was less and less willing to give in to his father's wishes and decisions. Not even his grandchildren, who merely thought of him as their grandfather, not as the master of the house, the fields and the stock, which is what he would have liked. Even the animals were different. Etienne had sold Brillant, and Rougette had to be finished off when she broke her leg. Inspectors had been sent by the government to examine the herd and perfectly healthy-looking cows, that Euchariste was proud to own, had been listed as diseased and slaughtered. Of course, they had received compensation and with the money Etienne bought pedigreed stock, black and white Holsteins, whose heavy dignified gait made Euchariste think rather longingly of his lively little Canadian cows.

Even the methods of working the farm had changed and each innovation seemed to Moisan to separate man from the soil and break that healthy contact that made for husky men and a friendly fertile earth. Gasoline engines had come in and replaced the horses, but they ruined the pastures with the fumes from their exhaust. Farmers were being urged on every side to give up mixed cultivation with its handy routine. Young upstarts, who had had lots to do with books but nothing or hardly anything with the land, tried to teach the old farmers their business.

The old farmers! How few of them were left. One by one those of his generation were dropping off. It started with the sicklier ones, who soon found their way to the cemetery. And now hardly a month went by without Euchariste hearing of the death of one of his boyhood companions.

"It's terrible how young folks are when they die nowadays. Look at Willie Daviau."

"But listen, Pa; Willie Daviau wasn't so young. He must have been going on sixty-one or sixty-two!"

"Yeah, he was only sixty-two. He would have been sixty-three this fall. When I was a youngster people lived till eighty-five and ninety."

He was quite convinced of this and forgot that of the generation preceding his he had only known the survivors. So he nursed this common illusion regarding the longevity of earlier years. He hadn't seen the children of those times decimated by epidemics of croup or their elders struck down by typhus and small-pox in such numbers that they had to be buried in a common grave.

What annoyed him and his cronies was that he couldn't keep track of the younger generation. If someone mentioned Amanda Paquette, he couldn't think who she was until somebody helped him out with: "Why, sure, Pa! You know—Ti-Bleu Grothé's daughter who married a Paquette from Labernadie."

Times had certainly changed; and the older he got the more attractive and pleasant the past seemed to him. He had now begun to talk about "the good old days," naïvely believing that the world had been young and green when he was so himself; and, in the same way, he attributed his decline and all his troubles to the age that witnessed his melancholy decrepitude. He never realized that his uncle had taken a similar view of things and his uncle's father before him and that in fifty years' time the same thing would happen to his sons and in a hundred to their sons too. In the same way he watched feelings that had been his appear in others, without understanding what it meant. He had been eager to take over the thirty-acre strip from Uncle Ephrem and now Etienne was just as anxious to get his hands on it and supplant its ageing master, who could no longer work it to the best advantage. But that seemed an outrage to Eucha-riste Moisan now.

This bred a hidden enmity between father and son, which flared up every time anything had to be decided; the very fact that this antagonism was ordinarily suppressed made it all the more bitter. Euchariste stubbornly opposed his son's methodical usurpation. He had reached the stage where he no longer dared complain of the least ache or pain or the most natural fatigue, for Etienne never failed to remark condescendingly, "Why don't you stop working, Pa, and take a rest? If you keep on this way, you'll kill yourself."

Take a rest! With times getting so hard!

The evenings brought him some peace of mind, because then he could be with Etienne's children, his grandchildren. In their company he didn't mind forgetting he was head of the family and boss of the farm; he was content to be just a grandfather. Though he wouldn't allow anyone else to think of him as an old man at sixty, he took a quiet delight in making himself seem older than his age for the benefit of the latest batch of youngsters.

"Grandpa, tell us a story."

"All right! . . . Once upon a time, when I was no bigger than you are, Bernard . . ."

He told them stories of bygone days he had heard from his elders, all the old tales of adventure from the heroic age of the shanty-men and the lumber-camps: the "Flying Canoe," the "Banshee of the Saint-Maurice," the exploits of Jos Montferrand who, to point out his house to a bully who had come to fight him, just lifted his plough up by the handles. And then there was Felix Poutré, the Patriot, who escaped from Colborne's prisons by pretending to be mad. That brought him straight to the glorious days of the Rebellion of '37 and to its heroes, some of whom he had actually known. And the children's eyes lost their sleepy look when he told them for the hundredth time how, when he was seven years old, he saw Louis-Joseph Papineau.

"Yes, children, you can take it from me, things wouldn't be the way they are if the Patriots had won in '37. We French-Canadians would be our own bosses and farmers' boys wouldn't have to go off to the States to make a living."

But he never mentioned the name of Ephrem, his favourite son.

"We wouldn't have the English sitting on our necks all the time and French-Canadians would stay good French-Canadians like in the old days."

Though he couldn't have explained it, this summed up his innermost feelings, all his horror of the changes that had come about little by little and that left him completely bewildered. People no longer measured in leagues but in miles; money was reckoned in dollars and cents instead of in shillings and pence. Etienne and those of his generation were always using English words they picked up from city people and tourists. Even the newspapers and particularly the catalogues of the big Toronto mail-order houses were crammed with foreign expressions that were speedily incorporated into the impoverished speech of townspeople and countryfolk alike. Their games were affected too. They had started a baseball team in the village and all the special terms used were, of course, in English. Every Sunday afternoon you could hear the umpire, who couldn't even say

"Good morning" in English, yelling "Strike two," "Ball one," and "Safe" with all the swank he could muster.

Like everybody else, Euchariste sometimes went to watch the matches played against neighbouring villages. On fine summer Sundays they all turned up by car or truck and, while the youngsters aped American baseball stars to the best of their ability, the old people exchanged the week's meagre news and hankered after the past. Perched on the fence surrounding the field, like a row of swallows on the telegraph wires, the young girls in their print dresses from Dupuis Frères flirted shyly with the tourists, who sometimes stopped their cars for a moment along the side of the road under the dusty beech trees.

It was a far cry from those Sundays of long ago, with the quiet empty afternoons spent on the veranda. The coming of the automobile had changed all that. There was one in every cart-shed now. The less prosperous farmers ran an old jalopy picked up on a second-hand lot, while in families where the sons were allowed to show off as much as they liked there were more pretentious cars. Every Sunday in summer the whole family would climb in, while the eldest son took his place sitting bolt upright behind the steering-wheel. In this way it took no longer to drive from one parish to the next than it used to take to go and visit a neighbour.

"Say, look who's here!"

Euchariste leaned over to see who it was. Under the haw trees, which the caterpillars had covered with their grey tents, a car had drawn up.

"Well! Hullo. . . . How are you?"

"Pretty fair, 'Charis. How are you?"

"Doing fine. How are the folks? They all well?"

"Thanks. They're fine."

"What's new?"

"Oh! Nothing special."

Conversation lagged. In days gone by they would have swapped news about their farms and about the haying, which had just begun. What was the use now? What was the use of find out what they all knew, of asking about work that was the same everywhere: the ploughing, harrowing, seeding, reaping and harvesting of their disastrous riches?

"Say, 'Charis, is it true you . . . "

There was a shout from the crowd of onlookers, thrilled by a spectacular play of the home team.

"What happened?" asked one of the old men.

"Don't know."

"Is it true, 'Charis, your boy down in the States got married?"

"Why, sure. He wrote us about it a while back."

"He must be getting on all right."

"Looks like it."

What Euchariste did not mention was that Ephrem had married an Irish-American girl at White Falls. Wasn't it bad enough that events had proved him wrong and Ephrem right? His son had been successful ever since his desertion, while the farm had betrayed those who gave it their confidence. It wounded the farmer in him more than anything else could that the farm hadn't placed a curse on Ephrem. He had refrained from doing so himself as he was sure his son would come back repentant.

"They're better off in the States than we are here," said young Bertrand, who was in mourning for his wife and wore a heart-shaped patch of black cloth on his left sleeve.

"No wonder," replied Moisan with sudden bitterness. "It was bound to happen with all these fine modern inventions: gasoline engines, machinery, imported stock. That's not all, neither; farmers think they've got to live like city folk now. Young fellows these days have to have an automobile to go and see their girls; and every cent they earn goes to buy clothes and things good enough for a millionaire."

The older men had gathered in a little knot round Moisan. Then some of the younger ones came up with their light-coloured felt hats cocked over one eye to see what was going on and what they were saying. But at the first good play and the first cheer from the crowd they went back to the game.

"What's old Moisan talking about now?"

"Oh! Just kicking for a change!"

Just then Toussaint Sansregret strode up in all his majesty. Everybody knew him and with good reason.

His shaggy mane of greying hair was worn brushed well up from his forehead. His neck was imprisoned in a very high starched collar, circled by a bright red tie with a paste horse-shoe stick-pin. This was surmounted by a thinnish face with two deep furrows on either side of his mouth. He inevitably looked a lot like Laurier, the idol of the French-Canadian Liberals; and to heighten this resemblance as much as he could, he copied the characteristic dress and even the carriage of the dead leader.

"Why, hullo, Toussaint! What's new?"

"Nothing special. Just odds and ends."

But as he said this he assumed the expression of a man who knows a great deal. He wanted to be coaxed. They all knew this and, to tease him, nobody said anything. He waited a bit and then, in his disappointment, blurted out the news.

"It's nothing special. It's just I heard they're really going to divide up the parish this time."

"You must be crazy!"

"Yeah. They're going to split the parish in two and build a church over by the butter-factory."

"God Almighty! That's something!"

But they all looked thoughtful, particularly those who lived in the part that was going to be made into a new parish.

The old church of Saint-Jacques had been standing for some time now and the debt had all been paid off by a series of levies, collections and church-fairs; the only thing left to settle was the cost of a new heating system. But the building of a new church and presbytery meant an outlay of at least thirty thousand dollars for temporary buildings; the hundred-and-fifty-thousand dollar stone church and the forty-thousand-dollar presbytery would come later. It all depended on the priest of the new parish. If the Bishop appointed an enthusiastic builder they were in for a bad time. Of course, there would have to be church-wardens and he, Euchariste Moisan, was certain to be elected. But he knew how useless it was to oppose the will of the priest once he had made up his mind to run his parishioners into debt for the sake of putting up something big and imposing.

"Where did you get those fool ideas?" he asked Toussaint.

The latter was offended and drew himself up to his full height and thrust out his neck above his tight collar.

"Fool ideas! Well . . . I promised not to tell, but seeing that's the way you take it . . . It's the notary told me and he's off to town today to see the Bishop about it. What have you got to say to that?"

Without drawing attention to himself, Euchariste slipped away from the group and strolled off towards the road.

As soon as he had passed the first house in the village he turned towards the notary's place and quickened his step. He might as well deposit the thirty dollars the dealer had given him for his eggs; it would be a good excuse! He could see about the note the priest had signed for his loan another time.

The notary's car was at the door. So he was just in time. He rang the bell. The notary himself came and opened the door with his hat on; there were two travelling bags standing in the middle of the hall.

"Good afternoon."

"Oh! It's you, 'Charis . . ."

"I'd have liked to see you a minute on business; it's about some money . . ."

But instead of asking him in politely, as he usually did, the notary cut him short.

"I'm awfully sorry, 'Charis, but you see I'm just leaving. I've got to catch the train. And I can hardly make it now."

"Yeah . . . well, I'd like to fix this up right away. And I wanted to ask you something."

But the notary was obviously in a hurry.

"Don't you see I can't today? Come back next Sunday."

"Oh! All right," said Moisan, scratching his head under his hat. "All right, I'll come back. But still I'd have liked to leave the money with you. You never can tell. But when it's with you . . ."

"Just to do you a favour then," said the notary after a moment's hesitation. "Come in, but we'll have to hustle. I'll make out a receipt."

A ray of sun shone through the wide-open window onto the polished floor. The shouts of the baseball fans could be heard coming from a long way off, muffled by the distance. Moisan crushed the thick pile of the carpet gently with his foot; he had never seen such a fine house.

As usual, when Moisan was in close proximity to the money he had tucked away in the big safe, he experienced a moment's perfect happiness; and such moments had been infrequent of late.

"Well, here's your receipt."

And before Euchariste had time to ask any questions about the current rumours the notary jumped into his car, which darted off with a roar like that of an uncaged animal and with all its chromium fittings shining in the sun.

The week went by, day after day, like so many other weeks: out of bed in the morning, work, breakfast, work, dinner, work, supper, work and then back to bed again. The day after: out of bed in the morning, work, breakfast, work, dinner . . . And the day after that; out of bed in the morning, work, breakfast . . .

On Friday it rained. Etienne had to go to the village to fetch a spare part for the car that had come by mail. When he got back Euchariste was in the work-shop humming to himself as he planed a plank, while the shavings themselves, smelling pleasantly of wood, sung their own song as they blossomed under his hand.

"That you, Etienne? Back again?"

There was no answer. Moisan was surprised; he looked up and . . .

Etienne was standing in the doorway, breathing hard, his shoulders hunched over like an old man's and with all the blood drained away from his face, which was as white as flour from the sifter.

Euchariste started to say something but stopped short. He felt some fresh misfortune was there, ready, like some wild beast, at the first word he uttered, the first movement he made, to spring at his throat and clutch him by the heart.

"The . . . notary . . ." gasped Etienne, after swallowing once or twice.

"What about him?"

"He's gone."

"Gone? The notary? And what . . ."

"He's gone. Yeah. He's gone. He beat it."

The plank and the plane remained balanced for a moment, then started sliding gently and came to rest in the bed of shavings. The beast had sprung, and yet he scarcely felt anything. At most there was a sort of aching numbness in his arms and legs.

"He's beat it, the bastard, with all the money in the parish. Our money too."

Etienne said nothing more, but the wild look in his eyes showed what he really thought.

These eyes shone venomously in his chalky face, as he twisted and turned the stake of his rancour in his father's breast—his father whose carelessness had ruined them, who hadn't known enough to guess that the notary would turn out a rogue and a thief!

But Euchariste was already out in the road, making frantically for the village like a runaway horse.

Suddenly his heart faltered and he stumbled; his foot had slipped in a mud puddle.

A buggy grazed him; but he saw nothing and heard nothing, not even Phydime who, as he passed, yelled out the old jest in a jeering voice : "Notary, take this down !"

He fell over among the weeds in a deep ditch that yawned open like a grave. As he fell he gulped at the air, which seemed too heavy to go down into his lungs. And then, as he rolled in the sodden grass with the gentle to-and-fro motion of a child being rocked to sleep, the dam burst at last. The rain streamed down his face and so did the bitter flood of his tears.

WINTER

Etienne alone would never have been able to persuade his father to leave. But the victory he had expected to achieve only at the end of a long campaign was won for him by force of circumstance.

The sleigh bumped along in the deep ruts and slewed sideways on the road an unusually mild February had covered with water. There was a thin drizzle of rain that froze as soon as it reached the ground and made dangerous footing for the horse.

Euchariste sat in silence; he was scarcely able to realize that it was he, Euchariste Moisan, going off like this.

But the burden of his humiliation was far more than he could shoulder. Least of all could he endure to meet the neighbours and feel their mockery stabbing him in the back; particularly Phydime, whom he was always running into, always seeing, as is generally the case with people one wants to avoid. He found even the atmosphere at home unbearable. At first he had given way to his anger and cursed the notary and declared he would have him arrested and thrown in jail, or sent to the penitentiary where the gangsters are, for wasn't he worse than a murderer? But his outbursts found no echo and so he sank into silence, gagged by the unfeeling lack of response of the family, of Etienne and his wife.

A few weeks of this were enough to make him give in completely, to relinquish everything and agree to all Etienne's demands. He "gave himself" to his son, deeding over farm and stock, assets and liabilities. He surrendered unconditionally and accepted the pension of ten dollars a month his son offered him. By so doing he disinherited his other children, who weren't there to protect their own interests; that is, all except Marie-Louise, to whom Etienne agreed to pay three hundred dollars. What would Napoléon say when he found out?

As a supreme act of cowardice and to postpone the inevitable storm of protest, he finally let himself be won over to the idea of going to the United States to visit Ephrem. For two months at the outside, just long enough to get over his setbacks.

He sat there glumly in the middle of the rain-soaked landscape. The branches of the trees on either side of the road were cased in ice; when the sun came out next day it would make each tree sparkle like a crystal chandelier. But for the moment the countryside looked unimpressive under this sleety rain which soaked in everywhere, even through one's clothes. The steaming horse shivered in the damp cold.

"It wouldn't be safe to make him trot, Pa," said Etienne. "I'm afraid we'll be late for the train."

What a hurry he was in to get it over with and return to the house, where he would be boss from now on. His father would be coming back, of course, but later on; in the meantime Etienne would be able to get full control of the thirty-acre strip of Moisan land with the buildings, the stock, and the house which draws its life from the farm and is the seat of authority. Besides, you never can tell. Perhaps his father . . .

Etienne was now the owner of a thirty-acre strip of good farm-land and the world seemed a pleasant place to him; even the countryside that stretched out on all sides, this stark plain with its rain-blurred horizon, felt nice and friendly.

"I did right to put the frost-nails on the horse's shoes. If I hadn't he'd have broke a leg for sure."

But Euchariste didn't answer. Was he thinking of the sadness of leaving, even for so short a time, all that had been his and would never be the same to him again—all these fields now muffled in their winter garments and which would emerge soon into the sunlight to deck themselves in the silks and satins of harvest? Was he thinking bitterly that it didn't matter to him any more, since he would no longer know the haunting fear of destructive hail-storms or the joyful hope kindled by a ray of sunlight piercing the clouds?

But soon Euchariste's mind was nothing but a complete blank, bogged down by the rain that soaked through the wraps.

They got to the station as the train was pulling in. He just had time to buy his ticket and climb into the coach with his bag.

When he had found an empty seat and settled down in it Euchariste peered out of the window to look at his farm in the distance, at what until now had been his whole universe. But it was too late; all he could see was a screen of trees standing in a pool of water and he couldn't make out where he was.

He didn't budge until they got to Montreal and sat hunched up in his 'coon coat, with his fur cap pulled down over his eyes, on the greasy wicker seat of a second-class coach, which stank of the fumes from the engine and the smoke from the passengers' pipes and was filthy with melted snow and spittle.

An hour before they got to the city an immense red glow appeared in the sky. From then on Euchariste kept asking at every stop: "This Montreal now?" until a kindly fellow-traveller promised to let him know when they pulled in.

There was a bridge and then houses set more and more closely together and stretching away into the distance, streets which showed as a double row of winking lights; then the train seemed to be going through what looked more or less like country again. This disturbed Moisan and he turned to ask his fellow-passenger about it; but he had disappeared. So he retired into his corner, worried but resigned, wondering into what unknown darkness the train was bearing him, towards what new and unfathomable misfortune.

And then the backs of houses appeared again in rows outside the train window; they were grimy with soot and streaked by the winter rain that froze as it fell. The windows of these houses were brightly lighted and nakedly revealed all that went on inside.

The panting of the engine slowed down and took on a deeper note as the brakes screeched to a stop. Moisan was swept along by the stream of passengers and found himself in a vast concourse stretching away into the distance.

He hadn't been himself since leaving home countless hours before, but at least all he had had to do was to allow himself to be carried along like a dead weight. Now he was forced to pull himself together. Lost and bewildered ever since his departure, he felt all right again. He took a firm hold; for he was alone now, more alone than he had ever been, adrift on the ocean of the city, whose waves he could hear beating close at hand.

The train for the States wasn't due to leave for another three hours. Carrying his valise, which seemed to get heavier and heavier, Euchariste started timidly to explore the station, looking for a corner where he could hide away out of sight. He finally found a waiting-room the size of a cathedral, where he took refuge. He sat there with his back to the wall in an effort to feel less lost and less lonely.

The hands crept across the face of the clock and he began

to feel hungry. At first he staved off his appetite with tobacco, filling his pipe time after time with his own strong black mixture. But it was no use and his stomach began to cry out again.

He went outside. A flight of stairs led to a concourse which gave right onto the crowded streets of the city. Brightly lit street-cars clanged their way menacingly through the throng. Electric signs stabbed the night as they flashed on and off and automobiles filled the air with the stench of their exhausts. Eucharíste saw a number of little shops on the other side of the street, with food displayed in their show-windows.

He decided to cross and, though cars whizzed by, almost touching him, he clung to his valise. He found the prices in the first eating-place disquietingly high; he went by two or three more and finally picked a cheap restaurant where for ten cents he got a watery bowl of soup that allayed his hunger. He came out to go back to the station, but the station wasn't there any more!

Still he was quite sure it had been there, just over to the right, not a hundred yards off. He started walking in that direction, thought he caught a glimpse of it at the end of a lane, and came out into a dimly lit street to find he had lost his way.

To collect his thoughts, he stopped for a moment and leaned, with his valise propped up between his legs, against a brick wall, hoping against hope to be saved by some improbable stroke of luck or the intervention of a non-existent providence. He waited in vain. Suddenly he looked at his watch and discovered his train was due to leave in an hour. What would happen if he missed it!

A chance passer-by, whom he stopped, looked at him suspiciously and went on without a word. Another muttered an oath which he didn't understand. A third, who seemed more agreeable, listened to what he had to say and then asked: "Do you speak English?" Moisan thanked him for his politeness' sake and stood there, weighed down by his fur coat on which the rain-drops were beginning to freeze in the cold night air. He was seized by a feeling of hopeless panic.

At that moment he thought he heard a low whistle. He looked round, but couldn't see anyone there.

"Ahem! Ahem!"

This time when he glanced back he saw a head outlined between two half-opened shutters. He turned in that direction.

"Hullo," said a voice. "Don't you want to come in?"

It was a husky sort of voice but quite pleasant. For a

second the lights of a taxi shone on a woman's head and lit up indistinctly the dyed hair, plastered down in ringlets, and the crude make-up on the cheeks and lips.

"Thank you, miss, it's very kind of you. But I'm looking for the station to catch my train and I'm scared of missing it!"

There were peals of laughter from behind the shutters.

"You big stupid," said the voice with sudden mockery. "The station? Why, you're right on top of it. It's the big dark building at the corner."

And so it was: its bulk loomed up in the night a couple of hundred yards away.

"Thank you, miss," said the old farmer, as he picked up his bag and hurried off.

The head disappeared into the house.

"Say, Violette, what did that country bumpkin want?"

"Oh, it was an old stupid that got lost. He was looking for the station."

"Huh! Must have been one of those hay-seeds from down round your way at Saint-Jacques!"

"He looked dumb enough all right," the girl answered.

Moisan settled down in an empty second-class coach, where the heat had not yet been turned on. He was there a good half-hour before the other passengers climbed in and took their seats. Then the train started off into the raw cold of the night.

Suddenly, with a dull roar, it ran onto the Victoria Bridge. Below, the broad highway of the river stretched away in either direction as far as the eye could see; it was frozen solid between the clusters of electric lights that seemed to meet away off in the distance. Above, the glare from the city dimmed the pale moon and the few sickly stars.

After Saint-Lambert, the train rattled on across the plain towards the mountains, whose jagged outline was already visible against the horizon. The squares of light from the coach windows shone on dazzlingly white snow, streaked here and there with patches of soot. Everything else was blacked out, but even the darkness was lit by a pale milky reflection from the snow-covered fields; the more sombre patches were groves of trees. There was a great red glow in the sky from time to time, whenever the fireman stoked up with shovelfuls of coal.

Once they had passed the immigration inspector, who examined their papers, the passengers in Moisan's second class coach settled down for the night by undoing their collars, taking off their shoes, and rolling up their coats to make pillows for themselves. The air was already heavy with strong tobacco smoke and the heat from the radiators made it almost unbreathable. Euchariste followed the example of the others and, balancing himself on one seat, with his feet up on the other, tried in vain to get to sleep. All he could manage was to fall into a kind of doze disturbed by horrible nightmares; every now and then he would wake up with an unpleasant taste in his mouth and an ache in his back from the ridge of the seat. He would drop off for five minutes or so only to be awakend by the jolting of the train, when the brakes were jammed on suddenly, or by the loud profanity of four men who had started a game of cards to while away the time. Most often he started into wakefulness frightened by the thought that he might have gone by his destination.

Finally he lit his pipe again and resumed his vigil by the window, watching against the background of the night the procession of unknown towns and villages with their rows of unknown towns and villages with their rows of lighted streets and their station-platforms, on which he occasionally glimpsed a couple of sleepy railroad men as the train flashed by.

A slow clammy dawn brought some relief. There were a good many farms to be seen now and that woke Euchariste up completely. It aroused the farmer in him and he felt alive again. He started sizing up farm-houses and out-buildings at a glance as they went by and, in places where rain had melted the snow, he tried to guess at the nature and quality of the soil. A fleeting glimpse of a stable was enough to tell him all he needed to know about the stock and what their yield was. And if he didn't actually imagine he could smell the warm stable smell, it was only because, having been born and brought up in it, he had never been conscious of its existence; it was this very smell that clung to his clothes and his body and even his mind. But all he now saw reminded him of the farm that had been his, of that thirty-acre strip which, at that very moment, slept under a frost-trimmed blanket of Canadian snows and tomorrow would mate with the sun and conceive again from the seed of former harvests.

His farm! Why ever had he left it to go off on this expensive and useless adventure, this trip to the States? Then he remembered what he was trying to escape: the contempt of the neighbours, his son's underhand hostility, the sudden collapse of his life, which seemed to have rotted and fallen from his overconfident hands. A sickening wave of anger swept through him to clutch him by the throat and he started mumbling curses against that crook of a notary. But he soon slumped down again, overwhelmed by the leaden shroud of his misfortune; and the knowledge of his humiliation gave him a kind of painful relief. Anyway, he remembered that of his thirty-acre strip of land, neither the house, nor the stock, nor anything else—not a clod, not a single head of cattle, not a plank—belonged to him any longer. He looked out of the window again at the countryside which seemed brighter and cleaner under the early-morning light.

The procession of farms began again; they were numerous and prosperous-looking and their brightly painted buildings were different from the unpainted or white-washed ones of Quebec, where wood costs so little that it is almost cheaper to rebuild them than to put on a coat of paint. The villages and small towns were closer together now. The latter all had the same checkerboard pattern of brick and wooden houses, the same green-painted stations, the same stone post-offices as the ones he knew and, instead of a tin-roofed church-steeple, a factory chimney with its early-morning plume of smoke. But the chief difference was in the amount of snow, scarcely deeper down here in the middle of February than it was back home at the end of March.

Now that it was the time when he usually got up in any case, Euchariste began to rid himself of the despondency he had felt during the night.

"Albany! Albany!" the brakeman chanted with a nasal twang

Euchariste stopped him and for the twentieth time showed him his ticket. The trainman nodded affirmatively.

He changed trains, but the countryside didn't change. It was broad daylight now and, after they left the city, he could see the same prosperous farms, the same small towns with very wide streets, along which workmen, swinging their dinner-pails, hurried with heavy Monday-morning steps.

At each place of any size Moisan got up and put one hand on his well-corded valise, all ready to get out. He kept a sharp watch for the grimy sign-boards on which the names of the stations were written.

At last came a town that looked larger than the others and was heralded by a clatter of wheels over switch-points, a fan-shaped stretch of sidings and puffing yard engines busy at their shunting. Euchariste suddenly saw the name "White Falls."

His cramped limbs were jostled by the other passengers as he got out, eager to breathe great lungfuls of the damp early-morning air which, even though filled with smoke, seemed fresh and pure by comparison with the stuffy atmosphere of the day-coach.

All around him on the platform were people hurrying along and calling out to each other. Moisan couldn't understand a word they said. From time to time he imagined he caught a few French-sounding syllables but, mixed with the twangy American jargon, they were unintelligible. In just the same way, he kept thinking he recognized a familiar face in the crowd, a face from back home where he came from; but he had only to look more closely for a moment to see his illusion vanish and be replaced by the features of a stranger.

Gosh! Suppose Ephrem hadn't come to meet him!

But he felt a hand on his shoulder. He turned round half-suspiciously, half-hopefully.

Those were certainly his son's eyes, those were Ephrem's eyes. But he hesitated a moment, as he hadn't seen his face for nearly ten years. Then it was as if the picture in front of him, which for a few seconds had seemed blurred, gave way to the picture in his own memory and merged with it feature for feature. And after a few moments' uncertainty he recognized his son's face and his voice as well.

"By God! It's Pa. Did you have a good trip?"

But how queer French words sounded on his lips, where they seemed to stumble as if they had lost the habit.

After the shaking-up he had had on the train, Euchariste would have liked to stay quiet for a little to regain his self-possession and re-establish contact with reality. When he saw his son he realized that at last the ordeal of the journey was over. But

Ephrem had already taken him in tow and he had to make his way across the station, which was littered with a residue of discarded morning papers. Everybody all around him seemed to be in a terrific hurry. A stream of workmen poured from a suburban local and each, without stopping, snatched a paper from the news-stand and jumped onto a street-car. Still quite bewildered, the old man found himself in a blue automobile parked in the little square.

"Not your automobile, is it Ephrem?"

Ephrem laughed a rich prosperous laugh and his gold teeth flashed like a beam from a light-house.

"Well, Pa, round here we all have cars."

By this time they were driving along a street which unemptied garbage-cans, newspapers of the evening before, and sweepings from front doorsteps—all the offscourings of a crowded urban centre—had turned into a sort of long sewer. It had been cold that night and the rivulets of filth had frozen along the edges of the sidewalks. Dominating all this was the heavy breath of the city: a choking stench of car exhaust.

Ephrem sounded his horn almost continuously; either to give warning when he grazed by a truck or another car, or from sheer good spirits when he had a clear road ahead of him for a moment. He was very proud of being able to show off to his father. And as he drove along he pointed out objects of interest.

"That there's the City Hall. Over on the right's the Public Library."

"The . . . what, Ephrem?"

"Well, the Public Library's where they keep all the books, thousands and thousands of books."

But Euchariste could hardly see anything. With death whizzing by every instant, he sat with his shoulders hunched up and his hair standing on end with fright, quite certain that the very next moment some disaster would smash them to bits under the wheels of a street-car. There was no change in Ephrem's triumphant gold-toothed smile.

A handsome red stone church rushed by at forty miles an hour; Euchariste thought he had better make an effort to say something.

"Say, Ti-Phrem, that's a fine church. What's it called?"

It had been left far behind before Ephrem replied.

"Oh! I don't know. . . . Look! Over to the left there, the big house . . . the stone one . . . over there."

He slowed down a little and pointed to a huge private residence ornamented with towers and pepper-pot turrets.

"The guy who lives there is Frank B. Somners."

He brought out the words as though they were so many silver dollars ringing on the counter.

"The guy at this corner's the richest guy in the whole crowd."

"Is he so very rich?"

"Rich! Wow!"

He let his arms drop to his side as if discouraged at not being able to find words to describe such splendour.

"What did he do to get so rich?"

"He made it out of booze."

Ephrem gave him a knowing, mysterious look.

Euchariste hesitated. He couldn't understand how anyone could make a fortune out of . . .

"Why, Ephrem, how did he get so rich just selling that?"

"Listen, Pa. Since prohibition there's nothing pays better round here than peddling whiskey."

There was the deafening shriek of a siren. The brakes were jammed on suddenly and Euchariste almost went through the windshield. The enormous bulk of a fire-reel thundered by.

The car started climbing a long hill and the engine began to roar. There were little workmen's houses on either side; their design was attractive enough, but the paint was beginning to peel off. Behind each one stretched a sloping patch of garden with a couple of vines on props.

"They're all Italians round here, Pa. They make their own wine."

"Gosh! That's fine for them."

"Sure, they're O.K."

When they reached the top of the hill Ephrem stopped the car.

"Turn around, Pa, and take a look down there."

Moisan did as he was told. Right at the foot of the hill and immediately below him, stretching almost as far as he could see, was a sort of black field crossed by hundreds of parallel lines that looked like well-ploughed furrows. He was pleased to find that in the States they managed to farm right in the middle of the city, and also that his son Ephrem had stopped to point it out to him.

"Do you know what it is, Pa? That," he went on without waiting for an answer, "is the roof of the shop where I work."

"The roof?"

"Sure. All that. And that ain't everything; there's a whole lot more further on. It's all part of the plant."

Then Euchariste realized that what he had taken for a well-ploughed field with parallel furrows was the endless roof of a factory that spread over acres and acres of ground and whose canted sections looked like the ridges of furrows.

The whole thing was a field of metal, a huge sterile meadow, under which men worked like moles, far from the friendly sunlight. To Euchariste all this was incredible. To his son it was magnificent.

"What do they do down there?" Euchariste asked finally.

"Its the biggest plant for making lamps in the whole world. There's Sunshine Corporation lamps every place you go. Why, do you know, Pa, our lamps back home was Sunshines; they was made right here."

"Huh! Many people down there?"

"Ten thousand!"

Moisan looked at this barren expanse of metal which had suddenly brought back his distant farm and the warm kitchen where the family gathered at that specially happy hour between work and rest when the lamps are lit: the old-fashioned kind that reek of coal-oil and whose glass chimneys are full of moths and insects lured by the open flame.

The car started up again suddenly and broke the thread of his reverie. They rode on in silence for a few moments.

"Is it far to your place?"

"We're just about there, Pa. I came the long way round to show you a bit of the town. Now we can go right through."

The car went up and down a few roller-coaster slopes and followed along beside the endless wall of a factory before reaching a level street with a double row of workmen's houses.

There were dozens of them lined up on both sides and all equally dismal. They must have been attractive-looking when they were new and freshly painted. But summer suns had cracked the paint and winter rains and frosts had peeled it off. Then soot from the factories near by had filled the chinks with a grimy deposit that ran down the corners of the walls and left long dark streaks.

But Euchariste was glad to be getting there. His night on the train had left him feeling rather dazed; and a kaleidoscope of unconnected images whirled round and round in his head. For the first time in his life he had lost the clear picture he always had with him, the picture of the restricted pattern of life as he lived it in his native Quebec. Adrift on this stormy sea of new impressions, he searched his memory for the lighthouses represented by the little grey roof between the two tall beech trees, the outbuildings and the meadows where he would have felt at home. But it was all confused and, no matter how hard he tried, he couldn't recall any of it clearly. He was exhausted and began to feel physically ill.

"I'll be pretty glad to get to your place," he said to Ephrem.

"Sure, Pa, we're right there."

At last he was going to be in some permanent place that was sure to be friendly and like what he was accustomed to; he'd be in his son's house with the members of his family. He could imagine what it would be like ahead of time; it would be very much like his own place back home, with somewhat the same furniture and the same pictures on the walls and the same settled calm that gathers round objects that outlast the brief span of a man's life.

But everything that surrounded him in this town was so different and so foreign by comparison with the only other town he knew : the one where he went when he took Oguinase to the college.

Poor Oguinase ! . . .

Ephrem took his father's valise and, crossing a lifeless patch of lawn with two forlorn winter-stripped flower-beds, opened the front door.

"Is that you, Jack?" came a voice in English.

"Well, that's a good one !" said Euchariste with a laugh. "I guess we're in the wrong house."

But Ephrem called back, in English too : "Hullo ! Elsie ! Come and meet my Dad."

"Give us your hat," he said to his father. "I'll stick it on the stand."

Euchariste stood rooted to the rug in the middle of the parlour. He cast about in vain for some familiar-looking object; something to make him feel more comfortable and put him at his ease.

The furniture in the room was both pretentious and shabby. On the wall hung imitation tapestries and enlarged photographs of people and landscapes he had never seen. The place of honour above the sham fireplace, where the gas-log was lit, was taken by the portrait in crayon of a man with spectacles whom he had never laid eyes on. He felt like bursting into tears.

The sight of his daughter-in-law's outstretched hand made him pull himself together. As she came into the parlour she smoothed out her dress at the waist where it was wrinkled by her apron-strings. He bent forward to embrace her and kiss her on both cheeks, as they do in Quebec. But she just left him standing there, floundering in his good intentions, with his lips pursed and his arms outstretched.

"Glad to meet my Jack's father," she said in English.

Euchariste took his daughter-in-law's hand, which was all covered with rings, and shook it vigorously.

"How are you?" he mumbled, at a loss as to what he should do. "Very well . . . very well." . . . Then he could think of nothing more to say.

"You know, Pa, you'll have to excuse her. She don't speak much French. It ain't her fault, she's Irish."

"Ah! She don't speak French?"

"Oh!" she said eagerly, making an effort to be pleasant. "*Je pou dire oune, do mots.*"

"Ah! Fine! Fine!"

"Take a seat, Pa. You must be all tired out."

Euchariste dropped into the nearest chair. He certainly was tired and he felt lost too; just as much as any traveller gone astray in the boundless Laurentian forest and hunting in vain for some mark by which to take his bearings.

Ever since he had arrived he, too, had that awful feeling of going aimlessly round and round in a circle in some unfamiliar wilderness.

"Well, Pa, how's everybody up in Canada?"

Moisan started in to give all the news, first about Ephrem's brothers and sisters, one after the other, and then about the neighbours, just as if he were telling the beads of a rosary. But he found himself at a loss for words, because the images of the people he was talking about seemed to become blurred in his memory as soon as he started to tell about them. The unfamiliar air he was breathing condensed into a fog that obscured the clearest picture he had ever possessed, that of the farm back home with Etienne and Etienne's wife and children and Marie-Louise and Napoléon, who was now in Quebec City, and all the friendly farm animals.

He was particularly eager for Ephrem to ask him for news of the farm and things about the land; this at least would give him a chance to re-establish the broken contact between himself and his son. But he didn't manage to steer the conversation into those channels. And, anyway, Ephrem was always interrupting him to translate a sentence for his wife's benefit.

"Oh, really!" she would exclaim politely in English. But it was quite obvious that she wasn't in the least interested.

Ephrem's questions became less and less frequent, and at last his eye lighted on the morning paper spread out on the table and he began to read it in stolen snatches. Euchariste realized that nobody was listening to him. Then Elsie went off to the kitchen and Ephrem and his father were left alone, more estranged than united by the desultory conversation they still managed to keep up.

"Where do you work then?" asked Euchariste after an unusually long silence.

"Well, I've a good steady job at the Sunshine."

"What do you do there?"

"I'm a flange borer."

"Oh!"

He didn't dare ask for an explanation. In any case, ever since he had started talking to his son he had felt puzzled and had often been unable to understand what he meant because of these strings of unfamiliar syllables, which, as far as he knew, might be foreign words or belong to some technical jargon or other. But instead of feeling critical of his son's uncouth speech, he was ashamed of his own ignorance.

There was a scurrying about upstairs that sounded like children running.

"Anybody else in the house?" Euchariste asked, not daring to put a direct question.

"Sure. It's the boys just getting up."

Moisan stopped and listened. A twittering of childish voices explained Ephrem's answer.

"How many have you got, Ephrem?" he asked with a new gentleness veiling his voice.

"A couple," his son replied triumphantly.

"Oh! Just a couple. That's not so many."

Why, he and his Alphonsine had had thirteen children, of whom eight were still living: Malvina and Eva, the two nuns in the convent; Orpha; Etienne and Lucinda that added up to eight, all right. There would have been nine if Oguinase . . .

And, in the same way, Etienne back home in fertile Quebec, the fruitful mother of men and harvests, would soon have his round dozen too. And here Ephrem at thirty-six still had only two children.

Euchariste remembered about his cousin Larivière, who had had the same number. What sort of creatures were these women in the States, anyway? If young Quebeckers migrated to this foreign country, why didn't they go back home for their brides and pick themselves soft-spoken fruitful women who would bear a son or a daughter once a year and fill the house with children, as Nature and Providence ordain?

"Just a couple, Ephrem! Moisans don't seem to do so well down here."

"Well, Pa, Elsie and me have only been married seven years."

There was a sound of unwilling little footsteps coming down the stairs, then Elsie's nasal voice scolding in English, and the door opened to admit her and the two boys. The elder, resplendent in a dollar-ninety-five child's suit and with his fair hair well plastered down, paused for a moment on the threshold with a look half of suspicion and half of defiance. But the younger one took refuge in his mother's skirts.

"Come on; be good and say good morning to Grand-daddy," said Elsie.

The old man stretched out his arms to them, visibly delighted. These fine-looking youngsters were his Ephrem's. How well dressed they were! They looked like real rich folks' children.

"Come and see your Grandpa," he said with a deep good-natured growl.

But the elder one just went on standing in the doorway, staring at this stranger who was supposed to be his grandfather, while the younger boy, terrified by the voice and the big moustache, began to howl.

"Come on, kids, be nice," Elsie encouraged them in English. "This is your Grand-daddy right from Canada."

Ephrem was obviously embarrassed by the lack of warmth in their welcome.

Euchariste tried again.

"Come on, kids, come and say hullo to your Grandpa."

Jack, the eldest boy, finally managed to overcome his suspicion and started over towards him rather reluctantly, while his mother gave him a push from behind. Patrick, who had been made to behave by a covert slap, merely went on snivelling.

"How old are you? Quite a big boy, I guess?"

"Well, you see, Pa," Ephrem put in with some awkwardness, "they don't talk no French yet; they're too young."

Jack, who had already summed up the new arrival, took advantage of this interruption to edge towards the door. Euchariste watched him go but didn't try to stop him.

He felt neither upset nor offended. It was just that he didn't understand. What was left of all he had hoped to discover, or rather rediscover here? All through the interminable journey he had thought of this house as a refuge and now that he had arrived it seemed inhospitable. Ever since leaving Montreal he had heard nothing but English, seen only English signs and English faces; and now, after crossing this desert, the oasis towards which he had been travelling appeared empty, waterless and without shade.

In addition to all this, he was beginning to feel rather dizzy; he had hardly slept and had had practically nothing to eat ever since he left. His eyelids felt heavy and even his mind was weighted down by a drowsiness that seemed to stretch a thick curtain of fog between him and his surroundings. The walls of the room and even the people in it seemed to float in the air and to shimmer like a landscape seen through smoke, and every now and then he felt as if he himself were floating and had lost contact with his chair. The talk between Ephrem and his wife came drifting into his consciousness like scraps of cotton-wool.

"By God, Pa!"

He woke up with a start.

"I guess you're falling asleep."

"Why, no, not at all."

He heaved himself up to shift the burden of his fatigue.

"What time do you go to work, Ephrem?"

"In fifteen minutes, Pa."

"Well, don't let me keep you."

"It's all right. It's all right," Ephrem muttered, lapsing into English.

Moisan began to feel strangely anxious for his son to go; he thought he might feel better if he were left alone. Just now he was aware of being intolerably tongue-tied, tense and weary. Like in a nightmare there seemed to be an invisible barrier between himself and his son.

Though Euchariste was far from being a chatterbox, there was the tale of all the everyday happenings back home waiting on the tip of his tongue for a question from Ephrem to bring it pouring out into the broad daylight of sympathy and understanding; but Ephrem asked no questions.

"Well, what do you do with yourself all the time? What's happened to you since you left home?"

"Well, all sorts of things."

Just then Ephrem's wife came in and she and her husband started speaking English.

"Jack, it's time for you to go to work."

"O.K. I'll beat it."

He stood up to go.

"See you tonight, Pa. We'll have lots of time to talk."

"Fine. Well, good-bye!"

Euchariste was left alone or practically alone all day. Of course, there was Mrs. Moisan; but as soon as Ephrem left she seemed to forget the few words of French she may once have known. And Euchariste fell asleep in the armchair, lulled by the even purring of the vacuum-cleaner as it went from room to room.

At lunch-time he ate with his head bent over his plate and only looked up from time to time to see if his grandchildren were watching him. But they went on talking to each other in English, apparently unaware of the presence of this farmer they didn't know but who was supposed to be a grandfather of theirs. Not the Washington Street one, who was a kindly old Irishman with gold teeth and gold-rimmed spectacles, expansive gestures, and a cigar that stayed clamped in his mouth except when he took it out to make some sweeping statement. He was a real grandfather who glowered at his grandchildren with mock ferocity and was always slipping them ten-cent pieces. This person sitting at table with them was very different from that typical product of the United States, the Irish-American; he was their other grandfather, who had come from away up North, from backward countrified Quebec, wearing a shabby suit and muddy boots. His eyes were submissive-looking and there were drops of soup on the drooping ends of his moustache. This grandfather smelt of the stable and not of the barber-shop.

For the first time in his life Euchariste found himself in a place where he felt completely useless and in surroundings that he understood much less than the common objects of a farm, though these can be complicated enough; he was with people now who were infinitely less in sympathy with him than his own farm animals were. Here he was, being dragged along in a current he could not fight against and that threatened to sweep him off his feet.

After lunch he thought he might as well go out for a bit. Oh, not far—just in front of the house, where he could watch the unending stream of automobiles go by and the occasional pedestrians.

The front garden, which was about the size of a pocket-handkerchief, was crowded in between the house and the side-walk. In summer there would doubtless be a few petunias in bloom, getting their nourishment supposedly from the soot in the air. He stood near the sickly-looking flowerbed and leaned against a tree, for these were relatively familiar objects to him. But he didn't dare sit down on the ice-cold doorstep or even smoke his pipe, as he no longer felt he knew what could be done and what couldn't.

Then a shower of rain sent him back to the house. When he tried to get in he found he couldn't; the door was locked. What kind of a country was this where even in broad day-light you had to lock up your house like a strong-box? He was almost ready to believe they had locked him out on purpose. He took refuge under the overhanging porch to wait for the rain to stop; it had now turned to melting sleet. Finally he slumped down on the doorstep and fell asleep.

Ephrem found him there when he came home from work.

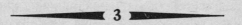

3

Back home, on the rare occasions when Euchariste Moisan had thought of the States, he had imagined towns and farms that were far away, perhaps, but very like the ones he was familiar with. And he thought of the whole country as being gradually invaded by Quebec. So many of the families he knew had emigrated there that this living and prolific stream must have spread out into an extension of the Laurentian home-land: a new, American Quebec. No doubt about it. Every year, when the celebrations on St. John the Baptist's Day opened the floodgates of national eloquence, pulpits, platforms, and the press resounded with the usual paeans on the fertility and vitality of the French-Canadian race. A million and a half "French" in the Eastern States alone, just in New England!

And now he was in his son's home, in a town where he had been told one-third of the population was of French descent, and yet everything was strange to him.

"Well, Pa," Ephrem explained, "here in White Falls the French-Canadians are all sort of scattered around. There's places like Lowell and Worcester where they're all together in a gang in their own little Canada. But it ain't like that here."

Euchariste had been there for five days now and each day he wandered about near the house, venturing further and further afield as the surroundings became familiar to him. And, without seeming to, he listened to the passers-by, hoping to hear them talk French. But they never did!

Finally, on Saturday evening, Ephrem announced to his father with an air of triumph: "Tomorrow's Sunday. We'll go to the French-Canadian church for Mass."

Euchariste was delighted. Not only at the idea of being among his own people again, but chiefly because this proposal allayed a half-formed suspicion that was beginning to worry him.

He had looked in vain on the walls of his son's house for a single one of those religious pictures that are so plentiful in Quebec homes. One day, when he was alone, he made a special tour of inspection, trying to find at least the certificate of the children's first communion. But there was nothing. And he got to the point of wondering whether his son had committed the dreadful crime of changing his religion. Why, he'd married an "English" girl, hadn't he, and the "English" were all Protestants and pagans, weren't they?

And now on Sunday even Elsie set off for an early Mass with her prayer-book under her arm and accompanied by the two children.

Euchariste and Ephrem decided to go to High Mass, which was at ten. As usual, the latter suggested they should drive. Indeed, ever since Euchariste's arrival and in spite of the fact it was winter, there wasn't a day they didn't dash off along the highways and byways as soon as they had hurried through supper, and Euchariste was whisked off into a mad dance, in which factory-chimneys waltzed about with lime-kilns, while garbage-dumps and hillocks slipped by to the backfiring of the engine, as the car climbed grades in low gear.

Moisan had had enough of it, so this time he insisted they should go on foot.

As it was Sunday, all the shops on Main Street were closed, but the show-windows were full of cheap finery: sleazy garments of artificial silk, panama hats at two-ninety-five, imitation gold jewellery. Each tenth shop was a drugstore, displaying trusses, patent lighters, "home-made" candy, kodaks and the latest best-seller.

With its two rows of assorted buildings of different heights, built for the most part of brick, but interspersed here and there with wooden shacks, and dominated by the twenty-eight stories of the New Hampshire Utilities Corporation Building, which rose like a tower above it, the main street had the temporary look of a midway at a fair, with the booths scattered about near the church to celebrate the feast day of a patron saint.

There were a certain number of French names. Some kept their original spelling without any false shame: Gélinas, Barbeau, Francoeur, Legendre; some were slightly disguised: a Martel changed to Martell, a Barabé to Barabey, a Lainé to Leney and there was even a Lapierre who had become La Pier! But there were still others Ephrem pointed out casually: a White who was really a Leblanc; a Delaney who had been Chapdelaine; a Cross, Lacroix; a Gault, Legault.

Sunday had not only emptied the stores but also the streets, covered with their late winter slush. There were a few loiterers only in the cigar-stores and the garages. At every second corner stood a filling-station which tried to attract customers by disguising itself as a Swiss chalet or a California mission.

They finally got to a little street that led to an open space in front of the church. A few married couples with their daughters dressed in their Sunday best, stood chatting in small groups in the damp March wind as they waited for Mass to begin.

Euchariste felt his heart-beat quicken: they were speaking French. Ephrem introduced his father to them right away and they shook him warmly by the hand one after another, exclaiming half in English, half in French: "Well! Well! Glad to know you!"

"That's fine! That's fine!" Moisan answered, overcome by a sudden wave of emotion.

All his bitterness had vanished in a moment. At last here were strangers speaking French, speaking the rugged familiar language of old Quebec. Everything else simply ceased to matter : time and space, his journey and these foreign-looking houses. A few ordinary everyday expressions had the magic power to make him feel at home again, as though he were back in some village of the St. Lawrence valley like the one he came from. And almost immediately he was surrounded by a little knot of men of his own age.

"So you've come right straight from Canada?"

"Sure. I've just been here a few days."

"Well, what do you know about that! Where are you from anyway?"

"Me? I'm from Saint-Jacques-l'Ermite."

"What! From Saint-Jacques? Can you beat that! My wife's from there too. She's a Lafleur, Ange-Aimée Lafleur."

"She any relation of 'Jésus' Lafleur?"

"Why, sure, of course. She's his cousin. Her father was Abondius Lafleur. Come here a minute, Ange-Aimée. I want to introduce you."

But the church-bell began to ring for Mass and the various groups broke up and started to file through the narrow doorway in an unbroken stream, like the sand in an hour-glass. Before going in, some of the men carefully crushed out their partly smoked cigars against the stone wall and slipped them in their pockets.

Euchariste was dazzled by the magnificence of the church. The reds and violets of a stained-glass window shone from the back. The filleted ceiling was studded with little angels, who clustered about the gilded plaster frame surrounding a huge Transfiguration.

The imitation-mahogany pews were quite well filled; the congregation was largely made up of women and young girls, the former calm and self-possessed, while the latter were all dressed up and kept turning round every now and then to eye the young men.

Euchariste felt care-free, relaxed and completely at his ease. It was just as if he had taken off a stiff new suit and got back into his everyday clothes, to which he was so accustomed he hardly knew he had them on. He felt he could move his arms and then turn around and twist his shoulders about with perfect freedom now he no longer bore the mark which set him apart as a pariah, a stranger.

"Say, Ephrem," he said, leaning over towards his son. "Are all these here French-Canadians?"

"Sure, Pa."

And, indeed, Moisan felt as if he were back again in the old church at Saint-Jacques, though, as befitted the States, this one was on a larger, newer, more prosperous scale. The celebrant went through the same universal ritual, but did it a little less sedately. Dominating everything was the heavenly and Catholic perfume of the incense.

When the priest appeared in the pulpit, Euchariste felt himself a humble and filial member of the congregation, his soul a part of the collective religious soul of his race; he even felt filial towards this very young man to whom a surplice lent a special dignity.

The curate took his wad of gum out of his mouth and stuck it carefully under the ledge of the pulpit before reading the announcements for the week. Every now and then Moisan found it hard to understand what he was saying. In addition to his American accent, the preacher had a curious way of swallowing his syllables! Euchariste felt more at home when proper names were mentioned, as these, even when slightly mispronounced, still had a melodious French ring to them, which was a pleasure to listen to. It made his whole body tingle. He felt as if he were immersed in a warm sea of friendship. In his new-found joy he was almost ready to get up and open his arms wide to all these people who seemed to welcome him.

So, when the priest took up the collection after the sermon, he felt generous and took all the small change out of his purse: a ten-cent piece and six or seven coppers, which he deposited in the plate.

The curate stopped dead. He looked down at the offering and then up at Euchariste. It was only then Moisan noticed that, aside from a few large silver coins, the plate contained nothing but bills. He turned to look at his son and saw he was blushing. So he sat there without moving and felt his happiness die inside him just as his bitterness had died a little while before; Ephrem quickly slipped a dollar into the plate.

Ephrem didn't say anything, but right up to the reading of the last Gospel Euchariste felt his son's annoyance burning into his side. His own embarrassment didn't abate until he came out onto the square in front of the church. There they met Euchariste's new-found friends again and, before going home, visited several of these hospitable Canadians. The women, who had remained more attached to Quebec than their husbands, spoke quite warmly of their country of origin, to which distance lent enchantment, and of friends and relatives whom they liked all the more because they hadn't seen them for a long time. They ended up at the home of Mr. Dagenais who, after a great many winks and high-signs, produced a bottle of *whiskey blanc* from behind the piano. The knowledge that they were breaking the law made them feel like fellow-conspirators and they drank down the rot-gut together in a religious silence.

There were people there of every age, but all belonged to about the same economic level : there were old men of Moisan's generation who spoke with a kind of nostalgia of the country they had left so many years before; Americanized French-Canadians in their forties who could still remember and who had acquired nothing in the States but a taste for a higher standard of living, a slight foreign accent and a corrupt way of speaking their own language. And there were even a few children who were shown off to Moisan as exceptional prodigies when, as was not often the case, they could be persuaded to speak the few words of French they happened to know.

"So you'd kind of like to go back home, would you?" Euchariste asked old Lessard, who seemed touched by the mention of Sainte-Anne-de-la-Pérade.

"Sure! I guess so. I guess I would."

"Well, why don't you come back with me? There's certainly plenty of room there. And they tell me the land round La Pérade is pretty hard to beat."

"It's the best there is! But I'll tell you, I wouldn't think of going back for good. I used to think I would when I lost my thirty-five thousand dollars."

Euchariste stared at him. He felt there was a bond between himself and this man who had also climbed the Calvary of ruin.

"I tried it, but living in Canada's too dear. It's not like round here."

A pale-faced little woman with drawn features came up to them quietly.

"All the same, Mr. Lessard, to my way of thinking it's better to be with your own folks than with foreigners."

"Oh! It ain't the same for you, Mrs. Léger. You don't speak English. You was married back home; you've never got used to it down here."

"Maybe so, Mr. Lessard, but to my way of thinking it's better to be with your own folks than with foreigners."

She was obviously homesick and would never get over it.

Still, she seemed to be an exception. They spoke of Quebec rather in the way you speak of a distant relative you are glad to get news of, but whom you wouldn't trouble to go and visit —a relative too insignificant to inspire any feelings of pride. Of all the Franco-Americans there, two or three at most pretended to any degree of warmth in their regard, or boasted of having gone back home a couple of times. But it didn't go beyond that. Their enthusiasm didn't seem very spontaneous and was more a mark of politeness towards the visiting Quebecker; it was just a thin thread of sentiment in the web of their self-satisfied daily existence.

Moisan began to feel that he wanted a little more than that. So he managed to drift over towards the woman they called Mrs. Léger.

"It seems you get lonesome for Canada sometimes, Mrs. Léger."

She gave him the answer he was hoping for: "Oh, yes, Mr. Moisan! You see, I can't seem to get used to it here."

Her words were as refreshing to Moisan as cool springwater to a thirsty man.

"And where are you from?"

"Me? I'm from Berthier, from Berthier-en-Haut. My maiden name was Boissonneault, Alice Boissonneault."

"Maybe you're related to the Boissonneaults of Maskinongé, the ones who live in the Trompe-Souris concession."

"I couldn't tell you. Probably."

"Have you been in the States long?"

"It'll be four years the twenty-seventh of April. When I was first married Frank wanted to stop in Berthier. But business wasn't as good as he hoped. Besides, he got lonesome. It wasn't the same for him; he was raised down here. So we moved to White Falls."

A wan smile like a piece of borrowed finery lit up the little woman's face.

"Well, well, Alice!" said her husband, as he came up to join them. "I guess you're pleased to run into someone from Canada. That's fine. You see I went to the Brothers' school in Berthier myself. And that's where I learned French and met my wife. You don't have to tell me Canadian girls are the best there is."

The group began to break up as people went off home for the Sunday midday dinner.

"Good-bye, Mr. Moisan. You'll have to come and see us. Are you stopping long in the States?"

"Why, no. I just came down to see my boy here and get acquainted with his family. I won't be here more than a few days."

"Sure you will, Pa," Ephrem protested. "There's no hurry."

And Euchariste went back to his son's house feeling much happier.

The days went by. He was expecting news from Canada, but it was a long time in coming: three weeks later, at about the time he had planned to leave for home, a letter finally arrived.

"Here you are, Pa," said Ephrem one morning. "Here's a letter from home. What have they got to say for themselves?"

But Euchariste was in no hurry to open it. He wanted to be alone when he read it, without anyone there to make him blush in case there was a reference to recent happenings, to the notary or his own ruin, matters on which he hadn't breathed a word to Ephrem. His son didn't press him to open it.

As far as actual news went, there was very little; but there was something about the notary, just a few words:

". . . as for the notary, they don't know where he went. And his wife's gone back to live with her folks in Grand-Mère.

"Old Touchette died of his cancer at last. The Onias Barrettes have moved away from here. They've gone to live with their cousins in town; he's got a job as a gardener at some Englishman's place. I haven't been paid for the eggs yet. So I can't send you your pension money right now . . ."

That was awkward. He would have to wait a little longer and stay on at White Falls. Why hadn't Etienne bought him a return ticket instead of putting him off by saying he might like it so much he would want to stay in the States longer? As if at his age a man could be happy anywhere else but at home with his barn and stable and his stock.

His . . . That's right, he had forgotten he had deeded away his property. That was something else he hadn't told Ephrem.

At any rate, all he could do was to wait a little longer and sit there doing nothing like the retired farmer he was.

And supposing Etienne didn't send him his money? How would he get back?

"Of course, we'd be glad to have you back home again. But if you could stay on a while longer at Ephrem's it would save a little money for the new binder.

"And Phydime Raymond was elected school commissioner to succeed old Touchette.

"Love to all the folks in the States."

Phydime a school commissioner! The man who had robbed him of a fortune and set fire to his barn! How Phydime must be chuckling!

Euchariste stood brooding, tasting his bitterness as he sucked at the ends of his moustache. His fingers groped instinctively in the envelope, trying to find something he might have overlooked: a postal order, perhaps, or maybe something in the letter itself, a few lines or phrases that seemed to be missing.

That was it. It didn't say anywhere that the farm and the family missed him. Or that things weren't running the way they should while he was away. He would almost have welcomed the news of some minor catastrophe.

He had only been away a month and yet so many days seemed to have gone by; so much must have happened in that time. For as he was out of touch with farm life now, he forgot how slow and measured its rhythm is, how unchanging its daily round.

When he left, one of the cows was just on the point of calving. And then there was the sow that had hurt herself on her yoke and didn't seem to be getting better. Part of the barn needed fixing, up near the rafters. Of course, Etienne wouldn't do anything about it until his father came back and had a look at the damage.

Ephrem's children were sprawled out on the rug in the living-room, surrounded by a litter of picture papers and coloured supplements. Their mother had gone out, leaving them in their grandfather's care.

But wasn't he rather their prisoner? Not that they paid any attention to him; they hardly ever noticed his existence. But today he had to sit there idle, when he would so much have liked to get away for a little and go out of doors and along Jefferson Street until he got to the place on the outskirts of the town where the street ran along beside a little wood that hid the houses and the factories.

Ever since he had discovered this little bit of make-believe country, he had got into the way of going along there, rain or shine, to renew his contact with nature. And nowadays he made it the goal of his daily stroll, stopping when he got there to look at the bare branches of the trees that the sun, which was getting stronger and stronger day by day, would bring to life again. Pretending to go out for a walk and only mildly interested, he would go up to a small maple tree whose lower branches he could just reach. He always waited to make sure there was nobody about.

Then he would pull a branch towards him and cradle one of the twigs—always the same one—in his thick hands. He would carefully examine the tip of the twig. For some days now he had noticed that the delicate bark was swelling mysteriously and becoming mottled. It didn't amount to much yet; just a slight bulge that you had to touch to be sure it was there, just a trace of red on the dark brown of the tip. But you could feel a suggestion of moisture from the sap that April was thawing out and that would start to run in May.

Every year back home at about this time he would go off across the fields that still slept under their winter covering. He used to say it was because he wanted to have a look at the fences. But what he was really after was some spot exposed to the sun, where the thin layer of snow had already melted and the grey tangle of last year's grass lay uncovered. Then he would look until he found a blade of new grass, a tiny slender blade, heralding approaching spring. And every year, with unconscious superstition, he built his hopes of a good harvest on the auspices of this blade of new grass.

The branch meant all that. . . .

The children started quarrelling all of a sudden and brought him back to reality. Outside a warm sun was shining that seemed to beckon man to his yearly mating with the fertile earth. But here he was a prisoner with the fetters of idleness clamped to his arms and legs. The calluses on his hands were beginning to soften because he had no work to do.

Elsie came in with her arms full of parcels and Ephrem got back soon after.

"Well, Pa," he said when supper was over. "What's the news from Canada?"

"Nothing special, son."

"Is it still pretty cold up there?"

"They don't say, but I guess it is."

There was a moment's silence. Euchariste slowly lit his pipe.

"Ain't they getting lonesome for you at Etienne's?"

Euchariste took a deep draw on his pipe and looked around in vain for a place to spit before lying with perfect composure.

"Well, they'd like me to come home because there's a lot to do on the farm in the spring. They miss me all right. But the snow ain't melted yet."

"Oh !"

"So, seeing as I don't often take a holiday, I'd like to stay on a few days longer with you folks."

"You can stay, Pa. You're no trouble."

So saying, he went out to the kitchen where Elsie was washing the dishes.

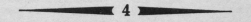

4

Euchariste had never expected Ephrem's wife to be very demonstrative. He would have been the first person to be surprised and even embarrassed by anything of the sort.

For he was accustomed to the gentleness of the farmers' wives and daughters in Quebec, where the long winters and the traditional struggle for existence have somewhat tempered the liveliness of their French blood. When French-Canadian women smile it is always with their eyes rather than with their lips.

But never once did Elsie throw him a kindly glance or give the slightest sign of filial affection. At first he put it down to her race and hoped she would thaw out gradually. He was content to wait and, with every suspicion of a smile that he noticed, he thought that the time would soon come when they would get used to his ways and accept him as one of the family.

He made little tentative advances, little secret moves to get into her good graces; and then one day he offered to come and sit in the kitchen to keep her company while she was doing the cooking. But she told him very emphatically that he would have to go outside if he wanted to smoke, and that was as far as he got.

Even his grandchildren seemed in no hurry to accept him or to show any signs of affection. So there was nobody left but Ephrem, and it was towards his son that he tried to direct all the tender feelings born of his loneliness. But he was always conscious of his daughter-in-law's hostile influence coming between them.

It almost turned into a sort of undeclared war, a guerilla of petty annoyances. It was enough for him to say: "If you like, Ephrem, we could go over and see the Légers this evening," for Elsie, who understood French well enough when it suited her, to remind her husband that they had to go and see one or other of their Irish friends.

He had never experienced such a long and trying period of loneliness, for he had always lived a collective sort of existence among people whose thoughts and decisions and actions were in harmony. These thoughts, these decisions and these actions were effects resulting from unvarying causes; the ups and downs of the land and weather conditions. Farmers don't have to say much to understand one another, for harvests, storms, deaths, or elections produce the same reactions in all of them. When Euchariste stood by himself in a field, turning the hay, he didn't need to look up; if he did look, he knew he would see a whole succession of fields just like his own with men just like himself pitching clover and timothy into the wind.

And it wasn't that neighbours visited one another much back home. When you've reached a certain age you don't go out to see people a great deal. However, a piece of news will travel from one end of the concession to the other in a few hours, passed on from neighbour to neighbour across the boundary fences. For farmers understand one another almost without saying a word, while people in the towns talk a great deal without really understanding each other.

It's true that during the three months he had been in the States he had plenty of invitations: to the Légers, the Benoîts and even to the Tyos who, in spite of their change of name, were still good honest Taillons from the lower St. Lawrence. But one day, when he turned up at an awkward moment, he discovered that you should telephone first. He tried to but . . .

"I seem to have a terrible lot of trouble trying to hear through that there contraption!"

"It ain't so tough!" Ephrem answered with a smile.

But no matter what he did or how frantically he glued his ear to the receiver and imitated the others by yelling "Hullo! Hullo!" he couldn't hear anything distinctly.

At first, to make himself useful, he tried to keep track of the calls for Ephrem and Elsie. But the results were hopeless.

He couldn't have made a worse mess of things if he had done it on purpose. He got to the point of envying his grandchildren, even three-year-old Patrick, who knew how to get his other grandfather on the telephone. It made him feel ashamed of himself.

"Say, Ephrem, I guess I'm starting to get hard of hearing; that's why I've so much trouble."

That was the excuse he invented to save his self-respect.

He sat around all week now waiting for Sunday, just as formerly he had waited for Sunday to be over to get back to his usual round. All his life Mass had been a matter of weekly routine and now it had become a pleasure to look forward to, almost a reason for his existence.

Though the officiating clergy took no special notice of him, he tried to curry favour with them by putting a lot of money in the collection plate. At first these offerings and his tobacco had been his only extravagances. Now he had cut down on his smoking.

When Mass was over he hung round in front of the church, drifting from one group to another and ready to accept the least hint of an invitation. A little group of the same few people showed some sympathetic understanding; they made him welcome and were kind enough to ask him in for a drink. He was grateful and wanted to do honour to their hospitality, so now he sometimes took a drop too much, though that sort of thing had hardly ever happened to him before.

When Ephrem was with him and it was raining, a card game was generally fixed up for the afternoon. But if the weather was fine they inevitably went for a drive in the car, so that every Sunday morning Euchariste looked anxiously out of his window hoping for signs of rain. It was no longer from a feeling of concern for the crops and the thirsty fields, but because he wanted to escape these long rides that shook him all to pieces; sometimes, however, he would be left at home on some vague pretext or other.

There was no news from Saint-Jacques. Each day's silence made him feel more helpless; he no longer stood upright on the solid familiar earth of his fields; he was being sucked down into unknown quicksands into which he felt himself sinking relentlessly. At times he even had that unbearable sensation of timelessness that comes to travellers lost in the forest. It seemed as if he would never, never get away from the place.

A bud began swelling on the branch of the maple tree and

burst finally to thrust out the green cluster of its newborn leaves into the soft spring air. From a distance everything still looked bare, but from close at hand each branch was taut and ready for the springtime explosion of its vital sap into leaves and petals.

In the new green of the underbrush, down in the little wood, a few flowers had already sprung up to brave the cold nights: stalks of spring beauty with their clusters of pink blossoms peeping out between their twin leaves, wild columbine too and liverleaf, reflecting the pale blue of the sky.

Further out, in the fields themselves, the flowers that Moisan knew well from having struggled against them were coming along fast: the tiny bridal bouquet of the shepherd's purse, the white sprays of penny cress and the green stalks of sweet hay. These comely agricultural pests were only a decorative and fragrant advance-guard for all the others.

Each year, as a rule, Euchariste was completely dumbfounded by the vigorous growth and flowering of the weeds. He couldn't understand it. The fact that Divine Providence made life easy for these pests, while useful crops needed so much work and care and worry and sweat, was the only thing that might have made him question it. And every time he came on an isolated tuft of field sorrel or plantain he would root it up with unconscious violence, though he let the daisies grow all over his fields. The paper told him all he had to do was to sow with clover and mow it early. But what was the use? There were too many of them.

And now today—a today that was so different from the yesterdays he had known—he found himself stooping to look with suppressed emotion at a single tuft of shepherd's purse, though he would never have stopped before the most lavish display in a florist's window. The fact was that this weed now reminded him of what he missed most keenly: that feeling of exhaustion after a day's ploughing or seeding, the anxiety at the sight of a storm cloud that comes to darken the spotless blue of the sky on the very last day of the haying, the many worries caused by the mysterious ailments of the stock. How he longed for all that now.

Because he had lived his whole life in contact with the land, he had adopted its rhythm. Towards the end of autumn a feeling of peace would pervade his whole being, a sort of torpor like the somnolence of hibernating animals, or the mysterious yearly lethargy of the seed buried in the soil which is merely a prelude to germination. And then, as with the animals and all growing things, when the sun returned from the South it would fill him with new blood that came bubbling up eager to cope with any weariness. This natural rhythm with which city folk have lost all contact had been an actual part of him for sixty years. And now that it was spring again he felt this deeply rooted instinct flowering within him.

There was a tiny yard attached to Ephrem's house.

"Do you know what, Ephrem, while I'm here I'd like to plant a garden for the kids."

"Well, Pa, suit yourself."

"You see, I'll fix the ground for them and sow some carrots and some parsley and some tomatoes. All they'll have to do will be to weed it a little once in a while."

The children received this suggestion with an outburst of enthusiasm and for the first time Euchariste felt he was really their grandfather.

With a coal-shovel instead of a spade, a rake and a broken kitchen-knife, he cleared the yard of its litter of old crates and tin cans. The space had to be carefully measured and marked out to leave the entrance to the garage free; but, by squeezing them close together, he managed to lay out three beds with sufficient exposure to the sun.

When the time came to plant the garden, it was the children who did the seeding under his direction. One of them dropped the seeds into the row of holes prepared beforehand and raked in the earth; the other came along and sprinkled the bed from a brand-new watering-can.

Ephrem came out of the kitchen and joined them.

" 'Take a look at that, Ephrem; they're working like real Moisans! They're farmers all right, honest-to-goodness little Canucks!"

"Where did you get that swell watering-can?" Ephrem asked his son Patrick.

But the child looked at him without understanding.

"Hey, sonny! Where did you get that?" he repeated in English.

"He gave it to me."

"Who?" his father insisted.

The child hesitated and then pointed at his grandfather. "That man!"

But fortunately Euchariste didn't understand.

The children's enthusiasm soon died down; their mother

saw to that. After she had scolded them a couple of times for coming into the house with muddy clothes, they stayed away from the yard and went back to their picture papers.

It was the end of May before a letter came from Etienne.

Marie-Louise still had a cough and was getting thin but wasn't sick enough yet to need the doctor. Napoléon with his wife and two children had come back home from Quebec, where there wasn't any work to be had. It was hard to find room for them all. It couldn't have happened at a worse time, either, because prices were away down. Still, Etienne was doing his best. He had bought some chemical fertilizer on the advice of the county agronomist.

Chemical fertilizer! As if the good Moisan land needed any of that poisonous stuff that just burned up the top-soil. A lot of good these chemical fertilizers did. He remembered the time Ti-Phonse Gélinas bought some "patented" stuff at that —to fertilize a field of potatoes. Three years later you couldn't grow anything in that field but water hemlock.

What else did he have to say?

"A government inspector came round and he said some of our hens was sick. He killed eighteen."

That would happen! Instead of keeping quiet and sowing his hay Etienne had to call in "agronomists," ignorant little squirts who think they can learn how to farm out of books. Euchariste remembered now : for the last three years Etienne had kept talking about "the agronomist they ought to get in," "the agronomist they ought to consult."

Well, one thing was clear anyway, things had got into a fine mess on the farm since he'd left!

He grumbled away to himself as he went on reading and turned the last page. "Regards to everybody, Etienne."

And not a word about his money, his pension !

He looked up from the letter. Seated in an armchair near him was Elsie, darning socks and looking as if she had been reading over his shoulder.

For once he was glad she didn't know enough French to question him. He got up, hesitated a moment, and then said: "Guess I'll go and take a little walk before supper."

She looked at him without answering.

He went up Jefferson Street from force of habit. In half an hour he was outside the town and on the other side of a knoll, which hid the place from him almost completely, so that only the factory chimneys showed like bare posts sticking up out of the ground. For once he had gone beyond the little maple wood without stopping. The country here was rather bare and sloped gently down towards a creek, invisible in the hollow below. On one side of the road rose a bank overgrown with bushes that had sprung up the year before and that May was just beginning to touch with green. On the other side, where the ground fell away, a score of junked car bodies lay piled together in a heap.

Obviously the news he had got from the farm wasn't very good. Now he was away they weren't doing any of the things they should have done and Etienne, egged on by that little runt of an agronomist who had never ploughed a furrow in his life, was doing all kinds of crazy things. Hadn't he once suggested to him, Euchariste Moisan, who had been farming for fifty years, that he ought to give up raising hay, which is an easy crop because it just grows of its own accord, and go in for imported seed all the way from Europe, or some place like that? But as soon as he got home he'd straighten it all out. . . .

Yes, but he'd "given" himself! From now on what could he do or say, supposing Etienne decided to put his own notions into effect? What if one fine day he made up his mind to harness the land and boss it instead of allowing it to lead him along to a comfortable and restful old age?

The mewing cry of a catbird from close at hand brought him back to earth. The road had led him into unknown territory, beyond the places he usually visited on his walks. Without noticing it he had crossed over into another valley.

The creek had broadened out and was almost beginning to look like a river; its banks were overgrown with reeds which caught and held long rainbow streaks of oil. There was a field over on the left and in the field a man harrowing. He happened to be down at the other end and was coming towards Euchariste, with his horse pulling sideways on his collar.

Euchariste stopped dead. The furrows stretched out in front of him in parallel rows.

"There's a fellow don't know much about ploughing," he said to himself.

To begin with, the furrows weren't straight and they ran slanting across the sloping of this low-lying, badly drained patch of ground. Besides, the sets of furrows were too wide. All this annoyed him.

The man was quite close now and was just about to turn; he stopped a moment and Euchariste felt sure he was going to say something to him, something like: "Well, you look as if you knew a thing or two about farming!"

But the man merely yelled something at his horse, turned his back, and set off in the other direction.

Euchariste looked at the harrow. It wasn't like the ones they used in Quebec; the teeth slanted backward. Why should that be?

A horn tooted and there was a screech of brakes. A car pulled up just beside him.

"For God's sake! If it ain't old man Moisan. What are you doing out this way? Did you get lost?"

"Why no, not exactly. I was taking a walk."

"Well, well. Hop in. I'll drive you back."

Euchariste hesitated a moment and then got in beside Mr. Dagenais.

When he got home he found Ephrem was already there, though it wasn't yet five o'clock.

"You're through early today. You don't seem to have to work so very hard in that shop of yours."

He was quite proud of knowing and being able to use an English word like "shop".

But Ephrem looked rather preoccupied.

"They told us today orders was a bit slack; we're going to have to loaf two days a week for a while. They've even fired a few."

"There's no danger that you . . . that you'll . . ." Eucharistte asked anxiously.

"Hell, no! No danger at all. I've been working for that outfit for six years. Besides, things won't be this way long."

The following Tuesday, which was one of his days off, Ephrem was very insistent on their going for a drive together.

"Shall we take the kids along too?"

"Not today. I've got to go to North Burma; it's twenty miles from here. Won't take long."

They started off. Ephrem obviously had something he wanted to say to his father, sitting there beside him, and found it hard to get it out. Finally he made up his mind.

"Had any news from Canada, Pa?"

Eucharistte braced himself against the back of the seat but said nothing.

"What . . . what did they have to say for themselves?"

Eucharistte began to reel off the list of petty local happenings. He spoke slowly and made the most of each bit of news, pausing every now and then to give full details about people and places.

"Sure, sure, I know," Ephrem interrupted. "Anything else?"

At last Euchariste found he had nothing more to say. He sat waiting for the questions he knew were bound to come.

Ephrem showed his nervous tension by driving along at sixty miles an hour.

"So they wrote you a letter, did they?"

"Why, yes. Didn't I tell you?"

"No, you didn't. . . . Listen, Pa . . ."

He couldn't finish what he was going to say, as they had to thread their way through a block in the traffic. There was an automobile toppled over on its side in the ditch and the stream of cars eddied round it like water that had suddenly been dammed up.

"Looks like a real accident," said Euchariste.

"Oh! That's nothing . . . Listen, Pa, you've been with us for pretty near three months now. I'm glad to have you, but you know I'm not getting much work right now. They've cut our pay."

Euchariste tried to change the subject again.

"Why? Ain't things going so well in the States?"

"Hell! That's not it. The country's too darn well organized for that. Best in the world. But some of those other countries are jealous and they don't pay their debts and it seems they want to put their tariffs up. Anyway, we're kind of hard up right now."

"Yeah! . . . Would you sooner . . . I went home?"

"Well, as far as I'm concerned, I'd like you to stay on a while. But . ."

There was no need for him to be more specific, Euchariste understood.

They had left White Falls and its outskirts far behind them. But every seven or eight miles the highway they were following ran through a smaller replica of the place they had come from. First there would be a wide street lined with fine-looking elms and houses set pleasantly in their own grounds. Then suddenly the trees and lawns and houses disappeared; lines of shops closed in on either side. There was first one, then two, then four, then ten filling-stations with garishly painted roofs.

Then came the detached houses again, surrounded by

lawns. And the road plunged back into the country until it got to the next town.

But Euchariste didn't see anything of this. He kept his mouth tightly closed and said nothing. He wanted, at all costs, to keep from pouring out the tale of his misfortunes and his humiliation. If he once started to talk and to explain that he hadn't received his pension money, he would be swept along and would have to tell the whole story : all about his lawsuit and Phydime and the fire and the absconding notary and his own surrender to his eldest son.

And as they drove along through scattered villages, up hill and down dale, his mind followed along the road that ran through his own life and paused at its stations of the cross. He tried to imagine what going home would be like, home to Etienne, now lord and master of the farm, with Phydime cock of the walk and all those who had respected him when he was rich and who would despise him now he was so no longer. It would mean going home to a farm that didn't belong to him any more and where he would count for nothing.

It made him forget the gentle friendliness of the earth and the skies of his homeland, its soothing peacefulness for those who are born there.

And he suddenly felt he hadn't the courage to face it.

Later perhaps, in a few weeks, or a month or two, but not now.

"Do you know, Ephrem, I'd just as soon stay down here a while longer. Maybe you could find me a job. It would give Etienne time to get things straightened out."

"Yeah, Pa, it ain't much fun sitting around doing nothing."

Ephrem was referring to himself, for, though it was a week-day afternoon, the factory was closed. But his father thought the remark was meant for him.

"Yeah! . . . It ain't much fun."

And when Ephrem didn't answer he went on : "It ain't that I don't want to work. The land round here don't look so bad. I've noticed that when I was out walking. I'm pretty sure a fellow like me who knows how to farm could get some kind of work to do. It wouldn't be so lonesome . . . and it would keep me busy till I go back home."

The two were sitting on the front steps, the old man smoking his pipe and his son a cigarette, as they enjoyed the soft fragrant air of early summer.

"Anyway, what I'd earn would be mostly for you folks. I don't need it."

That's what Ephrem thought too. His father must have quite a little pile salted away, up in Canada.

It might be worth their while to have the old man stay on with them. Yes, indeed: the farm for Etienne and the money for him. Share and share alike. All he'd have to do would be to make Elsie understand . . .

"Well, Pa, it ain't that I don't want you to stay on. But it costs plenty to keep the house going. Money! Money! There's the kids too. It ain't like on a farm. On a farm, if you want vegetables you can just go out and dig them in the garden. If you want meat, you can do your own butchering. And for clothes you can wear the same coat for years. The boys can go round bare-foot too; they like it better that way."

"Well, I'll be darned! Ti-Phrem, I bet you'd be glad to get back to the farm. You can't get the old Moisan place out of your system."

"Me? Hell, no!"

But he went on in a gentler tone of voice and tried not to show his feeling of superiority too much.

"I belong down here now; I'm an American citizen. You can have a swell time in the States: If I was up in Canada now, I wouldn't get a job where I could have a house like this and a car."

A robin with puffed-up breast and watchful eye, looking as pompous as a notary, was hopping about on the new grass on the lawn.

Ephrem threw a piece of twig at him.

"Maybe I could speak to John Corrigan about you."

"John . . . who?"

"Corrigan. He's the big Democratic boss. A pal of mine."

"Fine!"

It was about this time that Euchariste, to his surprise, noticed that Elsie was becoming gentler and rather more amiable towards him. She even managed to recall a few words of French and condescended to ask him to do little favours for her. He was only too pleased to run her errands.

One Wednesday afternoon, when Ephrem was at the factory and the children had gone out with Grandfather Phillimore, Elsie came and asked him quite nicely to take back some knitting that one of her friends had forgotten.

"It's quite a ways," she said apologetically.

"That don't matter. I'll be glad to, Mrs. Moisan."

He could never bring himself to call her anything else.

She gave him a scrap of paper with the address: 428 Revere Street. It would take him the whole afternoon to get there and back. It was at the other end of town, near the Catholic cemetery which he had visited on one or two occasions.

But it was nice weather. The sun, which was climbing higher and higher every day, bathed his skin in a warm balm and went right to the marrow of his bones to dispel the last shivers of winter. Euchariste walked along slowly, a little troubled by that sluggish feeling which, for some time past, he had felt after his mid-day meal.

As usual, Jefferson Street took him to Central Square. When he got there he wanted to take his bearings and put his hand in his pocket for the scrap of paper. It was gone. The darn thing must have fallen out a little way back when he took out his pipe. The only thing to do was to go back to the house, which fortunately wasn't far. He rang the bell.

For quite a time there was no answer. Perhaps Elsie had gone out! Then came the sound of muffled footsteps. Then silence again. He was beginning to give up hope when Elsie opened the door cautiously; she seemed out of breath and rather cross.

"Well! What is it?"

He explained with rather a hang-dog air.

"All right. Wait a second. I'll give you another."

She went to the desk in the living-room and, without saying a word, started scribbling rapidly. Then, just as she was getting up, came the sound of a man's voice.

"Is he gone, honey?"

"Hullo, you've got company, have you?"

Just then a broad-shouldered man in shirt sleeves, who seemed very much at home, strode into the room.

Moisan was too surprised to notice Elsie's dismay. And before he had time to turn and look at her she pulled herself together.

"Of course, this is . . . It's Mr. Corrigan. He just dropped in about that job for you. . . . Mr. Corrigan, meet my father-in-law."

The big man, quite unperturbed, almost wrenched Euchariste's arm from its socket and then exchanged a few remarks in English with Elsie.

"Well, Mr. Moisan, Mr. Corrigan just came to say he had a job for you."

Euchariste felt self-conscious and, after struggling in vain for words to thank him, took himself off.

That evening Elsie watched for her husband's return to tell him the news. She explained things to Ephrem at some length until he finally exclaimed: "You're real lucky, Pa. Corrigan took the trouble to come here and tell us he had a job for you. He wouldn't do that for just anybody."

Probably because old Moisan was at last going to work Elsie was quite affectionate to her father-in-law in the days that followed. Whenever she saw him settle down to have a talk with Ephrem she came and sat between them.

A week went by and then another and finally one day—
"Good news, Pa. I seen Corrigan today. You'll be starting work soon. He's found you a job."

"Is that so?"

But Euchariste's voice was lacking in enthusiasm.

"Sure, a soft job; a dandy."

"Yeah?"

"You're going to be night watchman in the city garage."

"Oh! In the garage?"

"Why, sure. All you'll have to do will be to loaf around and smoke your pipe."

Euchariste didn't answer right away.

Now that it was to happen so soon, almost at once, Euchariste felt frightened rather than pleased. When he had talked about working he hadn't really been serious; and, in any case, working, as far as he was concerned, meant farming—working the land. It meant guiding the horses across the sun-drenched fields with a train of birds swooping down onto the freshly turned furrows to look for worms.

And now he was beginning to feel very alarmed. It seemed to him that his fate hung in the balance and that the scales were weighted inexorably against his future happiness.

He had never belonged to anybody or anything except the land and even then it was to a restricted thirty-acre strip, which had been his whole world and his whole existence, and now he was to take orders from another man, from a boss, just like a clerk in a store. An ill-advised trip had brought him to this foreign country; a rash word had delivered him over, bound hand and foot, to a lot of foreigners and, worse, to people who had no use for the land, who only knew about

business—money, trade, all the city things. A fissure had suddenly opened in the smooth even surface of his life. He was
going to betray his calling just like the others.

Whatever made him suggest staying on in the States? Why
had he said anything at all? He had been tricked by words
again, though he had always suspected their treachery. They
had trapped him in their snare.

Why not just leave? Leave next week or even tomorrow!

No! It would be better to wait a few days for that letter
from Etienne that was bound to come soon. His pension money
was sure to be in it this time.

How could people of his race—how could his son—bear
to go on living in this country, which didn't belong to them,
where everything was hostile, or, in other words, different?
Why didn't they go back to that fertile ribbon stretched out
between the mighty furrow of the St. Lawrence and the
Laurentian ridge?

"Why, of course, Ephrem . . . On the other hand, I'm just
wondering . . . just wondering if it's a good idea for me to stay
on down here."

"Well!" said Ephrem, who was now thinking of something else.

"I tell you what, son," said Euchariste, taking heart. "I'm
kind of worried about the farm and about Etienne. He's still
pretty young. Not forty yet. When I said that about working,
I meant I might make a few dollars so I wouldn't have to ask
for money to go back to Canada. But maybe I'd better go back
right away. Because, the way I see it . . ."

But this time his son looked up at him suddenly.

"Well, I'll be damned! What's the big idea?"

"Listen, Ephrem, I was thinking. . . . The way I see it . . ."

"So you're putting the skids under us? John Corrigan went
to all kinds of trouble to do me a favour and found you a job,
a swell job. Now you don't want to take it!"

"Why, see here, Ephrem! It ain't that I don't want to
take it . . ."

"Jesus Christ! That'll look fine. I guess you think it's a
cinch to get a job, specially a job like that one. Why, you don't
speak a word of English."

"So you think I ought to stay?" said Euchariste rather
abashed.

"You should have made up your mind in the first place,
Pa," came the unsympathetic answer.

"Oh! All right, all right! I just wanted to talk it over with you."

He said no more but felt almost on the verge of tears.

Back home the seeding was probably long since over. Above the soil, broken up by the frosts and the harrow, the green shoots of oats and clover were beginning to show.

Ephrem said nothing, but he was quite obviously annoyed.

Euchariste Moisan wanted to put all this out of his mind and he made a great effort to call up the cyclorama of his house and fields. He closed his eyes, and suddenly it all appeared to him in such sharp detail that he felt he need only open them again to see the familiar countryside that had been the background of his whole existence. At his feet a field of rich black earth, crossed by the creek with its fringe of haw trees. A little further off stood the solitary old elm beneath which the animals took shelter. And away over there in the distance were the farm-house and the outbuildings, grouped together like a family under the arch of the two big beech trees.

He could feel the warm sunlight shining through his eyelids.

He opened his eyes again; but all he could see was the dismal prospect of the little house across the street, with its pretentious façade badly in need of a coat of paint and its hard unfriendly exterior.

Unconsciously he stretched out his old hands and spread his fingers to the sun's caress.

"Nice day, Ephrem."

"Yeah! It's swell!"

How the sun must be beating down on the fields back home, falling in a gentle life-giving flood of light and heat on the avid young shoots.

On a Monday evening three days later, Ephrem took him along to the place where he was to go to work. Euchariste was introduced to the foreman, in English of course.

Then his son said: "This is Mr. William Pratt, Pa; he's your boss."

"Fine. Now would he be related to the Prattes of Saint-Alphonse? You know, the one who married . . ."

"Well, Mr. Moisan, I hope . . ." began the foreman, and went on jabbering away in English.

"Don't he speak French neither?"

"Well, *pas beaucoup, un petit peu. Mon mère, il était du Canada.*"

Euchariste said nothing more. He felt quite giddy, just as he had on his journey. As on that occasion, he instinctively looked around for something real, something solid and familiar to cling to.

Every evening at a quarter to six Euchariste set off for the city garage, where he shut himself in until six in the morning.

Fortunately it stayed light for a long time; it was early July and the evening glow seemed endless in the western sky.

But when it did get dark he felt strangely ill at ease, though he had never before known what it was to be afraid.

Before he started he had understood that there were to be two watchmen. But his companion, a rather surly Irishman, slipped away towards nine o'clock every evening and only showed up again in the morning half an hour before they went off duty. He found this very peculiar.

"You know, Ephrem, you ought to tell Mr. Corrigan about it; I think that fellow's cheating him."

Ephrem stared at him, dumbfounded by so much simplicity.

"This is the States you're in, Pa. That means: Mind Your Own Business! You shouldn't get mixed up in other people's affairs."

"Yeah, but it ain't honest to get paid for doing nothing. To my way of thinking, if Mr. Corrigan . . ."

"If you want to get yourself bounced out, it wasn't much use my taking all that trouble to get you a job!"

What frightened him most at first was the idea that he might fall asleep and fail in his duty as a watchman even for a single moment. The first few nights he didn't dare sit down, he was so afraid he might suddenly begin to feel drowsy, or, worse still, that Mr. Corrigan himself might look in to see that he wasn't neglecting his job. Sometimes he did doze a bit, overcome by the heavy July nights when the glow from the city dimmed the light from the stars and it was so hot that the air you breathed was like a sickening lukewarm fluid. But before he had time to lose consciousness completely, a slight creak somewhere would make him sit up with a start.

Then he would peer with frightened suspicion into the huge garage where the monster trucks were herded. And every morning at daybreak he was surprised to see how moderate it was in extent, for at night in the darkness it yawned open like a boundless cavern.

Near the entrance was a small office with a desk, a spittoon and a greasy sofa. He finally plucked up enough courage to move in there and he felt better when he knew there was a glass door between him and the trucks. He spent the nights peacefully smoking his pipe.

One night when he was sweeping the floor he picked up a newspaper. It was a copy of the American edition of *La Presse*, left behind by some driver or other. Though he had never been much of a reader, he pounced on it eagerly.

And every Tuesday he had only to look to find the paper that some unknown providence seemed always to have left specially for him.

It lasted him a whole week. He devoured every bit of it, line by line, from the first page to the last. But it wasn't the main news articles that interested him most, not the ones with four-column headlines of which the city editor in the office back in Montreal had been so proud. Euchariste Moisan with his weakened eyesight passed over the murders and the political feuds. He would begin by slowly reading the headlines and the subtitles to make sure that there was nothing there that interested him. He could come back to those parts later when he had used up all the rest. Then he would turn to the inside pages and comb every nook and corner where they sandwich in the news of least importance.

What he was really looking for were familiar names, especially those from Saint-Jacques and Labernadie. There was a special section for parish correspondents, but they only wrote about American centres. He remembered this page in the local newspaper he used to subscribe to back home. The name of the patron saint of each parish was used as the heading and underneath was set forth that "Miss Délima Saint-Georges has come to visit for three days with her father Mr. Osias Saint-Georges of Saint-Anthime"; that "Mr. and Mrs. Adelard Legendre, who farm at L'Enfant-Jésus-de-Bagot, have given birth to a son christened Joseph-Ludovic-Moïse"; "that they have started rebuilding the school-house in the Pince-Bec concession"—all those trivial news items that cheer or worry or distress the little closed rural communities huddled round the church-spires that are strung out along the mighty river of French Canada.

If he looked very carefully, he sometimes managed to come across the names of villages near his own home, generally in connection with some accident like the violent death of a young farmer gored by a bull or a fire in the local convent. And at the time of the annual retreat for the clergy he was able to follow the movements of all the local priests.

Every Friday he was given his fifteen-dollars pay by his companion, the Irishman, who handed it over without saying a word. It wasn't a great deal of money, especially in a country where they paid such fabulous salaries. But the foreman had explained it all to him at the start.

"You see, Moisan, it's the boss got you this job. He was supposed to take on a night mechanic at thirty-five a week. But he fixed it so you could have the work, though there was plenty of men after it. If any person asks you about it, you just say you're a mechanic and you're getting thirty-five a week."

"Sure! I wish you'd thank Mr. Corrigan for me. It's mighty nice of him. You'll tell him that, won't you?"

"All right! All right! But if they ever ask you don't forget."

Fifteen dollars a week in nice new crisp bills! It was a lot of money for a farmer, but from the very beginning Ephrem got him to hand over ten dollars a week for his board.

"You'll be a rich man with the five bucks that leaves you. But I've got a wife and kids."

And sometimes round Thursday he would borrow another dollar or two from his father, but he always forgot to pay him back.

For the factories had fewer and fewer orders; Ephrem was only working two days a week now and at that his pay had been cut.

Summer was drawing to a close.

Every evening and, of course, on Sundays, too, Euchariste set off carrying his lunch-pail containing his midnight snack.

When he got back in the morning he went to bed. But he didn't sleep much. You don't sleep a great deal when you're getting old.

5

Old Moisan had few distractions. Especially now that he worked at night, he didn't see very many people. Occasionally, during the summer, one or other of Ephrem's friends would stop in on his way by for a brief chat. And for a while Mr. Léger came quite regularly; he even brought his wife along sometimes. They talked about home.

But towards the end of summer the days began to close in; Ephrem still showed up from time to time, but no one else now ever came to keep him company. As the depression got worse and worse, people seemed to want to barricade themselves in their homes. They hadn't enough money to do much entertaining and tried to hide their poverty, believing they were worse off than their neighbours and not wishing to make a spectacle of themselves. What was the good of meeting your friends if you could no longer talk about marvellous business deals and astounding profits and hundreds of thousands and millions of dollars? Everybody's existence was clouded by straitened circumstances and it killed their boastfulness and their pride in the American way of life.

A fog of depression lay heavily over everything, like the black pall of smoke which formerly hung over the cities. The most strident voices were now more subdued. People no longer told stories about smart successful business transactions, about clever schemes that would make you rich in a year, about new lines of business that, when they were opened up, would attract swarms of customers. For the first time in the memory of any American, everybody lived in the present and worried about unsold stocks of merchandise that cluttered up the warehouses, about whirring machines that fell silent one after the other, about factory chimneys that, at the rate of at least one a week, stopped belching smoke. It was as if this nation, hitherto so young in mind and heart, had been suddenly struck with old age.

Someone even said to Euchariste: "You're lucky, Moisan, you've got a good steady job!"

By comparison with this depression that poisoned the life of White Falls, Euchariste's own existence seemed more tolerable. When, on occasional Sunday afternoons, he met other French-Canadians, especially the older ones, he no longer hesitated to talk about home. From this distance and stripped of the uncertainties of weather and the seasons, farming seemed to wear a halo of stability.

He was fond of saying: "Back home in Canada it don't matter if the factories close, because there ain't no factories. It don't matter if the companies cut wages, because there ain't none. When we seed a field in hay, we harvest hay, sometimes there's a bit more and sometimes there's a bit less, but you always have enough to get by."

Some of the old men agreed with him.

"That's right, there's no depression back on the farm."

But the young ones looked thoughtful and said nothing.

Then one day he got another letter from Etienne.

"Times are pretty hard right now, Pa."

The refrain was a familiar one. Even in very good years he had always sung that tune himself when he grumbled about conditions.

"Napoléon is still living with us; he can't find work. That makes a lot of people to feed, because there are six of them now. His wife was sick again and this time it was twins. I think they ought to go back to the city, because it says in the papers they're going to give money to the out-of-works there. Of course, us poor farmers won't get nothing.

"The Touchette's farm is going to be sold up because they owe too much on it. It's the same with the Gélinas.

"My hay . . ."

That's right, it was Etienne's hay now.

"My hay from last year is still in the barn. I don't know where we're going to put this year's. It would have been better to sell it like I said. It may sound crazy, but eggs is down to thirteen cents a dozen. There's no money in it. I don't know what's going to happen. And Marie-Louise is costing a lot in doctor's bills and medicine."

So that's how things were; even the land no longer supported her children. And yet at first he had felt pleased for a moment at the idea that without him everything was going so badly. But then he remembered that, as far as the hay was concerned, it was he who had obstinately advised Etienne not to sell it.

The land was failing her own; the eternal earth-mother would no longer feed her sons.

Things were in a fine state nowadays. To be sure, the land could provide enough food, shelter and warmth. But people had to go and improve things and modernize everything, and all these changes, all these novelties, were the ruin of the farmer; he had to spend such a lot to operate his equipment, to keep up the strain of his pedigree stock, and to repair all the fancy new buildings.

The whole depression was the best possible proof of the falsity of this dangerous idea of "progress". As far as he, Euchariste, was concerned, the proper course was clear. What people would have to do was to go back to the sensible way of the past, give up all this machinery, and live on a thirty-acre strip of farm, content to expect nothing but what it could provide.

That was what he was going to do when he got back home. When he got back? But how old and helpless he felt.

When he got back? When would that be? He couldn't think of leaving Ephrem in the lurch for the moment.

"Money's pretty scarce, Pa," his son kept complaining. "Couldn't you help us out a bit more? I can easy pay you back when things pick up again. You don't need it. You've plenty of cash; you're well fixed."

And once again Euchariste hesitated to make a clean breast of things; he hadn't the courage to expose his own shame and his own failure.

"I think I'd do better to hang on to any cash I might have. You never know. But if it's any help, I'll stay on the job here till things get better. A couple of months or even a year if I have to. I don't mind giving you all I make. You need it worse than Etienne back on the farm."

For he hadn't shown him Etienne's letter.

So every night he set off for the garage and shut himself up until morning among all those mechanical monsters crouching like wild animals in a cage.

Gradually, without his knowing how or why, he began to lose hope. It seemed to him that his Laurentian homeland was getting further and further away every day and was becoming a province in the realm of the unattainable. He felt that each one of the hours he had lived through since he left was an infinity, an eternity he could never hope to retrace.

The fine weather was over. The autumn rains had come again, those cold and endless October downpours that mark the end of another cycle and the temporary divorce of sun and earth during which the farmer is useless.

In June, enjoying the first hot weather, he kept saying: "Dandy weather for the hay."

When in July it didn't rain for two weeks, he reflected: "If it don't rain in a few days the oats won't be so good."

And after a series of rain-storms in August: "If it keeps up this way for another week the potatoes will rot for sure."

But now that autumn had returned, there was nothing in his past life that found an echo in his thoughts.

What use was the farm to him now, his thirty-acre strip of good land, since none of it belonged to him any more? If he ever did go back, it would be to live apart from the land and outside it before finding a last resting-place beneath it.

For the first time in his life he was aware of the burden of his frail body and no longer felt indignant when he heard people calling him "the old man," as his daughter-in-law Elsie did.

He'd never be able to plough a field again. He felt he hadn't strength enough any more to lift a bundle of hay on the end of a pitchfork, right up above his head, level with the top of the loaded hay-cart, as they used to have to do before loaders were invented. Now that he had lost contact with the soil, he seemed to have been drained of all his vigour.

What did the future hold for him? A useless existence: sitting beside the stove in the winter and on the porch in summer, smoking his pipe while the others went off to work in the fields—the fields which had been his and now belonged to someone else—and chewing over the bitterness of his ruined life and the injustice of other people and the land. When he gave these folks his farm he gave them everything that was his; he had given himself to the land, body and soul, without holding anything back.

What was the use!

He lit the little stove in the garage office, for the nights were getting chilly already. He huddled close to it. Isn't that just what he would be doing if he were back home?

The snow came; it wasn't like real snow, white and firm and crisp, but almost like rain, and it no sooner touched the ground than it turned into puddles of muddy water or became a sodden grey slush.

So this was the States—the States that have beckoned to so many, many farmer's sons like a mirage. Beginning with his own son Ephrem. Towns full of houses coated with soot and s'ops that now stood empty, and dirty streets where haggard men wandered with trays of five-cent apples they tried to peddle to the occasional passer-by.

And back home? If what Etienne said was true, things weren't much better there. The paper too . . .

In the city, winter held sway once more with all its train : a coating of ice on the trees that broke down the branches, a north wind that cut right through you, cold that froze everything solid.

All he had to do was to sit there and warm himself at the stove; they gave him all the coal he needed. The trucks were asleep out in the garage and their guardian didn't have to look after them.

Big, ugly, tame animals.

All he had to do was to sit and wait for the pale dawn and for it to be time to go home and sleep and eat.

Christmas came and went. He had a specially good lunch on Christmas Eve : chicken sandwiches and a bottle of beer, which made him sleep better than usual. The thread that bound him to his Laurentian days was becoming more and more frayed. On Christmas Day, Ephrem and his family went to Grandfather Phillimore's.

In February a shop opposite the garage was destroyed by an explosion.

The birds came back in April. At dawn they twittered loudly in the branches of a solitary ash tree in the yard. And every night old Moisan saved his crusts of bread, which he fed to them in little pellets as they fluttered timidly at his feet.

In June he got the news that Marie-Louise had died of consumption. Like Oguinase . . .

The days got shorter with the last hot breath of August.

One evening—"Wonder what they're doing right now, back at Etienne's. Talking about me maybe?"

Back home at Etienne's, father and son were sitting in the warm kitchen. Outside, the night was gradually cooling down.

Etienne knocked out his pipe carefully on the edge of the spittoon.

"Say, Pa," suggested Hormisdas, "did you hear about the Scotchman down in the Eastern Townships who's making big money out of growing mushrooms?"

"Growing . . . what? Mushrooms?"

"Yeah! Mushrooms. Maybe we could try something like that right here."

"Why, what a crazy idea! Got any more like that? .. Listen, son, I've always been in favour of progress. But let me tell you, there's a gol-darn limit to everything. My farm don't need any of that kind of truck."

"Oh, well, Pa, I just thought I'd tell you about it."

But he said it with a slight shrug of his shoulders.

There was a moment's silence.

" 'Midas, we'll be cutting the field at the bottom of the hill tomorrow," said Etienne.

"All right."

Euchariste Moisan—old man Moisan—sat smoking and coughing in his garage at White Falls.

His sight had been getting worse for some time now, and his hearing too. But it was his legs that had begun to fail him more than anything. So now he could no longer go to visit the little wood right down at the end of Jefferson Street.

He hadn't given up hope of going back home to Saint-Jacques; giving up hope would mean he had made up his mind about it and that was something he hadn't done and probably never would do, would never have to do.

Circumstances had decided matters for him, that and people ruled by circumstance.

With November the rains came again and he lit a fire in the stove.

Every year brought spring. . . .

. . . and every year the valley of the St. Lawrence, which had lain asleep under the snow for four months, offered men its fields to plough and harrow and fertilize and seed and harvest . . . ;

. . . different men . . .

. . . but always the same land.

THE AUTHOR

PHILIPPE PANNETON, who writes under the name of RINGUET, was born in Three Rivers, Quebec, in 1895, and was educated at Laval University and the University of Montreal. During his college years, he was connected with a group of young French-Canadian intellectuals known as the *Nigog*. After he received the degree of Doctor of Medicine in 1920, Panneton spent several years in Paris doing post-graduate work. He then returned to Montreal, where he opened a practice, and later joined the staff of the University of Montreal as a professor of Medicine. He continued his interest in literature and writing, and was one of the founders and sometime president of the French Canadian Academy. In 1956, Panneton was appointed Canadian ambassador to Portugal.

Panneton is perhaps best known for his novel *Trente Arpents*, freely translated *Thirty Acres*, which was first published in Paris in 1938. This novel won the *Grand Prix du Roman* of the French Academy in 1939, and the *Governor General's Award* in Canada in 1940. It has been translated into German, Dutch, and Spanish, as well as English. Other works by Panneton include two novels, *Fausse Monnaie* (1947) and *Le Poids du Jour* (1948); a book of short stories, *L'Heritage* (1946); and two historical sketches, *Un Monde était leur Empire* (1943) and *L'Amiral et le Facteur* (1954).

THE NEW CANADIAN LIBRARY LIST